D0257455

# The
# Pink Ladies
# Club

Re
Pl
ma
re

Also by Emma Hannigan

*Designer Genes*

*Miss Conceived*

# *The*
# Pink Ladies Club

## EMMA HANNIGAN

POOLBEG

This novel is entirely a work of fiction. The names,
characters and incidents portrayed in it are the work of the
author's imagination. Any resemblance to actual persons,
living or dead, events or localities is entirely coincidental.

Published 2011
by Poolbeg Press Ltd
123 Grange Hill, Baldoyle
Dublin 13, Ireland
E-mail: poolbeg@poolbeg.com
www.poolbeg.com

© Emma Hannigan 2011

Copyright for typesetting, layout, design
© Poolbeg Press Ltd

The moral right of the author has been asserted.

1

A catalogue record for this book is available from the British Library.

ISBN 978-1-84223-492-1

All rights reserved. No part of this publication may be reproduced or
transmitted in any form or by any means, electronic or mechanical,
including photography, recording, or any information storage or retrieval
system, without permission in writing from the publisher. The book is sold
subject to the condition that it shall not, by way of trade or otherwise, be
lent, resold or otherwise circulated without the publisher's prior consent in
any form of binding or cover other than that in which it is published and
without a similar condition, including this condition, being imposed on the
subsequent purchaser.

DUNDEE CITY
COUNCIL

LOCATION
ARTHURSTONE

ACCESSION NUMBER
COO 933 944X

SUPPLIER
ASK

PRICE
£6.99

CLASS No.
823.91

DATE
22.5.2015

Typeset by Patricia Hope.
Printed and bound by CPI Group (UK) Ltd, Croydon, CR0 4YY

www.poolbeg.com

# About the author

Emma Hannigan lives in Bray, Co Wicklow, with her husband, two children and her cat Tom. A bestselling fiction and non-fiction author, her previous titles include *Designer Genes* and *Miss Conceived*. This is her third novel.

Emma has battled and beaten cancer six times, and is currently battling for the seventh time. Cancer is not her best friend, she wouldn't recommend it to her worst enemy, but she is quick to stress that fighting the good fight has turned her life around.

She is a glass-half-full type of person who believes that all things in life happen for a reason. Like most people, she finds lots of aspects of life confusing, but there are a few things she feels she has full clarity on. Chocolate is for eating. Coffee is for drinking. Cancer doesn't always have to win. Where there's life, there's hope. Life is for living and embracing the good times.

# Acknowledgements

For those of you who have read any of my previous books, you will know that I find these words the most difficult to write. It's a little like writing the speech for a milestone birthday!

A flurry of emotion rushes forth as I ponder and wonder what I can possibly say to the people who have surrounded me, supported me and made my life the joy that it is.

Firstly, I'd like to thank all the business people who make it possible for me to do a job that I adore. Writing is a pleasure and a privilege for me, but it couldn't happen without the hard work and support of Paula Campbell, Sarah Ormston, Gaye Shortland and all the team at Poolbeg. Thanks also to my agent Sheila Crowley of Curtis Brown UK. You all fly my flag and encourage me tirelessly. My humble thanks to you all for giving me the thrill of having my name printed on the covers of books.

Even though I do try and stick my head in my own armpit when my children bounce, point and yell, "Look, Mum, it's your book!" at the top of their lungs in shops, supermarkets and airports, the mortification is peppered with an indescribable inner pride and joy.

That brings me neatly on to Sacha and Kim. My books are my paper babies. My son and daughter are my house-wrecking, squabbling, PlayStation playing, Sylvanian Family supervising, Nerf Gun shooting, baking, rugby playing, hockey playing and filled to the brim with love, life and laughter children. They add a dimension to my world that I know I am blessed to have. No day is mundane. No hour is without a thought of them. They are the icing on the cake that is my sweet life. I am grateful for each and every day I can be their mum. (Even when we all argue on the way to school in the car – I'm sure that's character-building or something along those lines.)

Thank you to my ever loyal and supportive hubby Cian. I couldn't keep going the way I do without you. I will never do a triathlon, you live for the sport. You will never get a buzz from shopping, while I should be barred from all stores for my own good. My idea of swimming translates as twenty lengths of the pool, yours is two hundred. You drive like a maniac, I drive like a pensioner. You look good in lycra with a shaved head, I need well-cut tailoring and a foot of make-up. You love pasta, I'm gluten-intolerant. You get up at five in the morning and think that's normal. I crawl out of bed ten minutes after the alarm clock has gone off. None of that matters. You and I make a great team. As long as we continue to share our love, children, gin and tonic and many more years of laughter, I know we'll be okay!

My parents are the best in the world. Anyone who knows me will agree. My dad is the first to tell the referee to go to Specsavers at the children's rugby and hockey matches. My mum is the best at teaching six times tables minus a thirty-minute tantrum. Alongside all of that they are my cement. They bind my life and fill in the cracks when sickness and tiredness threaten to break through. Our lives would be hollow without you both.

Thanks to my extended family especially Tim & Hilary, Robyn & Joe, Steffy & Stan & Camille, Yvonne & Fionn & Evie. Thanks to my in-laws Orlaith & Seán, Eanna & Liz, Mary & Molly.

My friends are incredible and it never ceases to amaze me how willing they are to support me. I know there is a knee-buckling global recession, which is hitting us all. But there is no sense of cutbacks when it comes to friendships in my life. I am constantly reminded of goodness, kindness and just how caring my lovely friends are. Thank you all.

One person in particular who deserves a massive hug and a plinth surrounded by bright lights, with a massive firework display, is Cathy. I have dedicated this book to Cathy Kelly. She is known the world over as a brilliant and well-loved author. To me she is all the above as well as being my mentor, advisor and best friend.

Cathy, you are one of the kindest and most giving people I have ever had the privilege of knowing. I cannot imagine my life without you in it. Thank you for all that you do. But most of all thank you for being you.

For those of you who are not familiar with my previous books, I am a cancer survivor. I am currently battling for the seventh time. My survival is down to the watchful eye, brainpower and expert care of Dr David Fennelly (Saint David in my eyes) and his team of staff and nurses at the Blackrock Clinic. I cannot thank you all enough for all you do for me. Dr Michael Moriarty and the gang at St Vincent's Private Hospital are my radiation crusaders and I thank them from the bottom of my heart. Regina Quinn along with Mildred, Nuala, Margaret and all the staff at Cunningham's Pharmacy are the prettiest and most caring drug-dealers I know!

I am living proof that there can be a world outside of and also alongside cancer. I know I am one of the lucky ones. I am able to live my life and juggle sickness with health. For that I am eternally grateful. I know positivity helps, but I am more than aware of the fact that the wonderful advances in medical science and the team of talented doctors I have are my saviours. I owe you all my life. Instead of just saying thank you – I am clapping, waving, jumping up and down, whooping and blowing you all kisses. As my daughter's idol Justin Bieber would say – "I love you guys!"

My readers have blown me away. Putting it in simple terms – I am gobsmacked by the flood of positive letters, emails and warm wishes I have received from so many.

When I became an author it never struck me how many people would reach out and talk to me. I am astonished by how many of you have shared your stories and memories with me. That is a privilege that I will never take for granted. Thank you.

The story you are about to read deals with a diverse group of women of different ages affected by cancer. Fighting cancer is a continuous battle for me personally. I have days when I feel too weak to move, other days I have the energy of ten men and feel like I can take on the world. I hope I will win this current fight, and if anyone reading this book is affected by cancer, I am right there with you.

I hope you enjoy *The Pink Ladies Club*. Please continue to write and share your stories with me at **www.emmahannigan.com** or you'll find me tweeting away on twitter **@msemmahannigan**. Thank you all for buying my book and no matter where you are and what life is throwing at you, I hope you have plenty to make you smile. I wish each and every one of you love and light.

Emma

*For Cathy Kelly*
*With love*

*You are my cheerleader, soul sister &*
*most precious friend*

# Prologue

Zoe's palms began to sweat. The filtered Pan-pipe music, instead of inducing a sense of calm, felt like it was being produced via the invisible strumming of her nerve-endings. The corridor, decorated with a carefully chosen neutral carpet and inoffensive cream-painted walls, made her want to throw up. Closing her eyes for a moment, she willed herself to find the strength to deal with this surreal situation.

She hesitated, not wanting even to touch the door handle. She'd been in denial recently, kidding herself that she was fine.

Zoe could hear muffled voices and, much to her astonishment, laughter coming from the room. If someone was managing to laugh, then it couldn't be all bad, could it? With one final deep breath, as the hairs on the back of her neck stood up, Zoe placed her hand on the silver lever and pushed down.

There were actually only two people inside, so at least she wasn't being greeted by a sea of strange faces. Zoe pulled at the front panels of her shirt and yanked it to smooth it down. She'd tried on almost every item of clothing she owned that morning. What the hell was she supposed to wear to one of these meetings? She'd thought she'd nailed it, by going for the age-old surefire. Now, she wasn't so sure. Her skinny jeans felt too tight, her crisp white shirt too officey, her blue ballet pumps too sparkly.

"I'm Zoe Clarke. Dr Leah Philips sent me here." Her voice

didn't sound like her own. She shrugged and wished she was anywhere but here. She felt five years of age again, standing in her new classroom on her first day of school. Two pairs of eyes regarded the elfin-featured young girl. She was petite, with mid-length light-brown hair cut in soft fluffy spikes which framed her dewy-skinned face. Her huge brown eyes betrayed the fear she was doing her best to hide. Looking more like a stunned fawn than her usual bubbly, together self, she fumbled with the strap of her pale-blue Louis Vuitton shoulder bag.

"Hi, Zoe, you're very welcome, come on in and join us. Leah told me you were coming today. I'm Sian and this is Tanya. Please take a seat."

Sian was a warm smiley woman, who at fifty-three could easily get away with lying about her age. If she was to do one of those surveys on the street and ask one hundred people how old they thought she looked, her poll age would definitely shave at least five years from her real age. It was bizarre; the older she got, the more inclined she was to tell people how old she was. With glossy brown hair, cut in a well-groomed bob, perfect make-up and a "cared-for" skin type, she looked fabulous. But, that was becoming the norm for women these days. It was considered better to look after oneself. The dragged-through-a-bush-backwards look was off the agenda in her circle.

One of her friends had recently been outraged that her husband had organised a surprise fiftieth party for her.

"I've been telling everyone I'm forty-three – now the dozy git has ruined it all. People have memories like elephants too, so anyone who's anyone will be able to count back to tonight and know my real age," Claire had huffed.

Sian had laughed, but had understood her friend's dismay. Yet, while one part of her could see her friend's point, she also felt envious in another way. At least Claire had a husband who cared enough to go to the trouble of throwing her a party.

Today, Sian wore a simple linen trouser suit in a dull olive-green colour, which was lifted by a pretty white vest top and toning little silk scarf tied in a side knot at her neck. She was relaxed and happy in herself and her smile reached her eyes. Her movements were elegant and smooth. She instilled calm.

"I was just about to make a pot of coffee – would you like a cup or are you more a tea girl?" She was pleasant without being condescending and she made Zoe feel instantly relaxed.

Swallowing hard, Zoe felt the initial awkwardness disperse somewhat. "Coffee would be great, thank you." She disliked the sound of her own voice. She was like a strangled mouse that had been busy inhaling a tin of helium.

Cagily, she perched on a leather chair, and glanced sideways at Tanya. Without meaning to, she'd left two chairs' space between herself and the other woman. She began to panic inside, thinking she might have offended her. Should she get up and move closer, or would that be worse?

Tanya was looking straight ahead and pulling off her pashmina wrap, sniffing slightly. She seemed agitated and not altogether friendly. Luckily, Sian kept the conversation flowing.

"So this is your first time with us, Zoe. Tanya is here on her maiden voyage also, so you can start off together. The way we usually work this is we find a time that suits you and most people tend to stick to that. It means the patients can get to know each other a little bit too. Often sharing experiences can help. You're all in the same boat and it can be nice to know you're not the only one going through this."

Tanya remained silent throughout. She had that stunning auburn hair, which was long and straight with a glassy shine to it. Her skin, instead of milky white or the typical Irish bluish-doused-with-freckles look, was tanned and smooth-looking. As she glanced over at Zoe, her dark cyan-blue eyes licked her over, in a quick darting glance. Her trouser suit was beautifully cut, in French navy, and looked like it had been created by a slick-haired, dark Italian clothing genius. Her killer heels Zoe recognised as being Jimmy Choo. Even though it was mid-morning and not particularly warm out, she had teamed the suit with a boned cream and navy bustier. On anyone else, it might have looked a bit like overkill, or even as if she should be sitting in the church waiting for the bride. On Tanya, it all looked classically stylish.

Between Tanya and the bloomingly healthy-looking Sian, Zoe was beginning to wonder whether or not she was in the right place.

A knock at the door was a welcome distraction.

"Come on in," Sian called over her shoulder as she poured water into the cafetière.

The door opened. "Hi there, I'm Esme Mulligan, Dr Leah sent me to you." Booming with confidence and cheer, the newcomer waddled towards Sian and pumped her hand up and down, before plonking herself in between the other two women. "Hi there, delighted to make your acquaintance, I'm Esme." She grabbed Zoe's hand, and leaned the other way to do the same with Tanya.

Tanya looked at the Esme woman disapprovingly.

She was very like a pantomime dame, in her stretchy synthetic floral skirt and top, all purples and fawn mixed with a nasty shade of green. Her thick mottled-with-varicose-veins legs were coated by grey tights and garnished with old-lady, rubber-soled shoes.

Tanya knew her own make-up was flawless yet dewy, unlike Esme's cake-batter-textured stuff, which she'd finished off with a layer of bright-pink rouge like a shooting arrow coming from each ear, darting towards her nose. Tanya's lips glistened, while Esme's resembled two cloying peach horizontal lines, both of which ignored the shape of her lips entirely. Tanya had swept a glow of warm mushroom-toned Mac shadow on her lids, while Esme had opted for the clogging green-toad look. This nightmare was framed by the bushiest mono-brow and the worst-looking false lashes Tanya had ever seen. They were plastic and rigid, like ones from a child's play set. How she'd even managed to make them stick on was a feat in itself. She must have used either rubber-based or super glue.

But, unlike Tanya, Esme seemed comfortable in her own skin and oblivious to everyone else's stare.

The others introduced themselves somewhat awkwardly as Esme continued to chat away to no one in particular.

"Great to get here, was worried about finding the place, not great with directions," she babbled.

Sian set down a brown wooden tray with white coffee cups and saucers, a matching milk jug and sugar bowl and a pretty pink spotty plate, adorned with a selection of decent-looking biscuits. "Okay, ladies, let's start the ball rolling as they say." Gently pressing the plunger downwards, she smiled and shrugged her shoulders cheerfully. "I hate nothing more than instant coffee, so when I took this job I insisted they buy me a proper plunger," she confided. "Esme, are you alright with coffee or can I make you a cup of tea instead?"

"Not at all, that'll do me nicely. You don't need to wear yourself out, trotting around after me. I'll fit in with whatever. I've learned at this stage in my life, seventy next birthday, please God," she nodded at the others for approval, "if I don't know how to behave by now, there's no hope for me." Her blue-rinsed curls bounced as she chortled to herself.

The smell of fresh coffee filled the air. The milk-pouring and spooning of sugar all seemed too loud and exaggerated. It was like all the women wanted the mundane activity to go on forever. Anything to avoid the real reason they were all sitting here.

They all sipped the coffee, which, given the circumstances, even if it had been grown and harvested by a rare Pigmy tribe, with a net worth similar to gold, would have tasted bitter. Sian took the floor.

"The whole idea of this cancer support group is to give you all a sounding board. A time and a place to talk things over. To talk if you feel like it. To listen and learn, or simply to ask advice. You have all come here of your own free will, I hope?" Sian laughed and looked at the ladies.

Zoe and Esme smiled back, but Tanya just raised her eyebrows and looked at the floor with disdain.

"I hope that over the next few months you will find our meetings helpful and supportive. Often, it's good just to know that you are not alone. That you are not an island, so to speak."

Sian filled them in on her own background. She had worked for twenty-five years as a general nurse, until her husband of twenty years had died of cancer, eleven years previously.

"I went to a support group while Liam was ill, and found the people so wonderful. I couldn't face going back to my old job after he'd gone. I knew my life needed to change. I had to learn to live without him. I had to reinvent myself somewhat. So I decided to train to be a counsellor. So although I've never had cancer myself, I have lived with it, and now years down the road I have met lots of other women in a similar position to you all. I hope I can be of some help to you."

Sian took a gulp of her coffee and waited for a moment. Just as she'd experienced before, these first-time attendees were all reluctant to speak.

"Would you like to start off by introducing yourselves?"

There was barely a pause before Esme piped up. "I'll go first if you like?" She looked from one face to the next, expectantly.

"Sure." Zoe looked relieved she didn't have to start.

"Be my guest," Tanya answered, giving a sideways Simon Cowell type look.

Zoe was afraid to even glance in Tanya's direction. She found the woman scary. She was really wondering why Tanya had bothered coming if she was going to be so narky.

"Well, as I said, I'm Esme Mulligan, I'm sixty-nine years old, seventy in November, please God. I live with my husband Michael. I've two grown-up daughters, Nora and Tracey, both living across the water in London. Would never have thought when they were babies that they'd end up living so far away, but that's life, isn't it?" She nodded at Zoe. "Grand girls they are, fair play to them. One works in a hospital, the other in the bank. They must've picked up their number skills from their father. I was never very interested in the numbers. Now I'll sit from here till eternity at the crossword, but don't show me numbers," she chuckled.

Tanya shifted in her seat. If she was going to have to listen to this old bat rabbiting on about crosswords and her daughters with their yawn-inducing jobs, she was out of here. She had a million things to do today, and she really didn't have the time for this bullshit. Looking at her watch, she decided she'd give it another twenty minutes, then politely excuse herself and get the hell out.

At least that way, she'd have kept her promise to her husband, Alfie, so he wouldn't nag her anymore. She looked at that Esme woman. God, she'd top herself if she ended up looking like that when she was older. All grey-complexioned and saggy, with clothes fashioned from fabrics which looked like they had been designed by visually impaired gnomes. If she'd taken a bucket of LSD she still wouldn't come up with that combination. Shops shouldn't sell those types of things, they just shouldn't be allowed to exist. The woman's legs were the same width at the ankle as the thigh, and that blue-rinse thing going on – what the hell was that all about?

In fairness to her, she wasn't furry: no whiskers or moustache. But the earlobes were alarming. Tanya's hand meandered towards her own pert and tight lobes. Elderly lobes were definitely designed by the devil as revenge for bad doings in younger days. It was awful enough to have grey fur poking out your ear canals, but the wobbly, elephant's arse-cheek type things that hung as earlobes on the aged! It was all to be dreaded. The ageing process made Tanya shudder. Cosmetic surgery could fix a certain amount for sure, but unless she was planning on spending most of her time on the operating table once she hit seventy, most of it was inevitable.

Esme had tried to hide her elephant's-arses by clipping on big round gold button-type earrings, but it was no use. The big clots of gold just flapped and banged against her neck as she spoke.

Tanya's hesitant hand reached down to stroke her own neck, which was still firm and didn't move independently after she'd stopped moving her head like poor Esme's.

How had she ended up here, in this situation? Where she was having to do all this self-questioning? *Weakness*, that's how. Her own bloody weakness and her malfunctioning body had let her down. Her brain and her mind should never have allowed the breakdown. Tears of sheer anger pricked her eyes. Pinching herself on the side of her thigh with her left hand, she swallowed hard and willed herself to get a grip. Jesus, the last thing on earth she wanted was to sit blubbering like a fool in front of these strangers.

Zoning back into the conversation, Tanya sighed inwardly as she focused on the older woman.

"Tracey, that's my eldest girl, was home from London last month. She noticed I wasn't looking too well. I'd been having a bit of toilet trouble for a while, you know . . ." She wrinkled her nose and pointed at her bits.

Feck's sake, Tanya inhaled. Don't go there, lady, we don't need an image of your furry parts. The outside is scary enough. Then she instructed herself: Don't even let your mind wander to what happens with the lady parts when you're elderly . . .

"So she brought me along to see Dr Joyce. Lovely man, grew up in Tallaght, do you know him?" Esme asked the room.

They all shook their heads.

"'Well,' says he, 'it's probably nothing, Mrs Mulligan, but we'll run a couple of tests, on account of your age and all of that' – I'll be seventy next birthday."

"We know." Tanya couldn't help herself. It sounded a bit sharp, so she repeated it, trying to sound a bit kinder, "Yes, we know, you said already – how exciting for you and your family." She smiled fleetingly.

Esme continued, quite unperturbed by Tanya's acidity. "Before I knew which end was up, they had me in the University Hospital. Lovely place. Grand set of nurses over there. The food was grand too, lovely to have it handed up to you, I say." She chuckled to herself and looked into space for a moment.

What the hell is she doing now, Tanya wondered. Reminiscing about hospital Shepherd's Pie?

"In any case, they took bloods and I'd to wee in a bottle and everything. The next thing the surgeon came in, and what did he suggest only a col-ostomy." She blinked, stumbling on the big word.

"So you've had a bag fitted, have you?" Sian probed gently.

"No, dear, they performed a colostomy on me. You know, where they put a pipe up your jacksy like." She wiggled her finger around to show.

"Oh, I see, a colonoscopy," Sian corrected.

"Yes, love, that's what I said." Esme blinked, trying to get on with her story, wondering for a minute if that Sian girl was okay – all that repeating herself. She continued, deciding to give Sian the benefit of the doubt. "The next thing I knew, the doctors all came in. Now most of them looked young enough to put over your knee, if you know what I mean? 'Mrs Mulligan,' says one little one. She looked like she hadn't eaten a hot dinner all her life, pale and terrible thin. 'Mrs Mulligan,' says she, 'I'm afraid to tell you, we've found cancer in your colon.'" Esme clasped her hands together and rocked back and forth slightly.

"How did you feel when you were told that?" Sian probed.

"I was shocked, I suppose. I got out me rosary beads and said a few little prayers, and took a few deep breaths and decided that Holy God had made his plan for me. That he'd called me." She looked desperately sad for a moment.

An odd silence descended. Even though the others were obviously there because they had cancer too, it was still shocking and it still left an awkward silence.

Coming out of her brief daydream, Esme persevered with her story.

"That was all before I met Dr Leah. Sure she told me it's not a death sentence nowadays. That there's a whole shed-load of people walking, eating, sleeping and breathing, and they've all had cancer. So now I just trust Holy God and Dr Leah to mind me."

"Well told, and might I say, that's a great attitude to have, Esme," said Sian. "It will stand to you if you can try to remain positive. Good for you. Now, how about you, Zoe? Would you like to introduce yourself?" She turned in her chair slightly to encourage the young girl to speak.

Clearing her throat, Zoe looked like she wanted to run and hide.

"I'm Zoe Clarke, I'm a twin, I'm twenty-two years old and I have ovarian cancer along with a weird auto-immune disease called dermatomyositis. I found out two weeks ago." She tried to smile, but it wasn't really working. Instead her mouth was creasing downwards, all by itself. Shrugging her shoulders, she glanced at the other women fleetingly before fixing her stare on her glittery ballerina pumps. She knew she looked like a toddler when you snatch their lollipop, all wobbly bottom lip and pathetic. But she couldn't help it.

"Well done, Zoe. It's so difficult in the beginning to even say those words, isn't it?" Sian reached over and rubbed Zoe's shoulder.

The young girl took deep breaths and tried to calm herself, as Sian thankfully spoke again, moving all the attention to the last lady in the room.

"What about you, Tanya?"

"My name is Tanya Shields, I'm thirty-five years old. I found out a week ago that I have breast cancer. I have some surgery coming up, followed by chemotherapy, but I expect to be absolutely fine soon." The conversation was closed. She didn't smile, but she didn't flinch either. With the precision of a barrister addressing a judge and jury, Tanya took a confident sip of her coffee, indicating that she had finished speaking.

Sian didn't falter, and didn't make eye contact with anyone in particular. "Okay, well done. This first meeting, I'm told, is the most difficult. The fact that you've all come here today is a huge step. I hope you will be able to use our time together to vent your feelings and come to terms with the huge challenge you've all been faced with."

Although Sian had made this same speech a thousand times, she hoped that it didn't sound tired and like she was reeling off information. She went on to explain about the other services available at the cancer support workshop.

"We offer a lovely day called 'Taking Care of You'. This is run by a number of professionals including a make-up artist, a beauty therapist, a hair and wig specialist and massage therapist. The aim of the day is to pamper you and show you how to apply make-up and achieve the best results with your wig, should you choose to have one."

Zoe's eyes brimmed with tears at the mention of wigs. "I can't imagine losing my hair!" A sob escaped and her hands flew to her mouth in panic.

"Well, have the doctors told you that you will definitely lose all your hair, Zoe? Some of the chemotherapy treatments actually don't cause hair loss. At least not total. You hair may just become thinner for a while. Why don't you check that out with your team?" Sian stroked Zoe's arm as she spoke gently to the young girl.

"I did ask and Dr Leah said that she thinks the stuff they're going to give me won't make my hair fall out. She said she'll confirm the treatment after my operation. I've been offered a thing called the cold cap, in case my chemotherapy does cause alopecia. Do you know anything about it?" Zoe was shaking visibly now.

"Well, your medical team will give you all the proper information of course, but I believe it's a marvellous thing. It's like a helmet, which freezes the scalp so your hair doesn't come out as much. It could be a good option for you to try." Sian nodded positively.

"I know it must sound so stupid and meaningless to you, when I'm faced with battling cancer, but I can't help dreading the thought of losing my hair."

Tanya felt sorry for the petite girl. She was very young to have to face this kind of thing. It simply seemed more socially acceptable for that Esme woman to have cancer. This young, smooth-skinned, pretty little thing didn't look at all like the type of person who should have it.

"I'm having trouble understanding all this cancer thing." Tanya's words escaped from her mouth as if independent of her brain.

"In what way, Tanya?" Sian leaned forward, delighted Tanya was talking freely. This was more than she'd hoped for with this hard-shelled businesslike lady.

"Now, obviously cancer doesn't strike if you look a certain way. For example, if you have blonde hair and blue eyes, you're exempt. God knows I find it beyond weird that I've been tarred with this blasted cancer-brush, but this young, healthy-looking childlike person certainly doesn't look the type. What the hell?"

There was brief silence as Zoe's eyes again filled with tears. Esme just nodded a lot.

"Christ, I'm sorry, Zoe," said Tanya. "That was totally out of line, but I'm just so angry on all of our behalves. You too, Esme. You've raised your family and now should be your time to relax and go on bus tours or whatever it is you like doing. Why should you have to be sick? Where's the justice?" She found it hard to breathe evenly.

"Ah, don't worry about me, love. Kind of you and all that. But, sure, tons of people get cancer, so why not us, what?" Esme smiled.

"I wish I felt like that, Esme. Really I do, but I just feel deep-seated fury. Boiling rage at the injustice of it all."

"God bless you!" Esme shook her blue curls and tutted. "All I can say is that Holy God never closes a door without opening another. I believe that, love. I do."

"I'd like to find that second door too," Zoe sighed.

Sian handed out booklets and leaflets with information of all the services on offer at the support centre. Each person got a little folder with all the relevant numbers printed on the front, to keep everything together.

"We've actually come to the end of our session for today, believe it or not. So I hope to see you all at the same time next week. The first day is always a bit messy, but once we've introduced ourselves and got over the first hurdle, it's usually more productive from here on in. I have a little pink-ribbon notebook for each of you, and I would like to make a suggestion. Some people find this helpful, others don't take to it. It's a very personal thing." Sian grasped the candy-pink, shimmery, ring-bound, hard-backed notebooks.

"Oh, they're cute!" Zoe's eyes lit up at the pretty gifts.

"What I suggest is that every day you write one sentence, which is a positive thought, event or saying. Just one. Anything from 'The sun is shining', to 'I feel a step closer to being well again'. Do you catch my drift?"

"I know! We could call our little group 'The Pink Ladies' like in *Grease*!" Esme shrugged her shoulders in delight. "I already belong to an over-seventies group, and we're called 'The Golden Girls'. I love to have a name on things. What do you reckon, girls?"

Zoe thought Esme was a breath of fresh air, and although she hardly had the energy to breathe, she couldn't help but be drawn in by the older lady's enthusiasm. "That sounds cool," she smiled.

"Yeah, whatever you're into." Tanya had never been one for clubs or gangs, but she didn't want to appear rude. Besides, she wasn't even sure if she'd be back – ever.

"How exciting! Just wait until I tell my family and friends that I'm a 'Pink Lady'." Esme hopped up out of her seat, tucked her precious new book into her bag and waddled out, with plenty of waves and God blesses.

Sian watched Zoe struggle to stand up. The poor girl was in a bad way. She'd have to research that auto-immune disease she'd mentioned. She'd never heard of it but, by the looks of Zoe, it was causing her considerable pain.

Esme was a cheery soul. What you see is what you get. No malice and no hidden agendas.

Tanya was going to be more difficult to deal with. The more silent simmering type. A hard shell of an exterior, but experience had taught her that Tanya was the very one who could need this group more than any of the others. Her type often did. The ones who put up a front and boxed themselves inside were often the people who needed to be reached the most.

# 1

## Tanya

Tanya looked at her watch and realised she only had ten minutes to get ready for this evening's function. She always liked to be one step ahead of the game. And usually she was, but today she'd been dragging herself around, which was mildly puzzling, as she hadn't been out the night before or working late even. Little Jenny hadn't been awake during the night, so she'd had a decent night's sleep.

Tanya's company, The Main Event, organised private and corporate functions. Her edge was that she did them in people's homes. Unlike many other companies in the entertainment field, she was managing to ride the dreaded recession storm. As spare cash and budgets dwindled, Tanya's company had flourished. The fact that she would come and transform clients' own homes, providing the whole package from the food to flowers, candles and wine without the expense of hiring a venue or paying extortionate restaurant prices, meant she was in demand.

She'd started off doing dinner parties for up to twelve people and soon realised that doing a function for fifty was almost the same amount of work. Now, after twelve years in business, she had a decent turnover not to mention a fabulous reputation.

From a good Irish Catholic family of eight, Tanya was the eldest, and so spent all her time, until the day she moved out, minding other people. She couldn't even go to the corner shop without someone tagging along.

"Tanya, good girl, while you're picking up the bread, take Jamie and Seán with you – thanks, love."

Her mother had been sweet and unbelievably good-natured considering the multiplying family she'd had, not to mention the never-ending pile of washing. The woman was practically running a hotel, without the glamour.

Tanya had met her husband Alfie when she was only nineteen. He was her balance. Calm, sweet-natured and kind. They say a lot of women marry a man like their father – instead Tanya married the male version of her mother. He was the one who reeled her in from time to time. He was the one who told her she was pushing herself too much.

"Tanya, it's nine o'clock on Saturday night. Please, love, put the books away and come over and watch the end of *X-factor* with me, before I drink the whole bottle of wine on my own," he'd urge gently.

Their daughter, Jenny, was what Tanya termed a "surprise". Since her birth two years previously, the couple had adopted the role-reversal arrangement which had swept across many Irish houses since the global banking crisis.

It was five thirty as Tanya rushed to have a very quick shower, before changing into her usual little black dress to attend the evening's function. She'd bought new shower oil, which promised to moisturise as well as cleanse her skin. She thought it was a marvellous idea – it'd cut out having to slather cream on followed by dancing around waiting for it to dry. There was nothing more annoying than ending up with white marks or greasy stains on a freshly dry-cleaned dress.

As she washed under her left arm, she felt a slight sharp twang. Her initial reaction was to ignore it and keep going. But the nagging voice in her head made her place her hand on the area again. Prodding with her finger, she could feel a small hard perfectly round bump. A bit like a rubber pea.

The hot water continued to cascade down her back. The sound of the shower pump hummed on. She could hear Alfie and Jenny downstairs, singing and playing. Without turning around, she raised her hand backwards and bashed the shower water off at the wall.

Pulling back the glass shower-door, she grabbed a towel and patted the area dry. Quickly, she checked the other armpit for comparison, hoping there might be lumps on both sides. Maybe it was a muscle or a normal bit that she simply hadn't felt before. She wasn't usually an armpit-rooter, so maybe this was all perfectly normal?

There was no rubber pea on the other side. Would this have something to do with the dizzy feeling she'd had earlier on that day? Or the dreadful sluggishness she was experiencing?

Feck, it was ten to six. She didn't have time to stand around daydreaming. Robotically, she dried the rest of her body, dressed, put on make-up and got into the car to go to work.

"Bye, Alfie, bye, Jenny love, I'm sorry – I'm late, late, late – see you both in the morning – this one will go on until the early hours." She hugged them briefly and shuffled to the car, trying to balance her laptop, the client file and a pile of bunting for decorating.

As she settled into the early-evening traffic, she was genuinely puzzled. She certainly wasn't pregnant. She was on the pill and she'd taken each one meticulously. She adored Jenny, but she certainly didn't want to go through another pregnancy and birth. She'd heard that the pill could cause water retention and no doubt about it, her boobs had gone up a full bra size since she'd started taking it. Come to think of it, the bras she was wearing now were kind of tight. Well, the left side was in particular. She'd noticed a red mark on her left shoulder where the strap was digging into her skin. It hadn't done that before. The zip on her fitted dress had been more difficult than normal to close too. She must remember to weigh herself and see if she'd put on a lot of weight. God, if she was pregnant she'd be devastated. What the hell would she do? Would Alfie be able to manage another child?

All the while, she was trying to block out the image of that rubber pea under her arm. Within minutes, she pulled up at the venue for the party, just ahead of the eighty guests. With her wireless headset in place, Tanya didn't have a second to contemplate lumps or bumps.

By the time she managed to leave the party, it was three thirty in the morning. She was staggering with fatigue as she put her key in the door.

Pulling off her shoes, she found a cool cotton nightdress and ambled into the bathroom. The clients had been ever so grateful. Their party had been fantastic and she knew she'd get some business as a result. As she brushed her teeth, she tried to resist the urge to put her hand near her underarm.

She did very well until it came to cleaning her face. As she used the bits of cotton wool to rub off the make-up and grime of the day, she allowed herself to touch the area. Maybe it was gone. Glands can swell and infect. That didn't mean there was anything to worry about.

She found the spot immediately. No rooting necessary. It was definitely still there. Holding on to the side of the white porcelain sink, she exhaled. Standing on the weighing scales, she gasped as she realised she'd put on over four kilos, which was totally uncharacteristic for her. She'd make an appointment with her GP the following Monday. It was probably nothing.

She fell into bed and grabbed a book. Flicking on her itty-bitty book-light, so as not to awaken Alfie, she read a few chapters. She had no idea what the book was about. She was simply scanning the words and processing nothing.

* * *

The following day was Sunday, so that meant the usual dragging herself around to family and going to an overcrowded noisy restaurant for lunch.

"Look, Mama, a yummy from Jenny!" The two-and-a-half-year-old tried to shove a semi-regurgitated piece of bread at Tanya to taste.

"Yes, lovely, darling." She smiled fleetingly and pretended to nibble the soggy bread. She longed to go home and read the papers. She was tired after the late night and quite frankly wasn't in the mood for all the frenzied 'family' stuff.

By the time they got home, Jenny had fallen asleep in the car.

"Leave her there for a few minutes more," said Alfie. "Then

she'll have had a good forty minutes. She'll be in better form when she wakes." He got out of the car and gently clicked the door shut.

Unlike his wife, Alfie didn't do the tailored look. He was far more at ease in his jeans with a long-sleeved T-shirt and his beloved Converse runner boots. His surfer-style dark curls framed his dark eyes and he was what all Tanya's friends universally classed as 'sexy'. The fact that he was so unaware of his boyish good looks made him even more appealing. His easy demeanour and laid-back attitude to life balanced Tanya's go-go-go need-for-speed personality.

Tanya stared at their daughter. She had incredibly long eyelashes for such a tiny creature. She looked like photos of Tanya at the same age. The difference was the shape of her mouth. Tanya had quite thin lips, where as Jenny's were full and pouty like her daddy's.

That morning, Jenny had scurried over to Tanya with a pink hairbrush and some clips with little dogs on them. "Mama fix Jenny's hair," she'd said and clambered onto Tanya's lap.

Right now, dog-clips still in place, Jenny looked angelic and serene, sleeping with her head tilted to the side of the car seat, her flushed cheek resting on the checked fabric. She was very pretty, Tanya was delighted to observe. She had often wondered when she was pregnant if her child would be ugly.

"Alfie, what will we do if the baby looks like a pug? No amount of designer clothes will help. If it's butt-ugly it'll have to stay indoors until it's old enough to either wear make-up or have plastic surgery," she'd told her husband. Of course she hadn't meant that literally, but she really was stricken at the thought that the baby might be an eyesore.

He'd responded by roaring with laughter and hugging her. "You're so funny!" He'd obviously thought she was just joking.

She'd decided she'd better laugh too in case he thought she was a total bitch-cow, but she'd been genuinely concerned the child was going to look like an alien with a slapped arse.

Slipping out of the car, she made her way towards the house

with the papers. Alfie had already taken up position in an armchair by the window to keep an eye on their daughter in the car.

"Mama?"

Before she could make it inside, she heard Jenny's little voice calling hopefully. Dumping the papers on the doorstep, she returned to pluck her out of the car.

"Hi, Mama," Jenny said, smiling delightedly at her mother.

Even though she spent most of her time with Alfie, she loyally always seemed delighted to see Tanya. Wrapping her little arms around her mummy's neck, she hugged her tightly. Tanya stood for a moment and inhaled her childish scent.

"Hi, baby girl." Tanya smiled and kissed her soft head.

\* \* \*

By Monday morning Tanya was ready to get back to work. Much as she would have loved to be a stay-at-home type, she just wasn't. Unlike most people, Tanya did like Mondays. She liked having a fresh week ahead. She loved her job and getting her teeth into the next project.

She had a small office in a building in Dunlaoire, an airy seaside location. Her office consisted of two rooms, one for herself and one for Sally, her longstanding secretary. Most of her work took place at the chosen venue, so she didn't have a need for tons of space. She also had a warehouse on the north side of the city, where she stored the marquees, heaters, fold-down tables and chairs, delph and all the other paraphernalia.

Each morning, Tanya was at her desk by eight, ready to check emails and get that day's last-minute things organised. Flicking on the side-switch for her mini Gaggia coffee machine, she yawned as she heard it hiss into life. She had to drink real coffee. She couldn't abide instant. It baffled her entirely how anyone could possibly consume that dried nasty-smelling excuse for coffee. When she'd hired Sally, her secretary, she'd explained the coffee etiquette straight off. "It takes the same amount of time to make a plunger pot of delicious aromatic heaven. The other thing I don't ever do is paper cups. That whole stewed-cardboard, bendy-in-the-middle thing, or drinking from a plastic spout puts me in a bad mood. They remind me of a bad version of Jenny's sippy cups."

Sally had laughed and agreed totally.

For emergencies, when she knew she'd need coffee and was out and about, she had one of those thermal cups, in a smart chrome design with a removable lid, so she could feign some sort of a civilised ritual. Her ideal, which she had in her office and at home, was a china cup and matching saucer. She was never a big boozer, as in she didn't sit in pubs downing pints or shorts. She didn't smoke. She was very disciplined about what she ate. Low fat, high fibre, as much fresh fruit and organic produce as possible. She attended the gym a minimum of three times a week. Apart from the odd glass of wine, coffee was pretty much her only vice. Therefore, she took it seriously and accepted nothing less than the best.

That morning, she brewed her cup of coffee, using her newly acquired machine, added a small dash of milk, no sugar. She had turned Sally into a coffee neuroticist also, so she gave her a cup (and saucer) of delicious fresh brew too.

"Oh thanks, Tanya. The answer machine was almost at exploding level when I got in. The bride for this McEvoy wedding is a Bridezilla if ever I've met one. She must have pressed redial all weekend and left message after message. Most of it is verbal garbage, but I'd better listen to them all in case there's a point in there somewhere." She shrugged good-naturedly and sipped her coffee.

"Enjoy and don't fill me in unless you have to," Tanya smiled at her.

When she'd started out at first, she'd had to listen to all those messages as well as organise everything. She learned from very early on that she wasn't very good at neurotic people. She also found it hard not to take it as a personal insult that her clients seemed to feel the need to fly into a fit of panic coming up to their event. Did they not know she was totally anal about detail? Did they not realise that the money they were paying her included thinking of every eventuality as well as staying awake for hours at night crossing every 't' and dotting every 'i'?

Tanya had found Sally on one of those job-search websites. She was fresh out of secretarial college, twenty years old, and had the right qualifications. She'd been with her ten years now and, without it being said, they both knew Tanya would find it hard to run the place without her. She also possessed the pleasant-to-everyone gene, which Tanya had been born without. She could naturally endear herself to people and had the patience and empathy to calm people down.

This McEvoy girl who had left an hour's worth of warble on the answering machine would probably pull her business by the end of the morning if Tanya had to deal with her. Whereas Sally would call her and soothe her and make her feel happy and relieved she'd chosen them as her wedding organisers. True to form, it wasn't even nine o'clock and Tanya could hear Sally on the phone.

"I understand and you have every right to be jittery. But rest assured we have vast experience in this field and we are just as anxious as you are that the day is simply perfect."

Tanya could hear the smile in Sally's voice as she spoke.

"I'm glad you're happier now too, no problem at all . . . I understand . . . No, don't apologise . . . Sure, I'll talk to you soon. Let me know if you have any more concerns, that's what we're here for . . . You're welcome – you too – bye."

In the safety of her office, as the door clicked shut, Tanya eyed her mobile phone. She knew she needed to call her doctor. She had to have this lump checked. A niggling fear was prodding her psyche, telling her to sort this out. She dialled her GP's surgery, all the while convincing herself it was probably nothing to worry about.

"Doctor's surgery, Sarah speaking, how may I help you?"

"Hello, Sarah, Tanya Shields speaking. I'd like an appointment with Dr Gates as soon as possible, please." She held her breath. A part of her wanted Sarah to say that Dr Shields couldn't see her until next year, but the sensible part of her brain was willing her to have a free space immediately.

"Okay, Tanya, let me have a look . . . Right, she's pretty much fully booked both today and tomorrow . . . unless you could make it here in twenty minutes?"

"Done. I'll see you then." She clicked the phone off and drummed her gel nails on the desk.

Every second Thursday, Tanya ritually had her nails done. Her shiny French manicure was like an addiction. Her natural nails hadn't seen the light of day for years. Chewing the inside of her mouth with nerves, she sat in a slight state of trance for a few seconds. Okay, good. She would fly down to see Dr Gates, and be back at her desk ten fifteen at the latest. Perfect. It was probably nothing and she'd know she'd done the right thing.

Pulling on her coat and downing the dregs of her coffee, she marched purposefully out of her office.

"I won't be long, Sally," she called over her shoulder.

Sally didn't falter at the keyboard.

"Sure," she smiled and kept typing, without even looking up.

* * *

Dr Shield's practice was in the basement of her house, less than five minutes' drive away. The traffic was almost stationary as usual. Tanya urged it to get out of her way. What the hell were they all doing? Where was everyone going all at the same time? She flicked on the radio. She pressed each button in turn. The chat shows annoyed her that morning. The music all seemed to be the wrong tempo. She turned the radio off. Tapping the steering wheel in frustration, she edged towards the surgery.

At bang on the allotted time, she pulled up outside and slipped in.

"Hello, Tanya, just take a seat, the doctor will be with you in a second, she's just finishing a phone call," the secretary smiled.

It was just herself and the secretary, with nobody else in the room.

What a curious job, Tanya mused. She's not the doctor and yet she has access to all the files and knowledge of everyone's illnesses. Tanya suddenly felt relieved she'd never been in there to have treatment for a gooey vaginal fungal infection or scabies.

Promptly, the door to the surgery flew open and Dr Gates beckoned her inside. She'd been Tanya's doctor for years, and had seen her through her pregnancy and any other minor illnesses she'd had.

"Hi, Tanya, take a seat, what can I do for you?" She sat, clicking her pen.

She was direct and straight down to business. No bullshit, no let's pretend we're old friends. Tanya liked that about her.

"I've found a lump in my armpit. I discovered it on Saturday night, in the shower to be exact, and I'm concerned." Tanya swallowed and sat up straight, lowering her shoulders and trying to convey a nonchalant attitude. Inside, her heart was suddenly beating nineteen to the dozen and she was beginning to sweat.

"Okay, I'll take a look in one minute. A couple of quick preliminaries. Have you noticed any hot flushes?"

"Now that you mention it, I've had a few at night-time, but had kind of put them down to unwinding after late functions."

"Have you had any noticeable weight fluctuation?"

"Yes, my clothes are all feeling a bit tighter. My first thought was that I might be pregnant, which believe me wouldn't be ideal."

Dr Gates expression remained neutral. "Does the lump hurt?"

"Only when I press it hard." Tanya shuddered.

"Okay, let's have a look at you. Remove your top and bra and lie down on the bed over there." She motioned to the surgical couch with the paper towel draped over it.

Tanya did as instructed, her heart pounding.

"Sorry if my hands are chilly. Just raise your arm and take a deep breath in for me please, Tanya." Dr Gates bunched her fingers and placed them under Tanya's arm. Gently at first, skimming the surface of the area and then delving more deeply. "Okay, I can feel it alright. Is that painful?"

"Pain is the wrong word, it's more uncomfortable really, I – ouch!"

As Dr Shields pressed harder, Tanya got a sharp stabbing sensation which sent referred pain down into her elbow.

"Okay, I'm going to examine your tummy now. Deep breath in, please."

Dr Gates managed to put her hands so far in that Tanya was waiting for them to appear out her back.

"Good girl – sorry, I know it's uncomfortable for you. Bear with me. Another deep breath in, please, and let it out slowly."

Tanya winced in pain and had a dreadful urge to throw up. Dr Gates noticed the colour draining from the young woman's face.

"Well done, Tanya, you get dressed, and we'll have a chat." She pulled a curtain around the bed and went back behind her desk.

Tanya heard her pen scribbling notes on her file. Pulling her clothes back on, she joined her again.

"What do you think?" Tanya felt slightly sick and a little bit dizzy.

"To be honest, Tanya, I'm not sure. I'm going to refer you to hospital to have it checked out further. I think an ultrasound and possibly a scan will be called for. I'm going to recommend a doctor by the name of Leah Philips. I trained with her, she's straight as a die and I think you'll get on with her. You can trust her – she won't leave any stone unturned." Dr Gates was already writing a letter.

"Do you think this lump is cancer?" Tanya felt a straight question would warrant a straight answer.

"I don't know. That's the bottom line. I can't tell by touching it. You need to go and see Dr Philips – she's an oncologist and she'll be able to give you that answer. That's all I can honestly say for now." She held her hands up and looked Tanya straight in the eye.

Tanya sat, feeling a little dumbfounded, as Dr Gates lifted the phone and dialled a number.

"Good morning, Dr Gates here. May I make an appointment for a Ms Tanya Shields, a patient of mine? As soon as possible, please – she's presenting with a suspect node in the left axillary, and tenderness with abdominal swelling also to the left." She listened to the person on the other end of the phone. "I'll check – she's here with me now. Just a moment, please." She covered the receiver with her hand and whispered to Tanya, "Can you go in this morning? They have a slot. It's in the private clinic though so there'll be a charge . . ." She waited for Tanya to nod. "That's fine, I'll send my referral in with her – do you need me to fax it ahead?"

She continued to talk to the other person as Tanya's head began to swim. This was not really what she'd been planning. She tried to think of what she was supposed to be doing in work. How long was she going to be in the hospital? What were they going to do to her?

"Tanya?" Dr Gates was looking at her.

"Yes, sorry," she said, snapping back into reality.

"I'm going to fax the information through to the clinic. It's St Mark's private as opposed to the main public hospital. As I mentioned there will be a charge, but if we were to wait for an appointment in the adjoining public hospital it could take some time. Seeing as I specifically want you to see Leah, this is the swiftest route. Do you know how to get there?"

"Yes." Tanya swallowed.

"Okay, you head on in there, they're expecting you as soon as. Leah is fantastic, she'll have you sorted in no time. It's probably nothing to concern yourself with, but these things are better checked. Better to be safe than sorry and all that. I'll keep in touch. As I said, Dr Philips is an old friend, she'll keep me informed and she'll take a special interest." Dr Gates shook her hand and led her to the door.

Tanya paid the secretary and floated to her car. As soon as the Bluetooth found her phone and connected, she dialled Alfie's number. He answered and she could tell he was at one of those noisy indoor play areas. The sound of laughing mixed with screaming and crying boomed in the background. Tanya thanked her lucky stars she wasn't there. God, she hated those places.

"Hi, love, how's your day going?" Alfie shouted. "Sorry, it's a bit hard to hear, I'm in the play centre with Jenny! Good girl, Jenny, go down the slide again, I'll wait here to watch you – sorry, love, how are things?"

"Alfie, I've found a strange lump under my arm. I just saw the doctor and she's sending me into St Mark's private to see a breast specialist. I'm on my way there now. Just for a quick look, better to be safe than sorry, she says." Tanya tried to sound like it was a normal thing to do on a Monday morning, on spec.

"What do you mean you found a strange lump? When? Why didn't you tell me?" He sounded hurt and upset. Not what Tanya needed right at that moment.

"I only found it last night," she fibbed. "I was in the office and remembered it this morning and Dr Gates had a cancellation so I popped in, now I've been referred, yadda, yadda. Don't go all hurt and crushed on me. I'll be fine, I'm merely letting you know 'cos my phone will be off for a while. All okay there? Is Jenny alright?" She tried to sound even and in control.

"Jenny's fine. Listen, your mum could mind her – why don't I drop her off and meet you in the clinic? I don't like the sound of all this, to be honest with you." He was gentle and kind. The concern and love in his voice almost cracked her gruff exterior.

"I'm fine, love, don't fuss. You know I hate that. I don't want my mother or anyone else knowing about this for now. Unless it's cancer or something, there's no need to shout our business from here to Timbuktu."

"I won't be shouting it anywhere and your mum won't say a word. I'd prefer to be with you!" he yelled above the noisy din, mixed with tinny kids' music. "If it's nothing, great, we'll go to Starbucks and have hazelnut lattes and muffins as a sneaky together treat. If you need the support, I'm there. What's wrong with that?"

"I'm fine, just leave it, okay? I'll call when I know more. Talk to you in a while." She hung up before she started to cry. She wasn't going to allow him to drop the whole day and come running to her side. That was giving this thing more whack than it deserved. It was probably a cyst or some other manky growth. Besides, she didn't have time to sit around in Starbucks on a Monday morning eating muffins.

All the same, she had a dry mouth and a definite feeling of fear in the pit of her being as she found the right suite in St Mark's private clinic. She took the glass-fronted lift to the third floor and stepped out. The pale carpet and plants surrounded by white gravel, along with the piped music, made the place more hotel-like than hospital-like, which she appreciated. Each suite had a neat discreetly designed plaque, showing which consultant resided within. Scanning as she walked, Tanya found the name she wanted: *Dr Leah Philips*.

Reluctantly she pushed the heavy door open and went inside.

# 2

## Zoe

Being a twin, Zoe didn't have to do a lot of things on her own. Charlie was nearly always there with her. But since all this illness had raised its ugly head, she'd found herself suddenly alone.

When their mum, Diana, had been pregnant with them, she'd had a scan. They weren't as high-tech as they are now, of course. The doctors told her parents they were having two boys. When herself and her sister had popped out, Diana had had a bit of a meltdown.

"But I wanted to call them Charles and Christopher," she said, stricken. She'd got over the sex-change shock, but for the first few days the girls had been Charlene and Christine.

"Diana, we can't call them that! They sound like something from *Alice in Wonderland*," Steven their father had quipped.

Reluctantly, Diana agreed and the girls became Charlie and Zoe.

They were identical in every way to look at, and totally the opposite in personality.

The girls now owned their own clothing boutique in Blackrock, a wealthy suburb of Dublin. Set up at the height of the Celtic Tiger, with a little help from Daddy, the shop was their pride and joy.

When they'd gone to their father Steven begging for backing, he had been proud they were ambitious, but being an astute businessman he also wanted them to realise that dreams didn't come true by slacking off and thinking the world was a land of lollipops and lemon drops.

"Daddy, pleeeeease! We'll work so hard. It will be like a dream come true, to have our own shop. With Mum's friends and our friends alone, we have a readymade clientele." Zoe had fixed her big brown eyes on him and as usual melted his resolve.

"This is serious stuff though, girls – you're going to have to give 110% to this. You can't play shop for two months and decide it's too hard or too boring or too grown-up. If you take this on, you have to give me your word you'll commit totally." Steven was secretly delighted to see his girls hunger to start off in the world of business.

When Fashion Fiend had opened its doors, coming up to five years ago, the girls had come down to earth with a bang. For the first eighteen months, it was all work and no play for Charlie and Zoe. Not to mention no spare cash to pay themselves anything to write home about. They'd naively thought they could dip into the till and pop over to Starbucks for a couple of lattes, or even better snatch a fistful of fifties and trot off clubbing, courtesy of the shop. But that couldn't have been further away from the reality of the business.

It took a good while for them to get established and build up a loyal client base. The hardest part was keeping them coming back. So they took it in turns going off to shows and constantly trying to source new and defining pieces and labels. Stuff that fifty other shops didn't have. While at the same time stocking cuts and styles which were wearable and keenly priced. Suffice it to say, it was a balancing act. They loved every minute of it, so that was half the battle.

Life was ticking along nicely for them. They bought an apartment together and managed to work in the shop without too many fights – bar over the odd gorgeous item of clothing.

Then one day Zoe helped herself to a floaty Chloe top belonging to Charlie.

"Okay, sis, for starters, that's mine," said Charlie, "and,

secondly, I hate to say it, but it's not good on you. Does it look that tight on the arms on me too?" She walked around her sister, staring at her intently.

Zoe had noticed her clothes were getting seriously tight in odd places. The sleeves of her tops were tight. She had a pair of platform shoes, with a small leather ankle-strap. She'd worn them at the same hole-punch for eight months, but suddenly they were far too tight, until one morning she couldn't close them at all. That was when she realised there was something very iffy going on.

Next her sallow skin became mottled with an odd, pinkish, even purple tone in parts.

"I know during the winter, in the wrong light, we can tend to look like the Simpsons, which is the downside to having skin that tans easily. But I've never seen our skin go this shade, Charlie – can you check it?" Zoe showed her sister the top of her back where the unusual rash was spreading. She sighed, feeling like a leper.

"I have to go and open up the shop – you should go to the doctor and get that *thing* sorted." Charlie wagged her finger in a circle, with a look of distaste on her face.

Then the itching started. At first she thought she must be allergic to a shampoo or washing powder.

"Charlie, have you had any reaction to that shampoo I picked up in Duty Free?" she asked, scratching her head.

"No. You better not have nits or you can move out!" Charlie looked appalled as she strode over and started rooting through her sister's hair. "Jesus, Zoe, your scalp and forehead are all red and flaky." Pulling out her sister's top, she looked downwards.

"Hey, what are you doing? I'm not a bleeding chimpanzee, Charlie!"

"Zoe, it's all over your chest and across the top of your back too – gross! You need to go to the doctor and get some cream or something to get rid of that. Is it sore?"

"No, but really irritated and itchy. I'll leave it for a few days and chuck that shampoo in the bin. I'd say that's all it is." She'd shuddered and tried to convince herself it would all just go away.

Things went from bad to worse. The angry red scales travelled down her arms and seemed to skip the rest of her body, before landing to roost around her knees. Her hands were the most affected. The nail-folds at her cuticles went all red, with a thick yellowish kind of skin forming over them.

"That's gross, Zoe! Try soaking your fingers in soapy water and using an orange stick to push it all back," Charlie had suggested.

Zoe gave it a shot, but the pain was too much and the skin just didn't budge.

Then the weight really piled on. As in, one week she weighed nine stone and the next she weighed over ten. Just like that.

"Charlie, it's not fair," she sobbed, feeling utterly miserable. "I haven't changed my eating pattern at all. No pies or burgers for breakfast. No cream buns dipped in chocolate for lunch. No buckets of lard instead of coffee."

Charlie agreed there was no viable reason for the sudden hippo-itus. The final straw came when the purplish red rash crept all over her face.

As they were getting ready to go to work, Zoe broke down. "I know it sounds dreadfully vain and shallow, but I can't bear the thought of having to be in the shop looking fat and red and flaky. The rash is hideously itchy, so in my sleep especially I'm scratching the living daylights out of myself. I look like I've been boiled in oil and dipped in coconut. Charlie, I have to go to the doctor and find out what the hell is wrong with me. I can't go out in public looking like this anymore. Especially with the perfect, deflated version of myself standing beside me. The 'here's what it should look like' version, being you."

Charlie had bitten her lip. "I have to admit that you are starting to look like a mutant."

Only sisters can be that honest. So Zoe trotted off to the doctor, expecting him to say that it was a normal thing, like a reaction to washing powder and to use non-bio instead and take some tablets and stay in bed for a week.

Instead, he'd looked stricken and told her she needed to go to St Mark's Hospital, as he had a suspicion she had lupus.

"What? Lupus? What the hell is that when it's at home?" she'd scoffed, trying to hide the awful inner fear which was climbing up her body, threatening to reach her throat.

"Zoe, it's quite a serious illness. It's to do with your immune system and can cause some problems with the internal organs if not addressed." He'd done that clasping-together-of-his-hands and staring-over-his-round-glasses thing.

Do they all get those wire round glasses when they graduate? Zoe wondered.

"That's the huge scary public hospital near the city centre, isn't it?" Zoe said, looking terrified.

"Yes, St Mark's is the largest general hospital in the area and although it's not as aesthetically pleasing as the adjoining private clinic, you will have access to a large range of doctors. They'll need to run all manner of tests to establish exactly what's going on. I'm sure once you are appointed a specific specialist you could transfer to a private clinic if that's your preference."

"Eh, right. I'll go in to the big hospital then. Should I be majorly concerned here or is this a do-able thing?" She'd never been sick before. Neither herself nor Charlie had so much as had their tonsils out. They hadn't a stitch or a scar between them.

The doctor hadn't given her any reassurance. Only the tests could tell, he said.

She phoned her mum to explain about the tests.

"The doctor tells me it's more than likely that I'll have to stay overnight, for observation, and they'll probably let me out tomorrow afternoon," she told Diana.

"I'm coming. Pack your bag and I'll take you in. Dad is at work, but I'll let him know."

Diana was a lady-who-lunched, infinitely glamorous and poised. She'd had her eyes lifted, a breast augmentation and was a Botox queen.

"I'm merely helping nature along," she'd sniff.

"Nature isn't supposed to cost eight grand, Diana," Steven had scoffed after she'd had her breasts lifted slightly.

She'd failed to point out to her husband that her boobs had had an implant inserted at the same time.

"How can a simple lift cost so much? What the hell did they use? A tiny diamond-encrusted crane to do the job?"

"Don't fret and worry about it, Steven. It's done now, and I'll be the envy of our friends at the golf club. I'll be all healed and ready to show them off by the Christmas party. My eyes will be done and dusted by then too. I'll be a new woman, so you won't have to bother buggering off with a young one," she'd quipped.

"What do you mean your eyes will be done and dusted? What are you doing with them?" Poor Steven wasn't really able for Diana at times.

"Well, lovely Mr Chief has agreed to give me a little eye-lift next month. It's much less invasive than a full facelift and a fraction of the cost. I'll look so fresh and awake afterwards. It will cut down on the Botox too, so it's a win-win situation," Diana had said, hugging him.

"Hang on a bloody minute, Diana! Mr bloody Thief is more like it, and why have you been having Botox? Nobody told me about any of this. What does a fraction of the cost mean?" Steven took on that sad and upset look that men do when they simply can't comprehend the female psyche.

"We won't talk about it at the moment. Why don't I make us all a lovely fresh coffee. I have some of those delicious handmade eighty-five per cent cocoa-solid chocolates you love too, Stevie."

She only called him Stevie when she'd spent over a grand on a handbag or when she really wanted something she knew he'd say no to.

Glamour and glitz aside, Charlie and Zoe always knew they were the most important things to their mother. That afternoon, Diana strapped on her Guccis and drove her convertible TT over to the girls' apartment.

"Jesus, Zoe, that's a shabby-looking bag. Why didn't you tell me, I would've brought you one of my Louis Vuitton overnighters?" Diana eyeballed the battered rucksack in disdain.

By the time they'd parked, checked in and settled Zoe in a room, it was tea time at St Mark's public hospital. A tray with colourless unappetising limp sandwiches and a metal pot of tea arrived. The girl serving it neither made eye contact nor any attempt to make conversation as she dumped it on the wobbly narrow table. The whole atmosphere was horrible.

"I know it's a massive hospital and it's not supposed to be the Ritz Carlton, but the depressing air about the place is so awful!" Zoe began to cry.

"Hey, it's alright darling. We'll get through this." Diana put her fake-tanned, well-manicured arm around her daughter. "It might be an idea to reel in the VHI health insurance, however. Let's wait until the doctor comes around and we'll see about moving to a private clinic. There has to be a slightly *nicer* way of doing this."

Shortly afterwards, a doctor arrived and spoke like a robot, without making eye contact with anyone.

"You've been admitted for tests, am I correct? You need some bloods done immediately, as you have suspected lupus, am I correct?" His eyes darted around the room, a bit like a chicken in a yard.

"Yes, but would it be possible for her to move to a private clinic or somewhere a bit more aesthetically pleasing? It's kind of depressing here and it smells." Diana looked at him like he was something from the bottom of her shoe.

The look was returned ten-fold.

"Your daughter needs immediate attention. Once she's been diagnosed either way vis-à-vis this lupus condition, you can take a decision on who or where she attends. My advice to you now is to stay put and get your facts straight." He cocked his head and stalked out of the room.

Zoe spent the rest of the day being poked and prodded. Apart from moving her arms and legs up and down like a clockwork dolly, they all kept rummaging around her tummy. Pressing on it and asking if it hurt. Of course it bloody hurt. It was being leant on constantly for Christ's sake.

It was the following evening before Zoe got any information.

The door burst open and a whole nest of doctors in white coats, carrying clipboards, scurried in like mice with fixed expressions.

One white coat took the floor.

"Zoe, I'm sorry to have to inform you, but you have dermatomyositis."

"I'm sorry too," she said. "What the hell is that? Does it have a nickname or a short version, like HIV does?"

They all looked at the floor. There was an awkward silence.

"Well? What do you expect me to say? Ah yes, good old dermatamayo-thingamybob! Fuck me, it's a good while since I've heard of anyone having that. Shame really, having that. Damn and blast. So when does the electric-shock treatment and leech therapy start then? Do I have time for a quick shower or do you need to get cracking straight away?"

The speaking white coat took a step forwards.

"Zoe, I'm Dr Patrick Summer, please call me Patrick."

Zoe felt at ease instantly and a little sorry she had been so touchy. Knowing this doctor was opting for first-name terms from the offset made her feel that he was anxious to come across as personable rather than intimidating.

"I know this is all very scary and, yes, the disease has a very convoluted name," he said. "I'll do my best to explain things."

Actually, the doctors weren't the way Zoe thought they'd be. They all seemed incredibly normal and decent. It wasn't like years ago, after all, when the doctors were these God-like figures, with nuns shuffling ahead of them throwing holy water on the floor and bobbing and blessing the ground they walked on. Now, they wore trendy clothes, the men in divine Hugo Boss suits with cool shirts and quirky ties. Most of these white coats were good-looking and smiley and generally spoke to you in a manner which indicated they believed you had a brain too. The pleasant bedside manner they were all displaying instantly helped with Zoe's apprehension.

"Okay." Zoe felt like a small child in the bed.

"I'm a rheumatologist. I have seen your blood results and it's clear that you have got a rare auto-immune disease, called dermatomyositis. This basically means your immune system has broken down and turned on itself. That means that you've no power to fight infection."

"So my whole body is in severe danger of being utterly banjaxed. In a nutshell. Am I right?" Zoe tried to sound nonchalant.

"We can help to fix your immune system with steroid drugs. My main concern right now, though, is that this horrible disease is very often accompanied by cancer." Dr Patrick waited for the news to sink in.

"What? You think I have cancer along with the dermato-thing? But, I'm only twenty-two, I'm too young to have cancer. What sort of cancer? I don't have any lumps in my breast, I've checked." Zoe stared at him as if he was mad.

"Sadly, Zoe, cancer can attack at any age. The type of cancer that is very often linked to dermatomyositis is ovarian cancer. So you wouldn't necessarily feel it as such. I have arranged for you to have some scans. Until we have those results, I need you to start on steroids and sit tight. Have you any questions?"

"Yes, I'm sure I've about a million, but right at this second I can't think of a single one."

The team left Zoe sitting with a blank expression. Totally bereft of feeling. Like Botox to the brain.

The PET scan happened two days later. As she'd been so terrified and unable to sleep, Dr Patrick had prescribed some sleeping pills and some mild anti-anxiety tablets. The nurses had been in to try and help her stay sane. They were astonishingly kind and said all the right things, and explained about remaining positive and keeping her spirits up.

"It really makes a difference to your recovery if you can manage to stay on top of your feelings. If you can be upbeat and stay optimistic it speeds up recovery beyond any drug. I know you'll have times when you feel like jacking it all in and giving up, but don't ever underestimate the power of a positive mind."

Since she'd been taking the anti-anxiety pills, Zoe found it much easier to do all that. They didn't make her want to run a marathon or jump around singing and waving her arms up high, pretending she was at a rave. Nor was she exactly whistling 'Zip-a-Dee-Doo-Dah' out her arse-hole. They just helped to fluff the edges a tiny bit. Make the world slightly fuzzier and a tad less scary and cold. Fuzzy was good. She liked blurred edges. Cold hard light of day was just a bit too dreadful right at that moment.

Zoe hoped they'd let her take those tablets for the rest of her life. In fact, she wondered why they didn't just go ahead and put them in the national supply of drinking water. Why not? At some stage when she'd a bit more energy, she vowed she must campaign for that.

For the PET scan a nurse injected radioactive glucose into her arm and she had to lie in a darkened room for a while. They shut the door and turned on the 'sea sounds' swishy music. Instead of it all being calming, she found the whole thing brought on a panic attack. She closed her eyes and had visions of drowning. Instead of conjuring shoals of pretty coloured tropical fish, in her mind's eye she could see Jaws approaching and wanting to eat the lower half of her body.

She hadn't realised she was screaming until the door burst open and the nurse flew to her side.

"Zoe, what's wrong, darling?" she soothed.

"I'm going to drown and the shark is going to chew off my legs," she sobbed.

Zoe felt like a deranged lunatic, but the nurse soothed her and chatted to her until it was time to put her in the tunnel. Strapped to the bed, with an elasticated belt around her legs, tummy and forehead, she felt a bit like Hannibal Lecter in *Silence of the Lambs*.

"Is this so I don't jump up and knock myself out on the moving tunnel machine?" she asked the silent doctor.

"No," he said, "it's to remind you not to move. You must remain very still so we can scan you and get a clear picture."

Easier said than done. Jesus, why did they tell her not to move? Why did she then get an unmerciful itch on the sole of her left foot just as the scan started?

"The scan takes just over twenty minutes. I'll put on some music, try to relax." The doctor shuffled away.

Zoe desperately wanted to shout, "How the hell am I supposed to relax while strapped to a moving tunnel with an itchy foot and an urge to howl like a wounded wolf?"

Instead she decided to use the time to will her organs to be clear. She had a silent word with them. Asked them to try and not allow the cancer to have a party in them. She took them one by one, as the machine moved from her head down.

*Hey there, brain. Just like you to know how much I appreciate your allowing my whole body to function and all that. Could you possibly watch out for any loose cancer cells floating in your direction and tell them to bugger off?*

*Yo, neck, shoulders, breasts and lungs! How's it going? Same story, different area. Be on the lookout for this cancer stuff. Say no. Don't be timid.*

*Hi, all you big guys! Liver, kidneys, reproductive organs and general female bits not excluding Mr Stomach, bowel, intestines and any other gooey parts I don't even know I possess. If cancer comes knocking on the door, say you're not taking on any diseases at the moment and walk away. Don't get into any discussions and don't make eye contact. Blank the bastard. If we all stick together on this one, it's bound to work out. Thanks for your kind co-operation.*

By the time she'd finished talking to her toenails (she wasn't sure if one could even have cancer of the toenails, but she decided not to take any chances all the same) the background music stopped and the silent doctor reappeared and opened the straps.

"You may go. The porter will be down to take you back to your room."

"Okay," she said, trying to sound upbeat, "thanks a million . . . I –"

The doctor had already gone. *Prick*, she thought viciously. It's alright for him, being in a position to not give a toss and walk off when someone's in the middle of a sentence.

"*Bye then!*" she shouted like a mad old bat. "Sod you and the horse you rode in on," she muttered under her breath. Of course the nice and kind nurse had returned and was staring at her in bewilderment, wondering what she'd done to deserve such a torrent of abuse.

She felt her face flush. "I'm so, so sorry! I wasn't talking to you."

"It's okay." The nurse looked unsure.

Zoe decided to go with the when-you're-in-a-hole-stop-digging policy.

\* \* \*

Over the course of the next couple of days, while Zoe waited for the scan results, she tried desperately not to go insane. The clock seemed almost to tick backwards.

She was inundated with visitors. Charlie was missing her sister so badly she ached.

"You'll be fine, Zo-Zo. Besides, you don't look like you've got cancer. You don't have that papery old-lady skin which makes you look ill. I'd say it's just this dermato-thing."

"Dermatomyositis." Zoe looked as though she were dead inside as she drummed the word out.

"Wow, I'm impressed," Charlie faltered. "I'd say you just got this weird thing and they're only covering their asses saying that it might be cancer. They do that now, you know? They're all worried about being sued and stuff, so they say everything to you. They cover all eventualities, but you'll be fine, I just know it. If you'd had cancer, I would have known, and I didn't so it'll all be cool, yeah?" Charlie looked pleadingly at her twin.

For the first time ever, Zoe felt totally removed from her mirror image. Inside she felt like yelling at her, she felt like grabbing her and shaking her and telling her to get her head out of her arse and stop blabbering on about everything being fine. Fine had been and gone last week. Fine was retired with its feet up in the Seychelles. Fine was never coming back. Ever.

\* \* \*

Exactly a week after she'd been admitted, Dr Patrick and the team congregated in her room again.

"Zoe, there's no easy way to tell you this, but the results of the PET scan are through. I'm afraid you have ovarian cancer."

There. *Wham*. Defining moment. Zoe didn't say anything at first. She looked just past Patrick's head, out the window. There she could see a group of girls not much younger than herself, sitting on the ground with school folders strewn around them. In their itchy uncomfortable school kilts, with nylon blouses and knitted jumpers, they were nervously trying to cram in one more piece of valuable information before they walked inside and began their Leaving Certificate exams.

"Well, I'm glad I'm in here instead of out there with them. I still wake up after a recurring nightmare that I have to do my Leaving Cert, and of course I don't know anything. I'm sweating and some days it takes me a couple of seconds to realise it's only a dream. I know it's probably off the wall, but I'm happier to be in here dealing with what you've just told me, than out there with them." She smiled at Patrick and exhaled slowly. She hadn't even realised she was holding her breath.

"I'm sorry, Zoe. I wish the news could have been different." He sat forward on his chair at the side of her bed and looked at her. "Are you okay?"

"Yep. I suppose so. Shit happens, eh?" She felt terribly sorry for Patrick. "I'm sorry too that you had to come in here and tell me that. You got the shitty end of the stick, didn't you?" she shrugged.

"You get used to it in my job, I'm afraid to say. I'd rather never deliver this kind of news though."

They sat in companionable silence for a few minutes. The clanking and bashing and general activity of the large public hospital carried on outside the room. She'd been lucky to get a private room. Due to this lack-of-immune-system thing, she couldn't be near other people's infections. That was probably the only positive thing about the whole dermatomyositis disease.

"My colleague, Dr Leah Philips, will come in and see you this morning," Patrick said. "She's an oncologist, or a cancer doctor in plain English. She's brilliant and runs the oncology centre here at St Mark's. Your parents have reiterated that they would prefer if you are moved to the private clinic adjoining here. Dr Philips practises there also, so we can organise that transition. She'll go through all the plans and options with you."

# 3

## Esme

Esme had a big smile on her face as she shuffled onto the bus. She'd enjoyed her usual meeting with her Golden Girls group in the local church hall.

Ever since she'd found out about this cancer in her colon, she'd become a bit of a celebrity amongst the women.

Her husband Michael never went to any socials with her. "I'd rather stick hot pins in me eyes than sit listening to you lot talking about who brought her poodle to the hairdresser, or whatever it is you all do." He preferred to sit in front of the telly and watch the racing.

Her daughter Nora had known she wasn't right. She'd told her about all the noises in her belly. Some nights it sounded like a monster was trying to get out it was so loud. Now, Michael didn't pass any comment, but he was kind of the silent type so he wouldn't.

"Mum, he's as deaf as a post! If you had Nirvana playing in concert in there he wouldn't hear it," Nora had laughed.

"Well, maybe, but your dad was never a great man for discussing medical conundrums. He wouldn't know the first thing about women's problems or anything like that. Says gory details put him off his tea, and you know what your father's like when he misses his tea."

Esme and Michael didn't travel, apart from a bus tour once a year, and the furthest they'd ever gone was Wales. Michael didn't like foreign food.

"Why can't they talk proper, like what we can? All that sing-song business. They need to get a hold of themselves." He'd been irritable the whole time in Wales. It wasn't worth upsetting him. It had been a Sunday and they'd been served Shepherd's Pie, to add insult to injury. He never ate Shepherd's Pie on a Sunday. No, he usually had roast chicken on a Sunday.

When this tummy complaint had escalated, Esme had ended up in hospital.

"Was it terrible, Esme?" Rosaleen had asked at the Golden Girls meeting.

"Wait till I tell you. Girls, it was above and beyond what I could have imagined. The food was lovely and they even brought a menu so I could choose what to have. The bathroom at the end of the room was spotless. A little foreign girl came in each morning and scrubbed the place from top to bottom. A little dark-skinned girl, with lovely hair braided with beads at the ends. Now, it was the texture of wool, but she'd done a marvellous job of making it look pretty."

"Did she speak English, Esme?" another eager lady wanted to know.

"No, but she was very good at gesturing. The doctors and nurses were all very friendly. Particularly the doctor who told me I'd contracted the cancer. He was a lovely lad. A bit hesitant and needed to stand up for himself a bit more. A bit of a Mary-Jane. 'Pansy boys' they used to call them. But that's not allowed now. You have to call them 'members of the gay community'."

"Did you ask him if he's gay?" Margaret looked stunned.

All the Golden Girls had adjusted their hearing aids. The speed at which the biscuits were being dunked into mugs of tea accelerated.

"I know how to be politically erect. Don't worry about me," she'd reassured them with a wave of her hand. "I didn't ask him was he a queer. I'm sure it wouldn't affect his ability to be a doctor in any case."

"What did he say, Esme?"

"'Mrs Mulligan,' says he, 'I'm sorry to tell you that you've cancer of the colon.' 'Well, it's hardly your fault love,' says I. Then he got all kind of shuffley. So I told him to stand up straight and be a good lad and not to be fidgeting about as if he'd a ferret up his arse. Well, the look of shock on his face was priceless. But, you've got to be cruel to be kind, I say." Esme chuckled to herself.

All the others giggled too. Esme was a gas woman.

"What are they going to do now?" Mrs Murphy wanted to know.

"Well, hopefully he'll take the comment on board and try to keep still from now on," she sniffed.

"No, Esme, about the cancer."

"Well, that's just it, I've to go back to the hospital tomorrow and they're going to operate. I'll be in for ten days, so the doctor says. Then I'm having chemotherapy and all." She nodded, very pleased with herself.

The biscuits were finished and Esme was led out to the bus stop by the ladies, amidst a wave of "God bless you's" and "I'll say a prayer for you's".

The day only got better. As she shut her front door, the phone rang. It was her eldest daughter Tracey to wish her well the following day.

"I've been on to the hospital and they are very positive about your outcome, Mum, so I hope you're not too worried." Tracey hated being away from home at times of crisis.

"Ah, you're a good girl, Tracey, thinking of me like that. I've just come from my Golden Girls meeting. They're all off to Mass in the morning to pray for me. It's given us all something to talk about."

Although both Tracey and her sister Nora were delighted their mother wasn't distressed about her cancer, they did hope she wasn't in denial about it either. Tracey had had a good chat with the specialist and was confident they had a solid plan in place to care for Esme.

"The cancer is in the lower part of her colon and we hope to be able to remove it all. She'll need some chemotherapy to make sure there is nothing left hanging around."

"What's her prognosis?" Tracey had asked. "She's not a young woman." Being Esme's eldest child, she took it upon herself to do the talking.

"We're hoping for a positive outcome," the specialist had confided. "Your mother is as strong as an ox and has enough positivity to keep the whole hospital afloat. There's a great support group available too, which we'll tap her into. We hope to start her chemotherapy within six weeks. We'll move her to another ward, on the oncology floor, where she'll have more specialised care than the general surgical ward she's coming into tomorrow."

\* \* \*

The following morning, with her gown tied up the back, Esme was whisked into theatre. Instead of being upset or worried, she found the whole thing fascinating. She loved all the brown-skinned nurses patting her hand and telling her how great she was. Before she knew it, they were calling her name and telling her it was all over.

She was like a celebrity when they wheeled her back to the ward in a surgical bed. She got a great surprise – her Nora and Tracey were waiting behind the curtain which was pulled around her bed.

Michael was there too, wringing his hands and looking all upset. She wasn't able to talk much, she felt very tired, but she was thrilled with all the fuss.

The girls hugged her gently and stroked her hair.

"Don't try and speak, Mum," said Tracey. "You need your rest."

"The doctor fella was in with us, Esme. He seemed very pleased, said he got it all." Michael looked all overcome with emotion. "But he'd want to say it all went well, wouldn't he? Wasn't he bloody well doing it? He's hardly going to come in and say, 'We've made a pig's-Mickey of your wife's operation, and she's gonzoed!'" Michael was trying to be jolly, but his heart was breaking.

Esme had a catheter draining her bladder, two drips and was the colour of putty. Her normally styled hair was flat and stuck to her head. She looked old and vulnerable. Not the usual strong and confident lady they were all used to. Normally, she'd be the one straightening the bed and insisting the patient drank some tea. Tea held magical properties, of course. Even if your leg was falling off, a cup of tea could somehow fix it in Esme's eyes.

"Why don't you have a little sleep, Mum?" Tracey said and explained that they'd be right there beside her and she should close her eyes for a minute.

That seemed like a good plan, so she drifted off. What seemed like seconds later, the ward sister woke her.

"Esme, we have a bed for you in the new oncology ward, so we'll move you over there now if that's alright with you?"

"Yes, love, whatever suits you." She beamed, enjoying all the attention.

"I'll tell your husband and daughters where you've moved to. They've gone to have a snack, but they'll be up to see you in a while, okay?" The ward sister patted her hand.

The new ward Esme was brought to was even nicer than the first one. It was newer and there were only four beds, unlike the previous one which had six. The bed was electronic too. So fancy.

"I've never seen a robotic bed before, just look at that. You press the button with the picture of the man on it, and it moves all by itself. That's super," she commented to nobody in particular.

She moved the bed up to a sitting position, then all the way back to a lying-down position. Then she pressed the other button and the legs part went up in the air.

"Holy God, that's a great invention, isn't it?" she said to the lady beside her who only nodded slightly. She didn't say much. Wasn't much of a talker so far. Esme was a bit disappointed. She'd been hoping to meet some other women who liked a bit of a chinwag.

Another patient arrived back in the room and slowly made for the bed opposite. She nodded and smiled at Esme.

"Hello!" Esme sat herself up. The lady was in a purple quilted bed jacket, and a lovely floral flannelette nightgown with matching slippers. Her hair was kind of flat-looking, could do with a few curlers, Esme noted. She was limping slightly. "You seem to be having trouble walking there, love?" Esme nodded while looking down towards her feet.

"I've terrible arthritis in me knee. Now to add to it, they've told me I've cancer in me, you know, *breast*." She whispered the word and put her hand up to her mouth.

"Oh, right. God love you. Well, I'm not too well myself. Had to have an excursion myself last week. They put a pipe up me . . . you know," Esme pointed downwards. "They told me that there was cancer in me colon. So they're after chopping it out, thank God. A lovely young-fella's after doing it. I wonder if he's married, although he kind of had a bit of a way about him, if you know what I mean?"

The other lady introduced herself as Miriam. They hit it off from the first second. Esme was so thrilled with the other woman, she wasn't giving the post-surgical pain a second thought.

As Miriam was over her surgery a couple of days, she took it upon herself to be in charge. She told Esme what to order for her tea.

"The ham salad is terrible disappointing. Not like you'd do yourself. The ham isn't real stuff, it's that shop-bought plastic excuse. The pasta does be lovely. If you like that sort of thing."

They shared the odd snippet of idle chit-chat during the course of the afternoon, whenever Esme was awake. Miriam understood the other woman was groggy and undoubtedly uncomfortable so she kept their conversation to a minimum. Michael and the girls came back in during visiting hours and so did Frank, Miriam's husband. The two men were introduced. As the women were busy talking, the two men sat facing each other in armchairs with their arms folded, both looking at the floor.

"So do you follow sports at all yourself, Frank?" Michael ventured.

"Ah yeah. I'd watch anything. I like an auld trot into the bookies too. Not that I'm a gambler or anything iffy, just for the enjoyment."

"Oh yes. I do like an odd swift one myself. No harm in it, my son, no harm."

There was silence from the men for a further ten minutes or so.

"So do you take a pint at all, Michael?"

"I do. I do. A stout-man meself."

"Well, here's your brother." Frank rubbed his hands together at the thought of a creamy pint of the black stuff.

The nurse came in to tell the visitors that it was time to get going. The men decided to go for a quick one together on the way home.

"You don't mind if I do, love?" Michael asked Esme's permission.

"Sure what would I mind for? Aren't I stuck in here with me cancer in me colon? Where would I be going? You go and have a little drink with Frank and a chat. Don't miss the last bus home now, sure you won't?" she warned.

"We'll go too, Mum, and sit in the lounge part, and all head home in a taxi," Nora assured her.

Miriam tried not to compare these girls to her son, Declan. He was a good lad in a lot of ways. He never shouted or behaved in an aggressive way. He wasn't into drugs, unlike that thug of a son Mrs O'Gill had. He'd ended up behind bars, for selling stuff to school kids to sniff. Declan was fine, he just didn't make a huge effort. It wouldn't occur to him to drop in to the hospital to visit her. He certainly wouldn't bring her a bouquet of pretty pink peony roses, like the ones Esme's girls had lovingly placed on her beside locker.

She would even settle for a card, brought in by Frank. But seeing as Declan had never given her a birthday or Christmas card his whole life, he was hardly going to start now. She probably should tell him that he wasn't being that nice to her, but she didn't like to start a row. She hated fighting. Her own father had spent his time drinking and shouting.

Declan had a touch of his grandfather about him. A hot temper that could flare if he'd had a skinful of pints. It had only happened once or twice, but Miriam had been mortified. Frank had often said to her that the lad should be handing over some money towards the shopping and bills. But he didn't exactly earn a king's ransom on the buses, so she'd feel mean taking his cash.

"Sure he pours his wages down his throat, for Christ's sake, woman, why shouldn't he contribute? All he does is bring home a bag of soggy fish and a mountain of chips on a Friday evening, and you act like he's been to the North Pole and hunted down a rare breed of penguin and made it into pâté for you."

Frank was kind of hard on the lad, but he meant well. At least he was out of school, where he used to be in trouble most days, for being in the wrong place at the wrong time. He'd a job, which he turned into most days, he was able to look after his own expenses and he wasn't bothering anyone. He hadn't a string of illegitimate babies across the city and he never came home in a squad car. That was good enough for Miriam. Well, most of the time it was. Only in moments like today, when she saw how other kids treated their mams, did she feel a slight buried-away sting, in the depth of her heart.

At least she still had her son at home with her. Poor Esme's daughters had all fled to England. She said they phoned all the time and came home as often as possible, but that couldn't be the same. They were lovely girls both of them. Well turned out and lovely hair and make-up. Lovely speaking voices they had too. You'd know they were Irish, no two ways about it, but they had a gorgeous English tone to their accent. Just on some words. Declan's usual greeting to friends was, "Alright, horse." These girls had been chatting to pals on the phone and had answered with a posh, slightly high-pitched, "Hello," which they pronounced, "Hallou". Miriam vowed to practise that kind of hello as soon as she got home.

By ten o'clock that evening, the visitors had all been asked to leave. Miriam knew she probably should leave Esme alone, but she couldn't wait until the morning to get the proper lowdown on her surgery.

Popping her head around the corner of the curtain, she whispered, "Are you awake, love?"

"Ah hiya, Miriam love." Esme looked a little brighter than she had earlier in the day. "Come on in till I tell you all about the operation. Sit down on that chair there. Did you see the flowers, aren't they beautiful? Pee-knees roses, the girls called them. Sounds a bit rude, doesn't it?" she cackled.

Miriam sat on the edge of her seat as Esme filled her in on the operation.

"The tumour they removed was the size of a grapefruit," Esme fibbed. Now, nobody had mentioned grapefruits to Esme directly, but she'd heard it on one of the *Discovery* health programmes once before, so she thought this was the perfect opportunity to use it.

"God love you, Esme," Miriam kept repeating, tutting and shaking her head.

"Did you see all this plumbing work they've left sticking out of me? Did you have all this, Miriam?"

"No, love, I had a different one to you. When they removed my *breast*." Miriam had to whisper the word. She still couldn't say certain body parts out loud. "When they took it away, they gave me a drain. Awful it was."

"I even have a cataract in. Terrible it is. Won't be able to go to the toilet for a day or so. All the wee has to be taken into that bag, which they're keeping at the side of the bed. I had to tell Michael earlier not to look down. Would've put him off his pint."

"That's why men never have babies, Esme. They'd be no good at bags of wee or stitches in their nether regions, never mind all the blood. No. God definitely designed women for endurance." Miriam held her head high, proud of the fact that women should be encouraged to suffer.

\* \* \*

Esme stayed in a further six days, recovering from her operation. Meanwhile, Miriam had been sent home. Frank had come on the bus to collect her, but he had insisted that they went back in a taxi.

"I'm not sitting on a bus with all your bags and waiting for them stitches to burst as we go over all those bleeding ramps on the Stillorgan Road," he'd muttered.

# 4

## Tanya

Tanya was sitting uncomfortably in Dr Leah Philip's consulting rooms, to find out her scan results. She'd found out three weeks previously that the small rubber pea on the side of her breast was in fact cancer. Dr Leah had performed a biopsy, removing a tiny part of the lump, to determine whether or not there was cancer present. Tanya had taken the news in her stride. Deep down inside she'd been bloody furious with herself, but she wasn't going to show it.

Poor Alfie had taken it badly. He'd cried and physically shook and asked why repeatedly.

"Just leave it, Alfie, it happens all the time." Tanya had held his hand, as they sat in Dr Leah's office.

Dr Leah had explained that she would need a CT and PET scan to determine the extent of the cancer. "Once we have that information, we'll be in a position to decide on a suitable treatment. I need to know if this infected lymph node is on its own, or if the cancer is more widespread." Dr Leah's tone was kind yet firm.

On that same day she'd given them the support-group information too. Alfie had insisted she start attending this God-awful group. To appease him, as he was so devastated, she agreed. She felt guilty enough for having this blasted disease in the first place. The least she could do was try and keep him as placid as possible.

Now, as she waited nervously by herself, she prayed the scans hadn't shown any further spread of the disease. She hadn't told Alfie that Dr Leah's secretary had called the previous day. She'd tell him when it was all over.

Besides, they'd have to ask her mother to mind Jenny, so she'd know there was a problem. She didn't want anyone to know about this. She'd have the surgery or treatment or whatever she had to do and keep it to herself. People had no right to know her business.

"Tanya, hi, come through, please." Dr Leah called her into her office.

The doctor sat at her desk and motioned to Tanya to sit opposite.

"I'll come straight to the point, Tanya. The scans have shown the disease is in several parts of your body, I'm afraid."

"What do you mean by that?" Tanya sat bolt upright. *What? This wasn't what she was expecting.*

"There is no easy way to say this, so I'm going to be brutally straight with you." Dr Leah hesitated only momentarily. Her voice was even, yet sympathetic. "It's in your left breast, which would correspond with the lump you found. It's also in your axilla or underarm. It has spread to your shoulder, lungs and spine also."

There was gripping silence in the room, as Tanya's mind floated. Her eyes rolled and she felt a tightening in her throat, connecting with the whirlpool in her head. As she slid off the chair, Leah ran around the desk to grab her. She wasn't out for long, but she felt very confused when she came to.

"I'm sorry, how embarr . . . Oh dear. This is not great, my apolo . . ." Tanya struggled back onto the chair.

"Just sit still for a few seconds, Tanya. You've had a terrible shock. There is no easy way of delivering this type of news, I'm afraid. Can I call your husband?"

"*No!*" Tanya shouted, the whites of her eyes showing.

"But he'll need to know. You'll have to tell him. You're going to need extensive surgery and intensive chemotherapy, Tanya. You won't be able to do this alone."

*Wanna bet?* Tanya thought fiercely.

Dr Leah was amazing. She explained to Tanya that they didn't have time on their side, but they would do everything they could. The first step would be to perform a mastectomy and axillary clearance.

"This involves removing the breast and all the tissue, including lymph nodes, under your arm on the left side. As soon as you've recovered from that, we'll go straight into chemotherapy. I'll scan you again after a few weeks and we'll assess the other tumours at that stage."

Knowing this woman was scared out of her wits, but as tough as nails on the outside, Leah was taking the bereft-of-emotion approach. She knew if she pussy-footed around her, or was even too nice to her, she'd put up a brick wall of defence.

Tanya was dumbfounded. Here she was, at the age of thirty-five, talking about a mastectomy. Surely they were only for older women? People who had grey hair, crow's feet and dentures? Women who looked "good for their age".

"We can do reconstructive surgery at a later date, but right now we need to try and arrest the disease."

"So, I'll be flat on the left side. Like a deflated balloon?" She felt horrified. The thought of looking like a semi-pancake was terrible.

"Tanya, I know it's a dreadfully daunting thought for you. But you don't have a choice right now. I can go through the information here and show you some photos of other mastectomies, with women who've had reconstruction and women who haven't. So you'll have an idea of what to expect." Leah waited for Tanya to guide her with what she wanted to do.

"I want the reconstruction. I don't want to look like a freak, I'm too young to go through my life with only one breast." She started to shake and gulp. She didn't want to cry, but she simply couldn't hold back. This was a living hell. This fucking disease was eating her up from the inside out. She'd been going around oblivious as she was slowly rotting internally. "Am I dying?" her hollow eyes searched Leah's, willing her to say no. Lie to me if you have to, she thought.

"Your chance of survival is limited. The disease has spread.

We're looking at treatment to prolong your life, in my experience. But, miracles happen. We'll fight this every step of the way. I will do everything in my power to help you."

Dr Leah pulled out a large photo album. Tanya gasped when she saw the first picture. The torso showed an angry-looking purplish scar, which gathered the taut surrounding skin. The lop-sided flatness in comparison with the healthy plump breast on the other side was hideous. It screamed out *wrong, wrong, wrong,* to Tanya. Crying openly now, tears flowing down her cheeks, she slowly turned the pages. After the first couple of photos, she didn't find it quite as gruesome anymore. Nor did she feel like she was going to throw up. Which she had to admit she did in the beginning.

It was all so barbaric-looking. The ones who'd had reconstruction had no nipples. They looked like maimed Barbie dolls. Smooth and shiny, like people moulded from plastic. People who weren't real. A bit like that weird grumpy plasticine little man, Morph, who appeared on that art programme years ago.

"Bloody hell, Leah, they all look like they've survived a machete attack. Am I going to look like that?"

Tanya felt like she'd been run over by a steamroller. It was beyond awful. Nothing in the world had prepared her for this feeling. She shook like a leaf and cried. Tears of sadness, for her poor unsuspecting body and what it was going to endure. Tears of grief, for the innocence that she felt was being ripped away from her. An innocence that she had foolishly assumed was hers, health-wise, for a good few more years to come.

"Why is this happening to me? Why am I having to face this kind of thing? Why me? I know this might sound very callous and mean, but why couldn't it happen to someone else? An older woman, in her eighties who doesn't go out much and doesn't need to wear the next season's collection by Moschino? I need my body. I need to be able to go out to work. I need to be a wife and mother. I needed to be able to sit by a pool on holidays and not look like a freak. I don't want to be the type of person who freaks out little children. I don't want to be pointed at or have people back away from me because I scare them with half a flat chest, which looks like raw rashers. I don't think I can do this, Leah. I just want to go home and forget the whole thing. Can't I just leave it for a few months, at least until I feel like I can cope? Just so I can get my head around it and deal with it in a calmer manner?"

She was desperately clutching at straws, wishing and hoping against hope that there just might be some sort of a get-out clause.

"I know this is all huge and so much for you to take in, but the cancer won't wait for anyone, Tanya. You can't afford to sit around and let it continue to live in your body. We've got to try and kill it and attempt to stop it in its tracks. It's the only hope you have right now."

The tears sprang anew. Tanya didn't think she had any more. Where the hell were they coming from? She'd no idea a person could produce so much water.

"Your mastectomy is scheduled for the day after tomorrow. We act quickly once we have a positive diagnosis. Would you like me to call your husband so he can come and get you now?" Leah was staring at Tanya intently.

Tanya was finding it so difficult not to have a tantrum and run out the door. She didn't want to have this hideous conversation with anyone. She didn't want to tell poor Alfie she was riddled with disease and that she was going to look like a single-humped camel.

"No, I'm alright now. I'll drive home and talk to him there. He's a sensitive soul, he's going to be devastated. I don't want him to have a melt-down in public. He'd be embarrassed afterwards, and God knows he's going to have enough to endure in the next while. No, I'll go home." Tanya exhaled loudly, scrunching her shoulders and letting them drop. She dropped her head to one side and then to the other, stretching out her neck muscles.

Dr Leah went through the surgery procedure. It would take about four hours in total. She would be flat on the left side with a large flat scar across her chest where the breast used to be. She would have another scar under her arm, across her armpit, where the lymph nodes would be removed. There would be at least two drains in place to collect any residual liquid.

"We hope you will regain good function of your arm quite

quickly afterwards. I'll make sure the physiotherapy team is alerted. They'll get working with you as soon as possible. A big thing to remember is to try and do the stretches and the exercises they give you as soon after surgery as you can. A bit of pain in the beginning will reward you with much better results afterwards, trust me."

With a bag full of leaflets and a head full of information, Tanya emerged into the world, feeling like she'd been mutilated already. Her eyes burned and her nose felt like she'd inhaled a herd of angora goats. Both the bright daylight and the gravity of the situation blinded her as she made her way to her car. Briefly, she wondered if she should call a taxi but the thought of having to make polite conversation with a man who undoubtedly would want to discuss the plight of the taxi industry, spurred her on to the safe haven of privacy her own car provided.

Her mobile rang. It was Alfie. She didn't answer. As far as he was concerned, she was just at work as normal. She couldn't answer and pretend she was fine. Even seeing his name on her mobile-phone screen brought on fresh tears. She struggled to shove her ticket into the car-park machine. Why the hell did they have these things in hospitals? Surely the only reason anybody would be here was either have some sort of treatment or to visit a sick friend or relative? In either case, did those people need to pay any more than they were already paying?

As she pulled up to the front of her house a few moments later, she was met by a surprised Alfie and Jenny. They were in the front garden doing a bit of tidying up. Alfie had a big metal wheelbarrow and Jenny had her own red plastic Winnie the Pooh version.

"Mama, hi, hi, hi!" Jenny ran with muddy hands and launched herself at her mother before she could even get out of the car.

"Hi Jenny, are you helping Daddy, baby girl?" The softness of her downy hair and the baby scent, mixed with the rustic earthy smell of the garden, filled Tanya's senses.

"Down," Jenny wriggled free. She was on to the next thing, examining a snail on the side of the driveway. With her tiny finger pointed, she crouched down on her hunkers to have a better look.

"Hi, honey, what are you doing? Tanya, what is it?" Alfie caught her as she crumpled into his arms.

Sobbing and heaving, she couldn't control the flood of emotions rushing through her.

Alfie led her inside and quickly returned to scoop up a protesting Jenny.

"No, Dada, no! Down, down!" She pointed towards the garden and wriggled and writhed to try and break free. She'd been having such fun, she couldn't understand why she was being made go inside. Knowing she wasn't due to sleep for a further half hour, Alfie decided to put her in her cot with some gentle music playing and hope she'd calm down.

"Jenny out, no, Dada, out!" she yelled, standing up in the cot and shaking the bars ferociously. Alfie drew the curtains and turned on her little kaleidoscope which played a soothing tune and cast colourful images of animals onto the bedroom ceiling.

"Good girl, Jenny. You have a nice little sleepy and then Dada will bring you for a lollipop and a go on the swing at the park, okay?" He handed Jenny a soother, which she stuffed into her mouth.

"Num-a-num-a-num . . ." The little girl's eyes rolled as she sucked her soother.

Not for the first time, Alfie wished he could get such a kick from a piece of rubber. After rubbing her head, stroking and smoothing her forehead for a few minutes, he knew she was relaxed enough to fall asleep.

Tiptoeing from the room, he ran downstairs to talk to Tanya. He had never seen Tanya in a state before. The closest had been the day she'd discovered she was pregnant. But even then, it wasn't like this. There had to be something really awful happening.

"I think she'll settle. What's up, honey?" Alfie rushed to where Tanya was sitting on a wooden kitchen chair, motionless, staring into space, shoulders slumped forwards.

"Oh Alfie!" Fresh tears cascaded down her cheeks. "I'm sorry. I'm so, so sorry. It's all my fault. You don't deserve this. Neither does Jenny. I should go now – that way you won't have to deal with it all. Yes, that's what I'll do. I'll go. You'll move on. You'll find another love. You're such a good man. You'll be snapped up and Jenny's really cute too. We love her, of course we do. But strangers have said she's pretty. That's good. It'll make her easier to love. Easier for a strange woman to come in and *want* to love her. You could realise your dream, find a woman who wants a brood of kids this time. Don't ask her about it on the first date but, early on in the relationship, be blunt. If she's like me and doesn't seem interested, move on. You will, won't you?" Her eyes were darting from one end of the room to the other. Panic and fear mixed with her frenzy.

"Whoa there! One step at a time! What on earth are you on about? I've no intention of finding anyone else. Where is this nonsense talk coming from?"

She didn't answer. She was barely breathing, in fact.

"Tanya? Talk to me?" The fear was contagious. Alfie blanched. "What have you found out? Did you see the doctor again? Tanya? Tell me, please." He bent down and clasped her hands in his. Kneeling on the floor in front of her, he looked up into her eyes and waited for her to speak.

"The cancer has spread. It's in my breast, underarm, lungs, shoulder and spine. I'm having surgery tomorrow, to remove the breast and underarm one, but any treatment I'm having will only prolong my life. It's gone too far. It's too advanced. Dr Leah mentioned miracles," she scoffed bitterly, "but they certainly don't happen."

"Oh yes, they do. Look at us. Look at Jenny." Alfie was strong and determined.

Tanya had expected him to fall apart. She'd thought he'd have to be scraped off the tiles, like a big soggy limpet. Whinging and howling and shaking his head. Instead, he took on a determined expression. He held her hands even tighter than before.

"You will fight this. *We* will fight this, Tanya. Never say never. God is good, where there's life there's hope. Don't ever give up hope, Tanya, 'cos I sure as hell won't. Now, if you so much as mention me leaving or you going away again, I won't be responsible for what I'll do. No more bullshit talk. Another thing, don't you dare shut me out again. If you have an appointment at the hospital, you let me know. I want to be there too. You are not an island and you are not alone, so stop trying to be either. I love you more than anything in the world and I am not going to stand by and allow you to push me away. We are in this together, come hell or high water. Understood?" His eyes flashed, and Tanya knew it was futile to argue with him.

"Okay." The voice was barely audible. She didn't recognise herself.

"Now, you've had a terrible shock and no doubt you haven't had your coffee fix. Go inside and sit down. The paper is there, your coffee is on the way. Don't argue with me again and don't even consider trying to take all this on alone."

He stood up and pulled her hands to help her stand up. Wrapping his strong arms around her, he held her as if his life depended on it. The warmth of his embrace made the choked emotion she'd been trying to hold inside break free. She cried so hard her legs couldn't hold her up. He took the full weight and impact. Silently, he stroked her back and let her lean on him, in every way.

After she'd calmed down, they had enough time to talk before Jenny woke up. Tanya was adamant she didn't want too many people to know what was happening. She certainly wasn't telling them in work. She'd tell her secretary, Sally, but none of the others. She'd tell her family. No one else was to find out for now. Not until they had to.

"I couldn't stand the pity. I can't bear the thought of being looked at in that sorrowful way. That 'poor you' sentiment." She shuddered at the thought.

"Okay, love. Whatever you want." Alfie didn't think anyone would do that, but he wanted to try and keep her calm.

They discussed the surgery she was about to go through. Alfie, without prompting, told her he would love her no matter what she looked like. He repeatedly told her how much he believed God would mind her and watch over her.

As Jenny's little voice travelled down the stairs, she rose from the sofa. "I'll go. I'd like a hug now. At least she's too young to know what's going on, so she won't treat me differently. She won't pity me."

An hour later, Tanya insisted on going in to the office to talk to Sally, followed by a flying visit to a local shopping centre to buy night attire, a wash bag and a few essentials. Alfie put Jenny in the buggy and took her to the park for a lollipop and a play, as promised.

On the way home he popped into the church to light a candle, with Jenny in his arms. The toddler was mesmerised by the flicking, dancing candlelight. Putting a coin into the old-fashioned brass box in the church, Alfie let Jenny choose a little white candle with her pudgy paw. Guiding her, he held the wick against another candle to light it.

"Well done, darling. Give it to Dada now and we'll put it into the holder."

Not entirely happy about giving her new toy away, Jenny shouted out. "No, Dada, mine, ah-ah, bold Dada!" Her pout and determination to hold onto what she felt was hers made him smile. She was so like her mother at times it was scary.

Eventually he managed to coax the candle from her clutches and place it safely in a metal-pronged holder. Setting her down, he made his way to the nearest pew to say a quick prayer. Loving the echoing sound her clapping made in the empty church, Jenny marched around in a circle, bashing her tiny hands together and singing a gobbledegook song, with very few decipherable words. Every now and then, she'd throw in a 'dada' or 'mama' but mostly she sounded like a drunk, deaf person with a thick Scottish tinge to her accent.

As Alfie rested his elbows on the bench in front and clasped his hands together in prayer, he felt a presence above him. Looking up, he saw there was the lady in the headscarf. He had encountered her at the church before.

"God is good, keep your faith. He will be there for you all. He does nothing without meaning." Her little twinkling eyes blinked slowly and she continued on her way.

Alfie stayed on his knees for a few more minutes before rising and scooping up his performing daughter.

"Bye-bye, ta-ta, see-ya-soon!" Jenny called, waving like a maniac as they went back into the blinding daylight.

* * *

Tanya was in her office, trying to get her head together. She had a big function that evening. She wondered if it would be better to attend it as planned or ask her staff to do it without her. The answer came when her mobile phone rang. It was Marek, one of the Polish guys who erected the marquees for her.

"Miss-a-Tanya, I need new drill. This one no work. He broken. You can buy for me?"

"What do you mean it won't work?" she barked. Bloody hell, she didn't have time to piss about electrical shops looking for power tools.

"He stop. He make big bang. He smell like fire, you know?"

"Right, Marek, have you got the van?" she shouted into phone.

"Yes, he here with me."

"Okay, go to the electrical shop and pick out a drill and I'll meet you there. Go to the one in Sandyford. It's the nearest, okay?" She thumped the desk while glancing at the time.

"What?"

"*Go to the electrical shop – I will see you there!*" she yelled.

"Me have no money for drill."

"I know." She gritted her teeth and tried to stay calm. "That's why I'm meeting you there."

"Okay, you come too. I wait for you here, okay? You collect me, yes? Bye-bye."

The stupid git had hung up. She pressed his number and he answered. It took a while to get the message across. He was a brilliant worker, he always turned up on time and got the job done. He didn't get into small talk. Tanya never had to hear what his wife, granny, auntie or cat was up to. Unlike the dozen or so predecessors she'd employed to do his job, he just did what he was supposed to do. He'd also become like a mini employment agent –

he'd brought most of his extended family over to Ireland and she now employed them all in some capacity. Nearly all her waiting-staff, cleaners and cooks were Polish. She liked their attitude. They were hard-working and respectful. The only downside was the occasional language barrier.

She met him at the store. He was standing at the till with the new drill.

"Hello, Miss-a-Tanya. Drill." Marek didn't smile. His personality didn't often extend to unnecessary pleasantries, which suited her perfectly.

They paid for the tool, then Tanya decided to drive to the house where the party was being held. Everything was under control. The only thing that was missing as far as Tanya could see was the cake. It was a wedding-anniversary party and they had paid through the nose for a custom-made cake in the shape of a yacht.

A feeling of excited expectation filled the air. The tables were being finished off with flower arrangements. Tanya had chosen low-sided square bowls, which were filled with Oasis and studded with cream roses. The couple wanted pictures of them on their wedding day forty years previously to adorn the tent, so she'd had them printed on canvas and suspended like old-fashioned scrolls along the side. The sepia-coloured shading she'd chosen showed the pictures in a soft dreamy way. The bottles of mineral water had custom-made labels with the same photos. The lighting consisted of tiny twinkling blue LED lights, set into fine chiffon in the roof. The place looked wonderful. It also smelled faintly of grapefruit, as Tanya had a thing about marquees smelling of trampled grass. She felt people were paying over the odds to hire them as a function room so they didn't need the circus-tent smell. She always made sure that small oil burners were lit randomly around the tent to create a delicate fragrance in the air.

"Where's the cake?" she shouted, pacing up and down. She knew she was being aggressive and bad-tempered. Not that she got much response. Everyone was so busy they didn't answer.

"*Hello?*" Tanya yelled, one hand on her hip and her foot tapping. One of the girls came over and paid her some attention.

"Where's the cake? Has it been delivered? Your white shirt has a mark on the collar, you'll have to sponge it clean." Tanya looked her up and down. She knew she was being a bitch, but she couldn't help it. She genuinely didn't care if any of them liked her or not, she just wanted the job done correctly. She never became 'friends' with her employees, but at the same time she was polite and civil most of the time.

Sally appeared, looking hassled.

"Sally, there you are. Where is the cake?" Tanya glowered.

"I spoke to the delivery man just now, it'll be here in ten minutes. Are you okay, Tanya? You look kind of peaky."

"I'm fine, Sally. I have a bitch of a migraine and I might have to leave you to it here."

If Sally was shocked that her boss was abandoning a function, she didn't show it. "No problem, Tanya. It's all under control here. So you go on if you like. I can always call you if needs be. But I don't envisage any hitches at this stage."

Sally got a strange feeling as she watched Tanya leave. It was unheard of for her boss to go home at the start of any function. She hoped Tanya was alright.

# 5

The second 'Pink Ladies' meeting came around alarmingly quickly. Sian was putting the finishing touches to the coffee tray when Tanya and Zoe appeared at the same time.

"Good morning, ladies, you're very welcome. Come on in and sit down, coffee's on the way. Esme should be along any minute now." Sian flicked the kettle on to boil. God, she needed the coffee this morning. She'd had another sleepless night. She'd tried to fool herself into feeling fresh and awake by wearing bright colours. The shocking-pink and turquoise linen dress she'd chosen was doing its best, but she was knackered. It might be time to go the doctor and see about getting something to help her sleep.

Not for the first time, she thanked God for the invention of make-up. Without it, she simply couldn't have gone out in public today. Anyway, she figured all the people she was seeing today had far more on their minds than the fact that she looked like she'd been at a three-day rave.

Ever since Liam died, she'd had trouble sleeping. That was to be expected. They'd been married twenty years when he'd passed away, his body not much more than a skeleton, eaten up by cancer. When she'd taken this job, it had been as much a comfort to herself as to the people she was counselling. The awful fear she carried with her had abated ever so slightly. But in recent weeks, it had all escalated again. The amount of young women presenting with cancer was increasing – at least more of them were coming to her groups. It wasn't just elderly ladies, with long lives behind them.

Although she appeared all bright and breezy, positive and divil-may-care to the people she met, she was quivering inside. Her inner fears were heightened at night-time. More often than not, Sian would wake at three or four in the morning, with the deafening sound of silence taunting and terrifying her. Her apprehension turned the shadows in her bedroom into monsters looming towards her with grasping claws and gnashing teeth. Although she knew the figures were merely a figment of her imagination, that didn't stop the palpable fear that gripped her. Sometimes she was so rooted to the spot with panic she couldn't even muster up the courage to turn on the bedside light.

She'd tried leaving the light on, but then the room was so bright she'd absolutely no hope of getting to sleep. She'd go to the doctor and see if she could get some sleeping pills. Just enough for a few nights, to get her back into a sleeping pattern. She'd a drawer full of hippy pills from the health-food shop. But none of them were any use. One of the boxes said not to take more than three at a go. She'd swallowed five one evening and spent the night saucer-eyed, staring into the darkness. The only positive result she could report was that they'd upset her stomach slightly, which meant she'd had four bowel movements the following day. She'd gone to bed the following night feeling like she'd lost half a stone.

"Hello, girls, nice to see you, to see you nice!" Esme was shuffling in the door with a plastic bag on her head. "I'm a couple of minutes late because I was at the hairdresser's having a set. I was leaving and it started to drizzle, so I went into the butcher's next door, lovely lad in there. 'Now,' says I, 'I know it's not politically erect and all that, but would you have an auld plastic bag?' 'Mrs Mulligan,' says he, 'you're not supposed to put bags on your head – did you never see the ad on the telly with the children suffocating?' 'But I'm only after a set,' says I. 'I think I'll take me chances.' So I put the bag on me head. No point in paying for a set and ending up like a string of misery five minutes later." She chuckled as she untied the two handles of the crinkly bag, which were knotted under her wobbly chin.

Tanya looked at her as if she was utterly insane. Zoe smiled. The last day she'd found Esme a bit noisy and irritating, but the more she saw of her the funnier she found her. She was kind of batty, but she was her own woman.

As they all sipped a fresh cup of coffee, Zoe started to speak.

"I won't be here next week, just so you know. In case you're all sitting here waiting for me. I'm having surgery, so I won't be able to come." Her brown eyes looked too big and wide for her thin waif-like face.

"Okay, Zoe. Sorry to hear that. Would you like to tell us about it?" Sian was gentle. She busied herself with the tray as she spoke. She didn't make eye contact with Zoe, thus giving her the opportunity to say no if she didn't want to talk. There was nothing worse, she felt, than having a pair of eyes boring through to your very soul, making you not want to divulge information. At least if she wasn't staring at her, Zoe might feel happier about opening up.

"She told me I have to get my ovaries taken out." Zoe was rocking back and forth now. Her face was the colour of putty. Her eyes were staring into space. She wasn't focusing on anything in particular.

"Who did, love? Who would say that to you?" the older lady piped up, looking highly affronted that anyone would suggest such a thing. "Tell Esme all about it."

"Dr Leah. I have ovarian cancer, as I told you last time." Zoe's eyes fleetingly made contact with Esme's, before she resumed the unseeing stare and gentle rocking.

"Oh Mother of God, isn't that shocking? Shocking and unfair. You'd wonder why Himself," she pointed a wizened finger towards the roof, "you'd wonder why He wouldn't feck up my old prunes of ovaries and leave your young ones alone."

"Like I said, this dermatomyositis brings ovarian cancer with it a lot of the time. So when they diagnosed the auto-immune disease, they scanned me for cancer and there it was. Silent and evil. Eating away at my ovaries. So now I need my ovaries removed and then they'll give me chemotherapy." She spoke quietly but her words were clear.

There was a brief silence in the room. Tanya looked at her feet and tried to swallow the large lump of emotion which was creeping up her throat. Whatever about Esme, the Dame Edna look-alike, Zoe was so young and sweet. It was so unfair it made her feel incensed with rage and bitterness. She knew she had contracted this cancer thing due to her own weakness. Esme was old. So that kind of fit the bill. But Zoe was young, pretty and vibrant, it didn't fit.

"Dr Leah came to see me in my room so she could tell me all about the plan of action. I loved her outfit, a layered teal-coloured dress with cool wedge sandals in a stunning red patent. Her toenails were painted blood-red and her lipstick matched. She smelled of fresh vibrant cologne and her dark skin and thick dark hair has that healthy glow which looks gorgeous against any colour. She asked me how I was doing. She pulled up a chair and sat down, crossing her legs. Her voice was gentle and kind. She told me . . ." A frightened and exhausted Zoe was barely speaking above a whisper.

"Go on, love, let it out," said Esme. "You make her sound like something from Hollywood, by the way, and you're right – she's lovely. I like a woman who takes pride in her appearance." She patted her freshly curled hairdo, clearly including herself in that bracket. "But go on, tell us what she said."

Zoe closed her eyes and tried to control her tears as she recalled that entire conversation. She wasn't sure if it was the scenario of someone being so nice to her, or if the whole thing just hit her at that second, but she had burst out crying. "I'm sorry, Dr Leah, I don't know what prompted that. I'll be fine in a second."

"It's perfectly normal to feel scared and shocked right now," the doctor had said, her voice soft and calm. She stroked the young girl's arm and waited patiently until the sobbing subsided.

The bawling had set Diana off too. Tears flowed down her perfectly made-up face – although they looked like theatrical tears due to the amount of Botox and fillers in her crow's-feet, smile-line and between her brows. She couldn't quite stretch to much facial expression.

To make matters worse, her dad and Charlie arrived at that moment.

"What the hell's going on?" Charlie had screeched.

"It's all awful, Charlie," Zoe had sobbed. "I've got cancer."

Charlie had launched herself at Zoe and they hugged and rocked back and forth. Her parents hugged and cried. Dr Leah had just sat and looked at her notes calmly. A serene swan, in the middle of a sobbing pond of sniffling gannets.

Zoe zoned back to the Pink Ladies meeting.

"It was terrible. Charlie and I had never seen Mum and Dad cry before. I felt ashamed that I'd brought this sorrow into their lives. Charlie was hysterical. She clutched my body so tightly it felt like she was afraid if she let go, I'd drop dead on the spot. I will never forget the terror in her eyes." Zoe looked traumatised at the memory of her beloved twin.

Sian and the Pink Ladies sat silently as the young woman spoke.

"Dr Leah discussed the results of my PET scan. The first time I heard the name, I thought that sounded quite nice. I imagined a machine covered in white fluff with a pink twitchy nose."

"Lovely," Esme nodded.

Tanya raised her eyebrows and exhaled slowly.

"It wasn't quite like that though, was it?" Sian encouraged.

"Not a floppy ear in sight. It was a detailed scan which basically looked through every layer of my full body, from my skin right down to the bone marrow. They needed to make sure the cancer hadn't spread anywhere else." The bunny image in Zoe's mind had been rapidly replaced by a big scary worm-type monster. A worm, called cancer, which might be having a full-scale rave through every organ she owned.

"Did you find the scan scary?" Tanya found her voice for the first time that day.

"A bit, but it was mostly my own imagination that freaked me out, as opposed to the actual procedure."

In her mind, Zoe could still hear her dad questioning Dr Leah. At the time she'd known they were having a conversation about the chemotherapy. But her mind wasn't fully in the room. She was floating high above the situation. She was in the clouds, she was petting Rosie, the dog they'd had when they were children. Then, she was thinking about the shoe collection they were taking into the shop next month. She was aware of Charlie's arms around her. She'd felt like she was in a little bubble as she'd tried to concentrate on the comfortable feeling of her twin sister's embrace.

Then, from nowhere, she'd heard her own voice: "Will all my hair fall out?"

"That is a possibility, Zoe." Dr Leah had leaned forward. "Listen, it's all an awful lot to take in right at this moment. There are many different types of chemotherapy now, some cause alopecia or hair loss and some don't. As soon as I study the full test and scan results, I'll be in a position to let you know the particular side effects you can expect. I have a wonderful lady called Anna, who is fantastic at dealing with patients and helping them to come to terms with all the changes you might expect. She's a psychologist, but she's specially trained to deal with cancer patients. Would you like me to arrange a meeting for you?"

Zoe had felt like a dam had burst in her brain. "I don't want to be a cancer patient, I don't want to be bald and most of all, I don't want to die."

The whole room, bar Leah, had dissolved into fresh sobs. If it hadn't been so dreadful, it could almost have been funny. It was like Zoe had been given a remote control, which allowed her to switch her family's tears on and off willy-nilly.

"We have lots of medicine available to us now, Zoe. We are going to fight this cancer. I need you to believe that. You are young and we are here to help you beat this." Leah had held her hand. "Once we study the PET scan results, we will start you on your treatment. The sooner we begin this fight, the sooner you can win, okay?"

The Pink Ladies, silenced by poor Zoe's grief, all tried to absorb the sad tale. Zoe rocked back and forth gently. Eventually, Sian spoke.

"Did you meet the psychologist, Zoe?"

"I hated the idea of the psychologist, having to sit all alone in a room with a stranger. I'd be too paranoid that she'd turn around and tell my parents I was mental and needed to spend ten years in a straitjacket, in a room with squashy walls. So I opted to come here instead. I thought it might be less pressurised. That the focus needn't be on me if I didn't like it. Now look at me, taking the floor and blurting out my entire story. I'm sorry. I hadn't intended dumping on you all like this. Someone else please talk."

Zoe felt guilty. Again. She'd felt nothing but shock and guilt since this whole nightmare had begun. Shock was obvious, but the guilt was an emotion she'd never have anticipated. She felt rotten to the core for upsetting Charlie and her parents. That day, when they had dropped the cancer bomb, she had wanted more than anything in the world for someone to come in and tell her she was going to be alright. Someone to look her in the eye and tell her she was going to live. That the cancer wasn't going to eat up each and every organ in her body, and sap the life out of her. Even better, she wanted Jeremy Beadle to jump out of the cupboard and shout, "*Ha, got you! It's all a mean joke!*" But the wardrobe door remained stubbornly shut. Not a beard or camera in sight.

"What about the auto-immune disease you mentioned?" Sian probed.

"Is that the reason you walk funny? And why you've that red stuff on your cheeks and chest?" Esme looked more closely, scrunching up her eyes.

"I think the poor girl feels bad enough without you highlighting it all so brashly!" Tanya felt almost violent towards Esme. Why did the nosey old battle-axe have to be so insensitive?

"I'm only asking out of interest, you know? The girls at my Wednesday evening session do love a bit of news, so I want to get it right." Esme glanced at Tanya, oblivious to the other woman's dagger stare, and continued to almost climb into Zoe's top for a good look.

"It's okay, Tanya." Zoe smiled at her, before turning calmly and answering Esme. "The auto-immune disease was causing me more pain and concern than the cancer. Actually the cancer isn't sore as such. It's more like a silent monster, lurking in my body. The whole thought of it festering there is more scary than anything. By the time Dr Leah left my room, I was exhausted. My phone had been ringing and beeping with messages non-stop. I knew if I called any of my friends the conversation would be too emotional and frenzied, so I decided to send a text message. This is it here." Zoe passed her phone around the ladies.

> Hi all. Bad news, unfort have auto-immune disease and cancer. In St Marks. Waiting 4 scan results. Scared shitless but docs r all gr8. C u all soon x x Zoe

Tanya stared at the screen on Zoe's phone.

"Was that too cold and shocking for my poor friends to receive? My hands were so swollen and sore from the dermatomyositis I really wasn't in a position to either hold the phone or send longwinded personalised messages. So I did a send to many and pressed the button."

Tanya had huge admiration for the girl. She had buckets of courage and strength. She would never in a million years have the nerve to tell the world, via text message. No way. Her cancer was her own dark secret. She had no intention of telling anyone apart from family about it. If she had her way, she'd get through her treatment and continue with life as before, without anyone knowing. She didn't want sympathy and definitely not anyone's pity.

"What did your friends say? How did they react to the news?" Sian asked.

"They were all fantastic really. Within minutes, I was flooded with texts. I cried at each one. Friends old and new said gorgeous things." Zoe tried to smile, but her face crumpled and the tears began to flow. "I'm sorry. God, I'm so sick of crying."

"It's good to get it out, Zoe. If you bottle it all up, it's not going to do you any good," Sian stroked her hand.

"I wish I wasn't in this position. I want to be in the shop telling someone that blue isn't in fact her colour and maybe she should try the orange, and might I suggest going up a size? What is it about us women that we'll actually spend exorbitant amounts of money on clothes which don't even fit, just so we can convince ourselves we're a smaller size?" A small watery smile played on her lips.

"True," said Tanya. "You'd never find a man buying a pair of jeans or a suit in a size too small. They don't even get the uncomfortable shoes thing. Women can be a strange breed, not that we would ever admit it to our men." She smiled with warmth for the first time.

"I've been a size sixteen all my life and I'm as happy as Larry," said Esme. "Some of the young ones I see strutting around now look like they need to eat a decent dinner. My Michael has always said he likes a woman with something to hold on to!" She giggled. "But what's the story with that dermatology you have, Zoe?" She shifted in the chair to make herself comfortable. She loved this whole idea of coming and having big chats about herself and other people. Nowadays, people weren't that friendly. There was very little talking and hearing the bit of news over the fence. Since Mrs Daly next door had died and Mrs Moore had gone off to live in that retirement village, young ones had bought up the houses. They drove flash cars and wore terrible-looking dark clothes. That girl in Mrs Daly's was more like a man than a woman. She looked like something from the undertaker's. All dark trouser suits and polio boots like the poor children used to wear years ago. Maybe she was one of those lazerbeam girls. She'd read about them in her daily newspaper. Women who never liked men. Preferred to go with other women. Some of them even got married now. Esme had nothing against them, each to their own and all of that, but she had to admit it was all very different to the way she'd grown up. She'd asked Nora a couple of years ago if she was one of them. Tracey had a fella, but Nora never seemed to.

"I don't mind if you're a lezzer, if that makes you happy, but maybe we won't tell your father. He's a bit old-fashioned. You know yourself if he even gets his tea at the wrong time it upsets him, let alone trying to explain to him that you're a lazerbeam." Esme had felt very modern and with it, thinking she was being very new age and open-minded.

"Jesus, Mother, I'm not a lesbian!" Nora had laughed. "Not that I've any objections to them, but I'm not one! I just haven't found the right man. Working in the hospital and doing a lot of nights limits my time off. I'm not hung up on having a man, but I'm certainly not gay!" Her mother was hilarious. She was very old-fashioned in ways and yet she was so open to frank discussions at the same time.

"Oh right. Fair enough, I suppose." If she was honest, Esme was a bit disappointed. She'd told some of the ladies at the Golden Girls what she'd suspected. Now she'd nothing to report. Oh well, it might be better for Nora. Maybe being gay had its limitations too.

Esme shook herself and zoned back to the room. Zoe was telling everyone about her auto-immune disease and how its progress had suddenly accelerated.

"The main symptom it carries apart from the obvious rash is a problem with movement. The dermatomyositis has basically tried to stop my arms and legs from working at all. It takes me a good fifteen minutes to get out of bed, shuffle to the bathroom, lower myself onto the loo, stand up and get back to bed. Then I fall asleep for half an hour, totally involuntarily, before waking up and feeling like I've run a marathon. The whole shower and hair-wash thing is like scaling a cliff, backwards in bare feet, whilst being beaten with a heavy blunt object. It's painful, exhausting and I feel like the Tin Man in *Wizard of Oz*, before he got the oil. I especially can't lift my arms up above my head, so I have to attempt to bend double in the shower and wash my hair upside down. This, just in case you've never tried it, is not as easy as it sounds. I also know what all my shampoos taste like, from all the ingesting I've been doing. I either get totally drowned, if I'm facing inwards, or my arse stung by the cold of the tiles, if I face outwards. The pain is so bad at that stage that I have to sit on the edge of the bath and wait for the burning, tightening sensation to ease in my muscles. After a few minutes, I can just about manage to tie a towel around my dripping matted hair. Brushing it just isn't a consideration until at least half an hour later, followed by another bout of the aforementioned crash-out sleep. By this time, my hair's dry and looks like it's been styled by a visually impaired two-year-old. The only reason I can manage to make it in here is because my mum can drop me at the door and it's not far to walk down the corridor." Zoe exhaled, relieved to have got that much of her story out.

"That sounds utterly horrendous, Zoe. What are the doctors going to do about it?" Tanya asked softly, feeling desperately sorry for the young woman.

"The dermatomyositis can be treated with high doses of steroids, and the chemotherapy will help arrest it also. But until that all takes effect, I pretty much feel like I've arthritis in my limbs," she said with a shrug.

"Bless us and save us, what a dreadful thing for a young pretty little girl like you to have to deal with," said Esme. "Please God things will improve soon. Please God!" Her head dropped to the side in that well-known sympathetic gesture people automatically make in times of sadness. "Sheee-ock-in!" She clapped her hands together and muttered a little prayer, finishing off by shooting her hands upwards, as if to send the words off up to the Great Man above.

"With regards to your cancer diagnosis, Zoe, you mentioned at the beginning that you need to have your ovaries removed next week," Sian probed.

"Yes, Dr Leah told me that the cancer is contained to the ovaries. The good news is that it hasn't spread to any other organs, but I'll obviously lose my fertility."

"Well, could you not have HIV in years to come?" Esme asked. "I know a friend of my daughter Nora's and they tried and tried to have a child and in the end they went for the HIV and now they have twins, no less. Two for the price of one!" she chuckled.

"You mean IVF surely?" Tanya really wanted to box the old bag.

"That's what I said." Esme didn't even look at Tanya. She was busy focusing on Zoe and her story. One thing at a time was all she could concentrate on. She needed to remember every detail of Zoe's story for telling the Golden Girls.

"I don't think that'll be an option for me. Right now, Dr Leah has told me that we have to act quickly to stop this cancer. I asked her straight out if I was going to die." Zoe's voice was strangled as she tried to get the words out. "Dr Leah was very sweet and said I would most definitely die at some stage, but hopefully not from ovarian cancer."

"Well, that's very positive, Zoe," Sian soothed. "Doctors don't lie, they simply can't. She wouldn't have said those things to you if she didn't believe it."

"Yes, I suppose you're right, thank you." Zoe smiled gratefully. "Once the surgery is over, I'll have a couple of weeks to recover before I start six months of chemotherapy. I'm sorry. I feel like I've taken up everybody's time today. Please, someone else feel free to talk." She looked glumly at Esme and Tanya.

"Don't you worry, pet, sure I love a story. I'm just as happy to sit and listen – sure haven't we plenty of time for telling our stories over the next while?" Esme patted her hand.

"Absolutely, and good luck with your operation, I'll be thinking of you," said Tanya. If she was honest, she was delighted she didn't have to speak. Glancing at her watch, she was relieved to see the time was almost up. "I hope you'll all excuse me, but I've an appointment and I have to run. I'll see you both next week." She looked from Esme to Sian. "Zoe, I'll see you when you're feeling stronger." Before anyone could even answer, Tanya had scooped up her bag and fled the room.

With long purposeful strides she made it to her car. Exhaling slowly, she put the key in the ignition and flung the car into reverse. She did have an appointment with a surgeon, but not until that afternoon. She'd go to the office, go through the diary with Sally and make it into the appointment.

The only reason she was going to that blasted group was to keep poor Alfie sane. It seemed to mean an awful lot to him that she tried to help herself. In reality, she didn't have the time or the headspace for sitting in rooms with strangers. Just so long as they weren't all expecting her to do Tanya's Fireside Story next time. She'd no interest in furnishing that old bag with fodder for the cloth-eared old-bat society she kept mentioning.

# 6

*Today I am starting my chemotherapy. I hope to meet
a nice group of people to chat to. I love a bit of news!*

Esme was thrilled with her little notebook. She'd bought a little
fine-nibbed pen, which she attached to the side of the spiral
spine for safekeeping. She wasn't sure if they were supposed to
bring the book in for Sian to read out or if it was a private thing.
She secretly hoped they could all have a look at each other's books.
That would make more sense.

She returned to the hospital for her post-surgical check-up.
They said she'd recovered well, that her bloods were good, so she
could commence her chemotherapy as planned. She was to come
into the chemotherapy day unit the following morning and they'd
start her.

Michael went with her and sat looking like he was in pain,
rustling his newspaper and clearing his throat loudly.

"Stop that, Michael. Jesus, you sound like a fecking bin-man
hacking away there. Why don't you go off and I'll ring you later on
and tell you how I'm getting on? You don't like this kind of thing.
You'd be happier at home in front of the telly. I've left your lunch
in the oven – just heat the plate at one o'clock and take a slice of

Vienetta out of the freezer for your dessert. I'll be home in time to do the dinner. Before you start, it's only soup and a sandwich this evening, so you needn't be sitting there thinking of steak and kidney pie. I know it's Tuesday, but on account of this," she gestured all around the room, "it's soup and a sandwich instead."

"Right, love. I'll head off then. See you when I see you." He bent down to kiss her. Not sure what to say or do, he added, in a kind of confused manner, "I could do the dinner if you're not well."

"Don't be silly, Michael. I'm not dead yet," Esme scolded him.

He put on his overcoat and hat, tucked his rolled-up newspaper under his arm and shuffled out muttering.

Things went from good to better. Miriam pitched up. The two were delighted with the reunion. A snotty dark-haired woman with too many diamonds and not enough personality had been parked beside Esme.

"You don't mind moving to the chair over there, do you, love? I want my *friend* here to sit with me." Esme used her telephone voice and her menacing stare to get rid of yer wan. Luckily she seemed delighted to go over the other side of the room. "Sit down, Miriam love. How have you been? How's your chest since they lopped your breast off?"

"Not too bad, Esme, and how are your *innards*?" Miriam couldn't bring herself to mention the body parts. She admired Esme being able to say the word *breast* in a public place, but she preferred to just skip over it all.

"Never better, love. A lot of the toilet trouble has eased and I'm flying it now, to tell you the truth."

The ladies were brought a cup of tea and a scone, which they devoured.

A nurse came in mid-morning and told Esme she was going to "commence her treatment". She felt like a diplomat or one of those VIPs. The worst part was putting the thing in her vein.

"We're going to insert a cannula in your arm now, Esme. This is a little needle which goes into your vein. We'll use the cannula to feed the chemotherapy drugs through your bloodstream. Is that okay?"

"Grand. Thanks, love," Esme nodded as the nurse went off to get her trolley of implements.

Miriam appeared from the bathroom.

"This'll interest you love, you'll be after me. They're putting a canal into my arm and pumping my blood with drugs." Esme looked very proud.

"Lovely. I'll probably be next, as you say." Miriam went over to her seat to settle herself in a comfortable position to watch the proceedings.

It took a while to find a vein.

"Mrs Mulligan, we may decide it's a good option for you to have a portacath fitted. This is a little porthole device which we put into your lower neck, upper shoulder area. It stays there for the duration of your full chemotherapy treatment, and means we can avoid having to search for a vein in your hand."

"Lovely," Esme nodded.

As the nurse brought in the first bag of chemotherapy drugs, Miriam looked on eagerly. The clear bag of fluid was hung on the metal stand beside the bed.

"It's a bit like a coat-hanger for all the world, isn't it?" Esme said.

"Sure is," said the nurse. "This will take about half an hour. This is your pre-med. It's anti-nausea medicine, to stop you from feeling sick. If you feel any burning or stinging around the cannula, just press your buzzer immediately, okay?" The nurse smelled of that Spanish cologne the girls used to buy on holidays.

"Thanks, love." Esme watched like a hawk as the nurse started up the drip. She could feel the cool liquid entering her vein. It wasn't sore or unpleasant, just odd.

"What's it like?" Miriam was sitting up straight now.

Esme was delighted to be the first of the two of them to experience the chemotherapy. "Well, it's like having an injection, only without the stabby pain bit. All cool and runny like. Sort of makes you want to wee," she concluded.

"My God," said Miriam, fascinated.

She didn't have to wait long to experience it for herself. The nurses put her cannula in and started her drip too.

"It's not bad, Esme, you're right. I don't know what all the fuss is about chemotherapy. Your hair still looks the same too." Miriam looked down at her own shoulders. "Is mine still there?"

"Yes, love, all there."

Just over half an hour later, the nurse returned to do a "flush".

"What, like with the toilet?" Esme looked a bit alarmed.

"No, Esme, it means we flush a little bit of saline, which is sterile salt water through the cannula to clean it out before we put the first chemotherapy drug through," the nurse calmly explained.

After that was done, she put another bag, covered in purple plastic, onto the drip stand.

"You're having a mixture of three chemotherapy drugs today. This is the first one. It's called gemcitabine or Gemzar. Once again, please call me if you feel any stinging or burning near the cannula site. You're doing really well, Esme. Well done." The nurse connected the drip and started the liquid.

"She's after flushing me canal and now I'm onto the first of the chemo drugs," Esme reported to the eagerly awaiting Miriam.

"Fancy." Miriam looked suitably impressed as she nodded, sticking out her bottom lip for effect.

So far, the whole chemotherapy thing was fine. Esme had heard all the stories of people vomiting and having diarrhoea and all that. But the doctors had assured her that was all in the past.

"We have wonderful anti-nausea medicines now. So if you're feeling sick, let us know and we'll give you something."

"We were just saying between ourselves, love," Esme addressed the nurse, "that none of our hair has fallen out so far. Is it a delayed reaction, or will it be gone by the time we get home this evening?"

The nurse was very calm and explained it all clearly. Both ladies were surprised to learn that they wouldn't lose their hair. Most of the new drugs didn't cause alopecia nowadays, she'd said.

"Alopecia? I thought that was when you were born with snow-white skin and hair and pink eyes!" Esme looked astounded.

"No, Esme, that's when you're a bambino," Miriam corrected.

"That's actually called albinism, ladies, but you don't need to worry about that or losing your hair right at the moment."

It would be better to keep her hair, Esme mused. She didn't fancy wearing a wig really. Michael had one. He put it on sometimes going to Mass – it had belonged to his Uncle Willy who'd died over ten years ago. They'd gone to the house after the funeral and Michael was told to pick a memento to remember him by, so he'd chosen the wig. It wasn't really the same colour as the remaining hair on Michael's head – it was kind of mouse-brown really, the wig. But he felt good with it on, so Esme told him that was the main thing.

"I feel dressed up with it on," he'd said. Along with his new teeth, he looked very smart. But it was only a small wig, which sat on top of his head, so it wouldn't have done Esme.

She'd been given the three types of chemotherapy and it had all gone very well, so they told her. She just believed them, because she didn't really know what happened when it didn't go well. Miriam was grand too, and by five o'clock they were allowed to go home. They discovered they lived only five minutes away from each other, so they'd shared a taxi.

Esme felt pretty much the same that evening.

"How do you feel now?" Michael had asked her, stooping to look into her eyes after they'd had their soup and sandwich.

"Grand. Do I look any different yet?" She stared up at him, with her eyes wide.

"No." He shook his head and shuffled back to his armchair.

She was to go back in for more chemotherapy every three weeks for six months. If it kept going like this, she'd be delighted. The girls were on the phone every day to check up on her. Nora was planning a visit and then a week later, Tracey was coming over.

"So far, so good," she said. "As God closes one door, He opens another." She smiled as she thought of seeing her daughters. "When the girls come, maybe we'll go to the cinema and to that burger place again."

Michael didn't look too thrilled.

The last time Tracey had come home they'd gone to the pictures. You weren't allowed call it that anymore though, Esme reminded herself. It was the 'movies' or the 'cinema' nowadays. They'd gone to a burger joint after for their tea. Michael didn't like it too much. It was a Thursday. He usually had chops on a Thursday, so he hadn't liked eating the burger instead. "It's not the same as your dinners, Esme," he'd said. He'd slid about on the red plastic seats. The music had been too loud as well. None of the people serving them had spoken proper English either. The whole experience had left him feeling a bit shaken. But he'd put up with it to please the girls.

Tracey seemed to think it was all normal and had ordered buffalo's wings. Now, granted she'd never seen a buffalo up close, but the small orangey yokes Esme saw her daughter gnawing at looked iffy. But Esme had loved the place. Thought the soap in the toilets was gorgeous. They gave little wet tissues in a packet to wipe your hands at the end, and she'd thought it was the best invention ever. She'd taken a few to keep in her bag.

"They'd be brilliant for after your sticky bun on a Friday morning," she'd said, nudging Michael.

She was great that way, his Esme, Michael thought now. Always thinking ahead. Always looking after him. He got a bit tearful when he looked over at her. She was thumbing through one of her women's weekly magazines. She loved those books. Loved to know who was doing a line with who and what they were wearing while they were at it.

Once Michael got his chops tomorrow night, he'd be happy. She wasn't that hungry these days though. She might only have one potato with it and a small splash of gravy. She always did two types of veg – she'd make carrots and spinach for tomorrow evening. Michael wasn't mad about spinach, but Esme reckoned if it was good enough for Popeye, then it was good enough for them. She'd make a jam roly-poly with hot custard for afters. That'd cheer him up. Once he was sitting in front of *Who Wants to be a Millionaire* with a cup of tea and an After Eight, he'd be as happy as a pig in what's-it. So far, so good, she chuckled to herself.

\* \* \*

The only thing Esme had noticed, since her operation and the start of the chemotherapy, was that the toilet trouble had got a bit better. She'd been in a bad way.

She'd phoned Tracey at work a while back. "Tracey, can you talk, love?"

"Sort of, go on, Mum." Tracey stopped typing and concentrated. She'd told her mother a thousand times that she worked in an open-plan office, but Esme didn't really get the concept.

"I wanted to ask you a bit of a personal question . . ." Esme had hesitated. "I don't know if it's normal for a woman of my age, seventy next birthday, please God. But, when I'm on the pot lately I'm doing a number two at least six times a day. Now it's not sloppy, it's long and thin like a big chocolate snake, but my whole gut is like a ball of fire. What do you think? I haven't eaten anything unusual either, not since the burger that time with you." Esme was biting her lip. Tracey would know what to do, she was very clever, her Tracey. Nora worked at the hospital and she'd probably have all the answers, but she wasn't in a position to take calls during the day. She'd have to contact her bleeper, which was too much trouble.

"I don't know, Mum. How long have you been like this?"

"A couple of months, I suppose. None of my skirts are staying put anymore either. They're spinning around – the front bit ends up at the back, like. I'm getting a bit scrawny-looking, like Mrs Daley over the road. She looks like she needs a good dinner. I wouldn't want people to think I'm not feeding myself, you know?"

"Why don't you go and see Dr Joyce and he could put your mind at rest? Nora will be home next week – maybe wait and go with her." Tracey felt terrible. She loved living in London, but at times like this, when she knew her mother needed her, she wished she could call over and be with her. As her parents were getting older, she was noticing more and more that they needed someone to be there for them.

"Right, love, good idea, I'll wait until Nora comes back and I'll have an appointment lined up."

It had all taken on a mind of its own after that, between the scans and tests and being in the hospital and starting the chemotherapy. She was looking forward to the next meeting in the cancer support clinic. She was dying to get more details about what was wrong with the other women. The Golden Girls group had been asking.

"And can you bring a friend or do you have to have cancer to go?" Bridie wanted to know.

"No, I don't think you're allowed go if you don't have cancer. Pity really, because the girl who runs it makes a lovely cup of coffee. She'd gorgeous biscuits too. Dear ones now. Not just custard creams or anything like that. But, it's all talk about cancer and all that, so you might feel a bit left out, Bridie, if I brought you, on account of you not having any cancer, you know?"

# 7

*Today is D-day. My surgery awaits. I know I'm supposed to write something upbeat, but I feel like a dark cloud has settled over my head. I hope I have the courage to get through this.*

Zoe closed her notebook. Even though it was pink and sparkly, it still scared the hell out of her. Sian was adamant this worked as a form of therapy, so she'd give it a go. Zoe had been dreading coming into the private clinic for her surgery. She was still finding it hard to come to terms with the fact that she had cancer. At her parents' insistence she'd been transferred to the smaller and quieter private clinic adjoining the main hospital of St Mark's. As Steven and Diana accompanied her to the desk to check in she spotted Tanya. Not sure whether or not she should say hello, she hesitated for a moment. She found the other woman a bit scary really.

"Oh, hello, Zoe. Don't we always meet in the most wonderful places?" Tanya smiled and held her hand out to greet Diana and Steven. "Hi there, Tanya Shields. I know your lovely daughter from the cancer support centre."

Zoe watched, speechless, as Tanya chatted to her parents and explained she was in for a mastectomy. She didn't seem that spiky now. She wasn't doing her sighing and acting as if she hated everyone around her. For the first time, Zoe could fathom how this woman ran a successful business. When she wanted to, she could talk the talk and walk the walk.

"I'll be in room Number 302, Zoe. If you feel like a chat any time, drop by. I won't bother you, so I'll leave it up to you. Depending on how you feel, you might prefer to be left alone. If I don't see you before, I'll meet you at our next 'session'," Tanya made quote marks with her fingers. Touching Zoe's arm, she lingered for a second and wished her luck, before clicking up the handle of her wheelie suitcase and disappearing around the corner.

"She seems lovely, Zoe." Diana had instantly liked the other woman.

By the time she'd had her blood pressure and temperature taken followed by more questions than Mastermind, Zoe was exhausted. She'd turned off her phone. Her friends meant well, but she just couldn't have another conversation about her impending surgery. She'd run out of positive things to say about losing her ovaries and her fertility at the age of twenty-two.

She just wanted the whole thing over and done with. She even felt distanced from her twin Charlie. They weren't on the same wave length at the moment. She hated to admit it, but Charlie was irritating her beyond belief. Zoe knew she was only trying to help – trying to distract, trying to be kind, but it was all so trivial and boring.

"Did I tell you Katie snogged Rory last night? I just can't believe she'd do that, and Sandra was there and she just like made a move and was so totally all over him. She knows that Sandra hasn't hit closure with him yet, and she just didn't care. She's so, so, gone down in my estimation. I'd say by the time Sandra's finished dragging her name around, no other guy is going to touch Katie. It'll serve her right too, everyone knows you shouldn't shit on your own doorstep." Charlie was examining her nails as she spoke. "Do you think I should get the other girl, you know the blonde one, to do my nails the next time? They're a bit iffy-looking from the side, aren't they?"

That had been this morning. Zoe had been lying on the sofa in her parents' living room. The room smelled of furniture polish and lilies. Stretched out on the chocolate-coloured, goose-down-filled cushions of the oversized sofa was like resting on a big piece of marshmallow. Her limbs were so sore from the dermatomyositis that she found it increasingly difficult to get comfortable in spite of the soft surroundings. She'd just been about to drift off to sleep, when Charlie had burst in the door, rabbiting on about Katie, who Zoe barely knew.

"I don't know what you should do with your nails and I really couldn't give a toss about Katie," she said. "In fact, I wouldn't care if she'd stripped naked and done the fandango with an incensed orangutan in full view of the President of the United States last night. I'm in too much pain and I'm about to go to hospital and have my insides gouged out. If you want to make yourself useful, would you get me a Diet Coke?" Zoe knew she sounded like a bitch, but Charlie was living in cloud-cuckoo land.

"Well, ex-cuuuu-ze me! Sorry for breathing – not! Zoe, you need to keep check on yourself. You are in serious danger of ending up on Lonely Island, with no-mates.com as your new email address. Chill the hell out, Zo. I know you're sick and all that, but it's not my fault, is it? I'm just trying to help. But, I get the plot, you don't want me near you and everything I say is like soooo twisted by you. So I'm outta here. You," Charlie pointed a false nail at her twin, "can call me," she stabbed herself in the chest, "when you learn to be normal again. *Ciao*, Zoe." Charlie had flicked her hair and spun on her Juicy Couture kitten heel and stomped out of the house.

Instead of being upset or incensed, like normal, Zoe had just been relieved Charlie had left. She needed to get her head around what was about to happen to her body.

Now, as she lay between the rough stark white sheets of the hospital bed, Zoe gazed around her. How had it come to this? How had she gone from being a girl-about-town to a patient with a terminal illness? The hospital room was as nice as could be expected. At this private clinic she didn't have to share a bathroom with strangers and, fair enough, the walls were painted in an inoffensive shade and the bathroom was spotless, but it still smelled like illness to Zoe. That far-too-clean and no-room-for-deadly-bugs aroma was hanging in the air.

Eyeing the tiny wooden tray on her bedside locker, Zoe stretched her arm across to take the miniature plastic cup. It was clear plastic and looked like a mini shot glass, except this thing hadn't been brought here carrying a Tequila or Peach Schnapps – instead it held a sleeping pill. Zoe winced as she forced the seized-up muscles of her arm to stretch out and grasp the tablet. Managing to manoeuvre herself around enough to take a small glass of water, she took a deep breath and popped the pill into her dry mouth.

She couldn't even bear the noise of the television. So the room was silent, apart from the many muffled noises penetrating from the busy corridor outside, and here in her little cocoon all by herself she could finally be alone with her thoughts. Tomorrow the surgeon was going to open her up and dig out her ovaries and this potentially deadly disease. Laying her head gently back onto the pillows, she forced her eyes to close. She tried to make her mind wander. She tried to dredge up memories from her childhood. Days by the sea in Spain. Evenings spent sitting in a crisp cotton sundress, in a matching outfit to her twin, legs swinging on a wicker chair, drinking fizzy orange through a straw.

All thoughts of Charlie and her babbling, mixed with an image of the stressed, worried faces of her parents, seemed to blur into a nice fuzzy cloud. The next thing she knew, the nurse was calling her name.

"Good morning, sleepy head! I need you to run to the loo and put on this gown, then we'll take you straight down for your surgery, okay, honey?"

"Right now?" Zoe felt muzzy and a bit confused.

As she staggered to the bathroom and tried to put on her surgical gown, her heart was beating in her chest. At least she wasn't being made sit in the room on her own all morning, waiting and wondering. That'd be worse, she figured. At least this way, it would be over and done with before she knew it.

\* \* \*

After the operation, it took five days for the main results to come back. Dr Leah walked into the room with her team of white coats in hot pursuit.

"How are you doing today? Has the pain eased in the shoulder?"

Zoe had expected to feel sore inside. She knew her tummy would be swollen and tender. But she'd never anticipated the nauseatingly dull thudding agony in her shoulder. Dr Leah had explained that during the laparoscopic procedure, which involved putting both a camera and operating instruments through her belly button and a small incision in her tummy, they'd need to blow up the abdomen wall with gas, to raise it away from the surgery site. "In most cases," she had said, "the gas is absorbed into the body. Sometimes, however, the gas rises and pushes against the diaphragm and can exert pressure on a particular nerve. When this happens, it can produce a severe pain that extends to one or both of the patient's shoulders." In Zoe's case this had happened. The pain was unbelievable.

"I think it's starting to ease," she told Dr Leah now. "Between that and the pain in the muscles along with the swollen tummy, I reckon I'll have clocked up enough pain points to get at least a free microwave oven by the time I get out of here. Please tell me you have a pain-points catalogue somewhere, so I can at least claim a prize for all this agony."

"I'll suggest it to the hospital board. Sadly we don't give away toasters or Juicy couture track-suits in lieu of pain, but it's a damn good plan." Dr Leah smiled.

She went on to explain that the department of pathology had been in contact. The results confirmed that the ovaries were indeed blocked by cancerous tumours.

"We are confident that we've got it all. It definitely hasn't spread either. The surrounding areas all looked clean and clear. The surgeon had a good poke around while he was there. So once you've recovered a bit more, in say four weeks, I'd like to get you started on your chemotherapy."

She knew it was all happening, but every time Zoe heard the word *chemotherapy* she felt gripping fear. The whole notion of having to sit in a room with other sick people and have drugs pumped through her veins filled her with horror.

"I'm going to use three specific drugs on you, Zoe. Gemzar, Avastin and Carboplatin. I will leave you some booklets, which explain all about the drugs. The main side effects include loss of appetite, fatigue, lowering of white blood cells, mouth sores, a change in bowel movements, swelling of the ankles or hands and alopecia. Having said that, in your particular case, due to the dermatomyositis, you might actually feel better initially. The chemotherapy will kill any cancer cells, which may be hanging around, but it will also arrest the dermatomyositis. So unlike other patients, who can feel immediately worse on these drugs, you should hopefully feel better than you do right now."

"That wouldn't be hard," Zoe agreed.

* * *

Zoe was inundated with well-meaning visitors over the days that followed, so she felt like all her talking batteries were flat by the end of each day.

By day four, after she'd had a good snooze, she decided to emerge from her room and have a wander. Then she spotted Tanya shuffling towards her with a drip on a wheeling stand and a large plastic bag attached to her side. Zoe got a fright when she saw the other woman's complexion.

"Hi, Zoe, glad to see you have that same lovely green tinge to your skin as I have. I reckon if we all stay in here long enough we'll look like clones of each other. With your big brown eyes and tiny frame, you look like a skinnier version of Yoda from *Star Wars*." Tanya winced as she tried to stand still.

"Cheers, you're looking pretty hot yourself. I see you're using the same engine-oil look in your hair as I am. Amazing how your body starts to sort of melt from the hair down when you can't shower or move much for four days." Zoe found herself smiling genuinely for the first time in a few days.

"Do you feel like sitting in my room for a few minutes and ignoring all my flowers and chocolates instead of your own?"

"Sure," Zoe agreed immediately. "I'm sorry I got a bit of a shock when I saw you just there."

"I know I'm scary without make-up and I suppose along with all the stuff they're pumping into me, garnished with vile pyjamas, a drip and a drain, I look a bit like something from *Dawn of the Dead*. For the record," Tanya cursed under her breath as she tried to push her door open, "you look like shite too. That's the only reason I'm inviting you into my room. I'm sick of nice-smelling, well-groomed visitors, who waft in pretending to be upbeat. Well, it's actually only Alfie and close family if I'm truthful as I haven't exactly sent out a press release as to my whereabouts. God love them, what the hell are they supposed to do?"

Zoe, in spite of herself, started to laugh. "You look worse than me," she giggled as she perched painfully on a chair.

"That, my dear, is a matter of opinion. So what's the story? Have you any results and plans of action?" Tanya managed to get back onto her bed, guiding all the wires and appendages as she went.

Zoe filled her in on when she was starting chemotherapy and how the doctors were assuring her she would be fine.

"My only regret is that I won't be able to have kids. I know it's not that relevant to me yet, but I suppose it's the fact that my choice has been taken away that makes it hard."

Tanya listened and watched the young girl as she spoke. She seemed so young and innocent in one way and yet wise beyond her years in another.

"I never wanted kids. In fact, Alfie and I nearly broke up because of it." Tanya looked out the window, caught up in her own thoughts for a while.

"So you obviously changed your mind then – you have a little girl, don't you?" Zoe pointed to the photo of a little girl in red wellies holding a bucket and spade.

"I didn't. Jenny changed it for me. I found out I was pregnant and Alfie was so enthralled, I couldn't have an abortion."

The Tanya that Zoe recognised from the support group was back. The harsh look in her eyes, the screen of ice was back.

"But you obviously adore her now – you wouldn't change a thing, right?" Zoe studied her face.

The other woman didn't answer. She didn't move a muscle. She was totally silent until Zoe heard a small barely audible sound escape her pursed lips. Suddenly tears cascaded down her cheeks and she brought her hands up to cover her face.

"Tanya, I'm so sorry, I don't even know you, I shouldn't have asked you such a personal question." Zoe was terrified she'd offended her and was waiting for an attack.

"I'm sorry. The thing is, I was right all along, you see. I knew I shouldn't have stayed with Alfie, I knew I shouldn't have had a child. But I went through with it all against my better judgement, didn't I? I lulled them into a false sense of security. I made Alfie think he could have the dream. A wife and children. I let him believe his own stupid fantasy. And now, I will be the Wicked Witch I always knew I was – my black pointed hat and my gold-buckled shoes will out themselves. Just like the Black Fairy at the Sleeping Beauty's christening, I'm going to ruin everything." The tears flowed and Tanya did her best to curl into a ball. With the drain and drips it wasn't easy.

"But I don't understand." Zoe looked stricken.

"I'm dying, Zoe. The cancer is everywhere. They removed the breast and the tumour under my arm – but the stuff on my spine, in my shoulder, in my intestine, it's all gone too far. Even if they cut half my body away, it still wouldn't be enough. So you see. I've rained on the parade. I brought that sweet innocent little girl into the world, only to leave her without a mother." Tanya looked haunted.

Zoe was speechless. There were no words of comfort. There was no smoothing over the situation. "Is there no hope at all? Can't they do chemotherapy and radiation?"

"Oh sure." Tanya scrubbed her tears away and smiled. "They'll do all that. It might prolong my life by up to six months, but after that, I'm toast."

Zoe stayed in the room with Tanya until the daylight faded. After the initial outburst, both women sat in silence for a bit. Then Tanya told Zoe all about Alfie. What a good, kind and decent man he was. How he would be fine when she'd gone, because Jenny would distract him. She knew Jenny would get all the love and attention she craved from Alfie. There couldn't be a better father walking the earth. But she couldn't help feeling guilty and responsible for abandoning her.

"But, it's not your fault!" said Zoe. "There's nothing in the world you can do. You mustn't blame yourself. I know it's easy for me to say, but use what time you've got left to create memories for Jenny. Write her letters, take photos of the two of you together, create a journal to leave behind. Record your thoughts and hopes for her. Give her something she can open and read when she's older. A concrete book of evidence that her mother was a strong and wonderful human being."

Tanya nodded. She knew exactly why Zoe was suggesting she do a journal, but she wasn't sure she had the courage to go through with it. Could she possibly sit and write notes and paste pictures to a page, knowing it would be all her baby would ever have to remind her she'd had a mother who loved her once? This whole screwed-up situation was like a living hell. If there was a right or wrong way of dealing with it, Tanya longed for guidance.

Zoe found sitting and generally being out of bed painful and exhausting, so she eventually had to excuse herself and go back to her room.

"This is an odd one . . ." Tanya said, halting Zoe just as she was about to exit the room.

"Go on," said Zoe.

"At my funeral, will you tell Alfie that I don't want everyone wearing black? I couldn't bear it."

"You got it." Zoe instinctively returned to Tanya's bed and sealed her promise with a hug.

"And I detest nothing more than funerals where grieving people all have to congregate in a function room and sit at tables eating dinner. It's like being invited to your boss's wedding, where all you know is the bride and groom. In this case, the common denominator will be planted in a box."

"Tanya!" Zoe gasped, feeling a shiver run down her spine.

"I know, I'm evil." Tanya grinned and rested her head back on her pillow.

Knowing she was due to be released the following day, Zoe exchanged mobile-phone numbers with Tanya. Promising to call, they hugged, and Zoe hobbled back to her own room and crumpled into her bed.

So unbelievably grateful for the sleeping pills she'd become accustomed to taking, she waited for the sleep fairies to flutter by, gently closing her eyelids and enveloping her in their calm embrace.

Images of Tanya, Alfie and Jenny plagued her dreams. She twisted and turned as she tried to process all the dreadful facts in her mind. There she was, sitting moaning about not being able to have imaginary babies, with an imaginary partner, God only knew when, and Tanya was having to face the most frightening thing possible. Untimely death. This was worse than an accident. This was the worst possible combination. She had prior notice.

Zoe always remembered her grandmother telling them to "seize the day," as kids. "You never know the time or the day you might go, so enjoy your life, girls." Granny had happily worn as much leopard skin as possible, mixed with lashings of blue eye-shadow. She'd smoked untipped cigars and well before they'd been a craze, had consistently worn stick-on false nails and eyelashes. Zoe knew if she'd been alive today, she'd definitely go for gel nails with leopard-print nail art.

Now, while Tanya didn't know the exact day or hour, she did know one thing. It wasn't far away. The Angel of Death was tracking her. The egg-timer of life had been turned upside-down. The sands were running.

# 8

*My surgery is over. I have lived through it, but the clock
is ticking.*

Tanya closed the pink notebook. She could grasp Sian's idea of
trying to write positive messages. But she simply hadn't anything
upbeat to say today. She realised she was a terrible patient. She hated
being incarcerated in that God-awful room. She couldn't bear all
the nurses coming in and out constantly, day and night, poking and
prodding her. Why on earth did they need to know her blood
pressure at three thirty in the morning? She tried to be polite. She
knew it was their job. It wasn't their fault that she'd a bloody weak
system and a body riddled with cancer.

She'd decided not to tell Alfie how bad the prognosis was yet. What
was the point? She was causing enough trouble as it was. Besides, he'd
tell her mother. Then her brothers and sister would know. The phone
would ring incessantly. The conversations would be cringy and nobody
would have a clue what to say. What's the correct protocol when
phoning a dying sibling or daughter? "Sorry for your troubles, hope
it's quick and don't forget to take all the drugs"? Or worse still, she
might have people making requests for when she died: "Would you tell
my granny I love her?" or "Let my dead husband know I'm alright".

She'd told Dr Leah not to have in-depth conversations with Alfie. She'd made her promise to be vague and say that they were doing everything in their power to ensure a good outcome. That sounded proactive and promising. It wasn't a lie anyway. Wasn't death supposed to be the final release? What did her grandmother always say? "God takes the good ones early. Only the good die young."

Well, look at her now. Wasn't she the lucky one? She wasn't that convinced by the whole afterlife thing. Alfie was religious in a strange way. She knew he loved going into churches. She saw the difference in his whole demeanour when he'd been in a church. It calmed him, gave him inner peace. So that was a good thing. *She* just felt nothing – in fact the smell of the incense made her sneeze. She hated the darkness thing too. The rooms in their house were all painted in pale, space-enhancing colours. She never got the whole dark muted-tones thing. Why make a place look and feel like it was in eternal night-time? In any case, she didn't have time to think about the whole afterlife issue. The clock was well and truly ticking, so she needed to sort herself out while she still could.

The business was going well. That was a serious pisser. She wondered if anyone else would keep it going in such a meticulous manner. Alfie would need to be at home with Jenny though. She'd have to think of a way of keeping it going when she was gone. Alfie would need the proceeds even more than ever.

She'd been anally retentive about life-assurance policies all along. She'd have to look into it all and make sure that the bastards paid up when the time came.

Taking out her Pink Ladies notebook, she began to make a list. She always worked best against a list. She found little else more satisfying than ticking things off.

She headed it *"The Death Playlist"*. She underlined it. It made her smile. To a stranger, it would look like the title of an article in a teenage magazine. The following bullet points should be shaped like bockety hearts, with suggestions like, "See the Wonders of the World", or "Swim with a school of sweet dolphins", or "Sleep in a field, while coked to the eyeballs and swilling champagne by the neck, with a tall black man who speaks no English".

Instead she began to pen a very different list.

- Check life assurance
- Write letters/make a video for Jenny
- Do the same for Alfie
- Organise funeral, with specific instructions
- Clear away as many clothes, shoes and personal stuff as possible. Alfie will only hold onto them unnecessarily out of loyalty
- Find honest enthusiastic manager to run company (probably non-existent)
- Write out all bank details in easy format for Alfie
- Change all utility bills & mortgage to new account in Alfie's name (he'd never think of sorting it all, especially in time of grief)
- Withdraw all money from savings accounts and credit union "rainy day" account & put in trust fund for Jenny
- Write out all laptop and computer codes for Alfie to easily "find"

That would do for today. She shut the hard-backed notebook. Sliding down the hospital bed, she closed her eyes. Sleep evaded her. As usual. She'd finally agreed to take sleeping pills last night. She'd managed about four hours of obliteration. It was better than nothing.

"Might I suggest taking a mild dosage of anti-anxiety tablets? Xanax are very effective. They simply take the edge off everything. For seriously ill patients, I usually recommend them." Dr Leah had said it as nonchalantly as possible, while writing in her chart.

"No. Thank you, but no. At least not right now. I have a lot to do when I get out of here. I need to have my wits about me for the moment. When I'm reduced to a quivering mess, along the lines of a rotting cabbage, we'll talk about it then. Mind you, at that stage, I think I'll be entitled to something more fun. Isn't heroin meant to be the ultimate buzz? If I'm already on the road to nowhere, would I be allowed to have a few shots?" She smiled at Dr Leah, who was still writing.

Leah raised an eyebrow but didn't lift her head. "I'm not giving up on you, so don't you either."

"I'm not giving up, Leah, I'm just not doing an ostrich on it. There's no point."

* * *

Tanya was delighted to get home from the hospital, even though she knew she had to go back in two weeks' time to start her chemotherapy. Jenny was blissfully oblivious to the fact her mother looked terrible. Unlike Tanya's own mother, who wrung her hands and stood with a quivering lip, hugging and stroking her intermittently. Jenny was a comfort. She didn't do that "poor little you" look. She didn't care that Tanya's hair was lank, her skin dull and her already thin frame sinking into itself.

"Look, Mama, boo!" Jenny put her chubby hands up to her eyes and flicked them away. This was followed by hysterical laughing. Her contagious belly laugh made Tanya join in.

"You are like a soothing balm, do you know that, baby girl?" Tanya pulled the little munchkin onto her lap. Wrapping her arms around her baby tightly, she rocked her back and forth, humming a lullaby.

Thrilled to have her Mum's undivided attention, Jenny joined in loudly. "*La, la, la, la!*" She stuck her jaw out, allowing her only two pearly teeth to show themselves.

Alfie sidled in from the kitchen to stand leaning against the door jamb. He smiled to himself. Maybe this operation might have softened Tanya in some way. He knew it was an extreme measure, but she seemed to be calmer and more able to sit and spend time with both himself and Jenny. It might all wear off of course, but for now he was loving seeing her do the motherly thing.

Tanya realised her energy levels were low, so she made herself go for an hour's sleep at the same time as Jenny. When they both woke up, Alfie suggested they go to the shopping centre for some late lunch and a mosey around.

"It'll do you good to get out and about, even for a few minutes. Jenny loves going for pizza, so she'll be as good as gold, won't you, sweetie?" Alfie snuggled her.

Jenny nodded, her eyes as wide as she could hold them. "Pizza, Mama?"

"Okay, Jenny, let's go."

Less than ten minutes later they were walking slowly around the shopping mall. It was a Tuesday, so at least it wasn't like a cattle market.

"Jeez, I can sort of get why people like going shopping now," said Tanya. "Usually when I come here, under duress on Saturday or Sunday, to buy necessary clothes for work, it's utter mayhem. This is so much calmer and I almost feel like I'd be able to stay here for a while without the urge to run."

"I often come here in the morning with Jenny. I get her an ice cream and we go to the coffee shop. I get my caffeine fix and she sits in the buggy and proceeds to cover herself in an even coating of ice cream from hair to toes. It's a great game isn't it, Jen?"

"I-keem, Dada?"

"Okay, honey. We'll have a little look around the shops first and then we'll get you an ice cream, how's that?"

"Pink one?"

"Yes, Jenny, it'll be a pink one."

"And a brella?"

"Oh yes, we'll ask the lady for a little umbrella too." Alfie ruffled her hair and smiled down at her.

"Mama, push!" Jenny looked up at her mummy adoringly, delighted to have her in on the shopping trip.

"Are you able?" Alfie whispered.

Tanya winked at him and took the buggy. It was actually good to lean on – it aided her walking.

As they passed one of Tanya's favourite shops, Alfie hesitated and raised an eyebrow. "Don't you want to go and have a look in Zara? Surely there must be at least one thing in there you don't have," he grinned.

"Taking men shopping is a disaster. Mixed with a toddler, it's not going to make for a productive experience. You'll just stand looking uncomfortable in the doorway and make all the women look at you in a what-the-hell-are-you-doing-here way. Then you'll pick up something

I wouldn't put on the cat and suggest it would suit me. Then I'll think you have a very weird image of me. I'll think about that at four in the morning and wonder if you find me attractive or whether you see me as a substitute for your dead mother."

"'No', would have sufficed." Alfie grinned and, leaning over, kissed her passionately on the lips.

"Jesus, Alfie, what are you like? Snogging in the middle of a shopping centre!" she laughed, taken totally by surprise.

"I never did that with my mother." He squeezed her bum and walked on.

"I should bloody well hope not." She pushed Jenny forward to catch up with him. As he wandered into the electrical shop to prod widescreen televisions and play with the latest headphones, she held her breath. The nagging voice, with the horn and tail, in her head goaded her. *What's the point in buying new clothes? You'll be dead in a few months. They'll just end up in a charity shop, unworn, with the labels still attached.*

By the time they'd finished their coffee and Jenny was like a little pink milkshake with eyes, Tanya felt better. It was probably the chocolate and caffeine hit. Alfie was deft with the full-scale clean-up job of their daughter. He produced a packet of wet wipes from the underneath pocket of the buggy and managed to remove an extraordinary amount of ice cream. Jenny writhed and tried to move her face away from the wiping hand.

"No, Dada, yack wipe! Cold, cold! Bold Dada!"

"I know, honey, it's nearly over, then you're going to be all clean again. Like my little princess. 'Cos right now, you're hiding under all that pink sticky stuff. Where's my Jenny gone? Jenny?" He looked puzzled as he looked all around the buggy, while scratching his head. "Mummy, did you see Jenny?" The baby giggled, loving the game. All the while, Alfie stabbed away at the mess. Before she knew it, she was peachy and goo-free again.

Tanya watched the scene with awe and relief. She'd never been around for these little trips. She was always at work. This was a whole world she knew nothing about. Alfie and Jenny made a marvellous team. *Good*, she thought. *You're going to need each other when I'm gone.*

Her eyes were starting to burn. She was not going to make a show of herself and embarrass everyone around her by howling in the middle of the flat-screen TVs. Filling her lungs to capacity, she exhaled slowly and forced her mind to focus on the here and now.

She was totally exhausted by the time they got home. She fell onto the sofa and closed her eyes. Sleep didn't come, but she welcomed the relief from simply having to exist and function in public. Alfie and Jenny were in the small back garden. Jenny was digging in her little green plastic sandpit, he was pulling weeds. The sound of their easy banter washed over her, her baby's tinny voice weaving in and out of her husband's deep tones.

Not for the first time, a wave of prickly, heart-speeding fear washed over her. It was like the fear had crawled in under her toenail, like that advert she'd seen on TV for nail fungal infections. The fear clawed and scratched its way through every nerve and fibre of her being, invading its way until it gouged itself into her mind and brain.

Sitting bolt upright on the sofa, she looked around the room wildly. *Breathe in through your nose and exhale through your mouth,* she coached herself. She could do this. She could maintain control. She could handle this. She had to. Sitting down and lying still on her own wasn't good. She'd call Sally, her secretary, and see how she was fixed.

"Are you snowed under?" she asked.

"No, not bad now today. Things will kick off from tomorrow. You know yourself, once we pass Wednesday, the weekend functions come into play. We've that O'Connell wedding on Saturday, they confirmed the numbers at 285 this morning, but they're as happy as Larry, and the bride is still as cool as, so that's pretty much in the bag so far. The joint birthday bash is a tad trickier still."

"Are the mother and daughter still at loggerheads?" Tanya bit her lip. This pair of clients seemed to agree on nothing, could barely manage to be civil to each other, and yet they were having a huge shared celebration.

"I know the mother is a bit sharp but, Christ, if that child was mine I wouldn't give a toss if it was her twenty-first, I'd put her over my knee. In fact, a good beating wouldn't go amiss."

Tanya giggled. This was what she loved about Sally. She was dependable and very much a people person. She could do all the being nice to annoying customers, but underneath it all she was quite like Tanya really.

"Oh no, poor you! Tell you what, how would you feel about coming over to my house? I need to talk to you and it'd get you out of the office for the rest of the day. Just flick on the machine and let them all moan into that for the afternoon."

"O-kay. But don't you think you should take a break? There's nothing here that can't wait until next week at least." Sally assumed Tanya must be sore and tired, and all this week's events were well and truly under control. At the same time, she also knew her boss well enough not to argue with her.

"There are a few ideas I'd like to discuss with you, Sally, if you don't mind." Tanya rubbed her temples and willed the younger woman to agree.

"Of course. I'll just finish a quote and I'll be right over. Do you need anything brought? Any shopping or magazines or some chocolate?"

"No, you're terribly kind. Just bring yourself." Tanya smiled as she hung up.

Dragging herself outside to the back garden, she spotted Alfie in the furthest flowerbed, bum in the air, the crack of his arse on show, rooting out weeds.

"Great view, dear. Listen, I've got Sally popping over shortly to go through some stuff. There's a big wedding on Saturday and the bride is causing serious hassle. Sally was so sorry to have to annoy me, but needs must," she lied. "I know we're only back, but would you take Jenny to the park and give us an hour? It's just she won't understand being told to stay away from me, and Sally and I need to nail this."

"Of course, darling, but I'm concerned. You really need to minimise your stress at the moment, just until you get back on your feet."

He threw an arm around her shoulders as he walked her back down the garden towards the house. Kicking off his muddy Crocs, he led her back into the living room. She sat on the sofa and he crouched down and wrapped his arms around her.

"You're being so strong, I'm so proud of you," he said. "You're going to fight this bastard and win, you know that, don't you?"

She wasn't quite sure how she managed to hold it together as Alfie left the room. The love and hope and faith in his eyes would kill her quicker than this f'ing cancer. Tears of disappointment and stabbing guilt sprang afresh. She detested having to do this to him. He was going to be heartbroken and devastated. She was going to rip him apart, and there was damn all she could do about it. Right at that moment she hated and despised the cancer and herself in equal measure. *We're a likely pair,* she pondered bitterly, *Me and the cancer deserve each other.*

# 9

*Chemotherapy today, I hope to get a fruit scone with a bit of raspberry jam. Please God Miriam will be there. Over and out.*

Esme stuck her tongue out as she wrote in her book. She loved, loved, loved her little pink book. It was like a captain's log, and she felt all business-like writing in it each day. She was looking forward to her second round of treatment. The unit she attended at the hospital was really swish. All shiny floors, the type that came up lovely, with only a flick of a mop. Not like all those floors years ago that needed a good scrub to look anyway decent. The chat was mighty too.

"Ah hello, Miriam!" Esme was thrilled to see her new friend.

"Hiya, Esme love. How are you? I was terrible sick after the last one, so they said they'll give me more anti-nausea stuff this time." Miriam looked quite pleased with the complaint.

"God love you, Miriam. I was alright I must say. Now I did have to eat a poached egg for my tea the night after I'd been in. I did chops for Michael, because it was a Thursday, and he'd only be in a state if I suggested an egg, but I'd no appetite, not even for the mash and veg. How's the *breast?*" Esme whispered the word in case anyone should hear. She was well able to say rude words in a medical context, but she knew that Miriam had been ill at ease with the personal issues when they'd been in the hospital ward together. The girls were always telling her she'd the subtlety of a brick, which she'd taken as a compliment until Michael had explained that a brick doesn't have any, so it's really an insult in disguise.

"Well, you know, I told you before – they took most of *it* away?" Miriam looked all around to make sure nobody was listening in on the conversation. "Come here, wait till I tell you – well, they said they'd make me a new one if I like when the chemo is over." She nodded in satisfaction.

"Lovely. It's amazing what they can do. Sure I saw a programme where they grew an ear onto the back of a rat. Now, I don't know what a rat would be doing with a big ear on top of it, I'd say it must have been terrible sensitive to sound on account of having its own two to begin with. I'd say it was heavy too. But if they can give a rat a human ear, I'm sure they'd make you a grand *breast*." Esme patted her friend's hand.

A nurse came and sorted the ladies out, putting plastic cannulas into their veins. After drawing some blood, she explained they'd have to wait about an hour to make sure their levels were high enough.

"What's a level?" Miriam asked.

"Well, it just means we need to know if you have a good balance of white blood cells, red blood cells and platelets." The nurse tried to walk away.

"What's all that now, love?" Esme looked at the girl's shoes. A bit like men's shoes, she thought. She didn't really agree with those laced-up ones with rubber soles on women. Years ago, a nice court shoe would have been standard. None of the girls wore dresses any more either. All trousers, like a policeman, with a funny-looking top. Not a frill or a corsage in sight. Very masculine really. But, as Nora and Tracey kept telling her, she needed to keep up with the times. At least the girl had a bit of lipstick on, God bless her.

"Well, Esme. The white cells help to fight infection, the red ones carry oxygen and the platelets help to clot the blood, say if you get a cut." She scurried away before the ladies could ask any more.

"Jaysus, I had no idea blood could do all that, all at the same time. Brilliant really, isn't it?" Esme looked very impressed.

"You can see why it takes so long to learn medicine now," said Miriam. "If blood does all that, imagine what all the other organs do?"

Esme nodded. "'Awful' – isn't that the word for all those bits?"

"No, love, that's offal, and I think it's only the ones you eat are called that. Now I might be wrong." Miriam patted her arm.

One of the little foreign nurses appeared. "Can you come into the little side room for a minute, please, Esme?" she asked.

"Yes, love." Esme waddled after her. "And where are you from? I know you're foreign, but where do you come from?" She spoke very slowly and clearly, raising her voice a few octaves, to make sure the little one could understand.

"I am from India. My name is Amara," she said, smiling.

"Well, I never heard that type of name before. And did you train to be a nurse here, love?"

"No, no, I trained in India and then came here to work." She motioned to Esme to sit down.

"That sounds very exotic," Esme sighed.

"So I am going to ask you some routine questions, just to make sure you are doing okay."

Esme loved the whole session. She felt a bit like she was on the *Late Late Show*. The nurse would ask a question, she'd answer, and it was all written down. They covered everything from feeling sick, to how many hours of sleep she was getting, to all about poos.

She returned to her chair in the chemotherapy day unit feeling a bit smug.

"What did she ask you?" Miriam leaned in to hear the details.

"Wait till I tell you! We talked about everything, then she asked about stools. 'No,' says I, 'Michael needs a proper chair with a back on it.' Well, she was talking about poo! 'Why don't you just say poo then?' says I. Maybe it's the foreign way, but I told her in no uncertain terms that here in Ireland we refer to it as poo. 'Stools,' says I, 'are for sitting on.' I'm not sure if she understood. She's from India, you know."

"I'll have to ask her which takeaway she goes to. The odd time my fella gets a goo on him for a curry. I wouldn't know what to put in that and I don't trust them jars. Did you know Mrs Bulger from the Kylemore Road, Lord rest her?"

"No, love. Dead, is she?" Esme tutted.

"She died a few years ago, Lord rest her. Not from the iffy jar now, but I'd say it didn't help. She was stirring some foreign sauce into the meat and didn't she find a corn plaster floating in the pot. Now, she fished it out, according to herself, and fed the curry to Paul, her husband. She said nothing, but she told me on the quiet that he had the trots for two days after." Miriam nodded gravely.

"That's a shocking story, Miriam. I'm glad you told me that. My Michael has a very sensitive stomach. Doesn't even like going out to eat, to be truthful. We only dine out when the girls are home from England. But it puts him in a bad mood for days. Sends him off kilter. I'll keep that in mind though if the girls ever suggest using a jar of sauce. You wouldn't know what they put in them jars – could kill an innocent pensioner, couldn't it?" Esme patted her curls and straightened her blouse at the thought of death by curry.

The same girl approached them. "Miriam, please."

Esme winked at Miriam and tipped her nose, "Watch out for any *random* killer curry jars," she warned, using the biggest buzz word to grace the younger generation in years. With her Nora, everything was *random* – the word seemed to cover a multitude.

Just over an hour later, the nurse told Esme that her bloods were good.

"Well, I eat plenty of meat and on a Saturday we always have fried liver, so I'm not surprised to be truthful." She felt kind of proud of herself.

"That's great to hear, but the reason your white blood-cell levels could possibly be low is due to the chemotherapy. The medication is like a full internal wash-out. As well as killing all those bad cancer cells, it can often kill a lot of good cells at the same time. Plenty of patients suffer with a low cell count during treatment, so don't be alarmed if it does happen to you at a later stage. Luckily, so far you're doing well."

"Say for instance the good cells were gone, can you give me some more?" Esme scratched her chin.

"Yes. What we do is give you an injection which stimulates your bone marrow to produce new cells." The nurse hooked up the drip containing the first bag of clear liquid. "This is your pre-med – it helps with nausea," she explained.

"Why would you want to help me feel nausea?" Esme was shocked.

"No, dear, it stops you from feeling sick." The nurse turned the drip on and Esme could feel the cool liquid flowing into the vein in her hand.

After the nurse had gone, she whispered to Miriam. "I think she's a bit mixed up with her words. Lovely hair and skin, though, hasn't she?"

"Oh beautiful. She'd never need sun cream. I'd say she even gets away without tights when she's wearing a frock."

"It'd be very handy alright, wouldn't it?"

"Lovely."

Esme had a great day. The nurses followed the first bag of stuff with two others, which had a purple bag over them. Seemingly, the chemotherapy had to go in a coloured bag, so they'd know what was what. The girls even wore disposable gloves in the same colour. Esme and Miriam were very impressed by the co-ordination.

"If they even match their gloves to the medicine, imagine how well turned out they'd look at a wedding reception," Miriam commented.

At twelve o'clock, each patient got a bowl of soup and a sandwich. Now, it was lovely to have it handed up to her, Esme thought, but the bread wasn't the freshest. A bit curled up at the edges really. But they all got a pot of tea and twin pack of custard creams each.

"Grand, isn't it, Miriam? A bit like being on the train, except you don't have to pay? You can't beat tea and a custard cream, what?"

"You said it, girl. And with a bit of luck now, we'll see each other every time we come in – I'll look forward to that."

The two ladies chatted about years ago and how the times had changed. Miriam told her that she had only one child, a son, Declan. He'd never married and worked on the buses.

That was Esme's only regret – that her girls didn't live around the corner. They were good to her though. One of them rang her each day, and since this cancer thing, they'd come home a lot more. She loved to go places with them when they were home. They'd been in England so long now, they had beautiful accents. Tracey sounded a bit like one of the royal family. When they were little the girls had called her "Mammy", now they called her "Mum". She liked it. It was different.

Esme was very impressed by how well Tracey knew London too. The last time they'd gone over to visit her, she'd known all about the tube system. Esme and Michael would have ended up in China if they'd had to figure out where to go. She'd taken them to Fortnum & Mason, a stunning old Victorian-type place, with all posh tins of tea and biscuits. It was daylight robbery in Esme's opinion. Some of the tins had only a few scutty biscuits in them and they were forty pounds sterling. Some people obviously just had too much money. They'd sat at the teashop at the very back of the place, and ladies in black-and-white old-fashioned chambermaid-type costumes had served them. They'd called Esme, "Madam", which she'd enjoyed no end.

Her girls had a good life and were happy. So that was the main thing.

\* \* \*

Esme woke at about three o'clock in the morning, the night after the chemotherapy. Her head was spinning, yet she wasn't a bit tired. She got up and put on her dressing gown. She'd make herself a cup of tea, with plenty of milk in it. Her hand hesitated at the tea caddy. For a minute she was going to use the posh stuff, the one Tracey had bought her on that trip to Fortnum & Mason, but if she was truthful, she preferred her own Lyons Green Label.

The house was cold, even though it was August. The nights had already begun to get darker for longer. She'd take her cup into the sitting room and wrap one of her own hand-knitted blankets around her legs. She thought about turning the telly on, but was afraid she'd wake Michael. That wouldn't do at all. Even when the girls had been babies, when he was a much younger man, he'd hated to be woken at night. Now that he was getting on in years, he liked it even less. He'd only be confused and grumpy. Then he'd complain all day tomorrow. No, she'd sit in the quiet and drink her tea and go back up to bed.

The olive-green, velvet-covered three-piece suite, with big-buttoned detail, was soft and familiar.

"Would you not go for something a bit more contemporary?" Nora had asked the last time she'd been home. "That velvet yoke has seen better times. It must be older than me! Sure it owes you nothing at this stage."

"We like it and, besides, what would you suggest instead? Have your father slipping around on an oversized leather wallet? Oh Jesus, Nora, it wouldn't be worth the moaning. Anyway, the carpets are all marked from the feet of the settee – if we moved it now the whole room would need to be changed. That'd be too much upheaval for us both." Esme had shuddered at the thought of all that. Big dirty skips in the driveway, all the neighbours and the local gurriers looking at their private things, sitting all crumpled and dejected in the rain.

"But you could take the opportunity to have a total revamp. Tracey and I would pay for it. We'd like to. Imagine how modern and smart the place could be? If you go for bright colours instead of the dark greens and wine you have now, the house could feel twice the size."

"Ah, no. Your father would be too upset, you know what he's like about change." Esme always used Michael as an excuse when she didn't want to do something. Really he was a big old softie and was as easygoing as they come. Unless you were discussing his dinner. Then he could be quite forceful. Try and dissuade him from his chops and you'd have a proper fight on your hands.

Esme finished her cup of tea and sighed. It wasn't working it's usual magic. She still felt jittery and restless, yet her body was exhausted. Her skin felt dry too, like she needed to lather herself in thick comforting moisturiser. For all the trouble she was having sleeping, she still knew she wouldn't have the energy to cover herself in Nivea if she forced herself into the bathroom.

A picture on the mantelpiece caught her eye. Tracey's Communion photo. It had been a great day for them all. She'd gone to Arnotts to rig them all out. She'd worn a mint-green frock with a matching coat, and the biggest hat she could find. Michael was like Richard Gere in his pinstriped suit. Nora had a bit of a puss on – it was hard to be the little sister, the one *without* the big white dress and veil.

"You can't go up the church and get the holy bread. You'll have to sit on your own," Tracey had goaded her.

Nora had responded by boxing her sister in the eye.

So two days before the big day, instead of concentrating on sorting out the finer details, Esme had been like a woman possessed, trying to quell the swelling and bring down Tracey's shiner of a black eye. Everything was used, from frozen peas to gunge mixed in an eggcup, as recommended by Mrs Casey from four doors down.

"Ah Jesus, Mammy, what the hell is in that? It's fizzing the eye out of my head," poor Tracey had wailed, wincing.

"What's in it, Mrs Casey?" Esme had asked her.

"Bread soda and brandy, with a little bit of Andrew's liver salts." Mrs Casey had one hand on her hip, the other in the front pocket of her floral house coat, with an eternal fag burning in the left corner of her mouth. One eye was always squinted shut to avoid the smoke. Esme had never seen her in shoes. She always came out in her grey tights and men's tartan slippers.

"And it works well for black eyes, Mrs Casey?" Esme watched her daughter writhe around in pain. The other eye had started to water in sympathy with the fizzy one.

"I haven't a clue, Mrs Mulligan. I just made it up there five minutes ago, but if it does, I'll be onto a winner. Good girl, Tracey, how is it now?" Mrs Casey shouted in the child's face.

"It hurts and burns and smells funny – please, can we take it away?"

Feeling sorry for the whimpering child and not having a huge amount of faith in Mrs Casey's recipe, Esme led Tracey to the sink and dabbed the eye clean. Feeling it would be kinder to stick to a compress of frozen peas, Esme gave Nora a smack and sent her to her room and Tracey voluntarily went to bed early. Esme wasn't sure if it was the good night's sleep, the ice pack or indeed Mrs Casey's pungent fizzing goo, but the eye was a whole lot better the next day. By the time the veil and headdress went on, the day of the Communion, it was hardly noticeable.

"Just keep the veil down over your face for the day," Esme instructed the little one.

"But how will I take the holy bread and how will I eat my lunch?" Tracey had sobbed.

"By the time you get to the lunch everyone will have seen you. Just try not to look the priest in the eye, in case he thinks you come from a house where your parents beat you," Esme had instructed her.

She'd been fine in the end. Although Esme did notice the fear in Tracey's eyes, even through the veil, as she studied the picture all these years later. Of course nowadays it would be much simpler. She could bring her to a beauty salon. Didn't all the girls have fake tans and coloured nails and make-up and coaches and horses and all sorts of fairytale happenings? Lovely, thought Esme. Maybe one day soon, one of the girls would decide to get married and they could have all that. She'd even go for one of those pink Hummer things. They could play music, a bit like the ice-cream man, only make it the "Here Comes the Bride" tune.

She loved the idea of those ice sculptures too. Something classy like a swan or an angel playing a harp. The cake would be brilliant too. When herself and Michael had married, they'd had a bog-standard fruitcake, with a bit of royal icing blobbed on top. Just the normal snow effect, no fancy piping even.

She'd love one of her girls to have a big cake with three or four tiers, with a proper marzipan bride and groom on the top, with a little fountain flowing down the sides. She'd seen it in a magazine at the hairdresser's, so she knew it could be done. She'd never told the girls that she fantasised about weddings. She didn't want them to think she was being pushy.

Tracey was living in sin with her fella, Harry. You weren't supposed to call it that any more. You were supposed to say "living with her partner". And it was supposed to be all normal and cool. Nonchalant like. She tried to be like that about it. She kept her opinions on it all to herself – well, she'd told Michael of course. He didn't mind. He said everyone lived together now, Tracey was no different to any other young one.

"At least she's not a lezzer like Mrs Casey's daughter," said Michael. "She's like a man with tits, that one. She'll grow an Adam's apple if she has her way. She's scary, she is. All that weird dark-purple velvet she wears, and stockings with holes in them, and all those nails and bolts in her face. Has nobody ever told her she looks like a toolbox?" He shuddered.

"Well, I wouldn't like to – she'd probably head-butt you," Esme had warned.

Nora did have a boyfriend at one stage. He was foreign. From Wales. God, neither herself nor Michael could understand a single slur that came out of him.

"What's he on about now, Esme?" Michael would poke her at the dinner table.

Nora had brought him to meet them. He'd stayed in the box room, mind you.

"They can do what they like over there," Michael had poked his thumb behind his shoulder, "but unless they're married in front of Holy God, they can sleep in single beds under my roof."

"Stop, Michael, he's only Welsh, he's not deaf!" Esme had given him the look.

The fella hadn't said much after that. He certainly wasn't as nice as Aled Jones, Esme thought. They were glad when Nora took him away. She rang a few months later to say that she'd broken up with him. She hadn't brought anyone home since. That was over two years ago now. Esme was sure she had fellas over there that she didn't tell them about. Maybe she'd surprise them all and spring an engagement on them. She might even have it in Vegas. They could all go and maybe Elvis might be at the reception, and Nora could arrive on a unicorn, with Dolly Parton singing behind her. Lovely.

Yawning, Esme suddenly felt overwhelmingly tired. She shuffled back up the maroon-patterned stair carpet. She dipped her finger in the tiny holy-water font, just behind the front door, on the way. Outside she could hear young men shouting in the street. They'd built a new complex just around the corner. It had a nightclub on the upper level, so most nights drunkards shouted and roared and sometimes fought on her road. It used to be a quiet little cul de sac. Just a normal huddle of three-bed semi's.

They could move if they wanted. A young fella in a cheap suit had called to the door last year. From the estate agent's, saying their type of house was very sought after. A good starter home, he'd said.

"Where the hell would you like us to go? Climb onto a slab in the morgue and wait to die?" Michael had shouted at him.

Normally, she'd tell him not to yell at strangers, but that young pup had needed a bit of a talking-down. What would their option be? To go and live in an apartment? With lifts and stairs and no back garden?

"I'm not living in a dog box. Do you see a wagging tail, do I sit and lick my own bollox? No, I do not." Michael had poked the young spotty man with the clipboard. "Now bugger off and don't come back unless you want my foot, from my good starter home, inserted in your arse!" Michael had slammed the door. He'd nearly knocked the Virgin Mary statue over in the flurry, and the net curtain had got caught in the lock. He'd looked at Esme and the two of them had broken their holes laughing.

# 10

*Happy anniversary, darling Liam. Although I still miss you every day, time has healed the raw pain, even if only a little.*

Taking her own advice, Sian had filled many notebooks with positive thoughts to date. Due to Zoe and Tanya having operations, she had postponed the Pink Ladies meetings until they were well enough to return. She'd offered Esme the time on her own, but she'd declined gratefully, saying her daughter was coming for a few days, so it would suit her just as well to be at home.

Sian wasn't sure if it was a blessing or a curse to have a free morning. It was Liam's anniversary. He'd been the light of her life. Her soul mate. Even though it was eleven years ago today that she first stood at his graveside, she could still remember the pain as if it were yesterday. Of course, she didn't still have that raw, stabbing physical pain, day in, day out. That, thankfully, had passed with time. But when days like today came around, it was like the dormant monster of grief was woken, even if just for a while.

He'd been a real man's man, her Liam. He wasn't really in touch with his feminine side. He wouldn't have worn a pink shirt, or even a tie with pink or yellow stripes on it. Today, as the wind whipped up the back of her skirt at his graveside, she smiled through her tears, remembering the time she'd bought him a grey tie, with pink spots on it, to wear to a work function.

"Ah Sian, you're not serious, love. Are you trying to make me look like a puff in front of the people in work?"

"But I got it in Tie Rack. They're all the rage, patterned ties. I'll bet you all the others will have this kind of thing on," she'd tried to reason. "It'll look so smart on you."

"The others can look like gobshites if they like, but I'm wearing my white shirt, navy tie and my suit. What are you going to buy me next? A white suit, blonde wig and big teeth, and make me sing like I've my balls caught in a mousetrap?"

Today, to mark his anniversary, she'd brought a little tray of cacti. She'd never felt comfortable arranging lilies or chrysanthemums on his grave, though in the beginning she'd spent hours kneeling and arranging. She'd almost felt pressurised into it. All the other plots were like florist's windows. Some of the headstones had huge angels or elaborately carved patterns on them. She'd chosen a simple granite one, and had opted for plain black lettering. It was what she felt he'd prefer.

The first Christmas after Liam died, she'd gone to the grave, with a tiny potted pine tree. She'd swept away the dead flowers, brown and soggy from the elements. Although they looked bright and cheerful when they were freshly done, within hours the wind and rain would beat them to a pulp.

The little simple tree looked better. It fit in with his minimalist-look grave. So after that, she didn't bother with flowers any more. She stuck with hardy little shrubs and potted plants.

"I miss you, Liam," she said out loud, as she perched on her hunkers and stared at the black writing. The granite had grown some soft downy moss in places. She should probably clean it off. She'd seen other people with little buckets and nailbrushes, scrubbing gravestones. But she'd never felt the urge to follow suit.

"I hope you're having fun wherever you are. At least it's not this time eleven years ago. You struggled so much for breath. You fought until the end. At least now you're at peace. You are at peace, aren't you, Liam?" she urged the writing on the stone to answer her. "You'd have sent me a sign if you weren't, wouldn't you?"

In desperation, six months after he'd passed away, she'd gone to see one of those mediums. People who say they can communicate with the dead. She'd driven for two hours to a country cottage in the middle of nowhere to see this man. He was the seventh son of a seventh son, and was alleged to have the power to see and speak with the dead. She'd had to wait a month for an appointment.

"I don't take money, but I love a nice fruitcake if you're a baker at all," he'd told her over the phone.

The fact that he didn't seem to be in it for the money had raised her hopes. Obviously he did all this because he truly had "the gift".

The thought of talking to Liam again, even through a stranger, kept Sian going for the run-up to their meeting. She'd carefully baked a rich fruitcake, and wrapped it in brown paper and placed it in a colourful tin. Following the precise instructions, she found herself outside a small dreary-looking bungalow. She felt like a small child on Christmas morning as she made her way to the front door, tin in hand.

An ordinary-looking man, with greying temples, dressed in brown slacks and a short-sleeved nylon shirt opened the door before she could use the paint-spattered knocker.

"Sian?" he said, smiling at her gently.

"You must be Tomás." She realised she was shaking and standing like a stunned goldfish staring at him. Copping herself on, she thrust the tin at him and tried to look calm.

"Come on in. Thank you for the gift. I appreciate it."

The bungalow was darker inside than she'd anticipated. There were very few personal items on display. The narrow cramped hallway led to an open-plan living-cum-kitchen area. Two mahogany doors, with yellow mottled glass panels, led off the back of the kitchen. Sian assumed they led to the bedroom and bathroom. The house smelled faintly of turf and cabbage. The place could do with a good clean.

Tomás indicated to her to sit at the cheap-looking round table, with four plastic garden chairs around it. The brown-patterned lino was sticky under her feet.

"Tea or coffee?" He asked her, turning on a yellow-stained, once-white kettle.

The kitchen area was dank and cramped with a small four-ring electric cooker, two overhead and two under-counter cupboards, a small white fridge and a brown plastic crockery drainer at the side of the sink.

Not wanting to seem rude and desperately needing something to do with her quivering hands, she asked for a coffee. Not surprisingly, he produced a jar of supermarket own-brand instant.

"Milk and sugar?"

She was so busy trying to have a look around she wasn't focusing on Tomás.

"Oh yes, just milk. Thank you." She tried to smile, but her face was frozen with nerves.

Clicking the tin open, Tomás inhaled the scent of the freshly baked cake.

"Wow, that smells good!" He cut a couple of slices and put them on the table, served on the lid of the tin. Next came the plastic two-litre container of milk, followed by a bag of sugar and a single teaspoon to share. The mugs were chipped and kind of slimy. The coffee had a slick of what appeared to be grease on top of it. Under normal circumstances, Sian would have recoiled and found the whole place offensive. But this man was going to put her in touch with her darling Liam. He was like her telephone to heaven. Who cared if his house was a bit lacking in a woman's touch? He was going to reverse the heartbreaking silence she'd been forced into living each day, since Liam had died.

When he'd finished tasting her cake and adding milk and sugar to his coffee, he fixed his gaze on her.

"Okay, let's hope we'll be lucky today, Sian. I'm not sure if I told you over the phone, but sometimes people come to me full of expectation and go away disappointed. I have no way of telling whether or not anyone will come to communicate with you. You understand that, don't you?" He smiled, but his eyes were focusing behind her.

"I . . . no. I thought you could contact my Liam. I just assumed he'd be here. Isn't that going to happen?" She knew she was sounding like a spoilt child in a toy shop, but this wasn't the plan.

"I'm not Telecom Éireann, Sian. I have a gift, but I'm not a magician either. I can only communicate with spirits who present themselves. Some days nobody comes, some days three or four come at once. It varies and it is never possible to know what will happen. I've had the same person come and see me three times in a row, hoping to speak to her sister, but she's never come forward. So try and relax and we'll see if there's anyone here for you." He continued to stare just beyond Sian's head.

Hoping she might see what he appeared to be looking at, she swivelled suddenly to try and catch a glimpse of Liam. There was nothing there.

"There's no one here to see me, is there?" She felt crushed with disappointment. She'd been so excited and so sure Liam was going to be there. She'd so many questions in her head. She was going to ask him things and most of all tell him how much she loved him and missed him. She had felt sure things would be easier to cope with once she had one final chat with him. Once she knew he was happy and at peace. Once she knew he wasn't in pain any more. That he was free, and liked where he'd ended up. Then she could know it was okay to get on with what was left of her life without him.

Tomás was smiling now. His stare was fixed. He seemed to be honing in on something.

"Sian, there *is* someone here to communicate with you today." He flicked his eyes down to meet hers.

Her heart skipped a beat. "Liam, I knew you'd come! Where is he?" She looked around wildly.

"Please stay calm, Sian. It's not Liam. She calls herself Zadkiel. She is named after an Archangel and she brings a vivid violet ray of light in her wake."

"What? Who?" Sian felt her eyes brimming with tears. This wasn't what she'd planned at all. This guy was a fruitcake-eating freak. What the hell was he babbling about?

"She says she's your daughter." Tomás kept his gaze above Sian's head.

"What? But I never had children. Liam and I, we couldn't, well, it never happened. We wanted children, for years we hoped and prayed, but it just didn't come about. This is cruel. You're breaking my heart, I thought you were going to help me talk to my beautiful Liam, instead you're telling me the child we always yearned for and never had, is here. You're a mean and heartless man." Sian attempted to stand up and flee the scene.

"Wait, Sian. Please, just give me a few more minutes of your time. Zadkiel is trying to communicate with you. Please."

His eyes were kind, and for some reason, she found herself sitting down and listening to him.

"This is against my better judgment, but go on." She felt stricken and suspicious.

"Zadkiel is named after an angel as I've already said. Do you remember the time you fainted in the garden? She's talking about a rosebush and a wooden bench. You hit your head and Liam made you go to A&E to be checked out. The following day you woke up feeling nauseous and weak. You miscarried your baby. She's here now behind you."

Sian was stunned. She did remember the incident. But she'd never had any inkling that her hospital visit had included a miscarriage.

"I never got pregnant. We gave up hoping for a baby. This can't be right. I should never have come here." She wanted to run and get away from this man, but she felt compelled to stay. The scene he had just described had indeed happened. There was no way he could have known about it. But it was unfathomable to her that she had lost a child at that time. Rooted to the spot, Sian listened.

"Your daughter is here to tell you that she is with you. She will always be with you. She is your special guardian angel and anytime you need her, you must imagine her purple light and she will surround you."

"Well, if she's so much help, ask her to go and get her father. How about that then?" Sian felt fear and resentment in equal measure bubbling through her. She'd been a fool to come here with her fruitcake in hand, thinking this man in his musty bachelor pad could communicate with her darling husband. "I'm leaving now." She shoved the chair back and fled.

119

"Sian, wait! Please, don't go. Zadkiel is still here, she wants to help you." Tomás was standing at the door looking stricken as she turned around. Shaking her head, she got into the car and drove away as fast as she could.

Not only had she not found Liam, but she'd come away with fresh pain in her heart. Tomás hadn't offered her an iota of comfort. She'd been longing for one final conversation with her lost husband. Never in her most disturbing nightmares had she envisaged she'd end up being told she'd actually missed out on being a mother. The sceptic in her brain tried to tell her that Tomás was making the whole thing up. But how could he have known about that trip to A&E? With the details of the rosebush and the bench?

All her journey that day had done was rub salt on old wounds while simultaneously cutting a new one.

She shouldn't have driven the car, she was in such a state. But somehow she managed to get home. Unable to eat or speak, she crawled under her duvet, still wearing her coat and shoes, and curled into a ball and cried.

That was over ten years ago, and she still felt sorry for herself any time she thought about it.

"Things are better now, Liam. I'm better now, darling. My life is busy and I help people. That's good, isn't it?" She read his name over and over again on the headstone.

She'd never revisited the whole miscarriage thing in her head since the day she'd been to that medium. She couldn't afford to.

She gathered her bag and took a final look at the little row of spiky pale-green cacti, perched in a rectangular container at the edge of Liam's grave. They looked neat and fuss-free. Shoving her hands into her pockets, she walked towards the car. She'd go and have a coffee and a scone, maybe even treat herself to a couple of gossipy magazines. She was meeting her friend Joan at five. So she'd a bit of time to kill.

She'd met Joan shortly after Liam died, at a support group, a little like the one she ran now. Except this one was a grief-counselling one, with six in the group. Joan had lost her husband

Jimmy, also to cancer. Slowly the other group members had met new partners and some even remarried.

"Do you think they look at us as if we're two ageing lesbians?" Joan slurred out of the side of her mouth, quite squiffy, at the evening reception of a second marriage.

"Oh Jesus, the thought never entered my head. They wouldn't think that, would they?"

Sian looked so shocked, Joan roared laughing. "So will I take it from the look on your face you don't fancy me then?"

"What? You're not, well, you don't feel . . .?" Sian thought she was going to pass out from shock.

"Nooooo, I'm only pulling your leg! It just occurred to me that we're the only two who haven't found another love. Are we sad? Should we be off at singles-club dances? Or booking ourselves on to treks across Peru, in the hope of meeting an eligible widower to take away the pain of being alone?" Joan leaned her chin on her hands.

"I don't want anyone else. I've thought about it, meeting a new man, I mean. But I'm okay the way I am. The dagger-gouging pain has ebbed over the years. I know I don't have anyone who lights up my heart and makes the room spin, but I'm okay. You know? I don't feel like I'm being ripped to shreds by heartache either. Is that wrong? Am I cheating myself by playing it safe?" Sian searched her friend's eyes for an answer.

"I feel the same way, honey. Believe me, I think trucking along, not hurting anybody and nobody hurting me, is quite alright. Besides, until you meet Prince Charming, or Ageing-Widower-King-Saggy-Drawers, I'll stick with you. All the better if they think we're lesbians. It might give us a slight edge."

Clinking their glasses, they cackled with laughter and enjoyed their evening.

Today, as it was Liam's anniversary, they'd arranged to go out to a movie and a meal afterwards. She knew she could talk about him if she wanted, and Joan would understand – but just as long as she wasn't on her own, that was the main thing.

She felt weary. Like she was dragging herself around. The lack of sleep was really getting to her too. She'd mentioned it to the GP the last time she'd been for a check-up. He'd been kind and had told her that if it became a problem for her, he could prescribe something. She'd taken sleeping pills before, shortly after Liam had died, but she had soon weaned herself off them.

As she finished her coffee and scone, she made a decision. She'd give it another two weeks. If she still wasn't sleeping, she'd go back and ask for something to get her back in a routine. There were no prizes for being a martyr in life.

# 11

*I will never have to go on the pill again. I won't ever have to worry about getting pregnant. Do I feel positive now? Not really . . .*

Zoe was beginning to hate St Mark's Clinic. As she sat waiting for Dr Leah to come and chat to her, she wished to God she was anywhere else but here. She had recovered well after the operation, at least that's what the doctors were telling her. She was doing so well, in fact, that she was being allowed to start chemotherapy. For the first session, she was to stay in overnight, so they could monitor her progress. Her arms and legs were so swollen from the auto-immune disease she could barely function. The itchy red rash was like a dreadful case of sunburn.

"Zoe, hello. How are you doing?" Dr Leah breezed into the room, with her team in tow.

"I'm hideous, I look like a boiled chipmunk. Will this rash leave scars?"

"Hopefully not, but obviously the more you scratch it, the more chances you'll have of permanent marking."

Her parents and Charlie were all crowded into her room, ready to support her on her maiden voyage with the chemotherapy machine.

"Before we get going, I would like to talk to you about the cold cap, Zoe." Dr Leah pulled over a chair. "As with a number of the chemotherapy drugs now, the one you're going to be on shouldn't cause alopecia or hair loss. However, if you're particularly worried about your hair thinning and possibly falling out, we have an option."

Zoe looked from her parents to Leah.

"It's a system called scalp cooling. I know we mentioned it to you before, but so much has happened and you've had to take in so much medical information, I'll just run through the principle once more. Basically, when you have chemotherapy, the scalp heats up and, effectively, your hair follicles are fried and your hair falls out. This device, which looks a little bit like a cross between a helmet and an old-fashioned swimming hat, is put on your head. It's connected to a refrigeration device, which freezes the whole thing. We place it tightly on your head an hour before treatment, it stays in place while the chemotherapy goes through your veins, and we remove it an hour after treatment is completed."

Zoe felt the walls-closing-in feeling starting again. Any time Dr Leah or any of the medics started talking all the Scary-Mary medical talk, she felt like she wanted to run and hide.

Dr Leah went on to explain that the scalp cooling was quite uncomfortable, so they usually offered a little tablet to help the patient relax.

"Although it's obviously very cold and uncomfortable at first, it's proven to be quite effective. It works for in and around 60% of patients. If you want to preserve your hair, it's worth considering."

Dr Leah needed to finish her rounds with the other patients and make sure Zoe's bloods were healthy enough for treatment. Then she promised she'd be back to find out if Zoe wanted to go ahead with scalp cooling.

"Why would my bloods not be good enough?" Zoe looked terrified.

"One of the first side-effects of chemotherapy is that it depletes the goodness in your blood," Leah explained. "Your blood is made up of three main components: white cells, red cells and platelets."

"Okay," Zoe said.

"The function of white cells is to fight infection," Leah said. "The red cells carry oxygen around the body and platelets help clot blood. So if you get a cut for instance, the platelets kick into gear and help the bleeding to cease."

"Gotcha," Zoe answered, looking less worried.

"Your neutrophils are the most common type of white blood cell. They are the first immune cells to arrive at the site of an infection and so are responsible for the larger part of the immune response. Chemotherapy can deplete them massively, leaving you open to infection, so we're going to be pretty obsessed with your neutrophil count from here on in."

"How do you check that?" Zoe asked, biting her lip.

"The nurses will always check your blood mid-cycle. Which means you will have to pop in to see us about a week after each treatment. You're going to have chemotherapy every three weeks, for six months. So in your case, you will come in for a blood count on day ten after chemotherapy. Do you understand?"

Zoe felt like she was at a chemistry exam in school. It was all so much to take in at first. "I'm sure I'll get used to all this, but right now it all sounds quite complicated and terrifying to be honest."

"I understand. It's a seriously complicated process, but I know my stuff, so you can trust me. I'm here to look after you and to help you beat this. I will keep my finger on the pulse. Nothing will escape me or my team. All your appointments will be written down and you will be kept informed at all times. How's that? For now, have a chat with your mum and dad here and decide whether or not you'd like to go for the scalp cooling. I'll be back in shortly, okay?" Dr Leah patted Zoe's hand. Her skin was cool and taut against Zoe's hot, rash-burnt puffy paw.

Zoe wanted to crawl into the in-built wardrobe in her hospital room. So she could simply hide and not have to consider freezing her head to save her hair. She wanted to wiggle her nose like Samantha in *Bewitched* and make it all better again. She was so sore and, quite frankly, tired of being grown up. She wanted someone to take all the whizzing thoughts and decisions away. She wanted her life back to the way it had been.

She only realised now how simple and happy-go-lucky it had all been. It was sinking in with her why her mother had all this plastic surgery for instance. She'd never condemned her for going under the knife. It was her choice and she was entitled to do what made her happy. But a small part of her had always thought her mum's actions a tad mental. Diana was beautiful. Not just attractive, or lovely in her own way, or even what could be described as 'stylish' (which is really a translation in women's language for looking like a bulldog's arse-hole, but making the most of it).

Diana was a different story. She had huge brown eyes, sallow skin, a ski-slope nose, high but not sharp cheekbones, a neat rounded chin, with just enough shape to be soft, not a sign of Punch and Judy puppet going on. She was a perfect size ten, both top and bottom – unlike many women who could look fantastic sitting at a table in a restaurant, and they stand up to go to the bathroom and you think, *Holy shit, who stuck those thighs and bum onto that torso?* No, Diana was a stunner.

Lying here, looking like a pumped-up, boiled version of herself, Zoe would go to any lengths to feel better. Only now did she actually *get* what her mother had meant when she'd explained why she'd opted for some surgical "help" with her look.

"When I get up in the morning, I feel good. I have my shower, and get dressed. I go to the mirror to put on my make-up and the face that's staring back at me, is not the one I have in my mind's eye. It depresses me. I don't *feel* old. I don't *feel* the way I *look*. I know it's hard for you two to understand. But having this facelift will give me back my confidence. What's so wrong with wanting to appear the way I used to? That's what all this surgery was invented for after all."

Zoe and Charlie had shrugged and muttered, without making eye contact. Later on, in the confines of the shop, they'd discussed the fact that they both agreed their mother was gorgeous. To them, she hadn't needed any surgery.

"It's her choice and if that's what makes her happy, who am I to judge, but you wouldn't get me doing it." Charlie had been firm.

But they *had* been judging her. Zoe saw that now. When she was faced with the prospect of losing her hair a whole new understanding had enveloped her. Zoe knew growing old gracefully and losing one's hair from chemotherapy were two entirely different things, but it was all about perception. How strangers judged us.

If she was bald, she'd be "that poor girl with cancer". In a comparable way, her mother would have been put in the over-fifties bracket. Being labelled and put in a box wasn't a great prospect.

"I don't want to wear a wig that looks like a matted piece of road kill. I'm not doing the headscarf or baseball-cap look. I don't want to be a neon sign flashing 'cancer victim, drop head to side and sigh in sympathy'," Zoe burst out. "I'm going to try the scalp cooling. How bad can it be? If they give me more drugs to make it all feel okay, then I might as well go for it. In for a penny, in for a pound, eh?"

"I think you're right to give it a go, honey," her father said. "If you decide you can't stand it or you don't want to continue with it, at least you'll know you tried." He kissed her cheek gently.

"I agree," Diana joined in.

Zoe had a flash of realisation. Her parents were an amazingly strong unit. They were open-minded, loving and encouraging. Steven hadn't backed all Diana's decisions to have surgery but in general he was compassionate and supportive. So many of her friends' parents had separated, she knew it was almost unusual at this stage having her parents still together. She'd always taken that for granted too. Christ, her head felt like it needed to be cleaned out – she almost wished she could stick a feather duster in one ear and poke it out through the other, taking all the cobwebs and clutter with it.

This cancer was causing too many revelations to cope with.

When Dr Leah came back, Zoe told her she'd like to try the scalp cooling. A machine about the size of a mini-fridge was wheeled in. Coming out of it was a wide pipe, a bit like an electric-blue elephant's trunk, coated in foam. The pipe was connected to the back of a helmet-like cap. The inside of the cap was laced with little tiny lengths of that freezing gel that you can put into those cooler-bag pouches.

"Zoe, this is going to feel really cold. Like brain-freeze when you drink a cold drink too quickly. Are you ready?" the nurse asked.

"I think so." Zoe closed her eyes. She'd popped a little white pill, which was to help her relax during the brain-freeze. Bracing herself, she felt confident she'd be well able for all this. How cold could it be?

Beads of ice fell off the cap as it was fixed onto her skull. It was heavy, tight as bejaysus and a strap was fixed under her chin.

*Oh, sweet-divine-land-of-the-leaping-jaysus-all-the-angels-saints -and-holy-fathers!*

This was a new definition of cold. There was no word invented to describe the sensation.

"*Ugh, ouch!* I can't . . . I don't think I can . . ." Zoe yelped.

It was like having an enormous snowball mashed onto your entire head. The shock and heavy wetness was followed by a huge rush of appalling entire-head-encompassing brain-freeze.

"Holy fuck, this is horrendous!" Zoe yelled. It was hard for the nurse to hear her. She'd turned the machine on and it was as loud as a Hoover.

"Okay, honey?" The nurse did the thumbs-up motion.

Zoe simply sat riveted, barely able to speak. The freezing sensation rushed all through the bones in her skull. She caught her breath and tried to stay calm. With all her might, she wanted to rip the godforsaken thing off her head.

*Think of your hair. You don't want a headscarf. You don't want to look like a Lego man with a vile wig. You don't want to have a head that reflects the light. You don't want people talking to the headscarf.*

The nurse took her hand. "You'll get used to it in a few minutes. Try and relax and ride the storm."

As soon as the drugs trickled into her veins, she felt the effect. It was kind of muzzy and made her heart beat a little quicker.

"Is it like being drunk?" Charlie leaned forward.

"Jesus, Charlie, you're not going to feel the effects by climbing inside my face! Back off, will you?" Zoe snapped. Immediately she regretted sounding so narky.

There was a shocked silence. The girls had always been like two peas in a pod. But this cancer had wormed its way into their relationship. Charlie looked to the floor and muttered a weak apology under her breath. She hated all of this. Zoe having cancer wasn't right. It shouldn't be happening. She felt constant guilt too. Why had Zoe ended up in this terrible state and she was just as healthy as before?

All anyone talked about these days was cancer. She couldn't get away from it. Every single customer who came into the shop asked in a depressing way: "How is your sister?" It was like there was a ban on fun. Like smiling was in recession. She did try and act as if everything was wonderful. She'd tell the customers that Zoe was "doing as well as could be expected", and other such noncommittal answers. But the situation was horrendous. Her once natural and easy relationship with her twin had changed. Charlie felt helpless. More than that, she felt like she should just step out of the way.

The other thing that stung at her inner sense of guilt was the fact she'd come to realise she was utterly useless at dealing with all the hospital stuff. Everything from the thermometers to the drip equipment filled her with dread. For her, Zoe was Mother Theresa and Elvis all rolled into one. Before now, her idea of hospital had culminated in a gory episode of *Grey's Anatomy*. But even that show had Dr Shepherd, known as McDreamy, with his dark good looks and oozing sexual style.

In reality, hospital wasn't a soap nor was it a place where you could hang out in the coffee shop and wait for a delicious-looking surgeon to approach. Charlie allowed her mind to wander for a moment as she tried to envisage a more palatable scene.

"Is this seat taken?"

"No, Dr Sexy, it isn't, please join me. I could do with some company."

He'd sit and tell her how wonderful she was being, supporting her sick twin. He'd tell her that he had it on good authority that Zoe was going to make a full recovery and that everything would be okay.

"Why don't you join me for drinks in a cocktail bar, followed by dinner in a Michelin-starred restaurant?" he'd croon. "A beautiful girl like you needs to be looked after, especially in times of stress. Let me take care of you."

A shrill beeping noise pierced her dream and she was shunted back to reality.

"Oh God, what's happening? What's that noise?" She felt quite shaken.

"It's the chemo machine. One of the bags of stuff has emptied, so the nurse needs to come in and change it for the next medicine." Zoe looked up at the metal drip-stand, with the collapsed clear plastic bag hanging like a deflated balloon. She pressed the call button for the nurse.

Diana was flicking agitatedly through the large pile of magazines on the coffee table. Steven was pacing up and down, saying things like, "It's good to get the whole process started, I suppose."

Zoe felt guilt wash over her again. She wished with all her might that she didn't have to be the cause of all this anguish. Her parents had aged ten years in the last few weeks. Well, her dad certainly had. The plastic surgery, Botox and fillers didn't allow her mother to display her emotions. Her eyes were dull though. She was quiet too. Not her usual, down-to-business self. She was even looking through magazines without ear-marking pages for items she simply had to have or she'd die. Charlie was like a cat on a hot tin roof.

Zoe knew she was having to behave like a deranged parrot, telling people over and over again what was going on. This f'ing cancer wasn't just affecting her – it was interfering with all her family and their lives.

By the time she'd finished having all the drugs put through her veins – six bags in total, including the anti-nausea drugs and the "flush" – she was utterly knackered.

The freezing thing had eased slightly, but she was wondering if her brain was going to be permanently damaged by the process. Her jaw felt like it was about to snap in half under the strain of the under-chin strap.

"This needs to stay on for another while to ensure the chemotherapy doesn't frazzle your hair at the roots." The nurse patted her hand. "You're playing a blinder. Your first chemotherapy is finished. Well done!" With a smile she left the room.

Zoe felt oddly proud of herself. Amazing how completing a session of drugs could be satisfying, but it was. At least something was happening to kill this evil bastard that was trying to coil around her insides and squeeze the life out of her. Gritting her teeth, she urged herself to withstand the coldness for a little while longer. Fresh determination surged through her. She was going to fight this cancer tooth and nail. She was not going to let it win. Sod it. She would be victorious. The cancer and the dermatomyositis had picked the wrong girl.

"Fuck you and the horse you rode in on!" Zoe held her fist up.

"Pardon, darling?" Diana looked quite alarmed as she glanced at her husband.

"Nothing, Mum!" Zoe cracked up laughing. Once she started, she couldn't stop. Her limbs ached and her tummy felt like it would burst. Her head flopped to one side and then the other, with the weight of the frozen helmet. "Fuck you, and you and you!" She pointed to where her ovaries had been and to her swollen face. "Fuck the lot of you! You're all going to be obliterated. I am going to win. I am the Princess Warrior. I will overcome!" Her giggles switched to sobbing tears, gulping and gasping, her lungs burning.

Charlie rushed to Zoe's side and wrapped her arms around her sister.

"That's the Zoe I know and love. You say it as it is, girl! Besides," Charlie stroked her sister's cheek, "the new season gear from Paris is due in three weeks from now. That bright pink bandeau dress you fell in love with has your name on it. You'd better get yourself well so you can get at least two wears out of it!"

"I don't think I'd even get my big toe into that dress right now. Look at me! I'm like an inflated raft with eyes!" Zoe began to sob again.

"Remember what Dr Leah said," Charlie urged. "The chemotherapy will help with the dermatomyositis and the cancer. You'll be back to your own gorgeous self soon!"

131

"You did it! You said 'dermatomyositis'!" Zoe said, sniffing through her tears.

"There you go, sure you're almost cured then," Charlie said, getting onto the bed and lying down beside her twin. "Jeez, that thing is bloody freezing!" she gasped, wincing as some droplets of ice escaped and dropped onto her neck.

When the cap was lifted off her head and the tight gripping strap removed from her chin, Zoe felt overcome with gratitude. It was as if she'd been propelled into a Disney movie. Bluebirds should have been fluttering around her, pecking up the covers and laying them gently over her. Butterflies should be sweeping happily around her head.

"Oh my God, what a relief! It's nearly worth having that yoke rammed onto your head, just feel the liberation when it's removed." Sinking down onto the bed, she felt her shoulders relax and her head was as light as a feather.

Realising Zoe was a little less distressed, Charlie reluctantly agreed to head back to the shop.

"Anna is fine with the customers and all that, but you know yourself, people want to deal with the boss. I'll call you later on, sis." She bent and kissed Zoe's inflamed cheek.

"Text me any photos of new stock, I'm dying to see all the new bits and pieces," Zoe said trying to leave Charlie with as positive an impression of her as she could. "Talk to you later."

Charlie tried not to break into a jog as she left the hospital. It wasn't as bad as it could be – at least Zoe was in her own room and all that. The private clinic didn't have that dreadful antiseptic hospital smell and there was no accident and emergency area, so at least there weren't ambulances with maimed people rolling up at the door to freak her out.

Sticking her ticket into the machine in the car park, she felt like shouting out loud. Seven euro? She was only in there for a short while. They were bloody thieves! Why did you have to pay at a hospital car park at all? It wasn't as if you were there to watch a movie or have a boozy lunch. If she'd the time or energy, she'd organise a petition against them. Instead, she popped a chewing gum in her mouth and strode to her car.

She shuddered as the image of Zoe flashed before her. That manky-looking swimming-hat thing on her head. The creeping nasty red rash all over her face. All those drugs coursing through her veins. It was an utter nightmare, and there was absolutely nothing she could do to help. Bar sitting and keeping a positive expression on her face and trying to jolly her along – which she seemed to be failing at dismally, as their spats were full proof of.

* * *

"Is she going to die?" one of the gang asked over the booming music in the late bar.

"God no. She'll be grand. She just needs some chemo drugs and she'll be perfect." She went into the loo and sat there for ages.

"I'm going to wet myself, what the hell are you doing in there? Hurry up, will you?" An angry drunk person was doing a jig outside the toilet door.

Charlie grabbed her Chanel handbag from the hook on the back of the door, pushed her way past the queue of bursting revellers and went straight outside. She was lucky to find a taxi quickly.

"Blackrock, please." She sank into the seat and exhaled.

"Let me guess, fight with your fella?" The taxi driver was all ready for a chat. The pretty petite brunette looked like she'd the usual woes of the world on her shoulders. It was nearly always man trouble. He'd hate to go back to that stage again. Trying to find someone you could trust. Having to deal with all the queues, spending your wages on booze. He'd hated the whole going-out thing. That was why the taxi work suited him. He was never a drinker. He'd married young and was happy to provide for his wife and son.

"I wish that was all it was. My twin sister has cancer. What kind of a messed-up thing is that? She's in St Mark's, getting ready to be hooked up to God knows what drug machine. She'll never have kids and she could die. People die all the time from cancer, don't they?" Charlie burst into tears.

"I'm sorry, love. I'd no idea. If it helps you at all, my Aunt Maggie had cancer thirty years ago. They weren't as clever then as they are now, and she's fine. A tough old bird she is. I'm sure your sister will be just fine." He felt desperately sorry for the poor girl. Shit, he hadn't been expecting that.

"Your Aunt Maggie, did they tell her she'd be okay or what was the prognosis?" Charlie sat forward in the back seat to hear.

"Well, at the time, they just chopped off her breast and pumped her with drugs. All her hair fell out and she puked a lot. I remember that much. She was staying with us, you see. Me ma, God rest her, decided to care for her at the time. Sure, she'll outlive us all at this rate."

Charlie motioned for him to pull over as they neared the apartment block in Blackrock. She leaned forward and patted him on the shoulder.

"Thank you. I needed to hear something positive." She waved a fifty-euro note towards him.

"Have this one on me, love," he said with a smile. "I'll say a prayer for your sister. Go on before I change my mind!"

"Thank you, you're a kind and lovely man." Charlie got out of the car, feeling choked with booze and emotion.

As she staggered toward the apartment, the taxi pulled away. The driver exhaled, thanking his lucky stars he wasn't in her shoes. He was glad to able to say something to try and help the poor young girl. The image of his own mother, as she eventually gave in to cancer, two years before, flashed through his mind. He'd have given anything for someone to shed a glimmer of light on the darkness that cancer had shrouded his family at the time. He'd never had an Aunt Maggie. But right at that moment, the girl hadn't needed to know that.

# 12

*May the light shine upon my Pink Ladies. May our meeting bring them all a sliver of comfort.*

Sian used her notebooks almost obsessively. She never read over them, but she figured one day she *could* if she wanted. All the positivity would prevail surely?

It was a bit like a lame-duck convention rather than a support group, as Sian greeted Tanya, Zoe and Esme for their third meeting.

Zoe was looking better than she had before. Her skin was less angry and raw, and she seemed more able to move. Although she still shunted herself like a wooden doll, her movements didn't seem to be causing her the same level of pain.

Tanya looked hollow. She'd lost an alarming amount of weight and her hair was so thin that the glaring white of her scalp was beginning to poke its way through the auburn covering. It was like bits of pavement showing through melting snow.

Esme was as happy as Larry. She looked a little dark under the eyes, but otherwise, exactly the same.

"It's good to see you all again. We've had a break due to all the surgery. So we almost have to become reacquainted as such. How is everybody doing since we last met?" Sian threw the comment to the room.

"I've had three chemos by now, and I'm very good at it, so they tell me," Esme piped up. "It's every second week and in a funny way I do look forward to it. I've met a lovely girl in there, by the name of Miriam. She was in the bed opposite when I went in for the surgery." Esme took a loud slurp of her coffee.

Tanya shuddered. She hated nothing more than slurping. For her, it was on a par with chewing with your mouth open and picking your nose and eating it.

"Well, the first day of the chemotherapy, who walks in only Miriam. 'If it isn't yourself,' says I. Do you know, we've become firm friends. She even came over with her Frank for their dinner on Sunday. I do a roast beef or roast chicken on a Sunday. We'd a grand day. Frank and my Michael get on great, you know. Go for a pint together and all. They didn't actually talk that much on Sunday, but they ate every bit of their dinner and their crumble and custard and brought a cup of tea into the living room and watched the darts together."

Sian nodded gently and smiled at the older woman. "That's great, Esme. I'm glad you've found a friend who can share the experience with you. Chemotherapy can be a tough process and if you feel you have someone you can relate to, that's going to be invaluable for you."

"I've had my surgery and started my chemo too. I had the scalp-cooling thing," Zoe shuddered at the thought of it.

"How did you find it all?" Sian leaned forward.

"The chemotherapy was fine, but the scalp cooling was dreadful."

"What's that then?" Esme asked, entirely forgetting that Zoe had told them about it before.

"It's a thing that's supposed to make sure I don't lose all my hair. It's like wearing a snowball for three hours."

"Well, I've heard it all now! Why on earth would they want you to wear a snowball? They sound like they're a bit mental in your place." Esme helped herself to another biscuit. "Shouldn't really, but don't mind if I do. Seventy next birthday, please God, so I might as well treat myself. At this stage of my life, why not?" She chuckled away as she horsed through the chocolate-covered treats, dipping them into the coffee and slurping alternately.

"Will you continue with the scalp cooling, Zoe?" Sian probed.

"I actually don't know. I'm not sure if it's worth it. It was so unpleasant I can't say if I'll manage it again."

"Well, as you can all see my hair is falling out in chunks and as far as I'm concerned, I'll find a wig and be done with it." Tanya's eyes were shining with tears as she spoke. "What does it matter at this stage? I look like someone dressed up as a corpse at Halloween, so I might as well be bald as well as ugly."

"You don't look ugly, Tanya!" Zoe's hand flew to her mouth as she tried not to cry. Sure, Tanya looked a lot thinner. She looked haunted and exhausted, but never ugly. She was too beautiful to ever look ugly. Her glossy auburn hair was falling like autumn leaves. Her pale thin face was strained and her eyes sad. But she was still striking. Zoe looked at the floor. She'd wondered how Tanya was getting on. Had she told poor Alfie her prognosis?

"Thank you, Zoe. You are a little pet, but I'm riddled with cancer, not blind. I have mirrors. I can see the ghost of Tanya staring back at me. The only person who hasn't seemed to notice how wretched I look is my baby, Jenny. She still hugs me and puckers up and gives me tiny butterfly kisses. Alfie has an awkwardness about him now." Her eyes were focused on the floor as she spoke. "He pussyfoots around me. He used to argue with me or tell me to be nice. He used to hum a lot. He's quiet now. He just stares and tries not to jump when I talk. He looks guilty all the time. If it wasn't so depressing, it'd make me laugh."

"Things will improve, love," said Esme. "It's only a stage. A phase, as they say. A passing of time. Sure, this time next year, we'll all be hopping and skipping again, you'll see." She was about to chuckle to herself when Tanya interrupted her.

"This time next year, I'll be dead."

"I beg your pardon?" Esme looked shocked. "Don't speak like that, love, you mustn't think –"

"I'm not the same as you, Esme. I'm not being told it's a *phase*, the doctors are not giving me the 'keep your spirits up' chat. Instead we're talking about 'making me comfortable' and 'acceptance'. So you see, things aren't going to improve for me. Unless you're very spiritual, and then, hey, things can't get any better. I'm going to be compost, Esme. I've less than six months, they reckon. How's that for a timeframe? I've probably only another four months where I'll be able to function and then my body and brain will turn to mush before I slip away to the great unknown. Bid you all adieu. Auf wiedersehen. Goodbye. Me, myself and I, my own little Von Trapp 'Farewell'." Tears streamed down Tanya's wan cheeks.

The horrified women were silent. There was no answer to that. No up-beat, jolly comeback. Nobody could think of anything to say that didn't sound utterly futile.

Zoe stood up and went over to Tanya, then bent down and hugged her. The two women crooned and rocked for what seemed like an eternity.

"I'm not great at putting the right words on things. But I can listen and I can make dinners." Esme looked ashen-faced. "So if you need an ear or a hot meal with home-baked dessert, I'm your woman."

"Thank you." Tanya softened for a moment. Esme was not her type of person if the truth be known. Given a choice, she wouldn't sit in the same room as her. Her babbling and mispronunciations drove Tanya insane. But she was a good person. There was no malice in her. She meant well. It wasn't her fault she looked like a drag queen and talked incessant crap. She was just being herself. Jesus, I really am sick, Tanya thought to herself.

"I'd love to help in any way I can too," Zoe volunteered, kneeling on the floor next to Tanya's chair. "Maybe when I'm feeling a little stronger in a few weeks, I could take baby Jenny to the park or to a play centre? It might give you a bit of time on your own with Alfie?"

The mention of Alfie made Tanya start rocking again.

"He doesn't know yet. I haven't told him how little time I have left. The moment never seems right. What do I say? 'Can you get some milk when you go shopping and, by the way, I've phoned and organised my funeral. It's in about six months, so will you buy yourself some semi-respectable clothes?'"

"But you'll have to tell him, love. He'll guess and then he'll be terrible hurt you didn't let him in on it all," Esme insisted.

"Well, he will guess when I stop breathing alright. That's for sure. He's kind of clever in that way, my Alfie." Tanya stifled a sob.

"That's not what I meant, pet." Esme missed the sarcasm and tried to soothe Tanya. "He's your husband and he loves you. Why wouldn't he? A beautiful, clever and bright girl you are too. It's only fair to tell him the truth. That way you can let him help you. A problem shared is a problem halved. The other side of it is that he'll need the time to prepare too. He'll be the one left behind – at least give him a chance to say and do all the things he'll need to before you're gone. Don't shut him out and make him live out a whole lot of regrets." Esme held Tanya's gaze.

Tanya felt a new emotion towards the older woman. In spite of herself, she felt a tiny glimmer of respect creeping in. I still find you incredibly annoying, she thought. You talk a lot of shit, but there's a whole side to you I don't know.

Admitting she was wrong was something Tanya never did. Reluctantly, she was realising, she'd judged Esme wrongly. The woman had raised two daughters and had a hell of a lot more time on earth under her belt. She might not look or sound the way Tanya preferred, but she had to admit she admired the way the woman spoke her mind.

"I never thought of it that way, Esme. I just keep thinking it's going to crush him. I worry that he won't cope. I feel such deep and intense guilt. I'm leaving him and sweet little Jenny on their own. My own weakness is making me duck out of their lives."

"Oh holy God, where on earth did you get a notion like that, child? Who said you were weak?" Esme was getting on her high horse again. Wriggling in the chair, uncomfortable in her own skin at the thought of anybody telling this poor girl such dreadful things. "Whoever it was needs a good thrashing!"

"It is a pretty harsh thing to say, in fairness," Zoe agreed.

"Nobody said it as such. They didn't have to. I just know." Tanya grabbed at her cup of coffee, cold by now but what did it matter?

"Tanya, the cancer is not your fault." Sian felt her heart quicken. "You must know that. It's not to do with strength or weakness. This is a terrible thing that you have to face, but none of it is your fault."

"Yeah, right," Tanya laughed bitterly.

Sian was utterly taken back by the other woman's reaction. This was a serious situation. How was she going to make her understand she was not to blame? Esme was right, she needed to tell Alfie how little time she had left. She knew from experience that the last couple of months were usually pretty gruesome. So the next two months were going to be the ones she needed to make count. While she was still able to *live*.

"I have to go for a wee," said Esme, getting up and wandering towards the bathroom. "The auld waterworks are a bit on the leaky side at the best of times – I get the little stick-on nappy things from the chemist, a fantastic thing they are. Not that any of you girls would know about these things yet. Enjoy your bladder control while you have it." She paused at the bathroom door and looked back. "I tell you I didn't appreciate half the things my body used to do on its own when I was younger."

The other women waited until Esme had closed the door behind her, then looked at each other, an undeniable expression of disgust on each of their faces. But as they made eye contact they all began to giggle.

"There's one good reason to die young!" Zoe laughed. "Sorry, Tanya, that was below the belt."

Tanya dissolved into giggles again.

"I had no idea it was mandatory to wee down your own leg after the age of sixty," said Sian.

"Well, now you know!" said Zoe. "So enjoy your bladder control while you have it!"

"Too late for me," said Tanya. "I'll just have to think of it as a good reason to die young!"

As she spoke the bathroom door opened.

"Varacous veins, wiry hairs on your chin, grey pubic hair, saggy everything, less hair on your head than in your ears and your nose.

Failing eyesight and hearing. All loads of reasons to die young."
Esme plonked herself back down on the seat opposite Tanya, as a
short but distinct fart escaped her bottom. "Fatulance, the final
frontier," Esme grinned.

"*Flatulence*," Tanya laughed.

"That's what I said!" Esme joined in with the mirth.

It took a while for the women to regain their composure. Zoe
had slid onto the floor in front of Tanya. Sian was wiping the
streaked mascara from under her eyes. Tanya blew her nose loudly.

"Esme, you're a ticket," said Tanya. "I didn't think I would
laugh until I cried in here this morning. Anytime I feel sad now, I'll
conjure up a thought of weeing down my own leg, and I'll be
straight again." She felt exhausted but better than she had for a
long long time. Laughter really was the best medicine.

The conversation moved from bodily functions to the price of
diesel. It was as if a barrier had been broken down among the
women. They had all shared such private and intimate details of
their lives, in such an unexpectedly swift timeframe.

"I honestly only came here in the beginning to keep Alfie
happy," Tanya continued. "Never in a million years would I have
pictured myself sitting with a room full of people I'd never laid eyes
on before and spilling my innermost thoughts for all to hear."

"I know, I was utterly terrified the first time I arrived here," Zoe
volunteered. "I decided I would sit like a mouse and hope nobody
would try to make me speak."

"And how do you feel about our group now?" Sian probed
gently.

"I think it's a lifeline. All the worry I constantly cause my family
and friends doesn't apply in here. We can all empathise with one
another. It's a relief to be able to let loose," Zoe affirmed.

"Well, I live for my Golden Girls meetings, so I was a bit of a
pro at this kind of thing." Esme allowed herself to look a bit smug.
"But this lovely group hasn't disappointed me. It's great to talk, I
always say."

The chatter continued as the women opened up more and more.
Sian hadn't glanced at her watch for quite a while. She was sure

they had at least half an hour left. She was startled to hear a knock at the door. One of the doctors poked his head into the room with an apologetic look on his face.

"Sorry, Sian, I've the room booked and my patient is stuck for time today," he said with a shrug.

"Aren't we all? Stuck for time, that is," Tanya piped up.

They all dissolved into hysterics again. Sian realised they had been talking for over two hours. Apologising, she gathered the cups and began to clear away. The ladies agreed to meet again the following week. As they all filed out, sobriety returned.

Sian hoped Tanya would be alright. The meetings always varied so much. Things only came out if the attendees wanted to speak. Sometimes she clock-watched, wishing the time away. Other days like today, the time seemed to rush by. She'd never had such a giddy group before. Although it was wonderful to see poor Tanya laugh, she hoped it didn't all backfire. She was worried that the light-heartedness and black humour which had crept in would make her feel lonely and isolated later on when she was alone. She'd hate Tanya to think that her situation was being viewed as a joking matter.

Sian shivered. How would she feel if she knew her time was coming to an end? How on earth would you stop yourself from going insane?

# 13

*I now know laughter can help any situation. If only we could bottle and sell it.*

Tanya lowered herself into the car. Her back was very stiff from the tumours on her spine. Surprisingly she'd enjoyed the meeting no end. It had been a while since she'd laughed like that. Out-loud, tummy-clenching giggles. Good old Esme. The woman was a legend. She'd really changed her opinion of her.

Checking her phone she saw she had two messages. One from Alfie and one from Sally. She'd phone Sally first. It involved more brainpower, but less guilt. She knew she needed to tell Alfie the truth. But she just couldn't do it yet. She'd had lengthy discussions with Sally, and after the initial shock, she had agreed to consider taking over the running of the business when the time came. Sally would become a twenty-per-cent shareholder, with Alfie being the eighty-per-cent. He would obviously be an absent, silent partner. The advantage for Sally would be a portion in a profitable company, which ordinarily she wouldn't be in a position to set up on her own. She'd jumped at the offer straight away, but Tanya had told her she wasn't to give her final answer until two weeks later.

"I want you to go away and think about this. I want you to be sure you're not being bamboozled into anything. You must be certain you are willing to take this on and that you are happy with the arrangement. I will put in a clause that you are to have a decent wage increase every year, subject to profit. So there will always be proper incentive there for you." Tanya had worked it all out in her head.

"Okay, I'll think about it, but I know what my answer is going to be. Oh Tanya, how is Alfie doing?" Sally found it so hard to maintain her calm.

"Alfie is just fine. He doesn't know yet. I haven't told him. I will, just not yet. Nobody knows, bar you and a girl I met in hospital. Please keep it that way. I know I'm asking a lot, but also remember it's my life, or my death to be exact, so therefore my news." Tanya had clocked the stricken look on the other woman's face. She knew she was dropping a bomb and asking her to keep a dark secret, but she hadn't much time. She had to make some drastic decisions.

As she called Sally from the car, Tanya stared out the window while sitting in almost stationary traffic. The supermarket she drove past a dozen times a week, the people scurrying across the road, juggling bags of shopping, buggies and umbrellas. The world was still carrying on with its business. She was dying and it didn't really matter.

It wasn't going to change anything. There wouldn't be an impact on the traffic. The weather wouldn't change. Most people wouldn't know any different. Having to think about her own death had made Tanya feel so small. Not in an I'm-a-tiny-little-helpless-scrap way. In a speck-on-the-universe way. Alfie, Jenny, her family and a few others would be diversely affected by her passing. But all in all, the world would still keep on turning, oblivious to her untimely departure.

She found the thoughts of this and the great unknown to where she was heading, utterly terrifying. What was going to happen to her? How was it going to feel? Sure she'd heard of the "going into the light" thing. But what was going to happen to her after that? What if she could still see Alfie and Jenny? What if she ended up being an unseen, silent floating thing? What if it was like being in a coma, where people describe being able to hear everything that's going on, but can't communicate?

Maybe it was going to be utterly amazing. Maybe it would be similar, with shops and restaurants and occupations, like a parallel universe, where you meet all the people who've gone before you. But how would it work? Would everyone be the same age? Would the babies who died still be babies or would they have grown up? Would the old people be young again? Is God a man with a big white beard or is he really a guy in a tracksuit with dark glasses, gold teeth and signet rings? Is God a beautiful woman? Does He or She go around on a cloud or via angel transportation?

Every time Tanya began to think of all this, it made her shake with fear and trepidation. It was too much for her head to process. She'd never liked surprises. Her worst nightmare would be to walk into a restaurant and have sixty people with party-blowers, streamers and balloons, shouting "Surprise!" She would turn around and run as fast as her legs could carry her. This preparing-to-die situation was the worst combination. It was like knowing about the enormous surprise and yet having no control at the same time.

Maybe she was simply going insane. Maybe the cancer was in her brain too. She might actually talk to Dr Leah about those tablets. It could be anxiety. That would be acceptable in her circumstances. In the deepest part of her being, she knew it was purely the fact that the Grim Reaper was tracing her steps. She felt like she was beginning to quicken her step, yet all the time she was losing ground.

Finding a safe place to stop, she pulled the car over. She'd spoken to Sally. The office was fine. Searching the phone book in her mobile phone, she found Dr Leah's number.

"Dr Leah Philip's rooms, how may I help you?"

"Hello, it's Tanya Shields. I need to speak to Leah. I'm having a bad day, things are getting too much, I think I want the pills, I need some help, I want the feelings to go . . ." She started to cry and the words failed her. Her hands shook so much she was having trouble holding the phone to her ear.

"Tanya, where are you? Tanya?"

The secretary was talking but Tanya couldn't speak. She could hear but her jaw and her brain were frozen. Nothing was connecting. The sweat began to bead on her forehead. Her thinning hair became itchy on her head. Her skin was crawling, her lungs felt too big for her ribs. Flashes of colour fizzed in front of her eyes. She squeezed her lids shut. She could hear the intermittent swooshing of blood through her ears. It was like she'd become a mechanical dolly and she could hear and feel all the parts working individually.

"Tanya? It's Leah, where are you? Can you hear me? I need you to try and tell me where you are."

"Leah." The sound of her voice broke the spell. "I'm on the road outside Blackrock. I've pulled over. I can't do this anymore. It's not going to work anymore."

"What isn't working, Tanya?" Leah was calm but Tanya could hear the concern in her voice.

"The pretending-to-carry-on thing. The living until I keel over. The waiting-to-die thing. I can't do it anymore. It's too much for me."

"Tanya, stay where you are, I'm going to call your husband and ask him to bring you in here. Don't try to drive, just sit tight. I'll call you right back, okay?" Dr Leah waited for a response. "Tanya? Can you hear me?"

Towards the end of the sentence, Dr Leah's voice got very deep and droney. As the darkness enveloped her, Tanya felt herself relax and smile. *Oh, that felt nicer. More fluffy and relaxing. That was better than being scared and shifty and terrified.*

\* \* \*

"Tanya, can you hear me? Tanya, please, open your eyes."

"No, Alfie, it's the middle of the night, I don't have to get up for work until seven. Go back to sleep, love."

The rush of cold air was odd. She shifted her shoulder. Had Alfie left the window wide open again? It was too cold and windy to do that. Now she'd have to rouse herself and stagger over and close it. Feck it anyway. Then she'd probably need to go to the toilet, the bathroom would be freezing and she'd be wide awake then. Something was hanging over her. What was she forgetting to do?

"Tanya, please!" Alfie was shaking her.

God, why didn't he close the window if he was already awake? As she peeled her eyes open, she tried to focus on him. Why was he standing there fully clothed in the middle of the night?

"Alfie, what's the matter? Close the window, it's cold in here."

"She's awake, she's awake."

It wasn't Alfie at all. It was a man in a navy sweater. What the hell was he doing in her bedroom?

"Tanya, I'm from St Mark's Clinic, we're going to take you there in the ambulance now. We're going to manoeuvre you onto a bed, okay?"

She nodded, feeling it was the polite thing to do, but she really was going to have to ask this guy to get out of her house. He was going to wake Jenny. Then where would they be? She found herself on a bed. It was quite hard, but it felt good to stretch her legs out. She'd have to talk to Alfie about that bed. She hadn't noticed before how cramped it made her feel. This one was definitely better.

The whooshing sound came back. It was getting louder and louder.

Why was Alfie even staying the night? She'd only just met him. That wasn't like her, to allow someone stay over after a couple of dates. Still, she must have been really drunk last night, she couldn't remember a thing. He seemed to be confident about being with her, so she must have said he could stay. He seemed like a lovely guy, there was no point in being rude to him. She was knackered anyway. They'd all have to chat among themselves for the moment. She'd just have a few more hours' sleep and then she'd be well able to jump out of bed and get into the office before the rush.

The spinning got faster.

She must try and hire someone to help out. The client base was growing quickly. She really didn't have time to do all the paperwork and organise the events as well.

Things were not right.

She dreamed she was in the ghost train. She was seven and sitting beside her brother. The car was jerky and bumpy. The noises of the screaming monsters and images of mummies flashed before her. She screamed and tried to grab Andrew's arm.

"Get off, Tanya! I'm not coming out of here with my sister clinging to me. My mates are out there. They'll laugh at me."

Recoiling, she tried to convince herself this was fun. Really she was scared. She wouldn't go on this again. It wasn't as much fun as she'd thought it would be. She was only seven. She was too small.

The ride ended and a strange woman was standing smiling at her.

"Tanya, are you okay?"

"Yes, thanks. I don't want to go on the ghost train again though. Can I have candy floss now?"

"Okay, take her through to the examination room, contact radiology and set up a CT. She has all the symptoms of an aneurism. She's confused, lethargic and appears to be suffering memory loss. She's not recognising me."

The lady in the white coat was very pretty. Tanya wondered if she was a beautician. Maybe she'd have a facial. That might help with the pain behind her eye.

The pain was spreading actually. Now that she'd noticed it, it was kind of awful.

"Shiiiiiit! My head . . . it's . . ." The noise was deafening as the dull thudding ache ripped through her skull. Maybe she'd been shot? Christ, why would someone want to kill her? Was it a drug dealer? The sound became so loud, she couldn't bear it anymore.

Then it all stopped. A warm and comfortable feeling began to spread all over her. Myriad beautiful colours enveloped her. There was beautiful singing. It made her feel happier than she'd ever thought possible. Images flew past at a ferocious speed, but oddly she was able to process them all. Her second birthday, the day she rode a bike for the first time, her first kiss, her Alfie, baby Jenny. Her dad was here. He had his arms out. She ran to him and felt the warmth of his arms wrapped around her. Everything was going to be alright.

"Keep trying, recharge the paddles, you've got to try again."

Dr Leah was willing Tanya to stay with her. All the machines were flat-lining. None of the lines were registering. Sinking to her knees, Leah glanced at her watch.

"Time of death, 12.45 p.m."

# 14

*My girls are coming home soon. I know if I keep my pecker up, I'll feel better before I know it.*

Esme was beginning to feel the effects of the chemotherapy. Even the motion of looking down at her beloved notebook wasn't great. The doctors and nurses had told her she'd get tired and might feel a bit sick. After the first three goes, she'd been grand really. But this morning she'd been making the porridge and it had looked alarmingly like frog-spawn. She'd never noticed the musty, pungent smell off it before. Maybe it was gone off. It could be the milk she'd used. Grabbing the milk carton, she saw that it was well in date.

She'd try and manage a cup of tea and a slice of toast and marmalade. That'd be grand.

As Michael sat down to eat the porridge, she could smell it again. As he dug into the bowl with the spoon, the musty smell wafted towards her.

"I'm sorry, love, but I'll have to get you to eat that outside. It smells like untreated wool."

"What are you on about, woman? How could porridge resemble a sheep? Where exactly do you want me to go? Climb a tree and look over into next door while I feed myself like a monkey? Will I dig a hole to wee into afterwards?" Michael hated to be disturbed during his food.

She knew that, but this just couldn't be helped. "Here, I'll get you your coat and cap." Quickly she found the items, neatly stored in the cupboard under the stairs. Coaxing his arms into the sleeves, she pulled his hat on and grabbed his bowl in one hand and mug in the other.

"It's brass monkey's out here! What if the neighbours look out the window? The men in white coats will arrive. They'll think I'm a doddery auld git, sitting at the fecking round plastic picnic table in the cold. Why aren't you eating some? Who do you think you are – Paddington?"

Esme looked at her marmalade on toast and laughed. "No, I just feel kind of iffy from the chemotherapy and I fancied a bit of toast, that's all. I haven't put rat poison in the porridge or anything!"

She settled Michael at the garden table and went back inside. God love him, he looked miserable out on the patio by himself.

Esme tried the toast. Paddington she certainly wasn't. The taste of the marmalade was too strong and it kind of burnt her mouth. Giving up on the idea of eating altogether, she settled for a cup of tea.

Michael came in the back door a few minutes later muttering to himself, teacup in hand.

"Like one of those Chinese torture shows – freeze the bollox off your husband and see if he can avoid hypothermia," he grumped.

"Ah Michael, stop that now. It's my sense of smell. The doctor told me this might happen, they said it's like being pregnant."

"Well, you managed to have our two without me having to live in the garden. What are you going to do next? Tell me I've got to sleep in the shed because my aftershave is making you queasy?" Going out into the hall, he grabbed the newspaper from the letterbox, then shuffled in to sit in his chair and have a read.

She needed to hoover the hall, stairs and landing, but she wasn't sure she could muster up the strength. Mind you, she'd done it every Friday for the last forty years, so she wasn't about to stop now. Having drunk only half the cup of tea, she went out into the hall and bent down to pull the Hoover out from the cupboard under the stairs. The sweating started mildly at first. Her heart was racing a bit too. By the time she'd plugged in the Hoover, she was exhausted. She'd do it in stages. The hall first, then have a sit down and try the next bit. As the machine whirred to life, the smell from the old dust hit her nostrils. She retched. Flicking it off, she found refuge on the bottom step of the stairs.

Michael appeared, looking confused. "What's wrong with you?"

"I can't do it. The smell of the Hoover bag is desperate. I don't have the energy either. I'm wrecked, Michael. I think I'll have to go back to bed. I wasn't able to eat." Big fat tears ran down her cheeks.

"Ah now, love. Don't be crying. There's no need. I'll help you. How's about that? I'm sorry for saying you tried to freeze my nuts off. Don't mind me, I'm just a grumpy old git. You know me, I shoot my mouth off and think later. You go on up the stairs and I'll vacuum the floors. It'll be good for me to learn it all." He helped her up the stairs and stood awkwardly looking at her as she lay in the bed, barely able to breathe she was so tired.

Please go away and stop staring at me like I've a penis growing out of my forehead, she willed.

Eventually, he shuffled off in his slippers to do the housework. The noise and struggle which ensued nearly made her cry. Only she was so gonzoed, she would have gone downstairs to make him stop. He walloped the Hoover off the skirting boards in such a rough way, she expected to see lumps out of them later on. He also seemed to believe that giving out shite to the machine would help matters.

"Come here, you bollox! Wait till I show you who's boss!" As he made his way clumsily up the stairs she wanted to pull the covers over her head, so she wouldn't have to see him. There was an almighty struggle until he appeared on the top landing. His comb-over plastered to his face, he was florid and sweating.

"Howareya, love? Don't mind me. I'll get the better of this bastard, don't you worry."

Silence ensued. Followed by kicking of the machine and more curses. When he realised the plug had been pulled out, he stomped down the stairs waving his fist. He hoovered everywhere, including the bathroom, the box room and even the hot press. As he rounded the corner into their room, he gave her the thumbs-up. She felt like she was in a kayak after that. He knocked and bashed off the sides of the bed, making her jump with fright. The swaying motion she felt from the nausea and tiredness didn't help.

Turning the machine off, he came and sat beside her.

"Now, I won't mind, but do you think you'll be able to cook my tea?"

"I actually don't know, love. If I feel better, I will of course."

"Well, I was thinking I could go to the shops for you. I could get us a ready meal. Some of the fellas in the pub swear by them. Then you wouldn't have to cook. Can you make me a list and I'll head off to the supermarket and you can have a little sleep." He looked very pleased with himself.

"Okay, if you're sure . . ." She felt so uneasy with all this. Michael had never done the shopping on his own. He wouldn't know where to start. He'd go and get all upset. He wouldn't know the layout of the shop. She'd images of him wandering for hours with a trolley, that's if he even managed to put the euro in and get one out.

"I'll be grand. Can you think of anything you might like to eat? What about fresh bread or soup even. Don't sick people eat chicken soup?"

"No, love, I wouldn't eat a bought soup, only my own. Get some French bread and some ham. Not the packet stuff now, go to the delicatessen counter and ask for a few slices. I'm not sure I like the idea of ready meals. Miriam told me she knows a lady who bought a jar of foreign sauce once, and she found a corn plaster in the middle of it."

"Well, I'll tell the fella in the shop that we want something without any bandages, and none of that dog-food stuff that some people call meat. Full of lips and arse-holes, most of that mince they use in the pub. Sure if the worst comes to the worst, I could go to the chipper and get us a cod and chips. What do you think?" Michael didn't really know what to do next.

Esme didn't seem to care about their tea, which wasn't a bit like her. Normally she'd be all talk of what they'd eat and whether or not they'd have custard or ice cream with their dessert. Maybe she needed "time out". He'd heard Oprah talking about "time out". It was American for doing shag-all.

Esme felt even worse as Michael banged the front door, shopping bags in hand. This wasn't right. A man shouldn't be shopping and trying to make his own dinner. She'd made his dinner every day since they'd married. It was her job. She liked to do it. The phone rang.

"Hi, Mum, it's me, Tracey. How are you feeling today?"

"Hi, love. Not great, to be honest with you." To her horror the tears started again.

"What is it? Are you alright? Where's Dad?"

"Well, that's just it, your father's been doing the hoovering and now he's gone to the supermarket. It's not right, love. I even made him eat his porridge in the garden. The poor man will be traumatised. What if he runs off with a young wan? He's an attractive man, your father. He might decide to find a woman with no problems who won't make him forage for his dinner." Esme was devastated. The thought of her gorgeous husband running off to live with someone else, giving her the finger as he went, filled her with grief.

"Mum, first of all, I love Dad to bits, you know that, but he looks like Benny Hill. He adores you and he's not going to bugger off with a young one. It'll do that man good to get up off his arse and make himself useful. You treat him like an invalid. He's been waited on hand and foot by you for years. Let him mind you now. Doing a bit of housework won't kill him and let him buy some frozen ready meals to heat up."

"But they have used corn plasters in them!"

"What? No, they don't. Most of the world lives on them for Christ's sake. Listen, I'm going to ring around and organise a cleaning lady to come in twice a week to help you out for the next while. Susie from up the road has a lady, I'll see if she'd have a few hours a week to come to you. My treat, I'll look after it. She can do the bathrooms and change the bed and keep on top of the ironing.

Let Dad help out, but you know him – there could be a family of Gremlins living in the toilet and he wouldn't see it."

It took a bit of convincing, but eventually Esme gave in and told Tracey she could organise some help.

That evening, Michael cooked dinner for the first time in their marriage. It consisted of tinned spaghetti, ready-made Rogan Josh, frozen sweet corn and oven chips. The combination would have been hard to stomach at the best of times, but at that moment Esme was struggling.

She managed to shovel some of it in. But the dessert was the final straw. He had meringue nests, with tinned peaches, custard and mixed peel on top. As he chewed the soggy meringue and cold peaches, she could see him wince.

"Not great really, is it? You make it all look so easy. It's okay for a first attempt though, don't you think?" He looked crushed that it hadn't been much of a success.

"It's a fine art, cooking. You did great though. I'm just not too hungry at the moment." She smiled wanly at him, finding the slimy texture of the tinned peaches unbearable. She crawled back up to bed, as Michael proceeded to almost smash the dishes as he put them in the dishwasher.

He had to admit he wasn't feeling great himself. That curry stuff was like eating hot coals. It was probably going to rip the arse out of him too. As he sat down to watch *The Weakest Link* he felt kind of belchy and bloated. He had no problem helping poor Esme while she was sick, but he was kind of worried that he might end up dead himself. Poisoned to death by his own hand.

Miserable and lonely, sitting in the chair all by himself, he nursed a glass of fizzy tummy-settlers instead of his usual cup of tea and a biscuit. Although Esme was only upstairs in bed, he missed her. Maybe the nausea from the chemo was contagious, he mused. He'd get Esme to ask the nurses and doctors the next time she was in the hospital. This cancer thing was terrible. He hoped to God his wife was going to be okay. He didn't want to even let himself think of how empty his life would be without her. Not to mention how empty his tummy would be.

* * *

Tracey came up trumps. In no time at all, she'd organised a lady to come in three times a week to clean and cook a simple meal. She wasn't as careful as Esme about her presentation on the plate, Michael noticed. She was a bit rough too. Kind of banged the plate down in front of him. He'd seen her picking her nose too, which he found a bit off-putting, but beggars couldn't be choosers. Nobody would look after him the way his Esme did. That was for sure.

He'd taken to going to the park more often. He was kind of nervous of your woman, the helper. She was from some bunker in Russia and was called Fanny, which at first he'd thought was a joke. The lads in the pub had asked him if she was a lap dancer. But with the size of her arse and that mole on her chin, he didn't think any man would survive her sitting on them.

"She'd bend a fireman's pole in half if she tried to swing on it. I think she just doesn't know she's named after a woman's front garden. I'm sure as hell not telling her. She'd probably snap me neck in half." Michael had shuddered at the thought of her.

Esme had mentioned to Tracey that she was a godsend and a great help and well able to scrub the pan of the toilet. She ironed like it was going out of fashion and she mashed the spuds to within an inch of their lives, but there was a bit of a scary element to her. She never smiled or spoke really. She wasn't ever up for a chat and didn't volunteer any information. She wasn't married, which didn't surprise Esme. She was as hairy as next door's cat, both on her face and legs. She wouldn't appeal to any man.

"Why do you think I hired her?" Tracey said, astounded. "What did you want, some cute little doe-eyed young wan, who could come in and make you feel like an old unattractive bag past her sell-by date? We don't need some size-zero supermodel, waggling her fake tits in Dad's face as you lie upstairs retching in the bed. Fanny is like Shrek's auntie, she does the work and buggers off. Perfect."

Esme laughed out loud. "Tracey, you're a scream. You've a terrible suspicious mind for such a young one."

The whole idea of having "staff" was pretty brilliant. She'd told them all about it when she'd been in for the chemo last. Miriam was well impressed. Her son Declan wouldn't think of getting her a Fanny. Not in a fit.

"He's a grand lad. When I'm not able to cook, he brings home a bargain bucket from Kentucky Fried Chicken. He passes it on the way home from the bus shelter."

Esme could see that Miriam was a bit envious. She didn't wish the woman any ill, of course not, but she did feel a little smug secretly that her daughter was minding her so well.

* * *

Not that she was feeling very smug these days.

She'd been lying in bed, feeling okay, but needing to keep away from Fanny who was beating the mop around the kitchen, when her mobile phone rang.

"Hello?" Esme put on her telephone voice. "Esme Mulligan speaking."

"Esme, it's Sian from the support group. Is it a bad time for you, or can you talk?"

"Oh hello, Sian. No, my Fanny is mopping the floor, I'm well able to talk."

"Pardon? Em . . . right. Listen, I'm afraid I have very sad news, Esme."

"What is it, love?"

"Tanya has died."

"What? Holy God up in heaven, I don't believe you! What happened? She was okay the other day at the meeting! How did it happen?" All her posh telephone voice was gone. Esme was reeling with shock.

"They think she had an aneurism. Basically a bleed to the brain. They tried to save her, but couldn't."

Esme spoke to Sian for a few minutes longer and hung up. That poor girl! She'd a hard old road ahead of her, but to be taken so suddenly! It didn't seem fair. She'd a little baby and a husband too. They must be shocked half to death.

# 15

*I have Jenny. I know Alfie loves me. Nothing else matters.*

Alfie was reading the last thing Tanya had written in the pink notebook in her handbag. He vowed to ask that nice lady Sian what it was all about.

He'd felt relief flood over him as he heard Jenny's voice at a quarter to six that morning. Often he secretly wished she'd sleep for just one more hour in the morning. But today, after spending the entire night alone and traumatised, he welcomed the sound of his daughter waking up.

He needed to try and remain strong for her. Now, he was all she had left. He'd cried so much last night he thought he couldn't possibly have any fresh tears left. Until the day he died, he would never forget getting that phone call yesterday. He hadn't recognised the number as it flashed up on his mobile phone. He'd known Dr Leah's voice immediately though. She didn't sound her usual steady, friendly self, he'd mused. Then she'd dropped the bomb that had literally blown his world apart.

"I'm so sorry, Alfie. We did everything we could," she'd finished.

He could barely hold the phone, his lungs fought for air as he became engulfed in sobs. He managed to hold it together enough to call Tanya's mother. As she arrived at the house twenty minutes later, he was sitting on the stairs hugging himself and leaning against the wall. Jenny was in the playroom oblivious, watching Barney.

Danielle, Tanya's mother, fell into his arms and they clung to each other, sorrow streaming from every pore, the physical pain that ripped through them uniting them.

"I can't believe it, it's just not fair." Danielle searched Alfie's eyes for an answer.

"I know, she'd been through all that horrible surgery and now she fought for nothing." Alfie felt anger and bitterness flood through him.

By the time Tanya's sister arrived, Danielle had phoned a taxi.

"Lauren, can you stay here with little Jenny? I'll go to the hospital with Alfie to see Tanya."

At the mention of her name, Alfie shook with grief again.

"Hi Nana, hi Lala!" Jenny waddled out of the playroom into the kitchen, with her arms up to her granny and auntie. "Two here." She clapped, delighted with the visitors. Her tiny face fell as she drank in the sorrowful faces.

"Hello, darling." Alfie bent down to scoop her up.

"Ah-ow, Dada crying. Poor Dada, sad." Jenny wrapped her pudgy arms around his neck and patted his back.

"Oh Jenny!" Alfie felt like his heart was going to burst with misery.

\* \* \*

At the hospital, Tanya's body had been taken to a room where she'd been laid out on the bed, with her arms folded across her chest. The nurses had placed a small sprig of white flowers in her hand. They'd fixed her hair and wiped her face, before draping a white blanket over her. Folding it back to below her clasped hands, they'd straightened it out.

"She'd want to look dignified." Leah stroked her forehead gently.

This was the part of the job she detested. Of course she'd learned to deal with it, she'd no other choice, but that didn't mean she found it any easier. Some patients touched her more than others. She'd clicked with Tanya. She loved her elegance, her strong demeanour and her fighting spirit.

As she lay here now, stiff and cold, her spirit and life finished with, it hit Leah as always how the body is simply a shell for holding the personality and life within.

She heard Alfie's voice approaching in the corridor. Straightening her jacket, she inhaled deeply, closed her eyes and prepared herself to face him. She opened the door and saw Alfie and an older, distinguished version of Tanya facing her. Poor Alfie looked shattered and on the verge of tears.

"Hi, Leah. Thanks for letting me know. I can't believe it. This is Tanya's mum, Danielle." He looked at the floor, as tears plopped onto the front of his T-shirt.

"Hello, Dr Philips." Danielle looked stricken.

"I'm so sorry for your loss. I can only imagine how dreadful it must be to lose a wife, a child. We did all we could. I wish it could have been different." Leah shook hands with Danielle. When she held her hand out to Alfie, he pulled her close to him, hugged her with all his might and shook with grief.

Choking with tears, she took his hand and led him into the room. As his gaze fell on Tanya, he called out, like a wild animal caught in a poacher's trap. Rushing to her side, he stroked her frozen waxy face, repeating over and over how much he loved her.

"You were my heart and soul. How am I going to live without you? Why did you have to leave me? I don't know how to exist without you. My sweet, beautiful angel! I hope you're in a place that makes you happy. I love you with every shred of my being. Rest in peace, my darling."

Danielle stood utterly motionless, with a river of tears streaming down her cheeks. This wasn't the way she'd ever planned it. It was so unnatural for a child to die before her parent. Her own flesh and blood, her baby, her defiant, defensive, determined child. Wiped out, just like that. One minute she was marching around, in her usual power-house, sod-the-world way, and now all that remained was this shell. Danielle hoped she'd found her daddy. At least they'd have each other, wouldn't they?

"My mum will mind her," said Alfie. "I'll go to the church on the way home and light a candle and ask her to find Tanya and take her with her. Maybe she'll show her around and introduce her."

"I was just thinking how I'd love her to meet her father – do you think he'll be there too, Alfie?" Danielle stood at the foot of the bed, terrified to step too close to Tanya's body. She watched in admiration as Alfie stroked and kissed and talked to Tanya. She'd no idea that he was so spiritual. This was a whole new side of him she'd never have guessed existed. She was glad for him that he was this way inclined. Maybe it would help him in the long run, or give him courage and a reason to carry on. Although she desperately wished Tanya was now at peace and in a paradise filled with beauty and serenity, she wasn't as sure as Alfie seemed to be.

"Of course her daddy will be there. They'll all surround her with light and love. She will drift on angels' wings and she will be in heaven, filled with ecstasy." Alfie smiled through his tears at the thought of it.

Danielle had never felt less hopeful in all her life, but she drank in Alfie's faith with all her heart, and wished that some of his belief would rub off on her.

Dr Leah walked outside the room and waited. The family would need time to be with Tanya on their own. She stood with her back against the wall and closed her eyes. Images of Tanya as she sat, face full of dogged determination, in her office opposite her, flashed through her mind. The look of anger and disbelief was palpable when she'd delivered the crushing blow of her prognosis. As she'd read the scan results, before Tanya had come into her room, Leah had dropped her head to her hands. "Sod it anyway," she'd whispered to nobody in particular. The cancer was so advanced and had spread to so many places. How a person so pretty and vivacious and full of life could be harbouring so much disease was always astonishing. Even though Leah was almost twenty years in the business now, she still found cancer shocking. Medicine had come such a long way, there were amazing advances, but cancer was still a deadly disease. It still defied the odds time and time again. Leah loved her job. She thrived on the challenge. No two people ever had the same prognosis. Constant advancements and individual reactions meant her job was evolving all the time. There were more and more positive results to be enjoyed. More people survived than ever before. More patients beat the odds. But every now and then, even the person with the best will in the world, the strongest fighting spirit and the most positive attitude, still lost.

Tanya hadn't actually died from her cancer, but Leah knew the odds had been firmly stacked against her. It was never a *good* outcome for a patient to die an untimely death. But in this case, looking at the broader picture, Leah had a small voice in the back of her mind suggesting to her that perhaps Tanya had been granted some small mercy by her sudden passing.

As a doctor though, Leah would always wonder. Could they have beaten the cancer? Would Tanya have pulled through? Would she have defied all the odds, if her brain hadn't bled and drained the life out of her?

Alfie and Danielle emerged from the room some time later. Looking beaten and stunned, Alfie shrugged his shoulders and blew his breath out, whistling as he did so.

"Not really what I was planning for today, but then again who ever contemplates their wife's death?" He tried to smile.

Leah gestured for the pair to follow her to her office. They sat in the chairs opposite her. Silence engulfed them. There wasn't much to be said at this stage, or so Leah thought.

With her eyes shining, and her voice quivering, she tried desperately to say the right thing. "I know this is beyond the pain barrier for you both right at this moment, and I know it probably isn't any consolation here and now, but maybe in the future you will both come to the conclusion that she at least didn't suffer. The prognosis was pretty bleak I'm sure you'll agree, so perhaps we should try and remember that. Maybe for Tanya's sake, this is the better route?"

"I can appreciate what you're trying to say, Leah, but where there's life there's hope. I think I'd always hung on to the fact that miracles sometimes happen," Alfie whispered.

"Why didn't you and Tanya discuss the severity of her illness with us, Alfie?" Danielle looked stricken. "After the surgery we thought there was hope."

"So did I," said Alfie softly. "And she didn't tell me otherwise. You see, Danielle, Tanya was very angry. She blamed herself for being sick. She seemed to have it in her head that cancer had spread due to personal weakness. I think she wanted to bear it all alone and spare all of us for as long as possible."

"Oh Alfie," Danielle embraced him. "I just wish you could've told us more so we could help. But knowing Tanya and how forceful she can be . . . was . . ." Danielle's voice broke.

As soon as they left her room, Leah let go. Tears of sadness and an overwhelming sense of failure flowed. Even though she'd done all she could for the young woman, she still felt responsible when a patient died. She knew from the first day at medical school that she would have to deal with death on a fairly regular basis. Especially when she decided to specialise in oncology. But it didn't make the human element any easier. Much as she tried to shut down the emotional hatch and stay unattached to her cases, it never worked for her. She knew from medical conferences and conversations with other doctors that everyone had similar feelings. Some were hit harder than others by the emotion, but they were all doing the job for the same reason – to try and *save* lives.

"Leah, you can't compare what you do with any other occupation," her husband Dan had assured her over and over. "I go to work and design houses and offices for people. If an architect like me makes a muck-up of a drawing, then any client would be well within their rights to rap me on the knuckles. That's not acceptable. If a room is too small to fit a bed and wardrobe, without the door being able to open and shut, that's a disaster. It's my fault. But what you do is in a totally different league. You are constantly fighting against the odds. And you're dealing with living variable organisms, not precise mathematical measurements. What you do is so much more vital than what I do. I don't go to work, hold up scans of human parts, see a tumour and know how to try and fix it. Leah, what you do is a vocation not a job. You're amazing. How many letters do you get thanking you for all you've done?"

Dan's words rang through her head at that moment. She knew he was right, but there was a small part of her brain that taunted her. Like a little gremlin dancing, putting his thumbs in his ears and sticking his tongue out chanting, "*You made a boo-boo, you made a boo-boo!*"

One of her lecturers in college had told her that she had what it takes to be a brilliant doctor. "You self-guess all the time. You're not going to be one of these people who thinks she's God. The day you become complacent and think you know it all, hang up your stethoscope and walk away. If the cogs stop turning inside that head of yours, you're no use to any patient."

Pulling her bottom drawer open in her big oak desk, Leah found her trainers and tracksuit. Slipping off her shoes and clothes, she put on the comfortable outfit. She'd go and walk along by the sea. Air and the wide expanse of the ocean always put her in her box. Compared to the massive swelling of the endless water meeting the sky, she always felt humbled and more grounded. It let her know she wasn't in charge of life – or death for that matter.

* * *

By the time Alfie got home with Danielle he was in a kind of daze. Danielle was proving how she'd mothered and raised eight children. She'd phoned an undertaker from the taxi on the way home. They were coming to the house at six to discuss funeral arrangements. Alfie hadn't thought about any of it. All he could focus on was the fact that his darling wife was gone.

Right at that moment, he'd have preferred any physical torture known to man. Hot needles in his eyes, having his skin peeled and rolled in salt, toes snipped off one by one with a pliers. All of the above would have been preferable to this all-encompassing internal grief. He'd never felt so helpless in all his life. There were no pills to make this go away. There was no treatment to wipe this hateful feeling of pain away. He now knew why people referred to heart*ache*. It wasn't an emotion, it was a physical sensation. A palpable pain, which he could taste. He tried to close his eyes and the feeling was worse. Swishing noises fired through his head, whizzing past his ears. The sound of grief.

He wanted to curl up into a ball and die. He wanted to follow Tanya to paradise. He wanted out of this contract they called life. There was nothing left now. His light had been quenched. The candle that lit his life had not only been blown out, it had been power-hosed into oblivion.

"Alfie, we're home, come on out of the car, love."

For a second, through the fog in his mind, he heard Tanya. Looking up, filled with hope, he saw Danielle looking down at him, her hand out. People had often said they sounded alike on the phone, others thought the mother and daughter were "the spit of each other". Alfie had never really thought about that. He'd just been so engrossed in Tanya – she'd been all he'd focused on. But now he heard it. They had the same dulcet rich tone to their voices. They also shared determination and strength. As his mother would have said, "It wasn't off the ground she licked her personality."

He took Danielle's hand and she stepped back a little to let him out of the car. Like a zombie from Michael Jackson's *Thriller,* he staggered up their short driveway. As he mounted the small step up to the open front door, Jenny shot out of the playroom like a bullet from a gun.

"Dada, dada, hi, hi! Hug!" Oblivious to her father's wan grief-stricken face, she jumped up and down with her arms up. "Oooh, Dada home. Hi, Dada?" Reading his sadness, she looked sideways at him. Alfie scooped her up. Cupping his face in her tiny hands, she squashed his cheeks together, making his lips look like a fish's. "Dada?"

"Jenny." He buried his face in her soft purple top, inhaling her scent. Dropping to his knees, still clutching to his baby daughter, he rocked her and cried.

"Poor Dada, sad!" Wriggling free, she bent onto her hunkers and smacked the ground beside him, doing what he usually did when she fell and hurt herself. "Bold!" she scowled. Running to the playroom, she grabbed one of her bears and shoved it at Alfie. "Hug," she instructed. He took the bear but still wept. "Dada, pop?" She bent down and looked into his eyes, offering him a lollipop. Alfie always produced one for her when she was inconsolable. When all the hugs and soothing didn't work.

He tried to pull himself together. "No, darling, thank you. A hug would be lovely," he said, holding out his arms.

The little girl brightened and thrust herself at him, pleased she was able to help her daddy. As Alfie cuddled her tiny body and buried his face in her auburn curls, he knew this little scrap was the key to his healing. Tanya was gone, but Jenny was here, and she needed her daddy more than ever.

Danielle was standing close by, watching.

"I have a reason to go on," he whispered to his mother-in-law.

"You bet you do," she smiled through her tears.

Shortly afterwards, the doorbell rang.

The two men from the undertaker's were kindly and efficient. They were dressed in pale-coloured suits, as opposed to black with top hats, as Alfie had imagined they might be. They knew the drill, how to word the death notice, which casket to order, which church to book, what flowers might suit the coffin.

Just as they began discussing the finer details, and how they could make the funeral reflect Tanya's personality, her phone began to ring in her handbag.

* * *

As soon as Sian had passed on the dreadful news, Zoe had had an unquenchable compulsion to tell Alfie what Tanya had said to her in the hospital room that day. One thing kept ringing through her head: *"Don't let them all turn up in black, I want colour and lots of it."* What was she supposed to say? How would she even introduce herself? How would she even contact Alfie? Something drove her to call Tanya's mobile. Praying Alfie would actually have the phone in his possession, she dialled the number.

Rushing to fish for the phone, Alfie mercifully found it and gazed at the screen. A name he didn't recognise popped up: *Zoe Pink Ladies.*

"Hello?" Alfie sounded flat and beaten.

"Hello, is that Alfie?" a young girl's voice came through.

"Yes."

"I'm so sorry to bother you. I'm so sad about Tanya. I met her at the cancer support group. We were also in hospital together a couple of weeks ago . . ."

"Okay . . . I'm sorry, what did you say your name was?"

"Oh, it's Zoe. Zoe Clarke. I wouldn't have called and I didn't have your number, so that's why I rang this one, and I now feel I've done the wrong thing. I'm sorry, I should go really. It's just that Tanya said that if she was ever to have a funeral, that she didn't want people dressed in black. I'm sorry, I'm sure the last thing you needed was me –"

"*No!* Wait. Please. Zoe, what did she say? I need to know, I'm trying to arrange things for the funeral. The undertakers are here at the moment. I'd like it done the way she wanted. I have very little idea of the way she wanted things done. She wasn't open to discussing it much with me, you see." He paused. "Obviously she told you she was dying?" He sounded strangled as he said the words.

Zoe felt the sweat beading on her forehead. Oh Lord, this was awful. Tanya had said that day at the hospital that she would have the whole funeral 'chat' with Alfie when she felt ready. Obviously time had run out quicker than any of them suspected it would.

"Well, I . . ."

"It's okay, Zoe. I know she was just trying to protect me. You see, Tanya was a warrior. A cheerleader. She kept everything going. She would have wanted to make sure things went on as normal for as long as possible. She did it because she loved me." Alfie sounded like a frightened child.

"She loved you and Jenny so much. She told me all about you, and how amazing you are with Jenny. She didn't talk much at the support group, bar the last session. But we met in the hospital and she opened up to me. She was a wonderful person." Zoe's voice cracked.

Alfie closed his eyes as he tried to hold it together. A silence ensued for the longest time. The only sound every now and again, was the gulping, shunting noise of both people trying to catch their breath and remain calm.

"Is there anything else you can remember, Zoe? I'd really appreciate it if you can."

"There was another thing. She didn't want one of those sit-down dinner things, after the funeral. She said they always gave her the creeps. All that having to sit and try to eat a roast dinner when you want to run out and away from all the sorrow. I don't know what you want to organise, and of course it's your decision – but she was so strong, so sure of her own opinions, I wouldn't have been able to live with myself if I didn't tell you. Please don't feel I'm interfering and of course ignore all this if you wish." Zoe's heart was thumping. She really shouldn't have called this poor man. He didn't need a stranger telling him what his wife would like. He must think she'd such a nerve, ringing out of the blue and shouting the odds.

"Zoe, I'm so glad you called. Thank you. It's like Tanya is having the final say, even from beyond. She'd like that, you know?"

She could hear him smile. In the midst of all the unthinkable heartache, Tanya was still telling him what to do.

Zoe talked to Alfie for a few minutes longer and hung up. Her hands were shaking and her heart beating like a drum, but she knew she'd done the right thing. It was the weirdest situation. She barely knew the woman and yet, somehow, she felt an allegiance towards her. As she took in what she'd just done, she shook her head. All these drugs and life-questioning things were changing her. No doubt about it, she would never in a million years have phoned a dead person's mobile and given instructions to a stranger on his own wife's funeral before.

* * *

People were always saying that life only hands you what you can handle. Only moments before, Alfie had felt he couldn't continue. That the aching sadness of having to organise Tanya's funeral was going to choke him. Now he'd been given the push he'd desperately needed to keep going, at least for the next few hours.

"Do you know any singers?" he asked the undertakers. "I don't mean the usual church, hymn-singing ones. You see, Tanya had dreadful taste in music." He smiled. "She had a secret love affair with Barry Manilow. Could you find someone who can sing 'Can't Smile Without You'? I know she'd probably kill me for telling everyone, but she'd like that."

"We'll see what we can do, Alfie."

The whole procedure took almost two hours, by the time they'd agreed on prayers, the rest of the music, a venue for refreshments after the funeral, a plot at the graveyard, the exact wording of the death notice, the cars to take the coffin and family. It was extensive. It was also going to cost a small fortune. Alfie had to call Sally to ask her about policies. She was the first person he had to break the news to.

"Sally? Are you there?" Alfie could hear faint noise in the background.

"Yes. I'm sorry. I can't believe it. Oh Alfie, how are you?"

He'd always liked Sally, she was dependable and he knew Tanya had thought the world of her.

"I'm okay. I have to be, I have Jenny to think of." His voice sounded steady, but empty.

Sally agreed to come over the next morning with the relevant paperwork. She'd also assured him that Tanya had covered herself to an extreme level, should anything ever happen. Much as she'd hated the morbid conversation they'd had only a couple of weeks earlier, Sally was now glad she'd had the chance to discuss it all with Tanya. She was fully briefed on what she wanted and how to obtain access to all her affairs.

She'd expected the mood to be sombre when she arrived. Instead, she was met by Jenny, who clapped and attached herself to her leg.

"Sally! Hurray!"

"Hi, Jenny-baby. Have you got a hug for me?" She smiled at Alfie as she picked her up. As she held the child, she was conscious of taking care not to crush her. Because that was what she wanted to do. She wanted to hug her so hard that she'd cuddle all the pain and hurt away. Jenny was too young to realise her mummy was gone yet, but she'd know in time. She'd know when she was older. She'd know on her first day of school. When she had a birthday party and her mummy wasn't at it. On Christmas morning when just her daddy was there to see what Santa had brought. The day she picked her deb's dress, her wedding day, the day she became a mother. All the wonderful times she had ahead, not to mention the days she needed her mother's love. It had all been ripped from her. It just wasn't fair. This sweet innocent little curly-topped angel was going to have to learn to survive from a very early age. Sally squeezed her eyes shut and willed herself to gain control, then opened her eyes and linked gazes with Jenny. She could see the questioning in the baby's eyes as her little face tilted slightly to the side.

"Have you any nice toys to show me?" Sally managed.

"Oh yes, look!" Jenny ran to the playroom the second Sally set her down.

Alfie wandered into the kitchen, with Tanya's pink notebook. Feeling like a thief, he opened it again and read some more of the lines of scribbled writing. Tears coursed down his cheeks as he heard Tanya's voice in the words.

One of the final entries made him want to curl into a ball and expire.

*My prognosis may not be good, but I will always have my Alfie and baby girl. If God wants a fight, bring it on.*

# 16

*Please stay with me, help me to get through today.*

Alfie clicked his pen shut. He'd spoken to Sian on the phone and asked about the notebooks.

"We encourage patients to use them by way of positive-thought therapy. It can work wonders for some people."

Feeling a little closer to Tanya if he continued her book, he embraced the idea.

He was in a slight state of panic. He knew he couldn't go to Tanya's funeral in one of his old work suits. Besides, none of them were even clean or pressed. On autopilot he put Jenny into the buggy, stuffed the changing bag underneath and set off for the shopping centre.

Knowing, that Tanya didn't want anyone in black, he was slightly thrown. He didn't want to look like he was going to a Caribbean wedding, in a white or pale linen jobby, but he didn't want to go against Tanya's wishes and look like an undertaker either.

He was still overwhelmingly sad that Tanya hadn't felt able to tell him that she was dying. That he'd had to hear her final wishes from poor Zoe and Dr Leah. He understood why. Unlike most other people in the world he *got* Tanya. He could work it out. She'd been trying both to deny what was happening and protect himself and Jenny. He knew that was the reason, but at the same time he wished he'd had even one conversation with her where he could have told her one last time how much he loved her.

As he came around the corner of the shopping centre, he spotted the suit in the window. It was a dark wheaten shade, teamed with a linen shirt. He marched up to the counter, gave the man his size and asked for the outfit and matching shirt to be packed up. Offering his credit card, he waited for the assistant to carry out his wishes.

"I strongly suggest you try it on, sir. We have a spacious fitting room, which will fit the buggy." She smiled encouragingly. She was used to men arriving in and not bothering to try clothes on. They all wanted the grab-and-run option, but getting them to try stuff on usually avoided their having to return and exchange.

"No, thank you. I will wear it whether it works or not. Please just take the credit card and put it in a carrier-bag." Alfie's voice was only barely above a whisper.

Deciding not to argue with the man, the lady did as she was asked. She was a bit disappointed as she was bored stupid. He'd been her only customer that morning. People were terrified to spend money, what with the recession and all the doom and gloom it brought with it. This guy was stunning too, and she figured he'd be knock 'em dead gorgeous in the pale suit.

Alfie paced home and stored the suit in the wardrobe of the spare room, ready for the following day. Along with some new shoes he'd bought recently, he knew he wouldn't let Tanya down at the funeral the next evening.

He'd decided not to do a removal, just a Mass and burial. He couldn't face having to put himself and Jenny through two rituals.

* * *

The dark looming limousine pulled up outside the house on the morning of the funeral. Like a large hunting shark, it halted and waited for himself and Jenny to climb inside. Danielle and Lauren were already sitting in the back seat.

"Nana! Lala!" Jenny was thrilled to see them both. "Mama?" She looked up at Alfie and back out the door to see if her mummy was coming too.

"Mama's not coming, sweetheart." Danielle scooped the little girl onto her lap and let her root in her handbag for distraction.

Alfie had sat beside Jenny's cot the night before and told their little girl that Mummy had gone to sleep. That she was now a star in the sky and living with the angels. Jenny had kept looking beyond her daddy, towards her bedroom door, waiting for Tanya to come in.

Much as he'd willed the baby to understand, Alfie knew she simply couldn't. He didn't blame her – he couldn't comprehend any of it either. How could he expect Jenny to?

Most of the funeral passed by in a blur for Alfie. He wished he could have grabbed Jenny and run down the aisle and out the door. He wondered if Zoe was here, sitting somewhere in the church, listening to Barry Manilow.

Tanya's sudden death had knocked the stuffing out of Zoe. As she sat on the hard bench in the church, she felt it was a living nightmare. Her poor husband Alfie had looked disbelieving and tortured, while little Jenny had been blissfully unaware of what was really happening. She was the only one who clapped and swayed from side to side as the Barry Manilow song "Can't Smile Without You," was sung.

Cheesy as the song was, it was obvious to everyone sitting there that it had been a favourite of Tanya's. As the words flooded the church, with a man telling a story of how he simply couldn't smile since his true love was gone, all eyes were on Alfie who sat silent, head bowed, dressed in a pale-coloured suit and looking like he didn't fit in.

When the time came for people to go up and shake hands with the bereft family, Zoe hesitated. Should she go up? They'd never met her. She'd heard about them from Tanya, but they didn't know her.

"Sorry, can I get out past you or are you going up?" a lady in a bright yellow dress, with puffy eyes and a tearstained face, asked her.

"Yes, of course." Zoe leaned back into the pew to let her pass. Feeling a little odd in a pale pink and turquoise ensemble, Zoe found herself in the line behind the bright yellow lady.

The death notice had read:

*Tanya Shields, 35, died suddenly, at St Mark's private hospital, Monday 20th September. She will be sadly missed by her loving husband Alfie, her daughter Jenny, mother Danielle, brothers, sister, colleagues and many friends.*

*Until we meet again, Tanya, may God hold you in the palm of His hand.*

*Removal to the Church of the Holy Father, followed by a funeral Mass, all on Thursday 23rd at 12.00 p.m.*

*As requested by Tanya, would all mourners please refrain from wearing black. There will be cakes, canapés and cocktails in The Acid Bar, with face-painting and live music after the burial. We wish to celebrate Tanya's life rather than mourn her death.*

Zoe had cried for an hour after reading the notice. Alfie had gone all out to do what he knew Tanya would have liked.

As Zoe neared the top of the church, her heart skipped a beat as she studied the tiny replica of Tanya sitting between her daddy and her grandmother. It was so wrong on so many levels that such a small child should be sitting on a bench at her mother's funeral. Jenny had Tanya's look of determination on her face as she watched all the people filing past. Although she must have been terribly confused, she remained calm and examined each person who shook her father's and grandmother's hand.

"Hello, Alfie, I'm Zoe." She gazed at him with her big brown eyes and willed herself not to cry. Ignoring the offered hand, Alfie stood and threw his arms around the young girl and hugged her. "Thank you," he whispered into her ear as they embraced. "I'm so glad you were able to guide me. Tanya will be smiling down on us all later. I'd love you to join me for a cocktail if you feel up to it."

"Of course." Zoe couldn't meet his gaze, her vision totally blurred as the tears streamed down her face. She didn't even shake hands with the rest of the family. She walked away as quickly as she could without running. On tip-toe to avoid making noise on the old church floorboards, she made it outside. She knew she should stay for the rest of the Mass and go to the graveyard. But she simply couldn't do it. She found her car and clicked the door open with the key's remote control, then folded herself into the driver's seat. Flopping her head onto the wheel, she bawled loudly. It was so bloody unfair. Seeing that little child and that lovely man, being dragged through hell on earth. Where was the justice in all of it?

With heart-stabbing determination, Zoe vowed she was going to beat her cancer and stay alive. Seeing that poor family and all those sad people in the church gave her the biggest reason in the world to avoid the same thing happening to Charlie and her parents.

"*As God is my witness, I am going to fight this bastard and win!*" Zoe said to the roof of her car, gritting her teeth.

# 17

*Watch over and protect Tanya, welcome her to Your love, may she rest in eternal peace. Amen.*

Zoe had felt she should turn up for the after-funeral event but decided to conserve her energy and nip home for a rest first, so it was quite late in the afternoon before she walked into the cocktail bar where the refreshments were being served.

"Hello, everyone." Zoe stood, looking uncomfortable.

"Hello, Zoe love," said Esme. "This is my husband Michael."

Zoe was thrust towards the man, who pumped her hand up and down without saying a word.

Sian hugged her and they all chatted about how sudden and shocking the whole thing was. A waitress passed with drinks on a round wooden tray, and Zoe took an orange juice. The room was filled with people, all shouting and laughing. A jazz band with a very skinny lead singer, dressed in a short pink frilly, prom-style dress, pumped out bouncy music from the corner of the room.

"Do you think I should tell yer woman that she's got holes in her stockings?" Esme poked Zoe in the ribs and nodded her head towards the singer.

"That's the look, the Amy Winehouse kind of style," Zoe smiled.

"And whoever's behind the bar must be pissed," said Michael. "They gave me what looked like a goldfish bowel with mouthwash in it. To add insult to injury, they came along with trays of cold rice with raw meat on it. Do I look like an otter or a seal? Why would they try to give us all zoo food?" He scratched the back of his head. "I asked them for a pint of stout. I was terrified it was going to arrive on fire playing a tin whistle version of the 'Halleluiah' but so far it's alright, thank God." He drank a sip of his drink, while eyeing the glass suspiciously.

"I didn't recognise any of the drinks they offered, so I asked for a sherry. Lovely it is." Esme took another sip and giggled. "My handbag will never be the same again – my Tracey bought it for me, pity that," she sniffed.

"Why? What happened to it?" Zoe asked.

"Well, we had to put all that fish food somewhere, so we've stuffed it into my bag. We didn't want to upset that poor lad, in case he copped on they were handing out raw food. The poor fella has enough to cope with, losing his wife like that. All the same, do you think we should warn other people? The light is iffy in here – what if they eat it and die of food poisoning? I tried to tell those lads over there, but they don't speak proper and they seem to be quite upset."

"They sound like they're talking backwards. Too many of them gold-fish bowels of detergent I'd say," Michael muttered.

Zoe looked over at the group of foreigners. With their dark skin, blonde hair and dark eyes. She guessed they were eastern European.

Sian tried to make jolly conversation but stopped as Alfie approached.

Esme gave Michael a nudge with her elbow. "Here comes the widower, God bless him," she muttered and moved forward to meet him. "Esme and Michael Mulligan, we're terrible sorry, love. I met your lovely wife, God rest her, at the cancer support group. I have cancer in me intestines. The drugs are going grand and please God I'll be grand. We'll say a novena for you and the little one. My heart goes out to you both." And she launched herself at a very stunned Alfie.

Tanya had mentioned this woman to him. Tanya had said she dropped serious clangers all the time.

"Thank you, Esme and Michael. I really appreciate you coming and supporting us today. In spite of your own sickness. Please God you will be fine soon." Alfie smiled at them and shook hands with Sian. They exchanged pleasantries before he turned to Zoe.

"Hi, Zoe, thank you so much for everything." He hugged her and tried to hold back his tears.

"You did a wonderful job of everything – I'm sure Tanya would love all this." She waved her hand around the room. "The church was lovely too. How are you doing?" She struggled to maintain her composure as she looked into his eyes.

Alfie and Zoe stepped over to the side to have a little private chat.

"I'm still in shock, I think," he confided. "It probably won't hit me until next week. It's kind of like she's gone away for a few days, you know? Jenny looked for her when she woke up this morning, but then she found her Barney and started to play. She's used to having me there all the time. I suppose that'll be a good thing." He clouded over and the half-smile he'd been forcing faded.

"I'm not working at the moment, because of the chemo and all that. If you want me to call over or if you and Jenny would like to meet up, I'd be happy to help. Only if you want." She felt awkward as hell and thought she'd die of embarrassment as soon as the words came out.

"Thank you, I might take you up on that. I'd say it's going to hit me next week when everyone goes back to their work and general daily lives. It's going to be strange, you know?" Alfie shoved the sawdust on the floor around with his shoe.

His suit was uncomfortable and itchy. It was beyond him how other men wore them day after day. Imagine having to stuff yourself into such restricting clothes all the time? It was almost like being in school again. The din of the room faded, the pockets of laughter, grouped conversations and clinking of glasses. He remembered the feeling of restraint and limitation on his first day back to school after the freedom of the summer holidays. He could almost smell the leather from his new shoes and that gorgeous smell wafting from the pile of new books. He closed his eyes for a moment and wished he was a young boy again. Instead of a grown man, being made to exist in a world which spiked him from every angle with pain and torture. The bubble of new schoolbooks popped and instead the image of Tanya's coffin being lowered into the ground replaced it. A shiny orangey-coloured wooden box, with brass fittings and a smooth rectangular plate, with her name engraved on it.

It was a cruel mocking sort of object, the coffin. It was beautifully made, the wood nicer than most household furniture. The handles were shone to perfection. It was all very odd really. Why, in this day and age, didn't they make them out of recycled plastic bottles or old pizza boxes? They were only used as a storage box for a day or two – it seemed such a waste and such a shame. But perhaps that was the whole point. The loss of his darling wife filled him with the same sentiment. She'd been so young and full of life.

Snapping back to reality, Alfie focused on Zoe. She was sweet and easy to talk to. She seemed genuinely crushed by Tanya's passing. He felt sorry for her. She was ill enough, having a shitty enough time, without having to come and witness the sorrow of people she barely knew.

"I'm sorry you had to be here for all this. God, I'd say you wish you'd never met her, then you could have been spared having to drag yourself here today, feeling sore and nauseous. I really appreciate you coming." Alfie kissed her on the cheek and, with a smile, turned to walk away.

"Wait, Alfie, please! I don't want you to think like that, not for one second. I was honoured to meet Tanya. She was strong and funny and she's given me the will to fight. I was beginning to drown, you see. I was letting this manky dermatomyo-thingymabob and the cancer get me down. Now, I've been jolted into touch. Life's too short. I'm not going to roll over and give in. I meant what I said too, I'd like to be there, if you need a friend. I could do with one too. All my friends and even my twin are scared to come near me, you see. Illness and sadness are an incredible deterrent. People don't know what to say or do, so they figure staying away is the best policy. So, just in case you want someone to *not* do that, give me a call." Zoe rustled in her bag and found one of the cards from the shop, listing her details. "I know you have my number from when I called the other day, but here's my card just in case."

Alfie took the card and popped it into the inside pocket of his jacket. "Thanks so much. I really appreciate your kindness," he said, taking her hands in his and squeezing them momentarily.

Going back to Esme, Michael and Sian, he thanked them once more for coming before moving on to the next group of mourners.

Zoe's head was thumping, her limbs were burning and she'd had enough. Sian asked if herself and Esme would like to continue with the group sessions.

"Personally I think we need it more than ever now," Zoe answered.

"Oh yes, well, I love it, don't I, Michael?" Esme gave him a dig in the ribs as he dove into a fresh pint.

"Esme loves a chat. God knows she's like a walking newspaper article. She knows who's married to who, where they live and what their babies are called. It gives me a chance to nip down the road to the bookies when she's out with yous, so I'm all for it." His cheeks were flushed, his eyes glassy and he was becoming more chatty. "It'll do all of you the world of good to be together. That's what women like. Whether it's in the saloon getting a set or down at your centre drinking coffee, girls love an auld chinwag. I should know, haven't I been surrounded by them all me life? Two sisters growing up, then I met Esme and we'd the two girls. If I didn't have the few lads at the pub, I'd probably be wearing a frock and have me hair in curlers by now!" Michael sniffed and downed more of his drink.

In spite of the dreadful situation, Zoe and Sian giggled. Michael stared at them as if they were mad, muttering under his breath about women being a different species, and thank God for pints.

"If you ladies will excuse me, I'm off to the jacks," he said and made a beeline for the bathrooms.

After the three women agreed to hook up the following Monday for a meeting, Zoe slipped away. Spotting an acquaintance waving at her across the bar, Sian excused herself to Esme and went to say hello. Esme approached the group of foreign-looking men sitting near the bar.

"Do you know who you look like?" She pointed her finger at one man, as she pushed her way into the group and clambered onto a stool. "You look like one of them lion tamers at the circus years ago. All them dark curls and eyes like little bits of coal. That all-year-round-tanned skin too. You're a lovely lad, did anyone ever tell you that? Esme Mulligan – you don't mind if I sit down, do you? Not as young as I used to be, seventy next birthday, please God." She looked from one to the next, examining every inch of them, from their shoes to their hair. Two of them were white-blond and looked like Action Man dolls. They smiled at her but didn't otherwise respond, making her wonder if they understood what she was saying.

"Do you speak English?" she shouted.

"He's only foreign, Esme, he's not deaf!" Michael had returned from the bathroom and shuffled over to join his wife. He simply nodded a silent greeting to the three men.

Esme didn't seem to notice that the men weren't hard of hearing – she had obviously decided that it would be easier for them to understand if she spoke very loudly.

"Yes, we have plenty English," one of the men answered.

"Well, don't be shy, introduce yourselves, why don't you?" she said, eye-balling one in particular.

"I am Merek and these are my friends, Fryderyk and Jerzy," said the circus-looking man.

"And do you come from Romania or somewhere?" Esme was delighted with them – wait till she told the Golden Girls at the next coffee morning.

"We come from Poland. We work for Miss-a-Tanya. We are very sad she will have die. She was good person. We will be sad for many day now."

"She was a grand girl, it's terrible, and that little child with no mother left. Please God that lad will marry again quickly and provide a new mother. That's what would have happened years ago. Sure I remember when Mrs Quinn from Shankill died. Her little ones were only babies, but Mr Quinn found a new wife in no time and they went on to have two more babies. Grand it was. Better than seeing the poor man depending on dinners sent in by the neighbours and those babbies half dressed and not properly washed. A man can't be expected to do that kind of thing on a regular basis. It's not right, you know. My Michael couldn't even make a pot of tea. He'd set fire to the house if he tried, God bless him. Although he did manage to rustle up a bit of dinner for me not so long ago, seeing as I'm not too well. But I think men should be minded and cared for."

Esme took a swig of the pink stuff in the cocktail glass. It tasted a bit like melted ice-pop but at least it was pretty. They'd given her a yellow umbrella and a green cherry on this one. She'd a good collection in her handbag now: two little plastic swords with lemon slices threaded through them, a blue umbrella and a little fold-out paper fan thing with little glittery things on it. She'd bring them along to show the Golden Girls. They loved that type of thing. Maybe they could put them on their cups of tea, to brighten it all up a bit, she mused.

"Can I offer you another drink?" a young girl held up a tray with some cocktails in Martini-style glasses on it.

"Don't mind if I do, shouldn't really." Esme stuck her hand out to grab a blue cocktail with crushed ice and a gorgeous little fake parrot on the top. "But, sure I might as well, you only live once, what?" She jabbed Marek in the ribs and snorted.

Esme and Michael stayed for another couple of hours, by which time they were feeling hungry. Although she'd forced herself to drink a few glasses of water, Esme hadn't eaten much. It was all small round things on trays.

"It's like doll's food really. It looks very pretty, but it wouldn't exactly fill you up, would it?" she whispered to Michael, who was looking at his watch.

He'd have had his dinner and dessert and a cup of tea with a biscuit by now, if he'd been at home. Still, it was proper order to support that poor lad with the child. He was too young to know how to provide a proper dinner. Sure he couldn't even manage to dress himself. That suit was hanging off him and he'd hair like a caveman. Looked like it had been combed by the cat. He'd a nice appearance under all that hair. He had kind eyes.

"We go now for food. You will come too?" Marek asked.

"Yez don't eat raw fish or any mad food like brains, do you?" Michael stared at them with a warning look in his eye.

"No, we go for kebabs," Jerzy laughed. Although, a kebab might well indeed include brains and even eyeballs, the only difference being they were cooked to a large greasy mass. But, doused in ketchup and mixed with enough alcohol to fuel a small aircraft, it would be as good as gourmet.

The unlikely group staggered into the local kebab shop and Marek went up to the counter to place the order.

"I'm paying, I insist." Michael tried to focus on the money in his wallet. It was all moving around a lot and it was proving very tricky working out how much each one was worth. Why in the name of God had they changed to this euro nonsense? Before all this, money was real. This was like Monopoly money. Years ago, when you'd a twenty note, it was big and crispy and you felt like you'd a decent bit of cash. All this fecky, Mickey-Mouse-euro business annoyed him. He handed over a king's ransom for the food and made his way to the table. The whole thing was like being a savage. All messy sandwich-type things, in a bleeding box. No plates or cutlery. The chips were in cardboard yokes, like the things the girls used to bring home from art class when they were little.

"What am I supposed to do with this?" he looked at Esme.

"You pick it up in your hands and eat it, like a picnic, it'll be fun. Go on, live a little," she giggled.

He prised the bread open a little. "Why are there bits of carpet underlay in the bread, and there's all rabbit food and baby sick in it." There was no way he was eating this. Even the chips had some sort of orange stuff all over them. Esme's homemade chips weren't this colour. The smell of the food was oddly enticing though. The others were oblivious to his suspicion. They were silent as they hoovered up the strange food.

Esme was looking a bit put out by that point too, so at least he could count on her to back him up. She tentatively raised the kebab to her lips. He wasn't sure if it was the booze or the fact that he was longing for a plate of roast beef, but he suddenly felt very emotional. What on earth would he do without his Esme? She did everything for him. From making his breakfast, to telling him what he wanted to order when they went out. He knew the girls wouldn't see him short, but he couldn't bear the thought of having to face the final years of his life by himself. They'd known lots of people who'd died from cancer. Esme kept telling him times had changed, that the doctors knew what they were doing now. That they'd be able to cure this, but what if they were wrong?

"Esme, don't leave me!" he suddenly burst out, from nowhere.

"I'm not going anywhere, you daft git! Sure I'm trying to eat this cabutz. We'll have to get a taxi home, in any case, we're too late for the bus." She patted his arm and told him to eat up.

Against his better judgment, he decided to trust his beloved and try the food. To his astonishment, he thought it tasted gorgeous.

"This is magic, lads. I'd never in my life have thought of putting all this stuff in a pouch. It's a bit like one of those jiffy bags, isn't it? But it's very tasty, in fairness." He couldn't believe how good it was.

"What kind of meat do you think it is?" Esme asked the lads.

"Lamb or beef," said Jerzy.

"Probably Alsatian or badger, more like," said Michael, chomping, "but after a skinful of pints and nothing but raw doll's food all afternoon, it's bloody amazing! I'll tell you what, Esme, while you're not well, I'll come on the bus and get this for our tea once a week. This is one of the nicest things I've ever had." He thought he'd died and gone to heaven.

Grand, Esme thought. I'll let him do this on a Thursday from now on. She got her chemo on a Monday, so by the Thursday she always felt tired and sick. She'd been having trouble with the chops. The smell of them cooking was terrible, let alone trying to chew them afterwards. Not easy when you feel sick.

"That'll be grand on a Thursday, love. I'd appreciate that. One dinner less is a treat, what? So I'll take that into account when I'm doing my shopping from here on in. Pork chops – strike. Kaboots – in."

"It's kebabs, Esme."

"That's what I said."

# 18

*I can't think of a single positive thought. I need some help.*

Sian hated funerals. Everyone did, but as all people who've lost someone really close to them knows, it raked up all the buried emotion. Although it was better as time went by, she still had a dormant monster of grief lurking in her psyche. She spent the entire week after Tanya's death awake and terrorised. All the raw fear she'd experienced when Liam had first died returned. It was so bad that she made an appointment with her doctor.

As she sat in the waiting room, she suddenly felt silly. There was one other man there, who looked really ill and in pain. She was just about to get up and flee with her head down when her name was called.

As she sat opposite her doctor, she found herself unable to speak.

"Try and take a deep breath and let me know what's going on. Take your time." Paula had been her doctor for fifteen years now. About the same age as herself and so approachable, Sian had ultimate faith and trust in her.

"I'm sorry. I've just noticed lately that my sleep pattern has become so bad. I'm not eating properly and I have this dreadful feeling of unease and fear hovering all the time. I thought it would go away, but it hasn't. What's driven me here really is the lack of sleep. I'm so tired I can't keep going anymore."

Paula took her blood pressure and a blood test, asking questions as she went. A good quarter of an hour passed before she went back around to her own chair and sat at the desk.

"Okay, Sian. The bloods will confirm it, but I reckon you are having a rough ride with the menopause. Your hormones will probably show that in the bloods. We'll know for sure in a week. Meanwhile, I need you to cut down on caffeine, include some omega-rich foods in your diet, such as ground flax seeds. In fact I have a list of good menopause-friendly foods here." She handed her a print-out, with things such as sweet potato, porridge oats, dark green leafy vegetables, cress and other sprouting seeds listed. "Some of these you probably know already, but it's never any harm to see them listed again to remind yourself. Would you like a prescription for some sleeping pills, just for a few weeks to get you back on track?"

"Yes, I think that would be marvellous. As you know, I'm still involved with the counselling sessions, and I don't feel I'd be any use to others at the minute. What use is a sleep-deprived basket-case to sick people?"

"Don't be too hard on yourself, Sian. You do a great job. I'm sure all your patients are grateful to you. Tell me, did something in particular spark this feeling of hopelessness you're experiencing?" Paula held her head to the side.

"Yes, now you mention it. One of the younger patients died suddenly, not from her cancer. She left a young baby and husband behind. At the funeral, I saw it again . . . that haunted look of desperate sadness in his eyes. I saw myself all those years ago. I saw that raw feeling of palpable, tangible pain, emanating from his very soul. It's been keeping me awake at night. I can't shake it." She shuddered. Once the tears began to flow, she couldn't stop them. It was a strange relief though, to open the dam and let the emotion out.

* * *

Armed with her list of "good foods" and her prescription for sedatives, Sian hoped things would improve for her. She took Esme and Zoe for a meeting. They, too, were shocked to the core by Tanya's death. A week turned into two. The sleeping pills weren't doing much to help, so Sian returned to the doctor's.

"Your bloods show you are in fact in menopause, which would explain the hot flushes and feeling of panic that goes with them. Some women sail through it all and some, like you, find it quite interfering. Have the sleepers helped at all?"

"No, I just spend the night waiting for them to take effect and get out of bed more despondent than before, feeling hung over to hell, without having had any fun the night before." Sian felt utterly miserable. She'd been really good about making stirfrys and eating as much healthy food as she could bear.

"Okay, I'll tell you what, we'll try you on a drug called Rohypnol for a wee while. It will help with the feeling of the blues and should make you sleep like a baby."

So that was how *it* had all started. What Sian referred to her friend Joan as "the funny business". In the beginning she'd thought she was imagining all the things moving around on their own.

She'd come down in the morning and find a picture from the wall sitting in the middle of the kitchen counter. One morning, the hallway looked like it had been savaged by the Andrex puppy. There were yards of toilet paper strewn around. Clean, thank God, but unravelled all over the place. It was so odd that she didn't mention it to anyone at first. Not even Joan. It all had to come out, however, when she woke up feeling kind of warm and sticky around her forehead.

*Am I sick? Do I have a raging temperature? Have I got vomit-soaked hair?* She took a deep breath and waited for the pain to engulf her. *Nothing. Right. That's good, so what the hell is wrong with me?*

Sian made her way to the bathroom and looked in the mirror. *Holy shit! What happened?*

At first she felt like crying. The shock of what was staring back at her hit her like a bucket of cold water over the head. As the vision began to sink in, she smiled at first, seconds later she was doubled over the sink in hysterics of laughter. She looked like a toddler who'd been at a birthday cake unattended. She was covered in chocolate. There were clumps of it in her hair, stuck to her forehead and even in her eyebrows. Peeping back into her bedroom, she saw her bed looked like a herd of wild buffalo on laxatives had danced across her pillow.

Grabbing a facecloth, she began to wipe furiously as she made her way down the stairs. In the kitchen, she saw two of the cupboards had been emptied on to the counter and the floors. Everything from tins and packets to plastic bowls had been flung around.

Still giggling, she dialled her friend's number.

"Joan? You're not going to believe what I've just done," she chuckled.

As the story unfolded, Joan felt like she was going to burst. The fact that Sian had been moving stuff around her own house was bad enough. But this midnight eating was another story altogether.

"Is that a normal reaction to Rohypnol?" Joan asked between splutters.

"I've no idea! What am I supposed to do, call the doctor and confess to going berserk in my sleep?"

"Isn't that the drug they dubbed the 'date-rape drug' in the nineties? It's apparently an odd one, as afterwards the person is unable to remember what's happened, and yet was fully functional at the time. That stuff is illegal in the States, you know?"

"I'm not bloody surprised considering what it's making me do."

The problem escalated over the next few days. One night in particular, she went on a really bad rampage. Not only did she manage to eat half a Christmas pudding from the freezer, which she reckoned might have been at least five years old, but she hadn't even bothered to thaw it out before she smothered it with mustard.

"Are you sure?" By now Joan rang every morning to find out what her pal had been up to the night before.

"Yes, there's an empty jar beside the bed and the duvet cover is yellow tie-died. I did another dreadful thing, Joan. I think I'm going to have to 'fess up to the doctor. It's getting dangerous now."

"What did you do?"

"Stop sounding so gleeful, you wagon, it's not funny," Sian sighed.

"Ah leave me alone, it's the best entertainment I've had in ages. What else did you do? Go on, I promise I won't laugh." Joan was already squirming to keep a straight face.

"I drank a bottle of Baileys and a quarter of a bottle of cooking rum." Sian sounded a bit miserable.

"Jesus, and do you feel hung over now?" Joan thought she was going to wet herself.

"Oddly enough, no, I don't."

"The pudding obviously soaked it all up."

By now, Joan was beyond having a conversation with. Sian told her she was phoning the doctor and she'd call her later, when she was more able to control herself.

Feeling quite pissed-off and more than a little embarrassed, Sian contacted her doctor. Later that day, she had a brief and rather cringing meeting with her.

"It's not that common, but I have heard of patients doing strange things," Paula mused. "You know it was used in a nasty way for a spate, where rapists would drop them in women's drinks in bars and take advantage of them."

"Yes, so my friend told me. God, how scary!" Sian shuddered.

"Look, we need to look at this more objectively. Are you getting any sleep, in between the eating and trashing your house? Maybe we can put you on a similar type of drug or a slightly smaller dose, and see how that works for you?"

"Well, to be honest with you, I don't think it's worth taking any more. For a start I've piled on half a stone, which is making my clothes tight and I'm as bloated at bejaysus. Although eating half a Christmas pudding would tend to do that," she sighed.

Luckily Paula was sympathetic and being a woman of similar age didn't make Sian feel like a moron. They agreed to try another type of tablet, for a while.

"These are called Temazepam. They work as a relaxant so they should help you to drift off. Do all the usual stuff, read a relaxing book as opposed to watching murder programmes before you go to sleep. Stick to cotton bedclothes and pyjamas, keep your room well ventilated. I've heard from a lot of patients that cutting out wheat can help with the hot flushes too. Soya is a big one. Try to include even one soya yoghurt in your everyday diet. If the sweats are keeping you awake, or you have to change your pyjamas or bedclothes, in other words if you wake up wet more than twice a week, let me know. There is medication available, but I don't tend to prescribe hormone-replacement therapy unless there's no other option."

They chatted for a further ten minutes, and Sian made the first move to stand up. Paula was always brilliant, in that she didn't have a full waiting room with that get-out-you're-taking-too-long look about her. She gave the impression she had all the time in the world to talk to each patient.

Sian went straight to the chemist to get her tablets, followed by a coffee despite Paula's warning that she should cut down on caffeine.

"Would you like a scone with that?" The young Italian girl, who worked in the café beside the support centre, instinctively reached out to grab a brown scone for Sian.

"No, thank you, Nadia, I'm on a new diet, which doesn't include wheat. Not sure how long it will last, but I'll give it a go," Sian smiled.

The girl shrugged and rang up the price of the coffee.

Oh, the innocence of her, Sian mused. When I was twenty and carefree I would have thought anyone depriving themselves of a scone was insane too. But after a certain age, your body doesn't work as well as it used to. You with your cappuccino skin, silky dark hair, bright wrinkle-free eyes and toned body, you don't realise how lucky you are.

Of course she didn't voice any of it. Holy God, she had to come here most days, and she didn't want the poor girl to have to dive behind the counter to avoid the mad old bag coming in to complain. Anyway, she wasn't old. She was fifty-three. It wasn't as if her life was over. Although, most of the time, when she thumbed through magazines, she felt slightly alienated. All the models were teenagers. Of course there was the new trend towards "mature models". But even they were stereotypical. Women with grey hair down to their waist, wearing chain-store clothes, marketed at the over-fifties. With captions saying it's okay to grow old gracefully.

Sian would rather die than go around with grey hair. Fair enough, it suited French women and even black women. But if she didn't turn up at the hairdresser every five weeks, she knew she'd look like a corpse.

Maybe this was her mid-life crisis – she was most definitely fighting with herself. Did she need a new direction in life? Should she take up a new hobby? Did she need a man after all these years? She wasn't sure what was going on in her own head, but she knew she'd have to try and change things a bit. If she was totally honest, she wasn't that happy at the moment. Perhaps it was poor Tanya's death that had given her a shake-up, but she realised, not for the first time, how short life was. How precious our time on earth. She needed something more to look forward to. That was it. She needed some excitement. Joan, bless her, was all excited about organising a holiday. She was obsessed with going to Egypt. Sian thought it would be lovely and she'd go if the price was right.

As she made her way to the support centre, she felt a little bit lighter inside. Apart from the possible trip to Egypt, she would try and figure out a project or plan of action to give herself a jolt. No more ticking along for me, she vowed. I'm going to shake myself up.

# 19

*Things can only get better. I am not where I want to be
and I don't recognise myself right now. But I will be
better soon.*

Zoe felt like she'd been hit by a bus. In fact, she felt like the bus
had driven over her and reversed just to make sure. She'd
moved home since Tanya's funeral.

The evening of the funeral, after leaving the pub, she'd gone back to
the apartment she shared with Charlie. Four of their friends, including
Simon, Charlie's new man interest, were in situ. Although spacious by
modern standards, the apartment had walls like paper. All Zoe wanted
was to be able to crawl into bed and hide. Not a hope. She was hugged
and engulfed in wine-whiffing, well-meaning love from Charlie.

"Come and have a little glass of wine and sit with us, you look
beat." She bounded across to the kitchen to get a fresh glass from
the cupboard.

"No, honey, thanks all the same, but I think I'm going to rock
on over to Mum and Dad's. I'm feeling the effects of the chemo and
I don't want to rain on your parade here. Just let me grab a few bits
and I'll be out of your hair." She laughed and tried to sound lighter
than she felt. "You don't all need to do the cancer thing right now."

Charlie's face dropped, but only for a second. "No problem, Zo-Zo. Whatever you like."

"We should go," Simon stood up, looking awkward.

The others looked suitably ashamed and began to shuffle about collecting up their phones and bits and pieces.

"Please, please, don't! I'd hate it if you all left. I don't want to make things uncomfortable for anybody. It's just unfortunate that I have to go through all this shit at the moment. Really, I'd be happier to be in my old bed and in a place where I can lick my wounds. You're not going to help me in any way, jumping up and running off like scalded cats when I appear. You all stay, drink the wine and have one for me. As soon as I'm finished with all this stuff, I'll be the last one standing again. You tell them, Charlie. I'm not usually like this. I'm sorry."

She tried to walk slowly into her bedroom, without bolting and slamming the door and flinging herself face down onto the bed and bawling. She'd love nothing more than to sit in her Juicy Couture trackie bottoms and tuck her legs under her bum and sink into a glass of cold white wine.

Before she'd become this sick person, Cancer Girl, she would have burst into the room and made everybody listen to what a shit day she'd had. She'd have told them all how sad the funeral was. Who was at it. What they wore. Where she'd been. She wouldn't have missed out on a pair of shoes or a handbag in her report. Simon's eyes would have glazed over as she went through everyone's hairstyles, even the delicious-looking Eastern European men with heavy lids and dark hair at the bar. No stone would have been left unturned. But now . . .

The Zoe she'd been forced to become didn't have the energy to even say where she'd been. She couldn't begin to describe the fear, anger and appalling events she'd witnessed.

Charlie and her new love and his two friends – one a kind of hippy girl who Zoe noted was doing that just-got-out-of-bed look, with high-end designer gear, and her open-faced boyfriend, dressed in Ralph Lauren from shirt to socks – didn't need to have the world of sickness and death imposed upon them.

If this Simon guy lasted, he'd get to know the real Zoe in time. Her arms ached as she tried to put some clothes and basic provisions into an overnight bag. The burning swelling in her limbs and face was beginning to deflate, but when she was tired, it all accelerated.

Charlie stuck her head in the door.

"Can I help?" She looked shy and unsure.

"Yes, please. Can you grab me some pyjamas and a couple of long-sleeved T-shirts and some track-suit bottoms?"

"Do you want your jeans?"

"No, I can't manage the buttons, my fingers are so stiff. It's elasticated waists all the way, I'm afraid." She tried to smile, but she knew that if she displayed any kind of emotion, she'd cry.

"Zo-Zo, I don't know what to say or do around you at the moment. I know I should be helping you more. But I feel a million miles from you for the first time. Please *tell* me if you need me. Guide me if you can?" Charlie's eyes were filled with tears as she sat on the end of Zoe's bed. "If you want me to clear this place and tell people not to call in for a while, just say the word. I don't want you to think you have to leave."

"Thanks, Cha, but right now I think I need to go home. I need to succumb to this thing. Not the cancer, I fully intend fighting that every step of the way, but I just don't have any energy left over to keep everything else going. Do you understand?"

As Charlie threw her arms around Zoe's neck and hugged her beloved twin, she wished with all her heart that she could understand the first thing of what Zoe was going through, but deep down she was flailing. Her sister was slowly melting away. This sore and frightened girl was not the person she'd grown up with.

"You fight, darling Zoe." Charlie held her face in her hands. "You beat this bastard and you show the world that you can win. You hear me? I can't imagine being in this world without you, so don't you even think about making me try."

"I'm trying, Charlie. Trust me, I'm trying."

Charlie helped her to the car with her bag and she was able to drive the short distance to her parents' house. Phoning ahead, she warned her parents she was on the way.

"That's perfect, darling. Your bed is all ready, see you shortly." Her dad was always so delighted to see either herself or Charlie. His voice always lifted when he knew it was one of them on the phone. As she drove up the driveway, he was at the open front door, as if waiting to welcome royalty.

He scooped up her bags and helped her inside.

"I'm glad you've come home for a bit, love. Mum and I didn't want to invade your privacy, but we'd be so much happier if you'd let us mind you for a little while. Just until you feel stronger. You'll get through this, Zoe." He hugged her.

As she lay in her queen-sized bed, looking up at the high ceiling of her old bedroom, she felt more able to relax. It was almost as if returning to her childhood surroundings had taken some of the pressure off her.

The intricate cornicing of the ceiling was about as much visual stimulation as she could take. The white rose centre, with the crystal chandelier suspended from it, was kind of hypnotising. The shards of coloured light, which cast tiny fairy rainbows across the ceiling and onto the flowery Laura Ashley wallpaper, all soothed her.

The familiar smell of her mother's washing powder, and the sense of enveloped stillness only a big old house can possess, all washed over her. Right now, she needed to be a little girl again. She needed to be minded.

The next morning, when she woke up, the dreaded feeling had hit her. She knew the pattern that the chemotherapy took now. She'd have her treatment on a Monday – by Thursday, she was floored. It was like the drugs had finally travelled through every vein in her body and made it to her tissue and nerve endings.

She was exhausted beyond belief. The thought of having to get out of bed to even go to the bathroom was dreadful. It would take her half an hour to push herself and swing her legs out of the bed and make her way down the hall to go to the loo. While she was up, she'd make herself stand in the shower. At least, she mused, her arms were beginning to loosen up which meant she was again able to wash her own hair. But, as Sod's Law would have it, now that she was able to stretch to scrub her hair, it had begun to fall out from the chemotherapy.

* * *

Zoe waved to her mum as she drove off. Taking a deep breath, she walked purposefully into the hospital. The day unit where she had her chemotherapy was actually quite nice. Well, as nice as a room where people's veins are shot with poison could be expected to be. The chairs were soft cream leather, with little tables stuck on to them, which swivelled around so you could put your magazine or book on them. A little bit like first class on the train.

The staff were so friendly and kind, they made the process as easy as possible.

"Hi, Zoe, how are you feeling today? I love your dress, it's a fab colour on you. I can never wear red, I just look like a cranberry, with this tummy and this arse." The nurse wobbled her bits with a sod-that look on her face. "Grab yourself a seat and we'll organise for your bloods to be taken and your cannula to be put in."

Within minutes, Zoe had been offered coffee and a warm scone, with tiny mouse's pots of jam and cream to accompany it. Just as she was finishing her scone and coffee, the phlebotomist called her.

"Zoe Clarke? Can you come this way with me?" she said, smiling. She was wearing a pristine uniform, with flawless make-up and lip-gloss.

"I reckon you are all picked for your looks in this place," Zoe lowered herself into the chair. Her limbs were still stiff and sore from the dermatomyositis, although it did seem to be improving from the chemotherapy.

The nurse was quick and deft at inserting the needle into Zoe's vein. Looking out the window, and humming slightly, Zoe took a deep breath and held it.

"Now a small pinch here, pet." She pricked her skin.

Zoe felt the now-familiar prickling followed by a dull hot rushing sensation as the needle entered her vein.

"Well done, Zoe, you're a great patient," the girl smiled, after she drew three vials of blood for testing. When the procedure was over, she attached a valve and a small tube, which the chemotherapy would later be dripped through. "Okay, pet, you go back into the day unit and I'll send your bloods off to be analysed. We should have the results in about forty minutes or an hour."

"Thank you." Zoe roused herself from the chair. The chemotherapy was making the pain in her limbs and the rash better, but my God did it suck the life out of her!

She made her way back into the oncology day unit. As she sat back in her chair, she decided she'd push it back, raise the foot rest and have a snooze.

"Hello, God bless, how are you? Nice to see you. Isn't it terrible that we're all stuck in here?" A man with missing teeth and nutty-professor-type unruly hair the texture of wire wool, was perching uncomfortably on the edge of his seat, leaning towards her.

Bloody marvellous, Zoe thought. This is all I need, a mad old git who lives with his cats and has nobody to talk to, so he'll want to tell me about fighting in the war and how tea used to be rationed.

"Father Jimmy, pleased to make your acquaintance." He stuck out a hand, which looked like it had been covered in lizard skin, doused in salt and left to dry in the sun.

"Zoe. Hello." She didn't smile or make eye contact. She really couldn't take all the bless-us-and-save us talk right at that moment. Her frosty reception seemed to work at first. She sat back in the chair and opened one of her many magazines. She was becoming an expert on who dated or hated who and what each celebrity ate for lunch. Keeping the magazine high up so as to cover her face, she used it like a shield. That was successful at first. She became kind of dopey due to the heat of the day unit, so she allowed herself to slip into a little sleep.

The millisecond she opened her eyes, Father Jimmy was eagerly staring in her direction. He looked like a puppy who'd been locked in a cupboard all day on its own, and had just been let out.

"Do you feel better after your little sleep?" He moved his seat on casters over towards her.

Inwardly, Zoe sighed. Piss off, I don't do ageing loony priests. Please just bugger off and talk to another bible-basher-type person.

Someone who'd love to discuss the Gospel, and how it relates to everyday life. I'm not in the mood. I'm busy having cancer here. Not only that, but I'm kind of trying to be in pain at the same time. Give me a break!

"I feel pretty tired all the time at the moment, but that's the nature of the beast, isn't it?"

Zoe tried to grab another magazine, but like a sprint athlete Father Jimmy jumped in there, trying to start up afresh.

"I feel terrible most of the time myself. To be honest with you, it's making me question my faith. Are you religious, Zoe? Do you believe?" His eyes were flitting and slightly panic-stricken.

Oh flaming Nora, you've got to be kidding! Zoe stared at him as if he'd just asked her to have sex with him.

"Pardon?"

"Do you believe in God? It's just, I wonder why we're going through all of this. It doesn't seem fair, does it? What do you think? I can't voice my thoughts at home. The other priests are all being so positive and keep encouraging me every step of the way. They reassure me that God will look after me. But look at me. I've lost stones in weight, I'm the colour of custard and I can't even eat as much as a four-year-old child. I can't face a drink of whiskey, which used to be my favourite thing in the world. I can't say Mass, as I'm too tired and all the congregation coughing on me is too risky, what with the infection thing." He held his hands up as if to say: I just give up!

"Em, I don't really give the whole God thing much thought," said Zoe. "At least I didn't until someone I know died recently. I didn't know her terribly well. We met at one of the cancer support groups. Since she died, I've been scared. At night-time when I'm lying in my bed and it's dark and still, sometimes I feel her in the room. I even talk to her. I ask her if she's okay. I actually think she wants me to do something for her, but I don't know what." Zoe looked at him to see if he was backing away, pointing and shouting, "Loony-on-the-loose!"

"She might be trying to tell you something. You need to pray to God and to her. You will get an answer, my child." He did a blinky, bowing-head thing that all priests seem to have instilled in them.

"Well, if you think that, then why can't you apply that logic to your own head?"

"I know – you'd think I would, wouldn't you? But that's just it. I can't. Every time I think I have it sussed and I'm sure God is minding me, I get the fear. This terrible gripping hand of ice around my heart, which makes me feel tingly with panic and fright. I feel like I can't get enough air, and then I have this overwhelming sense that God is not on my side. Do you think He's trying to tell me something?"

"I used to feel like that too, but it's gone now." Zoe picked at her nails as she spoke.

"How did you get your faith back?" Poor Father Jimmy leaned even closer.

Zoe recoiled. *Christ, back off there, what are you going to do? Try and sit on my knee next?* "No, I asked Dr Leah for something to calm my nerves. So I take Xanax twice a day at the moment. It's bloody great stuff. You should ask if you can have some too. All that feeling of panic goes away. I take sleeping pills too. It helps to fluff off the hard edges, then you have this knock-out, unconscious sleep at the end of it all. When they take you into the consultation room for your how-are-you chat, ask for some drugs."

He nodded, with his eyes a bit wide and his mouth open. She knew she was probably being a bit cold and mean, but she really didn't feel in a position to be a counsellor right now. She'd enough of her own shit to deal with, without trying to pluck God out of the sky and make him soothe a doubtful priest.

The nurse came over to talk to her.

"Now, Zoe. Your bloods are actually a little bit on the low side today. We will go ahead and give you the chemotherapy, but we might have to organise for you to get some injections in the coming weeks. You can administer them yourself at home, or you can pop in here and we will do them for you. Whatever suits you."

"Okay." Zoe felt a bit excited at the thought of giving herself injections. It would be a bit like being a nurse or even a junkie. Fantastic.

"We'll cross that bridge when we come to it."

Zoe had never been a pill-popper before now. She wasn't even into taking loads of painkillers when she had a hang-over. Now she had done a full three-sixty on the drugs front, what with the chemotherapy, Xanax, sleeping pills, heavy-duty pain medication, injections and a bucket-load of laxatives.

The laxatives were a must. Seemingly chemotherapy did one of two things to the bowel. It either made you shit through the eye of a needle or else it plugged you like a cork. In Zoe's case, she had spent six days in a row, sitting on the toilet, pushing harder than if she was giving birth, only to produce a single turd the size of a rabbit-dropping.

"Charlie, all this food is going in and there's nothing coming out," she'd told her twin. "What if I just blow up?"

"That's so gross, Zoe. You shouldn't be discussing your poo with me or anyone else for that matter. Just in case you think it's normal, it's not," Charlie tried to sound cross, but a faint smile was forming on her face.

"Listen, Charlie, anything I used to think was normal has well passed by now. You'd be talking about poo too if you hadn't done one in six days. I feel like I've drunk a bucket of cement. It's horrendous. To add to it all, when I do manage to go, there's blood in it."

"Okay, that's enough, Zoe. Twins or not, I can't talk about blood-infested shite. Next you're going to tell me you have worms. That's too gross. Now I'll be thinking about that all night. I'm going to have dreams about your bum and what it can and can't produce. Nasty. Now please, button it, before I vomit."

"That could be an idea, to puke that is. Would that make me feel better? I feel like I'm two years pregnant. Look at my belly." Zoe prodded her tummy.

Charlie had to admit, it was kind of like Play-Doh.

That had been two weeks ago. When Zoe had come in for the last treatment, the nurses had questioned her all about her bowel habits. Luckily they'd been very interested in her poo. They had a word for the whole process: "motions". They'd even given her tablets to take. One to soften the stools (the medical word for poo) and one to make it come the hell out of there. The relief of not being bunged up was euphoric.

"You've no idea how excited I am about being able to go to the toilet! I feel like I lost half a stone in one sitting," Zoe told the nurse.

"Well, it's good news all round, because your bowel can't stay healthy if it's not working. It also causes more nausea if you can't keep that food going through. So it's really important you stay on top of it all. What about the water works? Are you managing to pass water easily and without burning?" The nurse was ready to tick another box.

"Yes, that's all fine, no burning or anything."

Christ, if someone had told Zoe a year ago that she'd be sitting here with a nurse talking gleefully about her toilet habits in detail, she'd have died of embarrassment.

At least she was in a position to be embarrassed, she mused. Every time she thought all the drugs and hospital stuff were getting to her, she thought of poor Tanya.

"What do you think about the scalp cooler? Will you go for it again on this round of chemotherapy?" The nurse waited patiently for Zoe's answer.

Snapping out of her thoughts of Tanya, Alfie and baby Jenny, Zoe tried to focus on the matter in hand.

She'd endured that scalp cooling once, but she'd made a decision, she couldn't bear to do it again. It was so horribly uncomfortable and restricting, and the clamping tightness of the under-chin strap left her jaw feeling bruised and sore. She'd never have believed she'd choose to let her hair fall out, but that's exactly what she'd opted for.

"I can't bear that snowball on my head again. I'll just take my chances and see if I lose the hair," she'd told the nurse, as she wheeled the machine towards her.

"Are you sure, Zoe? The drugs you are on are not the worst offenders for alopecia, but there are no guarantees and I'd hate you to regret it in a few months."

The nurses were so kind yet firm. They also treated her like an adult. They made sure she was fully aware of what was going on, and kept her informed of all her options at all times.

"No, I can get a wig if I have to. I've always thought I'd like a pale sugar-pink bob, but never wanted to put my own hair through all that. This could be my chance to experiment."

Having both cancer and dermatomyositis was pretty hard to deal with. Zoe was already swollen and green-complexioned. Adding being bald to the mix was just another happening. She kept waiting for it to matter hugely, the getting bald thing. But it quite simply didn't. Nobody could have convinced her before that moment that losing her hair wouldn't bother her. But in the greater scheme of things, faced with a choice of being dead, or alive and bald, well, there was no contest.

\* \* \*

As the treatments went on, she lost more and more hair. By treatment number three, after she'd moved back home, and into her childhood comfort zone, she took one more step towards being the baby she thought she'd grown up from. In all their baby photos, herself and Charlie were as bald as coots. No mops of hair or even sprigs at the front of their heads for Diana to clip a little bow onto. Not a screed.

They'd suggested to her in the hospital that she cut her hair short, to soften the blow of losing it.

"It may even help to salvage it for a little bit longer, as long hair obviously weighs more, so a shorter style may help."

She'd understood the theory but, although it was probably sensible, she couldn't bring herself to cut her hair. She'd prefer it to be either the way she wanted it, or not there at all.

The morning that she'd decided she'd had enough of her stringy hair, she had stooped in the shower and leaned her cheek against the coldness of the tiled wall for comfort. A large frond of hair, saturated by water, loosened itself from her scalp and plopped onto her foot. Peering down at it, she tentatively raised her stiff arm up to touch the side of her temple from where the clump of hair had fallen. A strange feeling came over her. It wasn't anger and it certainly wasn't fear. She turned off the water and stepped out of the shower. Patting herself dry, she pulled on a towelling bathrobe and made her way into her parents' bathroom. Rummaging on the shelf, she found her father's electric razor, housed in a black zip-around pouch. Up until a few years ago, he'd sported a tightly shaved haircut, but Diana had always objected to it.

"Steven, you look like you're shaving your head because you're bald. You have enough hair to do three men. Most men of your age would be thrilled to have your thatch. All it needs is a bit of *Grecian 2000* and you'd look ten years younger." Always looking for a quiet life and eager to please his Princess Diana he'd eventually conceded and allowed his hair to grow. Now he was marched off to Brown Thomas to have his hair "done" every four weeks. Although he had zero interest in his tresses, it had become a nice day out for himself and Diana. They'd take in a leisurely lunch and have a look around the luxurious store.

Zoe fumbled through the different fittings of the shaver. Blowing away the small particles of hair that had stuck in the head of the machine, she made her way back to her own bathroom. Plugging the two-pronged plug in, she willed the razor to work. As it buzzed into life, she felt a little excited. The reluctance of her muscles to move was going to make this job difficult. But, hey, who said shaving your own head was supposed to be easy?

The large portion of hair which had freed itself in the shower had revealed a circular white patch on her head. No hair band was going to hide this. Leaning the heel of her hand on the sink for support, she raised the other arm to the front of her forehead. Starting at the middle of her fringe, she gouged a line right down the centre of her head. A bit like a ploughed field. The pale grey downy surface which she'd revealed made her gasp.

She'd made a complete hames of her head now, so she might as well keep going. All it took was half a dozen more strokes of the razor and she was bald. Not shiny-headed, but kind of like a little grey baby bird. Her hair lay listless in the sink. As she picked it up and let it flutter through her fingers, she was amazed at how light it was. The thinning had obviously been more severe than she had thought.

Scooping it all into a ball, she shoved it in the plastic bag which lined the white plastic bin.

"Zoe? Are you alright, love?"

Her mother's voice penetrated her thoughts and made her jump. She was cast right back to early childhood, with a feeling of trapped panic. Except as a child she'd have been worried about getting caught for stealing biscuits from the tin or mushing up one of her mum's good lipsticks. This one was a little different.

"Mum, can you sit on the bed in my room? I'm coming out now," Zoe spoke slowly and clearly.

"Zoe?" Diana couldn't hide the fear in her voice. "Is everything okay, pet?"

As Zoe creaked open the heavy cream panelled door of the bathroom, Diana was standing right there. Her eyes widened and her hands flew to her face.

"Oh sweetheart, what have you done?" Diana's hands shook as she pulled her daughter towards her. Sobbing and rocking her, Diana thought her heart was going to burst through her chest. Her beautiful little girl looked like a starved concentration-camp victim. Her chestnut eyes looked too big for her face, the shadow of where her lovely glossy hair used to lie making her look like she'd a layer of sand stuck to her scalp.

"It was all falling out. A big clump fell on my leg in the shower. I wanted to do it." Zoe looked at her apologetically.

"Okay, sweetheart. I'm sorry, it's just a shock at first. Oh sweet Jesus, you're so brave, do you know that?" Diana raised her hand and touched her child's bald head. Much to her surprise it was soft on the surface yet very bony underneath as it was so close to her skull. It was warm and fuzzy, just like when she'd been a baby.

"You actually have a nice-shaped head." Diana looked around the back, sniffing loudly. "No mad lumps or bumps sticking out anywhere, which is lucky I suppose."

"It's okay, Mum, Sinéad O'Connor I certainly am not. I don't think I can carry off the no-hair look. Will you bring me into the wig shop? I don't want to go around being a neon sign for cancer. I ain't doing the headscarf thing, nor am I doing the baseball cap with no hair underneath. I do think I'd like to try some new looks though. What do you think?"

"I think you're strong and amazing and, whatever you want to do, I'll support you, sweetheart. What would you suggest doing right at this moment?" Diana looked alarmed. "I have a couple of Hermes scarves – would you like to tie one on?"

"It's okay, Mum, I'm not going out to the shops like this – I'll put on a hat or something. I wonder should we phone the wig place and see if I need an appointment? They gave me the name of a shop off Grafton Street, at the hospital. I'll call them. My head is bloody freezing, I hope the wigs help with the cold." Zoe marched off to find the number and grab a hat.

Diana stood rooted to the spot. Never in her wildest imagination had she ever dreamed she'd have to look at one of her girls bald. She felt physically ill. It was the biggest punch in the stomach she could imagine. There were moments since Zoe's diagnosis where she'd felt like the walls were closing in on her. Like there was nothing good about the world. Why would God do this to her precious daughter? Not for the first time, Diana wished she'd been the one given the cancer instead. At least she'd lived more of her life. Fair enough, she was only fifty-five, and was certainly not ready for the scrapheap, but if the cards had to be dealt, why had the Ace of Destruction been put in front of Zoe?

She couldn't even bear to visit the whole thought process of what she'd feel if Zoe died. Herself and Steven had only had that conversation once, the day she'd been diagnosed. As they lay in bed that evening, Steven had stared straight ahead and spoken like a hypontised robot.

"She's not going to die, Diana, is she?"

"No, of course not." Diana hadn't meant to sound so menacing. But he was uttering the unmentionable. It was the big elephant in the room. They'd both remained silent for the longest time. The noise of the immersion switching off in the hot press was the only sound in their now empty Georgian house. Before the girls had moved out, there was always music blaring from somewhere. Or a TV left on in a room, with the mixed smells of shower gel, perfume, hairspray and nail polish wafting through the house. The landline rarely rang anymore.

Before the girls had gone, they'd had two lines to accommodate all the calls. Then, knowing it was futile paying rent on two numbers, they'd cancelled the second and the main line now remained mostly silent. In the beginning, they'd both found it so odd, being in their own home. They had to get used to living like that again.

"I'm a bit nervous, to be honest," Diana had confessed to Steven. "We haven't been on our own in this house before. We moved in when the girls were two. It's a big hunk of a house, it's meant to buffer noise and constant movement. Should we sell up and buy a sensible bungalow or a trendy apartment?" She'd bitten her Botoxed lip. *Better not do that, I might chew right through it and end up in casualty having it sewn back together*, she mused.

"I don't want to live in a dog box, just because the kids don't live here anymore. Why can't we just adapt and live here and enjoy having privacy and space? Is it illegal to have lots of rooms when you're just a couple?"

"No, but you know what I mean? It's just strange, isn't it?"

Diana hadn't known at the time that Zoe would be back, albeit temporarily. Like a cyclone following her daughter, as soon as she'd become ensconced again, the phone had jumped back to life. The wafts of shower gel were back. The music and TV hubbub were back. Not that they sat in silence and didn't have showers, but this was different. Young people arrived at the door again. Flowers and cards began to flood in. Although the situation was scary and their worst nightmare realised, having Zoe home, just for a loan, was fabulous in a selfish kind of way.

It was like they were being given a little gift, just for a short time. After the spell of her moving away to start her own life, they were being given a small window, where they could play Mummy and Daddy again. It was bittersweet at its best. Though both Diana and Steven willed their daughter's health to return, they were thrilled to be allowed to baby her again, even for a short time.

As she spritzed herself with perfume and pulled on a jacket, Diana heard Zoe call her.

"I'm in my room, darling, coming now!" she answered.

Zoe was standing in the downstairs hall, with a little fluffy beanie hat pulled onto her head. Wearing a tight fitting Juicy tracksuit and her favourite Abercrombie denim jacket, with a little red corsage on the lapel, she looked gorgeous. About twelve years of age, but beautiful.

"You look so lovely, honey, all set?" Diana stifled the urge to lie on the floor and thump her fists and kick her legs at the unfairness of it all. She wanted to curse like a tinker and fly around the hallway in a fit of rage, smashing mirrors and pictures and anything that got in her way. Why was her daughter standing here bald waiting to go wig-shopping?

Instead, she smiled and swallowed and opened the front door.

\* \* \*

As they entered the wig shop a short time later, Zoe wasn't sure if it was to make the clients feel comfortable or whether the girl was just zany, but the person who greeted them was outrageous – with a Mohawk of bubblegum-pink, nylon-looking hair and a haircut which would almost make you wish to be bald, shaved on one side and long and black on the other, every inch of her face pierced, and false eyelashes.

"Hiya. Come on in, how's-it-going?" She smiled to reveal a whole mouth of junk. From gold-covered teeth to jewels stuck on, she looked like she needed to brush her teeth with a spanner at nighttime.

Well, no matter what I put on my head, I won't look that scary, Zoe thought.

"Hello there, I'm Zoe, I spoke to you on the phone earlier." She hung in the doorway nervously, linking her mother's arm. Eyes darting, she took in the white porcelain heads sporting wigs. Long ones, short ones, dark ones, coloured ones, sparkly dressing-up ones, braided ones with hats attached. They had them all.

"I'm Baz, come on in. Have a wander around and tell me what you're thinking of. Hiya," she smiled and waved at Diana.

"Hello, I'm Diana, Zoe's mum."

"Yeah, guessed that. She's a ringer for you. Feel free to try stuff on, both of you. Some funky stuff here if you're having a bad hair day yourself, Diana," she nodded towards a purple *Addam's Family* type one.

"Eh, yes, thank you, em, Baz." Diana tried not to look like she was being asked to lick dog-poo, but that was exactly how she felt. The place was not her cup of tea, but Zoe seemed happy enough, and that was the main thing.

After a few minutes' browsing, they went to a small area at the back of the shop. Baz pulled a dark curtain around them and turned on the lights at the dressing table. She explained that the wigs started at around 200.

"That's for a synthetic one. The real hair ones are a lot more pricey, but they last longer and you'll be able to brush, style and wash them. Did you want a long or short one?" After she spoke, she chomped on the bar through her tongue, making a clunking noise, which then clicked off her teeth. Diana couldn't look at her – she kept imagining the metal slitting the girl's tongue in half and shooting on to the floor.

"I don't know, my own hair was kind of mid-length and light brown, but I might try a couple of different looks," Zoe mused, seemingly oblivious to the other girl's chomping and alternative appearance.

The first wig she tried felt like a sieve on her head with steel wool attached. It also sat just shy of the crown of her head without engulfing it, so there was a little hump at the top giving a slight cone-head effect.

"That looks like road kill. There's no way I would be able to walk around like this!" Zoe laughed out loud.

Diana thought she was going to vomit. Tears pricked her eyes. None of this was in any way amusing to her. She felt the bile churning in her stomach. A large part of her wanted to flee the room. Sweat began to bead on her forehead. Why were they having to experience this living hell? How did other people get through this kind of thing and remain sane?

"Mum? What do you think of this one?" Zoe was tipping her head to the side and posing with a big grin on her face. She'd put on a Doris Day candy-floss-pink bob. It made her already pale complexion look milk-bottle white. Her dark eyes looked like little craters in the earth, peeping out of the gaunt fuzzy cloud.

"Well, I suppose it's a bit of fun, isn't it? What do you think, lovie?" She didn't want to say the wrong thing but she hated it. It was clearly a wig. It was crass and cheap-looking and it screamed sickness at her. But Zoe probably saw it in a different light, so she didn't want to crush her.

"I know I'm a bit anaemic-looking in it right now, especially as it clashes with the red rash on my cheeks, but with a good lashing of make-up for going out, it's a bit of skit, isn't it?" Zoe's glassy eyes danced for the first time in weeks, the sense of young fun glinting through for the first time in way too long. She put her two hands up and waved them around, giggling with Baz.

The spectacle made Diana choke with emotion. "It's great, Zoe, let's take it. How about a couple of day-to-day ones as well?" Diana deserved an Oscar for her performance. The knife of grief and pain was twisting round and around in her gut, watching her darling daughter make light of this hideous situation. Not for the first time, she thanked God for the miracle of Botox. *Freeze my emotion and keep the heartache inside. Let it growl and dig and don't let my child see I'm dying in here,* she begged.

"Oooh, that's a good one," Zoe leaned forward and looked at the short, feathered-around-her-face light-brown crop. It made her look a bit less corpsy too, which was good. She felt this one would be a good warm colour for the days she looked like shit. "It helps with the make-up thing too. It's really hard to put on make-up when you're bald. Where do you stop? I was there earlier trying to put on foundation, and I was kind of sweeping the brush higher and higher. Christ, I thought I'd have to paint my whole skull and neck! How does Sinéad O'Connor manage to look so beautiful with no hair? She must have flawless skin." Zoe giggled.

Baz was brilliant. She pulled out drawer after drawer of wigs. Much to Diana's astonishment she was very clued in too. She'd obviously been working with wigs a long time and knew her stuff.

It took a good two hours before they settled on two made from real hair and the pale-pink synthetic one which made Zoe so happy.

"Now here's the bad news, I'm afraid. These don't come cheap. Do you have health insurance? You can claim a bit of the money back." Baz fished out a form to show them. "If you fill this in at the end of the year, they'll give you a few quid back."

The bill came to over two thousand euro. Diana handed her credit card over.

"What do people *do* if they don't have the money?" Zoe asked, shocked.

"They do have a system in the public hospitals where they give you a certain allowance as far as I know, but you wouldn't be getting three and they wouldn't cover the real hair ones," Baz shrugged.

Zoe was so grateful that she had health insurance. It meant she was in a private hospital for her treatment and now, due to her parents' funds, she was able to have these wigs. It stung her to the core that other people weren't as fortunate as her. For them, they couldn't simply decide they didn't want to go around in a headscarf or a baseball cap. They probably had no choice. If you didn't have a couple of grand knocking about spare, what else would you do?

"Cancer really is a bastard, isn't it?" she said. "Apart from the fear attached to the disease, you have to deal with the realities of the treatment. Here's another potential smack in the chops: if you've no money, you have to go around either bald as a coot or looking like you've a dead animal on your head. Where's the justice in that?" Zoe felt like crying.

"It's shite alright. I've never lost my hair luckily enough, but I have to say it must cut like a knife." Baz leaned on the counter. "You're very brave. When did your hair fall out?"

"Some fell out this morning, so I shaved the rest," Zoe shrugged.

"Fuck me, that's rough. Well, I think you're bloody deadly. I hope it grows back soon and for now, if you've any problems with your syrups," Baz said, using the Cockney rhyming slang 'syrup of figs' for the word wig, "give me a bell. Here, I'll throw in some special shampoo and conditioner for them. Just steep them in a sink and rinse them in cool water every five to six weeks – if you wash them too often they'll look matted."

Diana was puzzled how a girl with such odd hair could feel so passionately about her daughter being bald. Right at that moment, given the choice of having her hairstyle or Zoe's, she'd be hard pushed to make a choice.

"Thank you, Baz, you're so kind," she said. "Thanks for your time and advice too. I really appreciate it."

Zoe waved to Baz as they left the shop. She'd kept the short dark one on. Walking onto Grafton Street for the first time, in a wig, Zoe felt kind of vulnerable at first.

"Do you think everyone knows it's a wig?" she whispered to her mum.

"No, lovie, it looks great on you. I doubt anyone would cop it." Diana glanced sideways at her as they walked. She wasn't lying as such. Maybe a general passer-by wouldn't realise. But she really couldn't comment. In her own psyche, all she could see was her daughter's bald head. That image would take a very long time to fade from her mind.

As she walked down the street, people milled about, shoved past and bustled on. Zoe realised that the whole world wasn't looking at her head. The wind filtered through the mesh under the fake hair. Although it was of course warmer than having nothing on, she was surprised at how bare her head still felt. She'd have to invest in some hats to keep her warm. This was only September for crying out loud – when the winter set in she'd be frozen.

"How do bald men not perish? This is really cold," she shivered.

But by the time they'd had a bowl of soup and a coffee, Zoe was roasting. Her head was also getting really itchy. Not wanting to shove her fingers under the wig and frighten the living shit out of the other diners, she had to make do with digging her fingers into the wig at intervals in a makeshift needling sort of fashion.

"Zoe, what are you doing, lovie? You look like a monkey picking at your head. What's wrong?" Diana whispered, horrified.

"Jesus, it's so itchy. It's like I've got little balls of Aran-jumper type wool nipping at my head all over. *Fuuuuuck*, it makes me want to dribble it's so annoying. How am I going to get used to this? I wonder is it like breaking in a new pair of shoes? Will my head skin get tougher and the wig get softer? This is torture. We'll have to go

212

home, Mum. I have to get this off." Zoe looked like she was going to rub her head along the sofa she was sitting on.

Diana flagged the waiter and paid the bill.

As they were sitting in the car going home, Zoe couldn't bear the feeling like live nits on her scalp, so she pulled the wig off. Sinking into the car seat, she scratched her head and her eyes rolled with the sheer bliss of it all.

"Oh that feels so good, you've no idea," she purred.

As they pulled away at the traffic lights, Diana clocked the man in the car beside them looking stunned. "Zoe, look at the poor devil, I'd say he'll never be the same again."

The other cars were beeping at him as he sat frozen to the spot in the car, mouth agape in pure shock.

"The poor creature was minding his own business as his gaze drifted towards us. He actually jumped with fright as you scratched your head and then all your hair came off in one quick flick. Sorry, love, I know it's terrible, but he looks like he'll need therapy to get over that!" Diana squealed.

Zoe and Diana belly-laughed the whole way home. Even in times of extreme sorrow, laughter was truly the best medicine.

# 20

*Help me out, Tanya, I need your strength and support.*
*I don't know how to make it through the days without*
*you.*

Alfie was using Tanya's pink notebook almost as a method for speaking to her. He knew it was silly, but he felt that writing in it helped him to feel closer to her. He was beginning to dread the evening time. As soon as it got dark, the demons came out. He'd never been scared of the dark as a child, so this whole phenomenon was new to him. As September moved into October the dark came earlier. Alfie felt fine during the daylight. Jenny was there, making constant noise and chatting to him. He had stopped putting her in her cot for a midday sleep. Instead, he'd put her in the buggy and take her for a walk, or even let her sleep in the car for a while, rather than be alone. As the days passed, he kept hoping it would get easier, that the deafening silence and the hard pain in his chest might ease.

The fear of the dark was now beginning to get to him. He could see images and hear voices whispering to him as the shadows invaded his very being. At times he would imagine Tanya walking in the door so vividly that he'd hear the sound of her keys jangling in the front door as he put Jenny in the bath. In the middle of the night, as he tried to sleep, he'd forget she was gone and reach his arm out to drape over her. As he connected with the cold mattress, he'd sit up, sweating and terrified. Her face would dance in front of his eyes like a twisted cartoon in the dark. So, he'd taken to sleeping with the light on.

In the beginning he'd taken Jenny into his bed with him, but his tossing and turning was waking her up, so she'd be cranky and rubbing her eyes all the next day. He knew the toddler needed her own bed and her usual routine. It wasn't fair to make her suffer any more than she had to. She'd adapted so well to Mummy going away. But she still asked for Tanya, especially when she was playing in the bath in the evening. That used to be the time Mummy would come home.

"Mama home soon?" she'd ask with her little eyebrows raised hopefully.

"No, honey. Mama has gone to be a star in the sky. She's shining down and minding us from way up high," he'd respond.

Her little face would look crushed and the room would go silent, as her round blue eyes would search his for a reason for all this.

"I'm sorry, baby girl. I wish I could make Mama come back, but she had to go away. She didn't want to, but she had to. But Dada is here and he's going to mind Jenny and we're going be happy, isn't that right?" His nose burned and his eyes peppered as he tried to keep a handle on his emotions. He knew Jenny didn't even begin to understand where Tanya had gone. But he couldn't fathom it either, so how could she?

He knew there was a counselling group he could go to, which was supposed to be very helpful, but he couldn't bring himself to attend. It would also mean asking Tanya's mother to mind Jenny. He couldn't do that either. He wasn't able to let her out of his sight. She was like his life-line. It was as if she held the strings to his very soul. Without the crutch of having to carry on for his daughter, he knew he'd have curled into a ball and expired by now.

As he walked towards the shopping centre one Thursday morning, the heavens opened. Pulling the clear plastic rain-cover over Jenny's buggy, he began to run.

"Weeeeeee, run Dada, run!" Jenny kicked her legs in delight, loving the speed.

Feeling mentally wrung out, he decided to go to the coffee shop and have a cappuccino and get Jenny a hot chocolate. At least it would be full of people and it would kill half an hour. Unfortunately every other person within a ten-mile radius had the same plan. The queue snaked the full length of Starbucks and out the door. He was just about to turn around and go somewhere else, when he heard his name being called. Spinning around, he focused near the top of the line and saw Zoe waving tentatively at him.

Apologising to the other customers, he squeezed the buggy through the throng of wet people.

"Hi, Zoe, how are you?" he smiled.

"I'm good – how are you, more to the point?"

"Okay, you know yourself," he shrugged.

"I'm on my own and I'd love you to join me if that suits. Can I get you something? Hi, Jenny!" She bent down and stroked the baby's cheek.

"Hiya! Who's that, Dada?" Jenny turned around in the buggy to ask him.

"That's Zoe. Will we have hot chocolate with her?"

"And cake," she nodded furiously.

"You see if you can bags a seat and I'll get the drinks," said Zoe. "What do you want?"

He placed his order and manoeuvred the buggy towards a clump of tables. The place was packed and he wasn't the only one waiting for a space. An elderly couple gave him the nod – he was always amazed how nice people were when he had Jenny with him. It was like a small child was a swift pass to a seat. By the time he made his way over, got Jenny free of the buggy and settled at the table Zoe joined them with a tray of goodies.

"Here we go! God, I need this. I'm so tired at the moment, if I didn't have a coffee habit I'd be in hibernation."

She unloaded the tray and Alfie set up a chocolate muffin for Jenny, while sliding the bulk of the hot stuff away from her grasp. Then he quickly fixed up some hot chocolate for her, adding some milk to cool it down.

Zoe eased herself into the chair. Alfie noticed she was restricted in her movement as she lowered herself onto the seat.

"How are you doing? You seem to be stiff," he said, concerned.

"Oh, a little better than I was," she answered lightly.

"That's good to hear," he said as he sipped his hazelnut mocha. "This is delicious, thank you. I was about to leave when I saw the queue. This little lady doesn't have the patience to wait for too long. By the time I'd get the stuff, she'd be bored and acting up."

"Gosh, you're welcome. It's nice to have some company, isn't it, Jenny?" She smiled at the little girl who was silently busy as she shovelled little mouse-sized handfuls of muffin into her mouth.

Zoe told Alfie all about the chemotherapy and how she'd moved home for the time being. She told him all the news she could think of, from the wig-shopping to her last visit to the cancer support centre. She knew she wanted to ask him how he was getting on, but seeing as she didn't actually *know* the guy, she felt she should let him bring it up, just in case it upset him too much.

"Well, I hope you continue to feel better," he said. "You're having a pretty rough time. Chemotherapy is no picnic, is it? For the record, the wig is amazing. I wouldn't have known it's not your own hair. I thought you'd just had it cut. But having said that, I'm only a man," he smiled.

His eyes were so sad it made Zoe want to hug him. She could see he was making a huge effort to be upbeat and normal. His shoulders were hunched and he looked exhausted. He'd got very thin too. The strain and grief was palpable.

"How are you doing?" she asked tentatively, lowering her eyes to concentrate on her plate, so he wouldn't feel under pressure.

"I'm alright. Not great, to be honest. But there's no instruction manual you can follow after someone passes away. I wish there was a set of rules to comply with, even if it wasn't easy, a formula would be so much better than the empty uncontrollable pain. I'm sorry, Zoe, you don't need to sit counselling anybody at the moment. You've enough to cope with." He wrung his hands in the scrunched-up napkin on his lap. Crossing his legs, he sat back from the table and glanced around the café agitatedly, his foot hopping up and down.

"Believe me, Alfie, I am glad to talk to you. I'm so sick of talking about myself and cancer and dermatomyositis. No matter what the subject, so long as it's not about me, I'm happy to go there. I keep thinking about her too, you know? I didn't know her for long, but she made a huge impact on me. I still can't actually believe she's gone. We had a meeting the other day at the centre and we were saying what a devastating effect her sudden death has had on us all. I can't imagine what you must be feeling."

The noise in the coffee shop supported the silence which briefly followed. Alfie stared straight ahead of him. His foot still jumping up and down. The little girl was singing a little made-up song as she mushed up her cake and doused it with dribbles of hot chocolate from her straw.

"She knew she was dying, Zoe. That's what's so terrible." He was looking straight ahead, not at Zoe's face.

"Yes, Alfie, but she was very matter of fact about it. She talked to me about it when we'd both had surgery, as I told you. The main thing that concerned her in the whole thing was you. You told me that she didn't want to discuss it with you at length because it made her feel so guilty. She felt you didn't deserve all the hurt she knew she'd have to inflict on you. She was angry and annoyed with herself that she was being forced to leave you and Jenny alone."

"I know," he said softly. He didn't move a muscle. The noise of the other people's chatter milled around him like a soft cloud, enveloping him like a comfort blanket. Zoe's words washed over him, surrounded his head and darted into his brain.

She'd been a funny fish, his girl Tanya. A few years ago she'd left him, saying he should find someone better. He'd of course taken it as meaning that it was his fault. Or that she simply didn't love him enough.

Then they'd discovered she was pregnant with Jenny, and she'd allowed him back in her life. That time, those few weeks of his life without Tanya had been the worse Alfie could imagine.

"We split up for a while, you know? Tanya always told me I should find a nicer person, someone who wanted a brood of kids and could dedicate her life to me. But all I ever wanted was her. Jenny was more than the icing on the cake. Not only did I get a child of my own, but she brought Tanya back to me. I've never felt more desolate or alone than that time when she left me. Even now. At least deep down I know that Tanya didn't *choose* to leave me. She would have stayed if she could. That makes a difference somehow."

Alfie was miles away. Instinctively Zoe reached her hand out and placed it on his for a moment. No words passed between them, but the silence was comfortable.

"I believe," he continued, "that things happen for a reason. During that awful time of separation, I struggled to understand why it was happening. But now I know. It has given me a strange clarity for the here and now. I know Tanya and I were meant to be. Our time just ran out, that's all." He sighed from the depths of his soul.

Zoe wiped her tears and blew her nose. "Sorry, I'm as much use as an ashtray on a motor bike to you here. Don't mind me blubbing." She smiled weakly.

"Sorry, Zoe. You came to have a nice quiet coffee and we land on you and make you cry." He held her gaze. "Thank you," he whispered.

"For what?"

"Letting me talk. For not saying that time will heal all. For crying. That helps, you know? Selfish bastard that I am, it actually makes more sense to me to see you cry when I talk about Tanya. The rest of the world just keeps on turning. It's almost as if her passing didn't make a single dent in the world."

"Of course it did. Tanya's death has affected so many people – don't ever think she isn't missed. I only knew her for a very short time, but let me tell you, she has given me the determination to kick this f'ing disease. I'm doing it for both of us. Tanya didn't get a chance to fight, I have mine and believe me I have no intention of letting this cancer bastard win."

"When I found out from Dr Leah that she'd been terminally ill, that dreadful stabbing pain hit me all over again. In the deep dark recesses of my own soul, I'd always harboured a fear that our love was a tiny bit desperate. That I loved her more than she loved me, you know. But now, when it's too late, I'm positive that she loved me all along. She'd been just too bloody scared to show it. How crazy is that?"

"It's not crazy at all. It's damned sad. But does it make you feel at peace about your relationship at all?" Zoe leaned forward earnestly.

"Yes, in a way." He paused, looking dreadfully saddened. "Do you know, you're right, I need to at least attempt to take a more positive look at it all." He nodded. "In her own way, Tanya was a lot less self-confident than me. Ever since we met, I wore my heart on my sleeve. I was always able to tell her and show her that I loved her utterly. She'd run from her feelings, thinking she didn't deserve to be showered with unconditional affection. But I guess I have closure on all of that if nothing else."

Alfie still couldn't help the bitterness he was longing to quell. What a waste and a shame it was, that they'd been ripped apart. Oddly though, hearing this from Zoe, how much he mattered to her, how much she had shielded him, it helped. He knew he was repeating himself, and probably boring poor Zoe senseless with the conversation, but he *needed* to nail this point in his own head.

"I honestly had no idea she cared that much. She often left me guessing, you know? She was so controlled and sometimes even cold in her approach, if I'm honest. I knew she loved us, because she wouldn't have stayed otherwise. She didn't do anything she didn't want to do. But, there was always that nagging question in my brain that she'd only stayed because she'd become pregnant with Jenny." He bit his lip and exhaled, blowing his cheeks out as he did. "Although there was a sensible voice in my head that reassured me that she wouldn't even have had the baby or come back to me unless she loved me. You couldn't give Tanya advice or persuade her if she didn't want to know."

Zoe listened as she sipped her coffee. She'd bought a coffee slice, which had appealed to her at the counter. But now that she was faced with it, the smell of the sweet icing and the thought of the texture of the cream in her mouth made her recoil. She studied Alfie. He was entirely wrapped up in his own thoughts, so he wasn't aware of her staring. He was certainly not the type of man she would have put Tanya with. He was her polar opposite in fact. She was polished, beautiful, in a shiny-haired, flawless-skinned and snappy-dressed way. She was quite loud when she spoke, and outwardly self-assured. This man was kind of scruffy, what with his messy hair, edging towards being a little too long for tidiness. But his ocean-deep eyes were brimming with feeling. His full lips, surrounded by stubble, gave his thin face a softer finish. He looked like he'd be a great rock star. But instead, he was here in a coffee shop with his baby daughter, quite at home with the role of full-time parent.

"How did you decide to be a full-time dad?" Zoe cocked her head to the side.

"As soon as we knew she was coming along, I offered to mind her. Didn't I, Jenny?" He tweaked her chubby cheek and she grinned at him. "Tanya was all career and business, that's what made her tick. She could do the mummy thing, but only in bursts. Then I'd see her almost physically needing to be Tanya the Businesswoman again." He was matter of fact about it and not in the least bit bitter.

"I have to admit I find that unusual simply because my mum was always at home with us. I've a twin sister, Charlie, and Mum was always there for us as kids. But times have changed and so have parents' roles. I think it's great that you mind Jenny."

They chatted easily for another few minutes. Alfie then looked at his watch and jumped.

"Sugar, we've got to be at Baby Bouncers in ten minutes. I'm so sorry to be rude, Zoe, but we have this little class, which involves a bit of music and climbing and playing for Jenny. She really loves it and it tires her out, so I'd rather not miss it."

"Of course. It was lovely to meet you. Please do give me a call anytime you feel like a chat. As I've said before, I'm not in work at the moment, so unless I'm a couple of days out of chemo, I'm usually able to be around." She shrugged.

"Thanks, Zoe. I really enjoyed chatting to you. I'd love to hook up again soon. I'll try not to moan all the time next time." He instinctively leaned forward and kissed her on the cheek.

221

She smiled at him, then got to her feet and picked up her bag. "Bye-bye, Jenny. See you some time again!" She waved at the little girl, who responded by waving both hands madly as she babbled away to her dad.

As she walked out of the café towards her car, Zoe shook her head. It was so unfair that they were going through such hell. She'd thought Tanya and Alfie seemed like an unlikely couple, but he was such a sweetheart and so genuine, she could see why Tanya had loved him. She hoped with all her heart that he'd meet someone else in time, someone who'd look after them both. He deserved it.

As Alfie packed up the buggy and did as good a job as he could of cleaning Jenny, with the help of a packet of wet wipes, he thought of Zoe. That poor girl was so kind and lovely. She was having such a dreadful time of it, with the cancer and that awful immune-system disease. Yet another example of how strangely the world seemed to turn sometimes.

As he rushed towards the play centre, with little Jenny singing to herself in the buggy, he got a sudden clear image of Tanya's grave in his mind.

\* \* \*

He hadn't been in the church since Tanya's funeral. He'd come close only the day before. He'd gone out intending to go, but had found himself at the graveyard instead. This was the first time he'd managed to make his way to his wife's resting place. Up until that point he simply couldn't cope with seeing her name written in stone. He'd stood at the foot of her grave, the hole in the ground where Tanya lay sleeping in that shiny wooden box, deep below the surface which was still humped over with freshly dug earth. Not like most of the other graves, which were either smooth and flat or even concave. The gravestone had arrived. He'd gone for a simple granite one with black script.

*Tanya Shields*
*Died aged 35*
*A loving wife and mother, taken on angel's wings.*

Danielle had told him the flowers from the funeral had all turned to mush, the colours of the pretty petals all reduced to brown curled balls of death. Most people had opted for fresh arrangements rather than artificial wreaths. She'd gathered up all the lovely handwritten cards, but the flowers had been put on the large compost heap at the back of the graveyard.

It was a strange concept to Alfie, the compost heap. Use all the dead things to create food for other things to spring to life. The compost, he presumed, was either sold or used to grow the flowers which lined the paths between the graves. It was a cheerful graveyard, if that was at all possible. Well, it was nicely landscaped at least. The view of the mountains from the back was kind of mystical too.

He hadn't come and viewed the grave before the funeral. The undertakers had offered to take him, but he hadn't wanted to drag Jenny out and he couldn't have coped with standing and choosing a hole to bury his wife in.

"A lot of couples pick a grave together – they buy it long before it's needed," the undertaker had explained.

"What a curious thing to do," Alfie had answered. Imagine people in the full of their health deciding to purchase a grave? What on earth would provoke that? What did they do? Decide instead of going to the cinema on a cold Saturday afternoon that they'd go grave-shopping instead? Weird.

"Well, people like to have their affairs in order. It can make things easier for the ones left behind. Not the type of thing a lot of us like to think or talk about, but sadly death comes to us all. Sometimes it's just too soon."

The last time he'd walked away from this very spot, just after Tanya's coffin had been lowered into the ground, the whole length of the grave had resembled a florist's shop. There were only two things on it now. A bunch of lilies in a little glass bulbous vase, and a small window-box type arrangement with funny-shaped cacti in it.

"Ouch! Sharp!" Jenny pointed her little finger at them, as she crouched on her hunkers and examined them.

"Yes, don't touch those, or you'll prick your finger, darling," he warned.

Jenny didn't seem to question what they were doing there. She didn't seem to find it odd, all these rows of headstones and line after line of graves. Instead she ran to the top of the row and found a few shrubs, surrounded by dark wood chippings. Stamping on the wood chippings, she danced around the plants.

"Don't step on the plants, honey, sure you won't?" Alfie called.

Jenny's cheeks were rosy from the wind. One thing he had noticed, the graveyard was like the edge of the earth. Even on a calm day, the breeze would cut you in half when you were standing in there.

Crunching down on his hunkers, Alfie fingered the earth.

"Hi, Tanya, I miss you so much, darling. The house is so quiet, the bed is so cold. I still keep waiting to hear your key in the door. I imagine it so strongly sometimes I almost believe it's happening. Is it amazing where you are? I hope you're eating chocolate for breakfast. I hope they don't have cellulite where you are. Remember how you used to obsess about the cellulite on your thighs? I could never see it, but saying that just made you cross. You used to say I was only being nice. I'd give anything in the world to see your cellulite right now. I wish we could just have an hour to talk. Just enough time to tell each other all the unspoken thoughts we'd had. Why didn't I tell you how amazing you were more often? Why did I let even one single day go by without telling you how much I loved you?"

The wind in the trees and the sound of Jenny's tinkling voice, from the end of the row, was all that broke the silence. A silence which he felt would follow him for the rest of his life.

That was all that was left of his marriage, his lover and his friend. Silence. Alfie closed his eyes and conjured up her face in his mind. He could see her auburn hair, he could smell her perfume, and the cherry lip-gloss she loved to wear.

"It's like kissing Jenny after an ice-pop! Why do you put that stuff on? You'll never find a husband with that gunk on your face," he'd teased her.

"It's all about the high shine, Alfie – it makes lips look plumper," she'd scoffed.

Giving in to the discomfort of balancing on his hunkers, Alfie sat on the damp grave.

"Nobody tells me to brush my hair now. Or to take off my *Guns & Roses 1989 Tour* T-shirt. I almost went to the shop in it the other day. I could have, you know. But at the last minute I stopped myself. You won't guess what I did, Tans. I put on a shirt. A real one with buttons and stripes. The one you made me wear to Gillian's wedding last year. It was scratchy and uncomfortable and now I'll have to wash it and iron it. But I found it oddly helpful. I knew you'd approve. You know, the way you always said you hated people going to the supermarket in a tracksuit? You said it was the one place where you meet half the country, so everyone should make an effort. Well, I made an effort. Next time I might even brush my hair, or swap my trainers for some shoes. I still have a pair, don't I?"

An old grey, papery-skinned man strode by, wrapped in an old-fashioned trench coat, with a tartan scarf and bowler style hat. He nodded a greeting without speaking and kept walking.

"I know it's probably very narrow-minded of me and all that, Tanya, but he belongs here more than Jenny and I. He's old. He *should* know dead people. That's more natural, isn't it? I should be at home cooking your dinner and sending you a text to see if you've got a function on Friday night or will we go to the Chinese. You weren't supposed to die, Tanya. That shouldn't be in the game plan. Millions of rapists and murderers and really bad people are roaming around, causing injury and harm. Why didn't one of them die instead? Why was it you? Where's the justice in it all? If there are monthly meetings up there, will you go along and tell them I'm outraged? Will you put yourself forward and become a chairwoman? Try and stop whatever the system is in place up there. Try and change things for the better. Organise for the bad people to be taken away and the good ones to be left here, where they belong. Will you try, Tanya? Will you do that?"

"Dada?" Jenny went down onto her hunkers beside her daddy.

Looking up into his face, she put her little finger on his cheek. "Dada cry?" She looked worried.

"It's okay, Jenny. Dada is just talking to Mummy."

"Mama?" her face lit up. She stood up and looked around. Turning in circle after circle she looked up and down the graveyard, trying to see her mummy.

"No, baby girl, I'm so sorry. Mummy is a star in the sky – she's having tea with the angels up in the clouds, honey."

The little girl's face crushed like a paper bag as she pushed out her bottom lip.

"Why?" She looked into the sky, staggering backwards as she strained to see her mother.

"Mummy didn't want to go, but somebody thought she should go and have tea with the angels." Alfie felt all his strength and positive powers leave him. He didn't know why she was gone either. How the hell could he convince Jenny it was alright when he couldn't convince himself? He began to sob and that turned into hysterical tears. He hated himself for dissolving in front of Jenny, but he just couldn't take any more. It wasn't okay. It wasn't fine. It never would be again. Ever.

"Ah, poor Dada! Now, now, shush!" Jenny put her little arms around his neck as he lay on the turned earth above the corpse of his wife. "Pop?" She bent down to look in his eyes, offering him a lollipop to help with the tears. Not even three years of age and she was already clued in enough to know how to fix him.

"Thank you, baby – yes, a pop will fix Dada. Will we go to the shop and buy one?" He mustered up every fibre of strength he possessed to pull himself together.

"And Jenny too?" She looked at him sideways, squinting until he answered.

"And Jenny too." He put his hands on her cheeks, cupping her little cherub face, and kissed her.

"Nice!" She rewarded him with an impish grin.

Missing Tanya was so constantly painful and exhausting, it was like a cancer eating him from the inside out, but he'd no choice about how he conducted himself during the day. He simply had to drag himself into touch and be there for Jenny. He couldn't afford to let her down. He had to mind her for both of them.

Jenny ran towards the gate to the graveyard, like a little bullet. Knowing she had no road sense, he had to jump up and leg it after her. Nearly impaling himself on the empty buggy, he caught up with her. Seeing him approach, she ran even faster, giggling like a madwoman. Nothing in the world could warm Alfie's heart like hearing his baby laugh. In spite of feeling wretched and unbearably sad, he made monster noises.

"I'm going to get you, let me grab you!" He stamped loudly behind her, making sure he caught up with her well in advance of her reaching the dangerous road.

In convulsions, which were almost causing her to stumble, Jenny trotted ahead.

By the time they reached the newsagent's to buy a lollipop, Alfie was genuinely grinning. Jenny was like a loonie, spinning and flapping, chuckling like a cartoon character.

\* \* \*

Clicking back to the here and now, Alfie braced himself to walk into the play centre for Jenny's little class. As long as he had Jenny, he hoped to God he'd get through this hell.

# 21

*When one door closes, another one opens.*

Just as she finished hanging the clothes on the line, Esme heard the phone ringing. Grabbing her plastic tub, which she used for the wet stuff, she made her way into the kitchen.

"Mulligan residence, Esme speaking," she said, putting on her telephone voice. She'd always had one. It was much posher than her usual voice. But, she figured you'd never know who might be ringing. For all she knew it could be Pat Kenny, trying to call his wife and he might have dialled a wrong number. She'd hate him to think she wasn't able to speak properly.

"Mum, it's me, Nora. How are you today?"

"Ah hiya, love!" The telephone voice disappeared. "Wait now till I sit down and have a chat with you. How's England?" Esme kind of thought, in her own head, that the two girls owned the whole country.

"Great thanks, Mum. Everything's going well. Listen, I had a drink with Trace last night and we've something to put to you. It was going to be a surprise, but we thought you'd prefer to know and tell us what you'd like best. We want to do a seventieth birthday party for you. All expenses paid, in a hotel with music and a dinner and as many friends as you can muster up. How about it?"

"Oh, Nora, are you serious? Oh Holy God up high! Really? For me? Well, you know me, I'd love it. In a hotel, you say?" Esme was all overcome. She patted her chest to calm herself down.

"Yes, or a restaurant or wherever you think would be good."

"Or a restaurant? Well, I'm gobsmacked. Imagine me, in a hotel, having a real do."

Her mother's giggles made Nora smile. The two girls had thought of doing a surprise party, but they figured it might frighten the living shit out of her for a start, and besides, the build-up and the invitations and a couple of trips to the venue would give her as much mileage as the actual party. Their mum was such a social butterfly too and knew so many people, they'd probably leave someone out, and they didn't want that to upset her.

"Trace and I are coming home next weekend – we'll land late Friday night and fly back Sunday evening – so put your thinking cap on and we'll take you around on Saturday for a nose. With a bit of luck you'll be able to choose a venue. We'll take it from there." Nora sounded really excited.

Esme had always dedicated herself to her husband and kids. The girls loved her dearly and knew she'd thoroughly enjoy a party. Her actual birthday happened to fall on a Saturday, which was very handy. As it was already September, the girls figured they'd better get going with organising it. Tracey had suggested the big hotel in Blackrock, the Regal. It was newly done up and would have the right balance – neither dingy nor too modern and uncomfortable. They'd reckoned on around one hundred guests.

They finished the chat and Esme put the phone down and clapped her hands. Her very own seventieth party! Imagine that. Not for one second did she think that she didn't want anyone to know how old she was or that it might be too much for her.

"Michael, Michael!" She rushed into the sitting room where he was sitting doing the crossword. "That was our Nora on the phone. You'll never guess," she bubbled. "The girls are throwing a party for me. Imagine, I'm going to be the host!" She nodded, feeling very smug.

"How can you be Holy Communion?" He looked at her in confusion.

"No, love. That's what they call the person who's having the party. The host." She patted his arm.

"Does Jesus not mind?" He still wasn't quite getting it, but thought he'd better just shut up. The girls got cross with him sometimes when he didn't understand things.

Besides, if Esme wanted to be a Holy Communion, that was fine by him. She was on a high with the whole idea. She was babbling about hotels and dinners and tableware and drinks and music. He shifted in his chair. He was hoping it wasn't going to be a weird dinner. One with spicy stuff, which would burn the mouth off him.

"Don't pick any of that Indian voodoo stuff. I'll never forget the state I was left in after Nora took us to the place in Sandymount. Ripped the arse out of me. Johnny Cash must've written *Ring of Fire* after eating one of those voodoos."

He shuddered at the thought of it all. Not to mention all the men in white dresses and glittery slippers. Flying saucers on their heads and more jewellery than a girl. They'd even stuck Christmas decorations on their faces, for crying out loud. Nora said it was just their way of dressing. Fellas used to get beaten up in laneways for less when he was a lad.

"I suppose it's good if people want to wear glittery night-shirts that nobody kicks the living shite out of them on account of it," he'd mused.

"Daddy, be quiet, they'll hear you! Jesus, I'm mortified!" Nora had been very cross with him. Luckily the waiter didn't hear – he was probably a bit hard of hearing with all that jewellry and stuff clanking around as he danced in his slippers.

As Michael had belched repeatedly in the taxi on the way home, he'd patted his poor grumbling tummy. "Aladdin will be delighted with himself. Who needs a magic lamp when he can magic me insides into the bog in half an hour, with one mouthful of that fecking gunpowder he put in me dinner."

The taxi driver had laughed and joined in with Michael,

agreeing that there was nothing wrong with a chop, decent potatoes and two veg.

Michael turned his attention back to his wife, who was bubbling with excitement at the prospect of a party. Fair play to the girls, he mused. They always knew how to make their mother happy. They were blessed with those girls. It was just a shame that they didn't live around the corner.

"I'm trying to think of what kind of food I'd like at the party, Michael. What are your thoughts?"

"I don't know, love, whatever you think," he answered.

"I think we'll ask for a buffet – that way everyone can go up to the table and pick their own food, what do you think?" Esme felt very pleased to be able to talk about different methods of presenting food.

"No, I hate them. You feel a bit like you're in prison, standing like a fecking eejit in a line waiting for some auld one with a hairy mole to dump a spoon of potato salad on your plate. Bloody exhausting too, all that marching around the room with your dinner."

"Maybe you're right. Bridie from the Golden Girls is on a frame too – she might get the wheels caught in a chair and it'd be hard for her to balance the plate and steer around the chairs at the same time. You're right. We'll go for the silver service instead. I'd like them croquet potatoes included too."

"And what about prawn cocktail to start? We had that at our wedding breakfast and everyone thought we were the bee's knees." He was getting into the swing of it all now.

"Do you think they'd do a little one of them cocktail umbrellas on each one?" Esme's eyes were dancing at the thought of it all. The phone rang for the second time.

"Mulligan residence," Esme answered.

"Hi, Mum, it's Tracey. I believe our Nora was on to you about the party idea?"

"Oh she certainly was. I'm just talking to your father about the food. Wait till I get a pen and we'll do out a menu. Have you five minutes to chat?"

"Of course. You organise yourself and we'll come up with an idea. The venue will have all sorts of suggestions no doubt, but it's always good to have your own ideas too."

"Let them see we know what we're talking about," said Esme. "That's how you do it properly, leave no stone unturned." She licked the top of the biro before she started to write.

"Okay, what do you reckon for the starter?"

"That's easy – a prawn cocktail with Marie-Rose sauce. Do you think they'd do a little umbrella or one of those cocktail sticks with the tinsel hanging off it?" Esme mused.

"They will of course. If they don't have them there we'll go to a party shop and buy some," Tracey promised. "I think we should do a soup after that, it makes the meal part longer. It'll prolong the whole event."

"Right you are, love. Just so long as it's not mushroom soup. I always think mushrooms are too like slugs."

"No slugs then!" Tracey giggled. "Let's do a choice of main course. I'll ask them to have a vegetarian option, but we'll have two others as well. What would you like?"

"Chicken à la King is gorgeous, and I love a good Beef En Route," Esme said imagining how impressed her friends were going to be.

"*En Croute,* Mum," Tracey corrected gently.

"I'd particularly like croquette potatoes included in the veg selection – I love them."

"I can't see that being a problem, Mum. Let me guess – trifle for dessert?"

"Ah, sure you know me too well!" Esme giggled. "Will you make sure they offer real tea as well? So many places do that herbal stuff now. I think it just tastes like hay. Chocolates would be grand too, served on nice little plates with doilies."

"It'll all be fantastic, Mum. And will we get a DJ or a band? Do you think your friends would have a bit of a dance or would you rather go home after the meal?"

"Oh, music is a must. You might think it's only you young lot who can boogie the night away, but my pals will show you a thing or two. Some might need a Zimmer frame to dance around rather than a handbag, but we'll shake our stuff!"

"Sounds mighty!" Tracey laughed. "We'll have some booming music in that case."

"It'll need to be – some of the older ones are a bit hard of hearing!" Esme giggled.

"Ah Mum, it's so good to hear you laugh. This party is going to be a roaring success," Tracey promised as they ended their conversation.

Esme filled Michael in on the ideas. He agreed it all sounded wonderful until she remembered coffee.

"I'd better put it on the list in case the hotel doesn't offer it normally," she said, wanting to leave no stone unturned.

As usual, Michael had to disagree. In his opinion they didn't need coffee. Once people got a proper cup of tea, they'd be happy, he said.

"No," said Esme, holding firm. "Sian and some of the Golden Girls like real coffee and some even like a latte or a cappuccino." She was adamant.

"They sound like diseases. Christ, gone are the days when a cup of tea and a chocolate biscuit were the height of it all. People have all lost the run of themselves looking for drinks that you'd need a degree to pronounce. There's a recession still going on, Esme. Don't go mad altogether, woman."

Esme ignored him. "Then the ladies can all get up for a turn on the floor if they feel like it."

"After all those coffees they'll be swinging out of the light fittings! You'd better keep the music to a slow tempo or we'll have a riot on our hands. Before we know it we'll be stung with the bill for hip-replacements and knee-joints," Michael boomed, laughing.

"You make us sound like a bunch of hooligans. What would you know? Sure you won't even come to any of the tea dances with me. For your information, some of the Golden Girls are fairly nifty movers on the dance floor," Esme said, poking him playfully.

"Oh, I can see it now! There'll be head-banging and break-dancing. You and Rosaleen will be there in your glittery track-suits with the gold medallions swinging as you spin on your backs in the middle of the place," Michael cackled.

"Ah, put a sock in it, you grumpy old goat!" Esme grinned good-naturedly.

She'd organise a good variety of music. The ladies loved a bit of a knees-up. She and the Golden Girls often went to tea dances on the bus. It was lovely. They'd get dressed up in a nice frock and put on a bit of make-up and go to dances together. Nearly all the Golden Girls were widowed at this stage, and Michael would just get all upset at the thought of having to sit on a bus. Both himself and Esme would be all worried about what he'd be given for his lunch, in case he didn't like it. Those tea dances tended to cater more for ladies' tastes. Little dainty sandwiches and fancy little cakes either filled with Chantilly cream or topped with sweet icing. She could just hear her husband revving up about it all. "Do they think I'm a leprechaun or a garden gnome? Feeding me dolly's tea-party food? Not enough to feed a gnat! What's wrong with a plate of stew?" No. It wouldn't be worth it. He wasn't gone on chatting either. He wouldn't like the banter on the bus. He didn't like talking about hair and going to the shops. He just have a puss on and make the ladies feel uncomfortable. He wasn't great at sober sing-songs either. Give him a few pints and catch him in the right mood and he'd a grand voice. He could do a Ronnie Drew number almost as well as the real man, God rest him. But he wasn't partial to a verse of "The Sally Gardens" at half ten on a Tuesday morning, on a bus going down the N11. "Yiz are like one of them lezzer gang-bangs," Michael shuddered, when she'd been naïve enough to invite him a couple of years ago. He was too set in his ways. It was easier to leave him a cold plate of boiled ham and a bit of potato salad with a nice egg mayonnaise. She'd even exhausted the idea of trying to get him to microwave things. He'd either burn the mouth off himself, heating it for too long, or eat the food half raw. It was easier to leave nothing to the imagination with him.

Zoning back into the chat about her party, Esme realised he was still muttering under his breath about women dancing with women and what a stupid thing it was to do.

"Stop it, Michael. There'll be no smutty talk about my do. It's going to be the height of sophistication. I'm going to ask the girls if I can have a theme as well."

"What? Like Mickey Mouse going around shaking hands?" Michael looked horrified. "You're not Walt bleedin' Disney, Esme!"

"No, you big eejit, I mean that you co-ordinate the room with the napkins and the flowers and all. Make it all match." She sat pondering, wondering what theme to choose.

By the time Nora and Tracey arrived on the Friday night, Esme was in a spin with excitement. The chemotherapy was trying its damnedest to make her feel rotten, but the thought of the celebration was so fantastic she couldn't help but feel semi-human.

Nora was shocked at how frail her mother was looking. She'd lost weight too, which made her look even older. "You look tired, Mum, how are you feeling? If this is all too much for you, Trace and I can just go and book a place in the morning. We can use the computer to pick out accessories and all that – you can look at them online. There are fabulous websites now with party gear on them."

"You must be joking. You'll have to nail me into a pine box to stop me from coming on the lookout tomorrow. Are you mental? I'm dying to go around and chose my venue!" Esme hugged her younger daughter and smiled. "Thanks for thinking of me, love, but you know me – I'll be in my alley out and about doing the meet-and-greet thing with my girls. Daddy can come too and maybe we'll have our lunch out? I was kind of thinking of the hotel you mentioned. I'd say they've a lovely function room. Millie from the GG's has been in it. Not at an actual do, but her daughter-in-law brought her there for afternoon tea. You know the unfortunate-looking girl with the sticky-out teeth and the stringy hair? Nice little girl, but has a face like a bulldog chewing a wasp. Millie is always saying if they ever have a child, she'll have to cut eyeholes in a paper bag sending it to school it'll be so ugly."

"Mum!" The two girls looked shocked.

"What? I didn't say it, Millie did. It's not my fault if the girl looks a fright. I said she's nice . . ." Esme looked all affronted for five seconds, before switching back to her party. "Anyway, if you'll let me finish, Millie put her head around the door, the day she was there with Face-ache for tea and cake. She said the room is beautiful. A lovely old-fashioned carpet with a nice pattern and the walls are a kind of cream and gold stripe, with blood-red curtains. She said it's only gorgeous. So I know they'd all be mad impressed if I were to send out an invitation for there. Would it be too dear though?" Esme bit her lip. "Daddy and me could help out if you want?"

"No way, Mum. Nora and I have this covered. It's our present to you. I'll ring them now and arrange to meet someone at the hotel and book a table for lunch," Tracey assured her.

Michael shuffled into the kitchen, scratching his head. "It won't be weird, rip-the-arsehole-out-of-you-food, will it?"

"No, Dad!" Nora hugged him, giggling. "You really are turning into a grumpy old man," she teased. "I'll book the sit-down restaurant – they do things like roast beef and your sort of food."

"Less of the 'old' there, you," he smiled.

There really was no point in arguing with Michael when he set his mind to something. The Regal Hotel would be perfect though. They'd know how to look after a man and with a bit of luck they'd serve big portions. Once the men got a decent dinner, things would go well.

The girls showed Esme the party-planning websites too. Tracey had a little laptop the size of a book, which was able to plug into the phone line and come up with page after page of information.

The choice of theme and colour was endless. Esme loved the idea of a Hawaiian-style party.

Michael looked alarmed. "If you think that I'm going around looking like a haystack with two white wrinkly legs sticking out the end of it, you've another think coming!"

"No, you silly old fool, I'd just get the plastic flowers to put around people's necks and have all brightly coloured flowers and parrots and stuff in the room."

"Is it a zoo or a party? Ah Esme, you can't have a room full of old fogies dressed like morons, it wouldn't be right. What if Millie got the flower garland caught in the wheels of her frame and choked herself?" Michael bellowed laughing. "On second thoughts, go for it. Great idea!"

"*You. Out.* Get into the sitting room and watch the darts. That's just rude, talking about poor Millie like that. May God forgive you, Michael Mulligan!"

In spite of herself, Esme burst out laughing as soon as he left the room. The girls had tears rolling down their faces at the thought of all the GG's in hula skirts with plastic garlands and parrots on their shoulders.

"Especially with Millie's boobs! Christ, they might have been a huge asset in her youth, but they're like two enormous water balloons now. She must have welts on her navel from having them bashing around down there. The image of her topless and doing the conga is not a good one."

The three women cried with laughing, and decided that sticking to cream and gold as a theme might be safer.

"We can do a lovely tasteful display, with little tiny gold stars scattered on the tables, and have little posies of cream rosebuds," Nora suggested.

"What about a nice arch of gold and cream balloons around my chair?" Esme piped up.

"Eh . . . Well, do you think that might be a bit tacky?" Tracey asked gently.

"No, I think it would be pure class." Esme had a dreamy look in her eye.

The girls agreed that it was her party and she should have whatever made her happy. By the end of the viewing session, Esme had chosen everything from balloons to confetti to little bottles of bubbles in a tiny champagne bottle and love-heart sweets with her name printed on them.

"Oh, Holy God, the friends won't believe that I've got my very own sweets!" she cried, clapping, and although she was pale and weak from the cancer treatment, she looked so thrilled.

Nora took the party favours a step further and ordered little gold tulle bags with gilded rope to tie them shut. They could put the little gifts into the bags and people could take them home. They'd look pretty on the table and double up as a kind of grown-up "going home" bag.

Esme went to bed around nine o'clock, saying she wanted to be fresh for the visit to the hotel the following day. Tracey had spoken with the banqueting manager and made all the necessary appointments for the following lunchtime.

The two girls then revisited the party website and ordered some wine-bottle labels. If they emailed them a photo of Esme, she could personally appear on the front of all the bottles on the table!

"Why don't we sift through the old photo box and find some pictures of Mum from when she was a baby and right through the years?" Nora suggested. "We could laminate them and ask the hotel to put one on each place as a table mat. It would be a great ice-breaker and an instant talking point. Besides, Mum would love the attention."

"Brilliant idea, we could order a funny cake for her too," said Tracey. "There are a few novelty cake shops around now. What would she like?"

"Well, it has to be something that just says 'Esme'," Nora tapped the table with her nails as she pondered.

"A Hoover," Tracey giggled.

"A plate with meat and three veg," Nora laughed.

They decided they'd go into the novelty cake shop the following day, and find out what ideas they had.

# 22

*How much more of this can I take?*

Zoe was sitting on a chair in Dr Leah's waiting room. The oncologist had called her the day before to say she needed to see her. Fearing the worse, Zoe shuffled into the consultation room.

"Hi, Zoe, sit down. Don't look alarmed, I don't have bad news as such," Leah ventured.

"What do you mean 'as such'?"

"Well, I've been monitoring your bloods very carefully and I examined the ultrasounds I ordered last week. I'm satisfied the chemotherapy is going well. I've taken a decision to do some radiation therapy at the same time."

"Does that hurt?" Zoe looked terrified.

"No, not at all. In fact, we don't often do radiation on ovarian cancer, as it can cause concern with regards to organs in your tummy. But your full pathology reports show us that your cancer was very early stages, and we are pretty sure we got it all during the surgery. The radiation will just be a fail-safe, to make sure that there are no cancer cells lying around causing trouble."

"Isn't that what the chemotherapy is supposed to do?" Zoe's

head hurt. All this information and medical stuff was scary and confusing to say the least.

"Yes, you're spot on, but if we have the opportunity to use radiation as well, and I feel we should, it just nails the problem that little bit more. We need to make sure we use every possible angle to kill this cancer. Ovarian is a very aggressive type and I'm not taking any chances with it."

Leah gave Zoe a letter and told her to go to a different hospital the following day.

"We don't have the equipment here to carry out the treatment, which is why I'm referring you to the other hospital. They'll look after you."

That evening, Zoe sat dumbfounded on her bed. She was only getting used to the idea of the chemotherapy, now she had to get her head around this other radiation thing. It was never-ending.

\* \* \*

The minute Diana drove into the huge hospital the next day, Zoe knew she was going to hate it.

"Jesus, Mum, it looks like a forbidding old boarding school."

"I'll park – you go on in and I'll find you."

"Okay. According to Leah's referral letter, it's on the third floor marked 'Radiology Department'," Zoe called into the car as she got out.

Unlike the smaller clinic Zoe had become accustomed to, this place was vast and stank of disinfectant and general human decay.

Zoe found the correct department and was ushered into a room containing a large scanning machine. The radiologist asked her to pull up her shirt and remove her jeans.

"Do I need to remove all my jewellry first?" Zoe asked. "Usually when I have a CT scan I have to take all my things off."

"No, this is literally just so we can scope the area, to confirm where we need to concentrate the radiation. It's a surface scan rather than a deep-tissue scan. So you're absolutely fine leaving your things on."

The bed was slid into place, and the radiologist stood above Zoe.

"Now, I need to make some marks on your skin with a black pen, just to guide the machine. You will also need a couple of tiny little tattoo marks."

"What, you mean marks that will stay there for ever and ever?"

"Yes, love. We use a needle and black dye to do this."

"I have never in my life heard of anyone getting a tattoo when they have radiation therapy," Zoe looked doubtful. "Then again, it's not something I remember chatting to anyone about. I've never known anyone else who's had cancer to be honest."

The piercing of the needle was shockingly sore. Although it only lasted seconds and was very small, it was probably the surprise of the whole thing that made it all seem difficult to take in.

The actual scan was quick and painless, and didn't involve any dye being injected or Zoe drinking any contrast liquid, which the CT scan called for to highlight tumours. This little scan was purely to pin-point the exact spot where the radiation machine would direct its rays.

"Okay, that's it. We'll start the radiation on Monday morning. You will come every day for the next four weeks."

"What? How on earth am I going to have any sort of a life?" Zoe began to sweat, that dreadful panicky feeling that she was becoming oddly accustomed to creeping through her skin, prickling her senses.

"I know it's all very hard to take on board, Zoe, and your treatment is going to take up a large portion of your time for the next while, but it's all for a good cause. It'll make you better, please God," the nurse answered kindly.

"I understand. Sometimes I feel like a hamster on a wheel. My life as I knew it has altered, but I guess I need to realise that this is only transient," Zoe agreed bravely.

"I know it sounds really awful at first, but each treatment, which is known as a fraction, only takes a matter of seconds. In your case, each fraction will be forty seconds. The most time is spent lying you on the couch and lining the machine up in the right spot. The biggest pain is going to be trekking in and out of this godforsaken place." The radiologist smiled.

"What are the side effects? I'm having chemotherapy at the moment as well, you know?" Zoe bit her lip.

"Plenty of our patients do the two together. There's none of the horrible risks of infections or anything like that. The main thing you can expect is tiredness and reddening of the skin. Just like sunburn."

The radiologist handed Zoe a leaflet with all the information she might need. By that point, Zoe felt like she could open a library with the amount of leaflets she owned on cancer, treatments and side effects.

"Oh, there you are, love. I've been wandering from pillar to post looking for you. This place is vast and I'm terrible at following signs." Diana was looking very hassled.

Zoe linked her mother's arm and they made their way back to the car park.

"Apparently it only takes a few minutes each day," she said. "It's more the pain of having to travel in and out, or so they said."

All the same, Zoe had a sinking feeling inside. Four weeks seemed like an eternity right at that moment.

The weekend dragged. Every time Zoe put the whole thing out of her head, she'd get that nagging something's-bugging-me feeling inside. Then she'd remember, oh yes, the four weeks of hell that loomed ahead. The next session of chemotherapy wasn't due for another ten days, so the radiation was going to take over all her energies.

\* \* \*

Zoe's appointment was for eleven fifteen on Monday morning. She came to learn that appointments didn't always run to schedule. She ended up waiting for over an hour before she was eventually ushered into the room where the radiation was to take place.

Unlike the chemotherapy room, which housed large comfy chairs, this was more akin to an operating theatre. There was a small bed, rather like a beautician's couch, in the middle of the shiny-floored windowless space. On the wall facing her there was a large mechanical arm with what looked to Zoe like a flying saucer attached to it.

"That's the radiation machine, Zoe," one of the radiologists explained. "It's programmed and operated from outside using a special computer system. We'll get you set up on the couch and once we know you're comfortable we'll move out of the room. At all stages we'll be able to see and hear you, so if you feel panicked or upset just call us."

"Fair enough," Zoe said, trying not to stare at the large looming machine.

"Now, the first treatment is always the most daunting, but you'll be an old hand at this in no time. It's painless and really quick, I promise." The radiologist smiled kindly.

As she lay on the hard couch-type bed, a large round flying-saucer thing moved into place above her body. It had a glass surface with a little window. Bright green lights emanated from the flying saucer, which also housed a row of black slats, just like an old-fashioned slide projector. The two radiologists stood on either side of the bed and called out numbers to each other, just like they had done at the time of the scan a few days previously.

"I just need to make a couple of little marks with a pen to make sure the machine is in the exact position, okay, love?"

"Okay." Zoe was so used to being prodded and poked by then, she would've sat in a busy shopping centre and had surgery without batting an eyelid.

"Right, love, we'll just be outside. The machine will perform your first radiation fraction. Just stay as still as you can, but breathe normally."

Zoe lay stiff as a board as the green lights shone in straight lines like a laser show. A small knocking noise followed by a faint high-pitched siren broke the silence.

As she was wondering when the treatment was going to commence, the radiologists came back into the room.

"Well done, you. All done, first fraction over with."

"Down you hop!" The second radiologist helped her off the bed.

"Is that it?" Zoe was baffled.

"Yes, love. As we said, it's incredibly quick – the worst part is coming in and out. You will get tired from the treatment too. The other main side effect is pink, sunburnt-type skin."

"But I can't comprehend how that flying saucer and green light show can kill cancer cells. Chemotherapy, yes, I get that. It's a physical bag of poison being pumped through your body. But this is like a minute-long disco on a beautician's couch."

The radiologists laughed.

"I'm sure it all feels very odd but, believe me, it really works," said the first one. "The radiation kills all the cells, but unlike with chemotherapy, the good cells will immediately begin to renew. That's why you get so tired. It makes your body work really hard, creating all those replacement cells. Your clever network inside can renew cells within twenty-four hours. So while you're having this done, rest up. Give your body a chance to really get the job done."

Zoe shuffled out. Fair enough, she understood what the radiologist was saying, but it was still quite beyond her how the thing worked. She would just place her trust in them and hope to God this thing did what it said on the tin.

By the end of the second week of radiation, she was feeling exhausted as predicted. The nurses explained that the cumulative effect of the radiation would continue to build and make her feel drained.

"Actually the radiation only peaks in your system a couple of weeks after the fractions finish. So you will need to be patient with yourself even after you're finished with the visits in here," the nurse explained.

# 23

*The Regal Hotel, here I come. When one door closes, another one opens.*

It was absolutely lashing rain the morning Esme was to go and look at the venue for her party. The type of rain that soaks you straight through to your knickers in five seconds.

"Oh dear, is it too wet to go now?" Esme looked crushed as she tried to force herself to eat a bowl of cereal.

"There's no way it's too wet," said Nora. "We've a taxi arriving at half eleven and they'll drop us right up to the door of the hotel. Lunch is booked for after the meeting with the banqueting manager and we can stay in the warmth and relax until you're ready to come home."

"Oh wow, girls, you're amazing!"

"Would you try a slice of toast instead of the cereal, Mum?" Nora asked kindly.

"Maybe I will try a piece of toast. If I put a scraping of lemon curd on it, I might manage it with a cup of milky tea. I need to keep my strength up for my meeting with the banquet person." She flushed with pleasure.

She couldn't eat much, but she did drink two cups of tea. With the girls' insistence, she made her way back up the stairs to have a little rest before dressing herself to go out. Not that happy about simply lying there with nothing to do, she grabbed her phone and called Miriam.

"Hiya, Miriam. How are you today, love?" Esme asked in her telephone voice.

"Not too bad today. Please God I'll be more able to get out and about by tomorrow," she answered in her own telephone voice.

"Wait till I tell you," Esme began. She spilled the whole story of the party and the balloons and the banqueting manager and the proposed trip to the hotel for lunch.

"That sounds fantastic. Don't forget to ring me later on and tell me all about it. I'll be in today – it's too wet to go out so I'll be waiting for your call. That'll make my day now."

Miriam sounded rooted to the spot with all the news. Not for the first time, Esme felt sorry for her that she'd only the one son. He was a useless git if the truth be known. He'd more interest in spending his money on pints and fags, than looking after his poor mother.

Miriam was a really kind and giving person, Esme reflected as she put down the phone and lay back on the bed. She had become so fond of her since they'd met at the hospital. She'd even encouraged her to join the GG's. The other Golden Girls all agreed that she was a marvellous addition to their little group. Especially since Gretta had died last March. That was the main drawback with their little posse. All the members were aged and likely to die at any moment. So new members were always welcome. At least they all liked Miriam. Not like that awful one Stella who'd come last year. Foreign she was. At first Esme had thought she was great. She'd a lovely way of talking. She sounded different and a bit exotic. But, soon enough, she'd shown her true colours. A right cranky old bitch she'd turned out to be. Spent her time telling them how much better it was in Sweden and how they didn't know the half of it, living in Ireland. She'd a bit of a waterworks problem too, which she didn't seem to want to deal with. So she smelled of piss, to add insult to injury.

"I know we all have to wee, and that's understandable but, dear God, can she not get herself some of them adult nappies?" Esme had whispered while she was over making herself a cup of tea. "They're able to soak it all up and stop you smelling like a public toilet." Then she'd added with a sniff, "She never brings any biscuits either."

Things had gone from bad to worse. Stella had come on a coach trip to Wexford. They were supposed to be having lunch and seeing one of those men who can hypnotise people and make them eat onions and think it's an apple. They'd all been really looking forward to it. First of all, Stella had turned up half an hour late for the bus. Then when they were over halfway there, she'd had a turn and started to jerk about. She gave poor Betty O'Shea a terrible fright. After all the shunting around in the seat, she'd gone and pissed all over Betty's silk scarf. Her dead husband had given it to her for Christmas in 1972, and she'd loved that scarf. She'd bravely agreed to put it in a plastic zip-lock sandwich bag, provided by the bus driver.

In the end, they'd had to divert the whole tour to the General Hospital. Stella had behaved like a guttersnipe, shouting and yelling abuse at the paramedics and the nurse. The GGs had all been scarlet. By the time they'd admitted Stella and contacted her family, who all lived in Sweden, it was too late to see the man make people think they were dogs who'd lost a yellow puppy in the crowd. It wasn't as if she was even sick. It was only fecking indigestion because she'd eaten some sort of pickled cabbage on toast for her breakfast.

"Why couldn't she have a boiled egg like the rest of us?" Esme had mused.

Stella had kicked up such a stink that Wexford General Hospital had eventually told the bus driver to go on back to Dublin and that they'd arrange to have Stella transferred the next day. She'd need to be kept in for observation overnight.

She managed to redeem herself and ingratiate herself with the others ever so slightly at the GGs meeting the following week. She at least managed an apologetic face.

Betty O'Shea (of the pissy scarf) had very kindly asked her how she was feeling.

"I'm fine," she said.

"How did they treat you in that hospital, love?" Esme had asked, hoping by being a bit nice to her she might tell them all about it. Who she'd shared a room with and what she'd done for a nighty seeing as she hadn't planned on being admitted – that sort of thing.

"I don't want to talk about that dreadful place. It's not open for discussion. My life is private and it will remain that way." She couldn't even talk properly. She said "zat" for "that."

"Oh, right. Like that, is it?" Esme shifted in her seat and looked all offended. Who the hell did yer woman think she was? Any time she'd been in hospital, she'd come in and told the girls all about it. A problem shared was a problem halved in her opinion. Not to mention the fact that the girls liked to know what was going on. Not in a bad way, just as friends like. But maybe they didn't do that kind of thing where Stella came from.

"Do yous not believe in talking in Sweden? Is it like a national-tradition type thing, that you don't ever tell anyone anything?" Betty asked, settling herself more comfortably in her chair so she could see Stella properly. Betty liked a good story, not to mention a good look at people.

"In Sweden, people mind their" (zeir) "own business. Not like in this country, where you all seem to think nothing" (no-zing) "of asking very personal and nosey questions." She shoved herself back in her chair crossly.

"We don't mean to sound nosey, love. We just share here. We do like a good auld chat and we just thought you might be the same. We're all pals here. There's no badness in us, we just like to be friendly," Esme explained, smiling around at the others.

"I had indigestion," Stella stated. Her po-face indicated the conversation was well and truly finished.

There was a brief silence, before Betty made an announcement. She'd made a new Rachel Allen recipe of chocolate brownies. She'd seen the beautiful blonde girl on the telly and her daughter had given her the book as a present.

"Lovely girl, she is. She's a bit like a better version of a supermodel, if you like."

"What do you mean, Betty?" Esme leaned forward.

"Well, she's got the glamour and all the lovely way of talking and all that, but she can cook too. She's not one of them silent, useless stick-insect ones. I think she's fantastic. She's got children and all, so not only does she let the cameras into the house to watch her making the dinner or baking a cake, but she probably has to tell them to wait a minute while she goes down the road to get the kids from school. I think she's a marvel. In any case, I made these out of the book and I thought you could all give me a verdict." Betty offered the "*tuba wear*" container around.

There was nothing but munching noises for the next while. Not a crumb was left over.

"You've an empty box there, Betty," Esme said.

All the girls cackled at the innuendo.

"You're right there, me box has been empty for a good while," Betty laughed.

They all cried laughing, except Stella, who sat staring straight ahead, po-faced. One glance at her set them all off again. Usually Esme would try to explain what the joke was if someone didn't get it, but on this occasion she decided not to bother.

Now, pushing away all thoughts of Stella and her snotty face and her pungent pong, Esme hauled herself out of the bed to get ready for the visit to the Regal Hotel. Putting on a nice fawn-coloured pencil skirt and a fine cashmere twin-set Tracey had bought her in London, she felt excitement ripple through her. Putting on a bit of make-up and a good slick of red lipstick to match her top, she stood back. She'd never underestimated the power of a bit of slap. In her opinion, there wasn't a woman alive who didn't benefit from a little bit of colour.

The taxi arrived on time and they all piled in. The banqueting manager turned out to be a little blonde thing called Sue. She had on a neat navy skirt-suit and a spotty blouse. Her little ponytail bobbed up and down as she shook hands with them all.

"This is Esme, she's the birthday girl," Nora said proudly.

"Pleased to make your acquaintance, I'm sure. Seventy next birthday, please God!" Esme kind of curtsied as she shook the girl's hand.

"And well you look on it too! Why don't we go straight down to the function room and I can show you what we have on offer?"

They followed her down a long corridor. It was all beautifully lit, with real crystal chandeliers. The carpet was like it was made of pure velvet. Esme could feel herself sink in almost up to her ankles as she walked. It was one of those really posh carpets too. It was basically a royal-blue colour, then towards the edges there was a gold-and-red stripe, creating a framing effect. The walls were all papered in that thick stuff that looked almost like upholstery fabric. Esme thought it looked like the inside of a palace. As Sue flung the double doors open, a whoosh of fresh flower smell hit them. Inside was the most stunning room Esme had ever seen. It was decked out with round tables and old-fashioned spoon-backed chairs. The backs and seats were covered in the same royal blue. Snow-white tablecloths draped the tables and fresh linen napkins were folded to perfection at each place.

There were enough wine and water glasses to drown an entire town, and enough silverware to keep a large pawnshop in operation for a whole year. At one end, an oversized granite fireplace surrounded a roaring real fire. The same type of crystal chandeliers graced the ceilings. Turned down to a dim level, they made the room look warm and welcoming. Each table had an elaborate tall glass vase, which for all the world looked like an enormous cocktail. Spilling over the edges were different shapes and sizes of cream flowers and trailing ivy. It was classy and beautiful and took Esme's breath away.

"We have it set up for a wedding which is due to start in about two hours, so it's lovely that you can see the room at its best. Sometimes when it's empty with a Hoover in the corner and bare tables stacked along the wall, it's hard to imagine how magical it can look. What do you think, Esme? Is it what you had in mind at all?" Sue turned to look at her.

"Oh sweet Jesus, it's magnificent! I can't imagine having a party in a room like this. I can't believe it could be possible for me to fill this room with all my family and friends. It's like a palace or a fairytale, isn't it?"

Michael was over at one of the tables, bashing the cutlery around, pinging a fork off a wineglass, and lifting up the tablecloth for a better look at what was underneath.

"Michael, don't trash the table, that's for someone's wedding!" said Esme but her husband didn't seem to hear. "Jesus, you can't take him anywhere," she laughed.

The girls agreed the function room would be perfect for the night. At the end of the room, there was a little private bar area, with some high tables and high stools. They walked down to view it all.

"I don't know if any of my friends will use those. I can see them being carted off in an ambulance with a broken hip. One drink too many and they'd wobble off that and snot themselves," Esme laughed.

"Don't worry, Mum, the younger generation can perch on those." Nora rubbed her mum's arm.

"What about the flowers, Mum? Do you like that kind of thing or would you prefer something more simple down on the table itself?" Tracey asked.

"No, I think that cocktail look is real *Woman's Own*," Esme smiled.

"What do you mean by that?" Nora looked puzzled.

"You know, the way they use the name of that magazine to describe things that are real class?" She looked a bit affronted.

"Oh, you mean *Cosmopolitan*, Mum?" Tracey smiled.

"Yes, is that it? I get my words muddled sometimes – don't mind me, love." Esme batted Sue on the arm.

"The only things I might suggest, which can provide a lovely evening atmosphere, are candles," Sue said. "We have beautiful candelabras which can be put on the mantelpiece and on each table. It's stunning at night-time and we'll turn the lights down lower, to create a soothing ambience."

"That's grand, love, just so long as it's not like a bunker," Esme said. "There's nothing worse than being at a dinner or something and you've no idea of what you're eating. It could be rat soufflé and half of it ends up on your lap. There'll be a good few senior citizens too, and it'll be a shambles if one of them walks into the wall, just for the sake of a bit of ambience. It'll turn into *ambulance* fairly quickly if we're not careful!" Esme laughed at her own joke. "Not that yer woman, Stella, will be tripping on the way to the toilet. Bit of a filthy skunk she is. Terrible smell of piss off her," she added, leaning in to tell Sue, who looked stunned.

"Muuum!" Tracey gave her a dig in the ribs. "Stop, will you, we don't need to hear about her at the moment."

"I was only saying," Esme sniffed indignantly.

"I'm starving, when is the food coming?" Michael's voice made them all turn the other way. He'd plonked himself at one of the beautifully presented tables, grabbed a linen napkin and tucked it into his shirt collar. Drumming his fingers impatiently on the pristine tablecloth, he was looking kind of grumpy and agitated.

"Daddy, no, this isn't for us. There's a wedding coming in here in a while. We're only having a look and then going to the restaurant. Sorry, Sue, he didn't realise . . ." Tracey was mortified.

"That's quite alright, one of the girls will fix that in a jiffy. If your father's hungry, why don't we head over to our small meeting room and get some menus and prices and you can have your lunch and talk it all over? I'm here all day, so you can ask for me at reception if you'd like to make a booking or else call me if you'd prefer a bit more time."

They all trooped after Sue as she made her way back towards the reception area. Standing to the side she ushered them into a small cubby-hole type room to the right of the main desk. After arranging the chairs in a semicircle, they all sat down. From her leather-bound folder with the hotel name inscribed in gold, Sue pulled out a few sheets of paper and three-way folded brochure.

"Here are some photos of the room you've just seen and on the printout there's a list of prices. Obviously depending on what menu you choose, we can do up a price for you, when we have a rough idea on numbers. We ask for the final number four days prior to the event, and this is the price you'll be charged on the day."

"What are we supposed to do if someone drops dead or can't come at the last minute?" Michael piped up.

"Daddy, stop. That's the way all places work it. Let's just hope nobody thinks of croaking it between now and then," Nora grinned.

They asked a couple more questions and Sue escorted them to the dining room, where a table was marked *Reserved* for them, with their name written on a small cream folded card.

"Lovely, thank you. This is great." Esme grabbed the little card and stuffed it into her handbag. "I'll keep it and show it to the girls," she whispered to Nora.

They ordered their lunch and Tracey chose a bottle of white wine from the extensive list. Esme was very impressed. It looked a bit confusing to her, like a huge big phone book. But her daughter didn't seem in the least bit phased and was able to pronounce the name of it and everything. It all sounded like double Dutch to her.

"Is that okay for you guys?" Tracey asked.

"Oh yes," Esme and Michael answered at once. If the truth were known, it might have been bottled monkey pee and they wouldn't be able to tell.

Nora read out the menu options. They all sounded nice, but the one with the roast beef on it appealed to them the most.

"I always think if you get beef at a wedding or a do, it speaks volumes." Michael folded his arms. "If you go for chicken or fish, it's a bit scabby, isn't it?"

"I think we should offer fish as well – some people are funny about red meat these days," Tracey said.

"But all that mad cow disease is gone." Nora bit into a warm white bread roll.

"Not in our house, it's not," said Michael, jabbing Esme in the arm.

"Don't pick any pork either, remember that swine flu? We don't want to kill anyone before they get a dance," Esme sniffed.

They decided on the menu and all agreed the hotel and its gorgeous function room was just the right thing for the party. Included in the price, they were offered a list of entertainers. Esme wanted a band rather than a DJ, so they chose one that played rock and roll music.

"We don't want any of those mad ones who sing about sex and rude words." Michael's brow knitted. "Or lads dressed in women's frocks with mental-looking face-paint on. You think they're women and then they sing in a deep voice and frighten the living daylights out of old people."

"Don't worry, Daddy all weirdos will be kept away," Nora assured him.

Their lunch was leisurely and tasty. The staff were attentive and made a huge fuss of the older couple, which the girls appreciated. The wine was delicious and properly chilled. There were a surprising number of people in having lunch, from businessmen to other couples. It was always a good sign to see a place busy.

"At least the food should be fresh and not sitting in a fridge growing mould," Esme commented. "I like to watch the traffic coming in and out of a place. I feel once there's a good turnover of clients, at least they can't be keeping everything in a tuba-wear container under the counter, ready to poison innocent people."

Fuelled by the wine, the girls decided to take a taxi into the city centre to see if they could pick out an outfit for Esme for the party.

Seeing as she was having a good day, and her energy levels were fairly high, the girls wanted to make sure she was kitted-out before they went back to the UK.

Details with regards to the venue could all be sorted by email and phone, but they wanted to treat their mum to a special dress or outfit and they wouldn't be home before the big event. Michael was delighted to go along. He was especially pleased when he saw an old-fashioned little pub just across the street from Esme's favourite boutique.

"I'll just nip in here and see what the Guinness is like. You can come and collect me when you're finished." With a little spring in his step, he rubbed his hands together and entered the bar. "A pint of plain, whenever you're ready there, barman. I'm just going to wait here while my wife and daughters go off picking frocks. Not a job for a man, unless you're bent." Michael hopped up onto a high stool with the agility of a twenty-year-old.

"Right you are!" The barman began to pull the pint. The small dark bar, which was almost entirely made of old mahogany wood, like the inside of a ship, was empty apart from one other man. He appeared to be around Michael's own age and was already sipping a pint. He turned slightly towards Michael.

"How-r-ya." It wasn't a question so much as a statement and greeting rolled into one.

That was it, the ice was broken, Michael had been accepted into the fold. He was settled in for as long as he was allowed by the girls. It never ceased to amaze him how easy men were. Not like women. Men could go on their own into any establishment (with drink) and start up a civil conversation. There was none of this fickle bitchiness like with women. Complicated creatures they were. They had an awful habit of worrying about what other ladies were wearing and what colour lipstick they had on, and where they bought their knickers. Men didn't have to worry about any of that sort of thing. They just sat down, without noticing who got their trousers in what shop, and started to talk.

Anything was game too, from sport to current affairs. Some of the older fellas were open to an auld song from time to time, which Michael loved. A lot of the younger crew didn't know the words to the old Dublin songs, which was a crying shame. He was going to ask this gentleman's opinion on that subject. Shrugging his shoulders with delight, he settled himself and waited for his pint to be ready. He was a real barman too, he noted with delight. He wore a proper pair of slacks with a crisply ironed shirt, with the sleeves rolled up to the elbow for proper manoeuvring. Over the whole lot, he had a starched white apron, which was tied around his waist and knotted neatly. He'd a proper man's haircut, with no spanners or bolts hanging out of his ears or face. No tattoos or mad cult-looking outfits.

Not like some of those ones he'd had the misfortune to come across, untrained ones who fill the whole glass in one go. Treating the Guinness pump like a bloody power-hose for washing the car.

Shooting the wondrous dark liquid into the glass, with the finesse of a carthorse in clogs. No, this man was a true artist. Tilting the glass correctly and only filling it two-thirds of the way, and leaving it on the black rubber mat to settle. Yes. This was going to be a good pint. No doubt about it. Michael particularly liked when a barman put the pint where he could view it properly. Not hiding it under the counter as if it were dodgy. Tilting his head to the side, he watched the pale brown muddy liquid leap and crawl its way up the glass, leaving a deep smooth calm blackness in its wake. Only when the yeast had stopped working its magic and the entire drink was asleep, did the barman attempt to even touch the glass to fill it up. When he did so, it was with a serious and concentrated face. This was poetry. Only serious barmen could do what he did next. He used the tip of the nozzle from the pump to draw a shamrock in the creamy head – a head which was not too thick, mind you. Nothing more uncouth than a big flobby, bubbly-looking head on a pint, to put you right off. No, this baby was pure cream. Michael, his newly acquainted friend and the barman all watched in silent anticipation as the drink reached its peak. There was no loud thumping music, like a fecking car alarm mixed with a bag of strangled cats either. No, just a faint mumble of Radio 4 in the background. Civilised, it was, Michael noted gratefully. He had loved his lunch and knew that his Esme and the girls were delighted with all the table linen and tweety music. But right now, Michael felt like he'd come home.

"That, my friend, is art," Michael congratulated the barman. "Well done, my son!" He held his hand out to be shaken.

"William. And it's nice to have a man who appreciates the fine art of pouring a decent pint. Did you happen to know that in certain establishments in this fair city, wankers have been caught watering down pints?" William stood back from the bar, arms folded across his chest for effect.

"No way! Damien, by the way." The other man, dressed in a blue seventies-style suit with a bowler hat with a small feather tucked into the side, offered his hand to Michael.

"Very pleased to make your acquaintance, my man. Michael's the name," Michael shook his hand and nodded his head.

"Likewise, Michael. A pleasure, I'm sure."

"I shit you not, a mate of mine saw it with his own two eyes," William went on. "Now if anyone else had said it to me, I'd have suspected porkies, but this fella is straight up. Not prone to exaggeration, if you get me?" He shook his head gravely.

"Shocking that is, shocking," said Michael. "Imagine the gall of some people? Necks like a jockey's arse, they have. I suppose if they're serving young ones from Lithuania who weren't reared on the stuff, they might get away with it. But take a person in the know, like your good self and my friend Damien here. I'm not a violent man, but God knows, mess with me pint and it'd bring out the devil in me. If I was in the wrong mood it would make me cross for a week. More than that, it'd be like a stab in the heart. Feckin' up a man's pint like that. Shocking." Michael waited for a few seconds, pondering the sacrilege of wrecking pints on purpose, before zoning in on his own perfect one. "This is the type of moment that makes life worth living," he added, poignantly marking the moment. "*Sláinte*," he saluted and slowly raised the glass to his lips. Not a tremor in sight, for all his seventy-four years.

"*Sláinte bha*," the other two chorused.

Closing his eyes and savouring the taste, Michael sank a good third of the pint in one go. Resting the glass back on the counter ever so gently as he swallowed, he opened his eyes and met William's.

"Well?" William leaned forward.

"Spot on, William. Spot on." Chuckling, Michael shook hands with both William and Damien, and easy laughter broke out among the three men.

*  *  *

As her husband was having the time of his life in the small snug, so was Esme in Classy Lady, her all-time favourite boutique across the way. It was a shop which specialised in clothing for more mature ladies. It was a great haunt for Mother of the Bride outfits and gear for the races. They did the works, from suits, matching blouses, hats, coats, gloves and Esme's current favourite – fascinators. These were the little dinky hats, which could be pinned to the top or side of a woman's head, with pretty things like net and feathers sticking out. Classy Lady had a stunning display of fascinators in every shade under the sun and Esme had already secretly decided she was going to have the most impressive fascinator going. It would wow the neighbours and Golden Girls alike.

"Can I help you ladies or would you like to look around?" the girl asked politely.

She was a nice enough looking young one, around thirty or so, Esme estimated. She'd a nice matching suit on which looked like it came from the shop. That was always a good sign, when the assistant thought the clothes were good enough for herself.

"We're looking for a special outfit for our mum. She's throwing a big party for her birthday," Nora said proudly, hugging her mother.

"I'll be seventy in November, please God," Esme noted.

"And very well you look on it too," said the girl.

She was really very nice, Esme thought then. Mannerly. That was something that had gone astray a lot these days too, she mused. "Manners cost you nothing," she'd always say to her girls.

"Would you like me to make a couple of suggestions or would you like to have a browse first?" The girl clasped her hands. "And can I offer you all a little glass of sparkling wine?"

"Ooh, yes, please!" said Esme.

They all were delighted. Their previous fuel from lunch was actually starting to wane slightly. Some bubbles were just what the doctor ordered.

"I shouldn't really. I'm having chemo at present, as you might have guessed by the strange pallor of me." Esme patted her set hair.

"I'm so sorry to hear that, I hope you'll be feeling better soon. All the more reason to celebrate your fine age," the girl fumbled.

"Why? In case I'm dead by next year?" Esme thumped her on the arm and roared laughing.

"Oh gosh, no. I only meant . . ."

"Ah you're alright love, don't mind me, I'm only pulling your leg. I've a small bit of cancer in me jacksy, but I'll be grand. I'm in for the chemotherapy every three weeks, but it's fine. It's not going to make my hair fall out. The modern ones don't. Besides, me doctor has told me I'm very good at it. The chemo, that is. Which brings me on to the main article I'm after. A fascinator. I've a terrible weakness for them and I'd love one for my party, if that's not too much trouble."

"Yes, of course." It was all a little too much information for the poor girl, but she held her own. "Why don't you ladies have a little look around? I'll get your drinks and we can start to show you some possibilities?"

The woman and her two daughters thanked her as they began to flick through the rails. The poor girl ran to the refuge of the stockroom, where the small fridge was housed. Most people said no to a drink in the middle of the afternoon. It was usually only late Friday-evening shoppers who accepted the offer. Nevertheless, Marie opened the fridge and fished out a half-bottle of sparkling wine. In the little Formica brown cupboard above the tarnished little sink, she found three champagne flutes and divided the wine. She didn't know much about cancer, but she hoped the poor woman wasn't going to drop dead in the changing room, especially if she gave her champagne.

Fixing her smile, she carried the glasses out on a small tray, along with a bowl of crisps.

"We'd better buy something now, or you'll be taking our glasses away," Esme quipped.

"Not at all, there's no pressure on my part. It's just nice to be nice, isn't it?"

There were so many outfits and dresses that Esme liked, she decided to ask the assistant for advice. They established that she'd like a dress with either a cardigan or bolero or matching jacket. Esme had plenty of suits in her wardrobe and a dress would be a real treat. She'd wear it on Christmas Day too, she said, so already it was going to be "an asset" to her.

"An *investment*, Mum," Nora winked at her.

The clothes were perfect for her shape and age. Not too low-cut or skimpy. The colours were bright and flattering too. The one they all thought was a winner was an olive-green velvet shift dress, which had a slight stretch in the fabric. It was long and fitted, with a small neat bolero with lace embellishments. To top it all off, the assistant appeared from the back room with a stripy box. When she lifted the lid, Esme gasped. Inside, nestled in soft tissue paper, was the most beautiful fascinator she'd ever seen. Adorned with peacock feathers and tiny twinkling green beads, with a very fine, barely there shard of silk netting which came in a point to one side. Set on a green velvet hair-band, it was simply gorgeous.

"Oh, I love it. I wonder if it would suit me?" Esme was rooted to the spot, she was almost afraid to touch it.

"Let's pop it on and see what you all think." The young girl gently adjusted Esme's hair and rested the fascinator on top.

"Mum! You look divine. The Queen herself would have nothing on you!" Nora clapped her hands in delight.

"It's stunning, Mum, you have to have it." Tracey turned to the pleased assistant. "Do you have shoes and a bag which would work with the outfit?"

"Yes, of course. We actually have a little clutch bag, which also has the peacock-feather detail – it's in leather, but I think it would tone beautifully. We have some court shoes by the same label – what size are you?" She looked at Esme's feet for inspiration.

"A six please, love," Esme said excitedly. By the time she'd slipped on the shoes and held the bag in place, she really did feel like royalty. "Ohmigod, not since the day I married your father have I felt so special. I'll be sleeping with one eye open until the party, I'll be that excited. Do you think anyone will recognise me?"

As Esme reluctantly took off the outfit and accessories, her daughters fished the items out of the changing room and brought them to the counter.

"I'll put it on my visa and we can settle it between us when the bill comes in – fair enough?" Nora asked her sister.

"Perfect. Isn't it great to see her so happy. She's had a rough time with the chemotherapy and having to manage Dad at the same time. He's worse than a toddler in some ways. She never complains and never falters. Although his going to the takeaway once a week is like a blessing from God. You'd swear he was taking fifteen modes of transport from train to camel the way he goes on!"

Before she began to gently fold the pieces, the shop girl filled the three glasses, emptying the small bottle.

"No point in leaving it there," she smiled.

"Thank you, and please don't say the total in front of our mother. Just pass the card through when you're ready." Nora put her credit card on the counter.

The two girls sat on the little sofa and clinked their glasses. Esme appeared moments later, flushed with delight.

"Grab your glass, Mum, and come and squeeze in with us." Tracey smiled at her.

Esme defied her near-seventy years by cantering to the counter and swooping up her glass.

"Shouldn't really, don't mind if I do. Waste not, want not, I always say!" Joining her daughters, she sat and drank her sparkling wine. "This has been a most memorable and wonderful day. I've enjoyed every second of it, girls. Even if I didn't have the party to look forward to, this would be enough. You're very good to your old mother. Very good indeed. Not like poor old Miriam, with that good-for-nothing waster of a son of hers. A lout he is." Shaking her head, she thought about her friend. That son of hers, his idea of spoiling his mother was to offer her a swig out of his can, while she ran around the house making his dinner and washing his cacks. Before she knew her too well, Miriam had her thinking he was an angel. Helpful and kind. But as they'd confided in each other more, she'd realised he was a waste of space. Poor Miriam was just very loyal and probably didn't want to face the fact that her only child didn't give a rat's ass about her. She'd always hoped for more children, but it just hadn't happened.

"I never took any tablets or anything like that – it just wasn't God's will that I have any more," she'd told Esme with regret.

"Well, I took the contraptive pill for a long time. That was before I went through the change, you know?" Esme pulled a face and pointed south.

"*Contraceptive*, Esme love, not contraptive. What was it like?

Did it make you feel drunk or anything?" Miriam was very interested. She'd never had a friend like Esme before. One who didn't mind chatting about things, even private stuff. Of course, in their day nobody discussed anything like that. Sure she'd no idea what was going on after they'd been married. The whole conceiving process, pregnancy and birth were traumatic too. The nuns were very efficient and most babies arrived safely. The nursing homes and maternity hospitals were spotless – you could eat your dinner off the floors. In those days, new mothers stayed in for two weeks to recuperate after the labour and birth. Not like now. God help them, all the new mothers had barely their arses in the bed and they were thrown out on the street.

After Miriam showed such interest in the subject, Esme decided to treat the GG's to an account of her contraceptive experiences.

"Now, wait till I tell you about the pill . . ." Esme had a whole room of elderly ladies' attention. They were at their weekly GG's meeting in the church hall and Mrs Deveny had baked a lovely lemon sponge to go with the tea. She'd even brought a bowl of whipped cream in her wheelie shopping trolley, God bless her. "The packet has the days of the week written above each pill. The doctor told me to take it at the same time each day." Eyes half shut with the joy of all the attention, Esme waved her hands for effect.

"What would you do if you were on holiday and the time was different?" Mrs Deveny mumbled through a mouthful of cake.

"You'd have to work it all out and take it accordingly, and if you were to go somewhere like India or America, I'd say you'd have to be up all night counting the hours. Not that I ever went to those sort of places when I was on them!"

"Did you never feel guilty, Esme?" Mrs Keilly asked. "On account of it being against the Catholic Church and all? Like, did you still go up and receive Communion on a Sunday?"

They all leaned forward to listen.

"I got over my initial feelings of guilt. I made my peace with Himself." She pointed skywards. "I pondered it all, I won't lie to you. But in the end I took myself into the chapel one morning when the girls were still small and had a deep meditation session. I looked deep inside myself and I asked God to forgive me for what I was about to do, and I went straight down to Dr Joyce, lovely man." There was a rippling mutter of agreement around the room, as his staunch supporters nodded. "Only marvellous he was. Told me that hundreds of women were at it, taking them pills and that they worked too. That if I'd decided I was finished with my family, it was the way to go."

"I wish I'd had your modern notions, Esme," said Mrs Murphy. "Now, I wouldn't give any of mine back or anything, but twelve was an awful lot to manage. Now I know the older ones were a help with the little ones, but only after a fashion. Sure they all scattered to every corner of the earth as soon as they were reared. Australia, Canada, England, America. The only one that stayed on home turf was Lisa and she's as much use to me as an ashtray on a motorbike. With her shaved head and her big black boots. Lives in the back end of Kerry, speaking Irish and shacked up with a hairy-faced woman nearly as old as me. 'We're friends, Mammy,' she does tell me. Does she think I came down in the last shower? 'Why don't you just admit you're a lesbian?' says I. Or 'gay' as they call themselves now. Both men and women are allowed to be under the one umbrella now – gay."

Mrs Murphy was a terrible bitter little woman when she got going, Esme thought. Even in spite of Mrs Deveny's lemon sponge. Nothing would make that woman happy. Not too happy herself about having her thunder stolen by the twelve children and the lesbian saga, Esme thought it was time to make her party announcement.

"Girls, yous won't believe what my daughters are doing on my behalf," she said smugly, using her telephone voice for the occasion.

"What, Esme?" Miriam answered loudly.

"Sure I told you already, what are *you* looking so surprised about?"

"I know that, I'm only trying to play along for Christ's sake! To give the announcement a bit of umph!" Miriam elbowed her to get on with it before they lost the attention of the room.

"Tell us, Esme, before another one of us pops our clogs," Mrs

Deveny cackled. She'd a terrible crack in her voice on account of all the fags she smoked. She loved those fags though, so everyone had stopped telling her to give them up.

Apparently they were very bad for you, damage your insides, Esme had heard. Some people even said they gave you cancer. Now she'd kind of believed that for a long time, but look at her now. She'd never puffed on one in her life and wasn't she in St Mark's hooked up to the chemotherapy machine?

"I," Esme paused and held her palms out flat for dramatic effect, closing her eyes, "I, ladies, am hosting a seventieth birthday party – time to be disclosed, invites to follow – at The Regal Hotel, in November. There shall be aperitif drinks followed by a sumptuous meal with dancing to a live band no less. It will be the event of the year, and yous are all invited!" Opening her eyes wide, she clapped her hands in delight.

All the other Golden Girls clapped too and went off into a fit of babbles and squeals of delight. That was it. The chat and banter was mighty. The time had run away with them that day in the church hall.

The parish priest, old Father Moriarty, had to come and open the door with the aid of his spare key. "It's time for you lot to put the things away – the weekly flower-arranging group has been standing in the drizzle for over fifteen minutes. They say they've been knocking and calling, but nobody answered."

"Well, their flowers will be nice and fresh and perky," said Mrs Murphy.

There was a stony silence for a few minutes as the notion sank in that bitter little Mrs Murphy had actually cracked a joke. Jesus, there was life in the old bird yet.

The news of the party was a tonic for them all. Three of them had even vowed to buy a new rig-out.

"Even though I'm heading for eighty and probably won't get a whole lot of wear out of it, I'm going to dip into the post-office savings account," said Mrs Murphy. "No pockets in a shroud, isn't that what they say? Feck it! Feck it!" she repeated for effect. "It's not every day you get wind of a seventieth party in the Regal, with a live band and a big dinner served up to you." She didn't even care that the priest had heard her saying "feck".

To his utter shock, it took Father Moriarty nearly a further ten minutes to shift the Golden Girls group. To add insult to injury, they didn't seem to care about the flower arrangers and the drizzle. It was most out of character for them, but all the same it was actually rude.

As the last of them shuffled outside, Esme Mulligan caught his arm.

"Fr Moriarty, I just wanted to be the first to fill you in on my news." She had a twinkle in her eye. "My two daughters are throwing me a seventieth birthday party, at the Regal Hotel. I was just telling the girls. Of course, you're invited too, should you be able to spare the time," she winked. "November, aperitifs, sit-down dinner and live music to follow. A formal invitation will be sent in due course." She was using the telephone voice again.

"Oh, right. Well, that explains the change in character – you know, the ignoring the flower arrangers and all that. They were always kind of moany anyhow. Not like all you lovely ladies!" Fr Moriarty smiled, showing his yellowing horse's teeth.

Esme had never seen him smile before. She wasn't sure whether she liked it or not. She thought she actually preferred him being his usual sour-pussed self. It ended up with her walking away feeling a bit uneasy.

She soon got over it all as Miriam was waiting for her at the railings, looking like the cat that got the cream.

"That, my dear Esme, was *fantastic!*" she said, bouncing up and down in her little furry Dubarry boots and her checked tweed coat.

"It was pretty marvellous, wasn't it? Even if I say so myself. Are you coming back for a cuppa? I'll show you all the stuff I've got in connection with the party. I have a folder, you know. I keep it in the high cupboard above the fridge, to stop Michael fussing with it."

"I'd love to see the folder, Esme." Miriam was enthralled. She already admired Esme – she was confident and happy and had lovely daughters – but this party had escalated her to a whole new level.

# 24

*Things are on the up. Never underestimate the positive effect of a good old-fashioned solid night's sleep.*

Sian had started to take the alternative sleeping pills Paula had prescribed. She was getting a decent night's sleep, and the whole world seemed like a much better place. She was finding it easier to get out of bed in the morning, and didn't feel like she wanted to crawl into a ball and die by four o'clock in the afternoon. She actually felt *young* again. She felt like she had done before Liam died.

She'd forgotten what it was like to wake after a long deep sleep and open your eyes with a sense of hope. To actually look forward to the day ahead. Maybe it was a depression lifting, maybe she had finally come to the end of mourning Liam. She felt at one with the Sleeping Beauty. That girl must have been astonishingly chirpy when she woke up at first! First she got to sleep for a hundred years, with no one to annoy her, only to be woken by a rich handsome prince. Not bad.

Sleeping Beauty she may not have been, but she was so enthused that she decided to take herself into the city centre and buy a few things for the winter. She had a bright-coloured coat in mind. Not red, that'd make her look like a clown. She'd quite a high complexion too, so it wouldn't flatter her. Little Red Riding Hood had got a raw deal, in comparison to the other storybook characters. She just avoided being savaged and attending her granny's funeral. Perhaps a nice plum shade or even a green? She wasn't buying black, that was for sure. After a cup of coffee, still with no scone (she'd amazingly managed to stick to her wheat-free diet), she launched herself at the shops.

As she neared the window of Arnotts department store, she saw it. The "Hallelujah" music played in her head. It was the most exquisite, deep purple, soft frock coat. With just the right balance between vintage and modern. The little stand-alone collar and pinched-in puff-sleeves gave it a neat look across the shoulders. Nipped in at the waist, it fell beautifully to almost ankle length. It could be dressed up with a nice evening scarf, or worn during the day with a woolly beret and knotted pashmina. With a spring in her step, she pulled the big heavy door open and rushed in, looking up to read the signs. *Ladies' Outerwear* was pointing to the first floor.

The best part of the wheat-free diet was that she was now a comfortable size twelve. She hadn't dropped a dress size as such, she just felt much better in all her clothes. The coat was almost waving to her as she stepped off the escalator. Like the genie from the lamp, a shop assistant appeared from nowhere.

"Good morning, may I help you?" she smiled. Her eyes were very wide-looking and a little bit startling. For such a young girl she was wearing a serious amount of make-up. It took Sian quite by surprise. She had to stop herself from asking her why she was doing that. She had an urge to turn her to the mirrored pillar just behind them and point it all out to her. Why was she caking her dewy flawless skin in a thick leather-like coating of brown slick?

Shaking herself out of her reverie, she cocked her head to the side with a wicked grin.

"Yes, I'd like to try that purple coat in a twelve, please." She shrugged her shoulders and clasped her hands.

"Of course. There's a fantastic fitted dress by the same designer, in a French navy with a detail around the neck in the same purple.

I think it would be stunning on you if you'd be interested?" said Make-up.

"Why not?"

"Shall I put them in the fitting room for you and let you have a little browse around?" Before Sian could even twitch, Make-up had spun on her black patent heel and bobbed off.

With excitement bubbling through her, Sian hoped it was going to be one of those fruitful shopping experiences. As in, one where she managed to actually buy a few bits. Why was it that every time she had the money and inclination to buy, nothing suited her? Another day, when she was supposed to be looking for mundane things like replacement pegs for the clothes line or a gift for someone else, it was like the whole city was trying to jump itself into bags and come and live in her wardrobe.

Grabbing a couple more pieces, she made her way to the changing room. Pleasant piped music took away the silence. She found herself humming as she slipped on the dress and matching coat. Looking a bit stumpy in her stocking feet, she shuffled into the rock-hard pair of black stilettos provided in the fitting room, knowing that the extra height would elongate her legs, enhancing the whole look. Wobbling a bit, as they were the size of boats, she tried to envisage herself strutting her stuff in the outfit. She could understand that the shop used slightly bigger shoes, rather than a size three which nobody could fit into, but what was the story with these? Sian was a size six, which she deemed fairly average. These were of transvestite proportions and hard as the hobs of hell. Plopping them off, she turned and examined herself from the side, turned again and tried to do an owl on it and twist her head a full 360 degrees.

Yes, it was slimming and trendy, up-to-date without being mutton dressed as lamb. Great, she'd take it. She expertly contorted her arms around to the back of the dress and eased the zipper open. She'd become quite talented at opening even the most tricky fastenings unaided. It was one of the things that used to make her cry like a baby just after Liam died. The awful sad realisation that she had nobody there to help her pull up her zip had hit her like a ton weight. It might sound silly to anyone else, but to her it had been heartbreaking. She'd avoided wearing, and most certainly buying, clothing with back zips for a long, long time.

On this occasion, as she undressed, her gaze fell on her face. All creased up in a happy smile. The smile faded rapidly. It turned to a look of shock and disbelief. Where had that face come from? Since when did she look *old?* Sian didn't recognise the lady looking back at her. The hair was the same, the figure was improved if she was honest. But the face was wrinkly and baggy-looking. It wasn't working with the bones underneath. It was like her once firm and waxy face had been heated too much and it had all slid downwards, leaving a sad loose-fitting unstructured scrotum-type yoke in its place.

Raising a stunned hand to paw the scrotum, she found it to be almost jelly-like. Everything was turned downwards too. Her eyes, mouth, jowls, even the skin on her nose looked kind of runny.

Without her previous vigour, she tried on the other outfit she'd selected. She hadn't the heart to imagine what lipstick or tights would help it. Which accessories would jazz it up. Taking it off, she dressed in her own clothes and brought the first coat and matching dress out to Make-up.

"Any good?" The girl smiled too brightly.

"Yes, I'll take these please." Sian's voice was barely audible as she handed over her laser card. It was a rude awakening for her. Why had nobody told her that she'd turned into an old lady? As she made her way out of the department store, she decided she'd go online when she got home and figure out her options.

\* \* \*

As soon as the computer linked to the modem, she punched in the words: *plastic surgery*.

That was far too random. She'd have to redefine her search or she'd be there forever: *facelifts*.

That had narrowed it down slightly. She zoned in on Ireland and found a couple of places near Dublin. Their websites illustrated what they could offer, but none of them had any prices. Clicking on one of the private hospitals, she saw a list of plastic surgeons. She didn't recognise any of the names. Plenty of the people who came to her support groups had had reconstructive surgery, but it was mostly breast surgery, rather than facelifts.

She watched lots of those make-over shows on TV. Some of the women on them went to extraordinary lengths to change themselves. By the end of it all, they barely resembled the person they'd started out as. Small children in their families cried during the reveal, looking in a terrified manner at the new person who sounded a lot like Mummy or Granny. She didn't want that. She just wanted to look like she hadn't melted. One of the names jumped out at her. Dr Wesley Burke, plastic surgeon. Figuring he'd have a massive waiting list and nothing would ever come of it, she dialled his number.

"Dr Burke's office, Janet speaking, how may I help you?"

Sian took a deep breath. She felt her heart thumping and her throat dry as she explained that she was interested in some information on facelifts. To her surprise and relief, Janet didn't talk to her as if she was a freak, nor did she make her feel like she was an overly vain, silly old fool.

"May I take your name, please?" she asked politely, the clicking of a keyboard in the background.

"Sian Doyle." There. She'd given her identity away. Which was oddly difficult. Now it made it more real. She was a real person asking for information on plastic surgery.

"Correct me if I'm wrong, but you run the cancer support group, Sian, don't you?" Janet sounded pleased.

*Oh Holy God and all the angels and saints!* Sian wanted to hang up immediately, but seeing as this woman seemed to know her that would be slightly futile.

"Eh, yes, do I know you?" Sian shut her eyes, her cheeks flushing with embarrassment.

"No, but I know your name from my sister, Pamela Reilly. She attended your group a few years ago, do you remember her?"

"Yes, of course. How is Pamela doing?" Sian felt relieved this lady didn't know her, but mortified that one of her former members might hear about her silly vain phone call.

"She's great, thank God. Listen, seeing as it's you, I don't suppose you could make it in here this afternoon by any chance, could you? Dr Burke has a cancellation. I'm supposed to notify the people on the waiting list, but none of them are emergency cases, they're all elective surgeries, so you're in luck. You were so fantastic with Pamela I'd be glad to help you out in any way I can." Janet sounded sincere and not in the least judgemental. She certainly hid it very well if she thought Sian's call to be unusual.

"Oh right, yes. Yes, I'm free this afternoon, if that's okay with you and Dr Burke." She was in a bit of a spin.

"The best policy when you're considering surgery is to talk to a professional. Once you've spoken to Dr Burke, you'll at least have the proper information, straight from the horse's mouth. There's a lot of conflicting information out there and, to be honest, I would do exactly as you have done, by sticking with a surgeon connected to a proper hospital. There are a lot of cowboys out there."

Sian was barely focusing on the chat. She was still trying to come to terms with the sight she'd encountered in the dressing room earlier. Why had Joan not told her she'd turned into a toad? More to the point, how long had she been going around oblivious?

The two o'clock appointment came around far too quickly. Sian had toyed with the idea of telling Joan. She knew she'd have come with her, if she'd asked her to. But instead she found herself in St Mark's private hospital, looking on the name board to see which suite Dr Burke occupied.

"Sian? Hi there, how are you?"

Nearly screaming with fright, Sian turned to see Zoe from the support group.

"Zoe, hello, how are you?" she smiled, but her hands shook and her face was on fire.

"I was just in for a chat with Dr Leah. Everything seems to be going well, which is all I can ask for at this stage. Until I have a few more sessions of chemotherapy and further scans, I just have to plod along for the moment." The young girl was so caught up in her own sickness and prognosis, she quite obviously didn't notice Sian's discomfort. Nor did she think it odd, to see the older lady at the hospital. To Zoe, all the people to do with her cancer were under the same umbrella.

All the same, Sian felt such a sense of panic and, if she were honest, shame. Look at this beautiful young woman, she thought, trekking in and out of this hospital, fighting for her life. Here was she, silly old fool, who'd got a shock in a dressing room while treating herself to new clothes. Hardly comparable. She would have turned and left the building, only that Janet knew of her and had fitted her in so kindly. She couldn't *not* turn up. She said her goodbyes to Zoe and took the stairs to the second floor.

Janet looked remarkably like her sister, Pamela. The hair colour was different of course, but Pamela had been wearing a wig when Sian had known her. She had the same distinctive mouth, which turned down at the side when she spoke.

There was a man in the waiting room who'd looked over his paper to nod acknowledgement to her as she'd entered.

"Hello, I'm Sian Doyle," she whispered.

"Hi, Sian, how lovely to meet you!" Janet stood up and slid the glass partition right back in order to shake hands with Sian and chat to her more openly.

She handed Sian a thin black clipboard with a form attached and a biro studded in the top. Sian was to fill it out as best she could and Janet would be on hand to answer any questions or to help with some answers if she required. By the time she'd ticked the boxes and filled in the lines, agreed she wasn't allergic to anything and written in the large space at the end of the questionnaire why she was here (she'd simply scribbled "For information about a facelift") the heavy door flung open. A small thin man, with very pale skin and dark bushy eyebrows, a bit like that eagle puppet from *The Muppet Show*, appeared.

"Sian Doyle, please," he said very loudly.

It kind of unnerved her, as she was the only female person sitting there, yet he had felt the need to shout. Blushing furiously, she jumped up and followed him into his small oak-infested consultation room. Everything that could possibly be covered in dark wood was. The chocolate-brown carpet added to the conservative and slightly scary atmosphere.

"Sit. Pleased to meet you, I'm sure. Now I believe from your form here that you are interested in a, erm, eh, facelift." He clasped his hands together and looked at them. He didn't make any eye contact. He perched on a chair and shifted uncomfortably.

His apparent nerves were not doing much to instil confidence in Sian. She was strongly considering saying it had all been a silly whim and that she really shouldn't be taken seriously and that she'd just prefer to head on home. She was taking a deep breath and bracing herself to explain that she wouldn't stay, when he began to fire questions at her like a human cannon.

"Which parts of the face are you not so satisfied with?"

"All the baggy bits, especially the eyes, around my mouth and here between my eyes," she said, pointing.

"What kind of outcome did you have in mind?"

"Excuse me?"

"Were you thinking of looking fresher than you do today or did you want to alter your whole appearance?" He still didn't make eye contact, maintaining a constant jittery approach.

"Well, I don't want to look like Claudia Schiffer if that's what you mean. Like, I know you're obviously not a magician. I just wanted to look the way I thought I did." She thought her argument sounded so feeble.

"That's good. Yes, fine, okay. We can continue the conversation. As you mentioned I am not a magic man, nor am I God. I am able to work only with what's presented to me. You will still look like you, should you go ahead with surgery. I can certainly improve on the current look of the skin, but the general appearance will remain. Are we clear on all of that?" He was still looking at the mahogany desk.

"Well, yes of course. What did you think, that I'd have a photo in my handbag and ask you to make me into a sixteen-year-old supermodel?" She wondered where she'd found the courage to joke with such an edgy unapproachable man.

"You'd be very surprised what people come in and ask me for. Years of experience have taught me to be cautious and very frank." He smiled fleetingly.

Continuing his chat, he went through a litany of questions which he both asked and answered.

"Are you suitable for a facelift, yes. Would I suggest a full lift? No. What I would suggest is an upper and lower eye lift, with a chemical peel. What will this achieve? It will take away the tired look and rejuvenate the skin at the same time. What do you think?"

He'd stopped talking and was obviously waiting for her to step in.

"Oh, em, right. Well, I only noticed recently, very recently, this morning in fact, that I suddenly look, well, old. I wasn't quite sure what to do about it and hey presto, I've ended up here. I hadn't made up my mind as to what I wanted to do, so I'm open to suggestions."

"Well, a sudden look of skin sagging can be due to a number of issues. Sometimes weight loss, illness or simply the ageing process. Although the third doesn't usually cause a sudden change in appearance."

He was waiting again. She was supposed to speak.

"I have lost a bit of weight, but nothing major. I'm on a wheat-free diet, you see. I thought it might help with the menopausal symptoms I'd been feeling, and so I decided to –"

"Okay, so assuming the noticeable change is down to weight loss, I would strongly suggest changing your idea of a full facelift to the suggested eye lift. I will come around the table and show you with this mirror." He pulled a small hand-held mirror out of the desk drawer and came towards her. "My first incision would be along here . . ." He ran his nail along the middle of her eyelid. "I would then remove the excess skin and stitch – the scar will be absorbed by the natural line of the eye. The second incision would be under the eye or in the area commonly known as bags. I will do the same thing, removing the excess skin and stitching along the area just below the lashes."

"Oh," was all Sian could think of saying. She suddenly felt a little bit queasy.

"The skin will then be prepared for the chemical peel. This is an astringent chemical, which is brushed over the skin. I use a combination of glycolic, trichloric and salicylic acid. Depending on what I feel at the time of surgery, I mix a solution to suit your skin. The acidic reaction basically eats into the skin to produce what we term a controlled wound. The skin blisters in the process and the underneath skin which is revealed is usually softer and appears less wrinkled."

"Okay." Sian felt like she was going to vomit.

"With regards to recovery. Some people bruise very badly, and look like they've been on the receiving end of a baseball bat, others look fine. It's impossible to know how you'll react until the time comes. You will need to allow at least ten days of recuperation."

"You mean, ten days of hiding as I'll look like a battered panda?" Sian thought she was being witty.

"Precisely." Dr Burke didn't smile. By now he was back sitting behind his desk. "The next issue is price. The eyelift will come in at a price tag of five thousand euro, the chemical peel a further two. If you chose to go for both, I can do you a combined price of six thousand. Unfortunately none of this can be reclaimed on the medical health insurance, as it's classed as cosmetic, elective surgery. In the case of reconstruction due to an accident or medical emergency, it's different. In your case, you will have to fund the surgery yourself. Do you have any further questions?" His hands were clasped again. He was still looking at his hands, not at the face he was proposing to carve up.

"No, I don't think I have any more questions for now. I just need to go away and think about it all, if that's alright."

"Yes, I strongly suggest you do so. This is not a procedure you should consider undertaking rashly. It will involve considerable deliberation and you should be sure you are doing what you personally want. Without being swayed by a partner, friend or other." He gathered up the small amount of notes he'd splayed on the desk, which included her questionnaire and a page where he'd written some information for himself. Signalling their session was over, he stood up and offered his hand.

"Thank you for coming in to see me today. The ball is in your court now. If you wish to take this any further, you can contact, eh, my secretary."

They left the room. He looked mildly confused as he handed her, along with her file, over to Janet.

"I've only worked for him for the last twelve years and he still doesn't know my name," Janet whispered, looking totally unperturbed, when he had returned to his office. "Just so you know, he's an amazing surgeon, he just isn't so great with patients who are not anaesthetised, if you know what I mean?" She laughed easily as she motioned for Sian to sit on a chair beside her desk to settle up.

"Yes, of course." Sian tried to look like she thought it all very normal and funny. Inside, she was terrified. The thought of having her eyes slit open, filleted and sewn up, followed by her skin eaten alive by acid, made her want to run out of the place crying for her mummy.

She managed to get out of the room still holding it together. Janet was terribly nice, and had assured her that she would organise a prompt appointment for her, should she choose to go ahead. She'd smiled a lot, and Sian noticed she hadn't a line when she did so. She'd obviously been carved and boiled. She'd lived to tell the tale. Judging from her clothes and her general demeanour, Sian guessed she was in her late forties at least. She looked marvellous. There was a lot to be said for it. No doubt about it, Sian just needed to figure out whether or not the butchering part would be worth it for her.

By the time she picked up a few groceries and a magazine on the way home, the idea was surprisingly growing on Sian. The initial shock was dulling. She was getting used to it all. The image of the black eyes and peeling skin was fading and the end result, a fresh, new, rejuvenated version of herself was more at the forefront of her mind. Maybe it wouldn't be so bad? She would talk to Joan about it and see what she thought. Dr Burke's words rang in her ears – *"Don't allow yourself to be swayed by others."*

All the same, Joan was always a good person to bounce off. It wouldn't do any harm to phone her and ask her.

"Are you mental?" Joan scoffed nastily. "I wouldn't dream of doing anything so vain and stupid. Six thousand euro? Not a hope, I wouldn't spend it on *that*. The guy saw you coming. He must have thought all his Christmases had come at once when you pitched up!"

"Why are you so fired up about it? It's my face, my money. Surely if that's what I want to do, you should support my decision?" Sian felt stung by her friend's outburst.

"If you're so sure about it, why did you ask my opinion?" asked Joan indignantly.

They decided to change the subject. Joan was full of gossip about a wedding she'd been invited to. Pretty much a shotgun wedding, which they both agreed they'd assumed never happened anymore. Her neighbour's son had got a girl pregnant and her parents were insisting they marry.

"They're only twenty-two. I think it's crazy stuff, in this day and age. Why don't they simply try and live together and see how they fare? Marriage is a bloody messy thing to get out of in this country, should it all go pear-shaped." Joan babbled on about what a bad move it was to force people into a decision and how they should listen to the kids.

Yeah, like you listened to me just now? Sian thought. She felt a kind of kinship with the poor kids. Nobody wanted to listen to them or hear their point of view. Narrow-mindedness was a dangerous thing, no matter what the subject, she mused.

Once they'd finished the conversation, which was lengthy, as Joan had then gone off on a tangent about what to wear and whether or not she'd wear a hat, Sian felt at a loss. Normally, Sian would love to chat about such things, but on this occasion her friend had made it quite clear she had no interest in her facelift.

The only good thing to come out of it was the knowledge that she actually did want to go ahead with the procedure. She'd give it another couple of weeks, muse over it and sleep on it for a while. Then, she'd make her final decision.

Now that she'd noticed the wrinkles though, they were almost calling out to her every time she passed a mirror. They waved and taunted her. They yelled and screamed *"Old lady!"* at her.

At work, over the next couple of days, she scrutinised all the patients' skin. Some of them were a lot younger than her, so she knew she was foolish to compare herself to them. But she envied their taut skin. The men and women nearer her own age were a different story. One lady, it had to be said, had a face like a cheap handbag in a Moroccan market. Beaten and leathery, dotted with liver spots. Another woman, who Sian knew to be in her sixties, was in far better shape than she was. In fact, Sian found it hard to even listen to her properly as she poured her heart out. Instead, she was straining her eyes to see if there were any tell-tale scars.

"Are you alright today, love?" the patient asked Sian.

Embarrassed and disgusted with herself for being so dreadful, Sian knew she needed to cop on fast.

"Yes, of course, I'm sorry, I just have a bit of a migraine. It's been there since the other day. Must be the weather. It's been kind of muggy out, hasn't it?"

The other lady looked kind of confused. It was unseasonably cold outside and there'd been plenty of rain. The air was crisp and clear, certainly not what one would describe as migraine season.

A week after her initial consultation, Sian decided to call Janet.

"Yes, the middle of December would be fantastic. I think I can organise to finish work a little early for Christmas, and the usual holidays will ensure I'm not like a fright by the time I have to be in the general public domain again."

Putting the phone down, Sian exhaled. There. She'd done it. She was booked in. All she had to do was post a cheque with the deposit and the date was secured. Just so long as she didn't have a cold or any other sickness on the day, the operation was all set.

Although it was all quite sudden in one way, in another way she had been building up to this moment for the last eleven years. Ever since Liam had died, a huge part of her had gone with him. Oddly, this physical transformation she was about to embark on was a large step towards becoming the person she needed to be. The Sian who'd loved and lived with Liam was long gone, but until now she'd never managed to replace her with a new one. To some people, like Joan, it merely seemed like she was being a silly old cow. A person who had big ideas about her own appearance. But, to her, it was so much more than that. She'd tell Joan when the deed was done. Before then, it would be her own little secret. She still felt flutters of nerves at the thought of the actual surgery and the pain she'd have to endure. But rebirth was a huge process and a bit of pain along the way wasn't going to kill her. At least it would be physical pain. There were drugs available for that, and it would heal with time. Sian felt a sort of inner calm that she hadn't felt for such a long time.

# 25

*I must remember not to brush off the walls too harshly,
I might self-combust. Sellafield is probably more pure
than my blood right now.*

Zoe was getting to a stage where she felt radioactive. What with all the pills rattling through her system, the chemotherapy drugs flowing through her veins, and the radiation being lashed on top, she thought she must be able to glow in the dark.

The build-up of toxins was starting to really get to her. She felt nauseous most of the time. Waves of sickness hit her at random times, for no apparent reason. One day she'd be able to eat toast and honey with a cup of milky tea, the following day her poor mum would bring her the same thing and even the smell of it would make her gag.

The radiologists had warned her that her skin was likely to become red and sore, blistered even. But due to her immensely sallow skin, she just looked like she had the opposite skin condition to Michael Jackson. Instead of becoming white in patches like he had, she was growing darker and darker all around her pelvis. No amount of fake tan would ever cover this. Bikinis were out of the question forever. She'd have to invest in a wet suit for her next holiday at this rate.

At least the radiotherapy was finished, the six weeks of to-ing and fro-ing in and out of hospital were behind her.

Her mother was being amazing. Zoe's up and down relationship with food could have driven even the most patient person to drink, but Diana was more than understanding.

"I'm sorry, Mum, I can't control this," she said, watery-eyed, as Diana removed the offending tray at speed.

"Don't worry, darling. I was the exact same as this when I was pregnant with you girls. Your father would spend hours cooking dinners for me, especially towards the end of the pregnancy, and I'd have to leave the kitchen. I couldn't even bear to sit in the room with him eating the food, let alone try it myself. He used to sit and look like a puppy that'd been beaten with a rolled-up newspaper. Then the hormones would kick in and I'd feel like hitting him with one of the twenty pots he'd just dirtied in the cooking process." Diana went into a dream world as she remembered her pregnancy. She'd been so ill the whole time. She knew it was probably on account of it being twins, but she certainly never wanted to repeat the process. Steven had tried his best to support her at the time, but Jesus, he'd been so annoying he'd been scarily close to losing a limb at moments.

Like the time he'd decided to "help" with the housework. He'd cleaned out the fire into the plastic wheelie bin, which had duly gone on fire and melted in a black runny river down the drive and coated the neighbour's car tires.

Another day, he'd decided to put on the washing machine. Apart from boiling three expensive cashmere sweaters, he'd put in all her white underwear, which had of course ended up that revolting shade of pinky grey that only ever lives on spoiled clothes or mixed-up Play-Doh.

"Please don't wash anything else," she'd said through gritted teeth, as she tried to pull the boiled stringy jumper back into shape. "Where did you even find my sweaters?"

"I was putting some things away for you and I spotted them and thought it would be nice to freshen them up for you," he shrugged, looking like a reprimanded child. "I was just trying to make you happy. You're so fed up at the moment and I feel so helpless. I'm sorry."

She couldn't remain annoyed with him. He was trying his best. The day they brought the twins home from the hospital he'd stated that he was cooking dinner. With a kind of spring in his step, he'd gone into the kitchen where it sounded like a diseased donkey was buckarooing around kicking the shit out of the pots and crockery.

Sometime later, he called her in to eat. Wheeling the two tiny babies in their pram, she tentatively walked into the room. Every work surface was covered in food. Every utensil in the place had been used. The smell was not enticing.

"Mummy, please sit, your dinner is served!"

He looked so proud, she felt encouraged. Maybe he just wasn't a very neat worker. That didn't mean the food wouldn't taste delicious.

As she tried to eat the pasta, she began to retch loudly.

"What?" He looked at her, hurt and surprise all over his face.

"I'm sorry, honey. I'd say it's just after the Caesarean section. I'm still not too well," she'd lied. He'd overcooked the spaghetti, so it was like strings of worms. The chopped rashers he'd put over the top were like bits of tree bark, they were so burnt. "What's in your sauce?" she winced, as she wiped the gluey stuff from around her mouth.

"It's mayonnaise, with a bit of grated cheese, mixed with a tin of tuna. It came in oil, so I figured that would add an Italian feel to it. The Italians love olive oil, don't they? Doesn't taste too bad, even if I say so myself." He looked delighted as he tucked into the pasty sticky dish.

She had managed to make it out of the kitchen before she started to cry uncontrollably. She'd been starving and was so tired and shell-shocked after the birth and hospital stay, it was the last thing she needed to come home to a plate of fishy-coated worms.

Diana shook her head and smiled as she took Zoe's tray back to the kitchen. Her poor daughter had gone from swollen and red, to pale and stick-thin. She knew that making a fuss wasn't going to help her, so she simply brought what Zoe asked for and said nothing when she couldn't manage it.

The constant stabbing and cannulas in Zoe's hands were starting to take their toll too. As she pulled on a cardigan to go in for her mid-cycle bloods, she winced. Her arms were black and blue, the bruising starting just behind the knuckles on her hands and finishing above her elbow. She looked and felt like a junkie. In the beginning, the nurses had told her she had great veins. A compliment she'd never thought she'd hear. But as the weeks had passed, and she'd been stabbed over and over again, her veins had become more and more damaged.

In order to administer the chemotherapy, she needed a cannula put in. The needle with adjoining tube was one attack on the vein. Then a week later, she'd have to go back in to have blood taken to check on how the chemotherapy was affecting her body. Bang, another attack. Fair enough, the phlebotomist was very careful to alternate the arms, so that the bruising would have a chance to die down. But after a couple of months of treatment, the bruising wasn't going away. Her body was under serious strain from the harsh treatment and was busy fighting cancer, so doing menial tasks like healing bruised veins was much lower down on the schedule.

She'd never had a fear of needles before. She'd certainly never thought about them. But now, the thought of having her arm strapped so tightly that her hand turned blue, in order to raise a vein, filled her with fear. Most times, the phlebotomist used a heated compress, which she tenderly pressed over the fold of her elbow or the back of her hand. Warmer skin meant raised veins. Raised veins meant they protruded and made themselves readily available for a needle to find access.

"Okay, Zoe, a little pinch," the nurse would warn.

She'd close her eyes and take a deep breath, waiting for the sharp shunting sting, swiftly followed by a dull hot piercing sensation. Exhaling, she'd make eye contact with the phlebotomist.

"Are you in? Did the needle get into the vein?" she'd wince.

"No, darling, I'm so sorry," the phlebotomist would say. "The veins are there but they just seem to roll away to the side as I try to get the needle in. Forgive me, I'm going to have to take that needle out and try another vein. Can you bear with me?"

The phlebotomy nurses were so kind and always apologised for hurting her, and told her how well she was doing.

"We kind of expect the patients to hate us," one of them, Abbie, had smiled one day. "All we do is prod people with needles, so we're hardly the most loved team in the hospital, but we try to combat the hate by being so pleasant that you can't help yourself loving us." She'd shrugged as she smiled cheerfully.

"I don't hate you, I think you're amazing. I couldn't do what you do. I can't even look at you doing it to me, let alone manage to carry it out myself. I know I'd hit the wrong bit and make someone bleed to death, or hurt them so much they cried."

"I'll let you in on a little secret." Abbie moved a little closer as she deftly removed the failed needle and swabbed a new site on the hand with antiseptic solution. "The men are a million times worse than the ladies. Some of them cry, and most of them shout and scream as if you're banging a ten-inch rusty nail into their veins. Another little pinch now, pet."

Luckily for Zoe and Abbie, blood flowed from the vein this time. Abbie filled the vials of blood, using the little pressurised chamber. She labelled the tubes and removed the needle.

"Just press down on the cotton wool for a quick second for me, Zoe. I'll get you a plaster." Smiling, she patted Zoe's hand gently. "Well done. I know it's all getting very sore for you. Listen, I know it might sound a bit scary at first, but would you consider talking to Dr Leah about a port?"

"What's that?" Zoe looked wide-eyed and terrified. Needles were one thing, but this *port* word sounded larger and even worse.

"It might sound a bit worrying at first, but believe me, any patient who goes for it is delighted with the results."

Abbie arranged for the nurses to talk to Zoe about it all.

Zoe felt like the walls were closing in on her, as Kate, the sister on duty, sat down in the consultation room with her. She produced a small plastic torso, with a rubber front on it, which they used for demonstration purposes.

Kate was young, glamorous and confident. She always made Zoe feel at ease. This time, however, nothing would have made her feel relaxed. Kate explained that a surgeon would make an incision just below her collarbone. He would insert a small disc-like device, which would rest just under the skin. From this disc, a thin plastic tube would run to the jugular vein. A needle on the end of the tube would basically feed chemotherapy and any other medication into her veins.

"So the port, or 'port-a-cath' as it is called, would be used for both putting medication in and taking bloods out. There would be no more rooting around in the arm and hand, trying to chase your poor veins. If I was having chemotherapy, it would be the first thing I'd do, hand-on-heart." Kate held her hands up and looked Zoe directly in the eye.

"Okay. I'm not convinced – purely because it means more surgery. I'll be like a human patchwork quilt at this rate."

Zoe was miserable. This was the side of cancer and chemotherapy that she'd never have known about. All the extra things that can, and do go wrong. She'd never known that her veins could all sink, that she'd be in a situation where she'd have to think of having this port put into her. That she'd have reversed-Michael-Jackson syndrome and odd black-dot tattoos on her. Eyeballing the device on the rubber dummy, a silent blob with no arms, legs or head, sitting there like a poor severed victim, she shuddered.

"Will it hurt to have put in?" Zoe couldn't take her eyes off the device. It looked a bit like the top of one of those plastic sports bottles. Or two metal polo mints. The thin plastic line which would access her vein was kind of innocuous enough. For all the world it was like a plastic straw. It would take a bit of thinking about. She wasn't warming to the idea of having a foreign body sitting under her collarbone. She knew the nurse would probably think she was mad if she said that, so she tried to look and sound nonchalant about it all.

"You'll be sedated, but not under full general anaesthetic. You won't feel a thing and you won't remember it at all." Kate leaned forward to rest her elbows on her knees. "You'll have four little stitches at the site of the port and one, maybe two, where the line enters the jugular, just here." She pointed to the area at the base of Zoe's neck.

Vowing to think it over and let the hospital know, Zoe went back into the oncology day unit to take a seat and wait for the results of her mid-cycle bloods. It usually only took about an hour, so it must be nearly time by now.

Sure enough, Kate soon approached her. She wasn't smiling.

"Zoe, your bloods are a bit low today. You're what we call 'neutropenic'. It means that the chemotherapy has destroyed your white blood cells, leaving you with a very low count. If left alone, you are very open to infection and it would possibly mean you could get very sick. As you probably know, the white cells help the body to fight infection. You have none, so should you pick up even a cold, it could be very dangerous for you. So we want you to do some injections of a product called Neupogen, at home. Do you think you'd manage that?"

"I've never done injections before, I'm not sure if I'd be any good at it." Zoe wanted to run and not stop. She wanted to be a little girl again, maybe eight or nine years old. She wanted to be relieved of all this responsibility and illness. She didn't want to learn how to inject herself with Neupogen. She didn't want to decide whether or not to have a port put in her neck. She wished this cancer and all the trouble that came with it would just go away. She wanted to click her heels three times, she wanted to go to the ball, she wanted to be *just* Zoe again.

Kate brought Zoe a little tiny version of the yellow sharps bucket they used in the hospital for disposal of all used needles. A mini-version to take home. Although she was dreading the injection stuff, she had to admit the baby version of the bucket was terribly cute.

"The injections come fully loaded and ready to use. You simply remove the syringe from the box and pull off the lid, like so . . ." Kate popped the lid off, to reveal a fairly long, very sharp-looking needle. "It's a very fine needle, so it shouldn't hurt too much."

Kate showed her how to pinch up a good roll of flesh from the side of her tummy. At a forty-five degree angle, she was to push the needle in the whole way and slowly release the liquid, by pressing down on the top.

"You'll need to keep your Neupogen in the fridge, so if you think of it take it out about half an hour before you use it. When it's not so cold, it's less uncomfortable to inject. The other main thing is to try and do it at the same time each day." Kate waited to see if she had any further questions about the injecting, before she handed the spear to Zoe. "Okay, ready to try?"

"What, me? Now? Can't you do it?" Zoe looked astounded.

"Well, I need you to do it here with me, so we can decide if you're going to manage at home on your own. If you can't do it, we can organise for a nurse to call to your house each day. But it would serve you better if you can do it, so you won't be as tied down, waiting for help," Kate said gently.

"Okay, right. Yes, I can do this. I just need a second." Zoe exhaled, whistling. "Okay, here goes . . ." Breathing in, she pinched up a little bit of what flesh she had left on her tummy. Raising her hand up and bracing herself, she stabbed the needle into her own flesh.

"Good, Zoe, it's in, now you need to press the top of the injection and release the Neupogen. Slowly does it, great job. Now, release the squeezed flesh, and gently retract the needle. Good job. You did it!"

Opening her tiny little sharps bucket, Zoe popped the needle inside. "I don't think I'd ever make it as a nurse, but I actually did it!" She smiled, feeling a warm sense of achievement.

"Now, that Neupogen will get to work and stimulate your bone marrow to create some nice disease-fighting white blood cells. You might experience some bony pain. Which feels a bit crampy in areas of bone density, like your hips, lower back and even knees. This is normal and you can take a painkiller. Just make sure it doesn't contain paracetamol."

"Why not paracetamol?"

"It's just in case you get an infection. The main way we can tell if you do is by your temperature spiking. Once your body has any infection, the quickest way it can tell us is by creating a fever. Paracetamol brings down fevers, so stay away from it. We need to let your body tell us as quickly as possible if there's something wrong with you so we can make you better."

By the time Zoe left the hospital with her bag of injections, and all her instructions, she was exhausted. When she put them into the fridge, she felt kind of odd. The blue and white boxes looked strange beside the butter and yoghurts. Not something she'd ever imagined seeing in her parents' fridge.

By ten o'clock that night, she was lying in bed and she couldn't get to sleep. Despite taking her sleeping pill and even one of her Xanax relaxant tablets, she was uncomfortable and uneasy. Tossing and turning, she couldn't fall asleep. Reaching over to turn on the bedside light, she pressed the button on her electronic thermometer. Smiling wryly, she raised her eyebrows as she placed the device in her own ear. She'd never have owned any of these things before. Now, instead of lipstick and blusher in her handbag, she carried a thermometer and packets of anti-anxiety tablets and painkillers.

Her temperature read 38.6. Shoot, she was spiking a fever. The normal level of 37.0 was what she'd been hoping for. She knew she was supposed to phone the oncology unit immediately when she detected a fever. But it was ten o'clock at night. Her parents were just going to bed. Maybe it would go away. She'd wait for another hour or so and hope it was just a passing thing. She lay and tried to think whether she had any pain anywhere. There was nothing out of place, apart from her chest feeling a bit heavy. She wasn't coughing though, so she assumed she didn't have a chest infection.

By ten forty-five she was burning up. She had palpitations and she could barely crawl out of bed to alert her parents.

"Mum, Dad? Can you come and help me? I'm not well." Her voice cracked and the tears began to flow.

Her parents came rushing out of their room and to her side.

"What's the matter, honey?" Her dad looked terrified.

"I've got a fever and my whole body is shaking." She could hardly get the words out, her teeth were chattering so wildly.

Her mum phoned St Mark's oncology unit and they said to bring Zoe straight in. Packing a quick overnight bag, Diana's hands were fumbling as she went. "Fuck this cancer and all the problems it's dishing up to our darling daughter," she muttered under her breath. Where was the justice in all this?

By the time they got to the hospital and settled Zoe in a bed, she was physically jerking around from the fever. Her face was purple and touching her was like touching a radiator. The doctor on duty arrived, took one look at her and ordered immediate IV antibiotics.

"We need to try and get the fever down, but as we've explained previously, it can't be done using paracetamol. We have to get to the hub of the problem. We need to know what's causing the infection. Due to the fact that Zoe is neutropenic right now, with no white cells, we have to be extra cautious."

The phlebotomist was called to insert a cannula. After four tries on the left arm, Zoe was fighting back tears.

"I'm so, so sorry, Zoe, your poor veins are just hiding from the needles at this stage. I'll have to try the other arm. Bear with me here."

Eventually, after the fifth attempt, the phlebotomist managed to connect with a vein.

"Bingo, we're in! Well done. I know that was terrible for you. You're going to be bruised as well unfortunately, pet."

The antibiotics were connected into the arm and they began to pump through the accessed vein. As soon as the bottle of medicine was finished, another doctor came into the room. By now it was almost three o'clock in the morning. Her parents were sitting silently on chairs, shunting off to sleep and jerking awake.

"Why don't you guys go home? I'll be fine here. You need some sleep. Come back again tomorrow, the doctors will look after me now."

While she really appreciated her parents' support and them being there for her, she felt so hot and uncomfortable it was actually making her ill at ease having them sitting staring at her.

"Well, okay, love, if that's what you want." Diana stood up. "Come on, Steven, we'll go home for a few hours and come back, like Zoe says."

"No, I'm staying here." Her father wasn't open to any arguments.

"Dad, please." Her voice was barely audible.

Reluctantly her parents shuffled out miserably a few moments later. The silence, albeit only for a few minutes, was bliss. Zoe closed her eyes and took some deep breaths. A stingy pain shot up her arm. Peeling her exhausted eyes open, she rolled her head forward to look at her arm. The site where the needle was entering her vein was red and the entire length of her forearm was puffing up.

"Shit," she breathed.

Pressing the call button, she waited for a nurse to come into the room.

"Hi, sorry to annoy you, but my arm is getting stiff and the needle site looks red."

"I'll stop the drip. I'm afraid the poor vein has given way. We'll have to call the phlebotomist in to take that cannula out and have them put in a new one. Sorry now, Zoe." The nurse pressed her pager.

Zoe's heart sank. She was going to be subjected to more tightened straps on the top of her arm, followed by more prodding with needles. She felt rotten enough as it was, without this happening again.

As the phlebotomist jabbed her twice more, she felt like she was going to cry. Kate's words rang in her ears: *If you have the port put in, you won't look back.*

Maybe it wasn't such a bad idea after all. Nothing could be as bad as this. Already her left arm was black, with some yellow tinges beginning to show through, from the first round of pricks. Her right arm, which now housed the second cannula would end up the same by the following morning.

At eight o'clock next morning she was brought down for a chest x-ray. More bloods were taken, which meant more stabbing. Her temperature was still spiking and she felt like a wet rag.

"Zoe, good morning. I believe you came in to stay for a sleepover with us. How are you feeling today?" Dr Leah breezed in the door, wafting fresh perfume, with hair and make-up like a super model, oozing effortless elegance. To make Zoe feel more at ease, she perched on a chair at her bedside.

"I feel pretty terrible to be honest. My arms are black and blue from all the needles, I look like a heroin addict and I feel like a ton of bricks has been dumped on my chest."

"I'm not surprised. Your x-ray has just been handed to me. We can see that you've got pneumonia. I need you to try and produce a sample from your lungs. Are you coughing anything up right now?"

"No, I haven't had a cough at all. I'm just boiling and feeling like shit."

Dr Leah explained that Zoe had what they suspected to be a very dangerous form of pneumonia. She put a small plastic specimen bottle with a screw-on lid on the bedside locker. Zoe was to try and produce a bit of goo from her lungs to be tested. Every time she tried to force herself to cough, her head felt like it was going to burst. Her eyes bulged and she retched.

"It's okay, don't force it. We're pretty sure of what you've got, but it always helps to be certain, that's all."

Zoe was the one who brought up the port-a-cath this time. "I think I'm ready to go there now. I jump every time the door opens in case it's someone else looking for blood or to put in a cannula. The stinging and burning in my arms from all this stuff being pumped through me is getting unbearable."

"Okay, I'm hearing you loud and clear. I obviously can't let you have any surgery while you're fighting an infection, or while you're neutropenic. That would put you at too much risk. The other side is that you wouldn't heal very well after the surgery, if you go into theatre already ill. So we need to get you through this bout and then, once your bloods level out, we'll schedule you."

Zoe wished with all her might that the infection would go quickly and the port could be inserted. Her collapsed veins and ongoing pain were simply becoming too much for her to handle.

The pneumonia was severe and her system was so hammered from the chemotherapy and radiation, it took a long time for her to recover. The after-effects of the radiation were making her skin blister and inevitably bleed.

"But I finished the radiation weeks ago, so how come it's only blistering up now? My skin should have got sore when I was actually in the throes of having the therapy surely?"

"Well, some people do get sore at the time of radiation, but the effects come to fruition around six weeks after the fractions are finished. It's probably the effect of the starched hospital linen you've been grating up against during your stay here." The nurse shrugged her shoulders.

"What can I do about it?" Zoe looked at her poor boiled-looking pelvis.

"I'll go and get you some special steroid cream. That should help to relieve it. Don't let shower gels or any scented creams near the area, and certainly don't soak in any bath salts or bubble baths. Keep out of pools with chlorine as well."

"Well, I'm hardly in the mood for going to a pool right now. I'd be a right sight in a pair of swimming togs at the moment. Mind you, I wouldn't have to wear one of those uncomfortable hats, would I?" she sighed.

"I know you feel like it will never get better, but I promise you you'll be able to feel normal again soon. It's astounding what your body can recover from. I see it all the time, honestly."

The oncology nurses were such special and fantastic people.

As Zoe was in isolation she couldn't have friends in to visit. Although she almost felt grateful for that. Her head was shiny bald, with small patches of fuzz, her face was still quite red from the dermatomyositis, her arms were like two-week-old bananas and she could barely manage to string a sentence together. All in all, she wasn't exactly at her best, and having her stunningly dressed friends arriving in to make her feel worse (unintentionally) was not on her to-do list.

She'd every magazine known to woman in her room. Celebrities who she'd thought to be mingers suddenly looked stunning in comparison to what was gazing back at her in the mirror. Any time she had to shuffle into the bathroom, dragging the drip and the metal stand with her, she got a shock. The balding sick creature that stared back at her was not the image she had in her head. Sometime over the last couple of months, someone had come in and stolen her away, leaving this freakish-looking Halloween-type monster in her place.

The drip stand was a curse. "*Shiiiiit*," she started to cry one day, as she tried to manoeuvre it out of the bathroom. It was just like a supermarket trolley. She'd try and make it go in one direction and it would shoot off in the other. On this occasion, it had shunted sideways and yanked the needle in her hand with it. It hadn't come all the way out, but it was certainly dislodged somewhat.

Pulling the panic cord, she heard the nurses come running down the corridor.

"I'm sorry. I was only trying to go to the toilet and the bloody drip stand wouldn't do what it was told. It ran in the other direction – it was like it had a mind of its own, I'm sorry." Zoe's knees buckled and she squatted to the floor, tears streaming down her hot cheeks.

The nurses were kind and firm, raising her up and supporting her under her arms. Leading her into the bedroom from the ensuite, they folded her into bed. Working quickly, one nurse removed the sticky stuff holding the drip cannula in place and the other called the phlebotomist back, yet again.

Her breathing was so bad by that evening that they had to hook her up to oxygen. She felt like a patient on *Grey's Anatomy* as they wrapped the clear soft tubing under her nose and around her ears. Between all the constant drips of antibiotics, the noise of the oxygen pumping and nurses checking her blood pressure and temperature, she felt like she was in a train station.

\* \* \*

It took a full three weeks before she was allowed to go home. Dr Leah had explained that she would have to be fever free for a full twenty-four hours before they could consider letting her out.

It felt like the time would never come. She'd got so used to being in the hospital room that she almost gave up and became institutionalised. When Dr Leah finally came in and said she could go home, she sat in the bed, kind of dumbstruck.

"Really?" She looked from Dr Leah to the others in her team.

"Really," the doctor smiled.

Calling her parents, she could hardly contain herself as she asked them to come in and collect her.

"I'm escaping, I'm allowed parole!" she beamed.

"We'll be there as soon as the traffic lets us. We're only ten minutes away as it is!" her father shouted down the phone's loudspeaker in the car.

Meanwhile, Zoe crawled out of bed, at last free of the drip and being spiked for the moment. She felt a mixture of nerves and excitement as she pulled a tracksuit on. She'd made up her mind about one thing at least: she was definitely having the port thing inserted. She never wanted to end up having an experience like the recent one again. Her arms were swollen, bruised and unable to bend properly. Her skin felt like she'd been doused in chewing gum, there was so much sticky residual glue dotted around it from all the sticking plasters to hold the needles in place. The wigs weren't comfortable in the heat of the hospital, so she was wearing a little soft cap Diana had bought, made from T-shirt material, to cover her head up. She couldn't bear to be bald, even in a cancer hospital, where the staff were well used to the look. As she threw her belongings into a bag, she longed to be at home with her own things around her again.

# 26

*Who would have thought it – my very own event. I am*
*a true socialite!*

Esme had learned how to log on to their new computer the last
time the girls had been home. Tracey and Nora had bought it
for her and Michael for Christmas the previous year, and although
she dusted it every day and hoovered under its little desk, Esme had
never really had the nerve or the need to use the thing. Now, there
was no stopping her. She had a credit-card number which belonged
to Nora. At first she'd been afraid of her life using it, in case the
police came around and arrested her.

"Mum, they can't see if it's you or me over the internet. Once
you have the number and the three digits on the back, that's it. You
go online and find whatever you would like for the party and use
the credit-card number to pay for it," Nora had insisted.

In the beginning, she'd thought it better not to spend the girls'
money – it wouldn't be fair. They worked so hard and they didn't
need her coming in and siphoning it all away. So for the first week
or so, she just looked at things. It was astonishing what came up.
She'd type in just a word, like "party" and all sorts of websites
would pop up.

"I'm a bit confused though, Michael. What has a girl in her underpants and stockings with a rabbit costume got to do with a seventieth party?" Esme was a bit surprised at some of the websites that also popped up when she typed in the word.

"Maybe you can order one of them huge cakes and yer woman jumps out during the evening?" Michael looked amused.

"No." Esme wasn't convinced by that idea.

"Well, the men might like it." Michael looked sideways over his paper, where he was studying the racing for that afternoon.

"The men aren't having the party, I am. If they want to see that sort of thing they can go to Las Vegas, or some other seedy joint."

Michael guffawed and started to sing about Lola, and the Copa Cabana.

Once she'd managed to find the right sort of party site, she was mesmerised. They sold everything from balloons to party favours. Some of the gear was stunning. She'd found one particular balloon place, which was based in Dublin, and she made Michael go there on the bus with her on Tuesday.

All the shop sold was balloons. Every shade and size they had. She ordered a big arch of balloons in cream and gold to put around the door of the function room, a bunch of helium-filled ones for each table and a net filled with both balloons and streamers and little gold confetti in the shape of the number seventy. All those were to fall on the dance floor when the music started.

"I'll have some of the confetti for the tables as well, what do you think, Michael?" She rubbed her chin as she tried to imagine what the tables would look like. She'd flowers for the middle, just plain cream posies of roses. Then the balloons. Each place would have a little gold tulle bag, which would be filled with trinkets. A little going-home present for each guest. Really, she'd need the confetti as well, she mused.

"By the time you're finished, woman, there'll be no room for anybody to sit at the bloody table. That's if they don't float away in the first place," Michael chuckled to himself. He was secretly delighted for Esme. The girls were little stars for thinking of this party. It was keeping her mind off that horrible chemo. Even on the days when she wasn't able to eat her dinner, and she had to go back to bed with a cup of tea, she was able to talk about her party. The girls rang every day too, to check on her, and inevitably she'd end up on the party topic.

"Oh Michael, look at these!" Esme was bouncing up and down on the spot, pointing at what could only be described as obese people made out of helium balloons.

"What are they for? To make you feel like Cinderella next to the Ugly Sisters on the night?" Michael looked at them with distaste. They were foil balloons with arms and little legs with weights in them.

"They're the air walkers," the shop girl smiled. "They come in a few designs – we have nurses, doctors, builders, grannies, ones in bikinis, the list goes on. They're usually ordered to send to people. They come in a box and when you open it, they kind of pop out."

"Can I get the granny one?" Esme clapped. "I'll have her in a box and when the balloons fall from the roof, I'll get someone to let her out and she can kick off the dancing."

"Ah Esme love, you don't want to do that, do you? I'll be scarlet, with that fat yoke bobbing around the floor. People will think you've lost your marbles!" Michael looked a bit pained.

By the time they left the shop, Esme was unstoppable. She made him go to a coffee shop and sit eating cake, and he had to listen to all the ideas she had of bits of crap to put in the little going-home bags. He'd the *Daily Star* rolled up under his arm and he was itching to have a read of it. He hadn't even looked at the racing for this afternoon yet and it was after half eleven. He didn't want to upset her, but he really wasn't interested in this whole party thing. He'd go along on the night and have a few pints, of course he would, sure he wouldn't miss it. But apart from propping up the bar with a few of the lads, he didn't feel the need for all this discussion and fuss.

"So are you set then, love?" Esme was looking at him.

"For what?"

"Ah Michael, were you listening to a word I said?" She batted his arm.

"I was just thinking about the pints I'll have at your party. I hope the Guinness isn't stale in that little function-room bar. Some of those places can have gammy pipes, you know? They have people from God knows where working there and they haven't a dog's-arse-notion of how to treat a pint. I'd hate the lads to get an iffy pint." Jesus, maybe he'd better pay more attention to this party after all.

"Don't be worrying about pints, for crying out loud. That'll all be sorted by the banqueting manager." Esme stuck her nose in the air at the mention of banqueting. "Drink up that frappachino and come on, will ya?"

"Where?" He looked a bit scared.

"To buy a new suit! Did you not hear a word I said to you? Tracey was on last night and rightly pointed out that you haven't bought a new tin-o-fruit in fifteen years. On account of neither of the girls getting married yet, you've had no excuse. So we're going over to Louis Copeland now to get you fitted."

"I am in me bollox going to some gay shop to buy a bleeding suit. I draw the line at that now, Esme. It'd be a waste of money and God knows it's hard enough for us to manage on a pension as it is, without squandering every penny on a yoke that'll be worn once and then pulled on to me when I'm stiff in a box. Because that's what'll happen to it, you know. Mark my words."

"Stop that talk, and stop sounding like a grumpy old git. We're going to Louis Copeland and that's final."

Esme had her determined face on, with her lips pulled all thin and her handbag tucked under her arm. He knew from many years of experience there was no point arguing with her when she took a notion.

His newspaper would have to stay rolled up for a while longer, he sighed inwardly. He'd have to do what she wanted. The girls were "sponsoring" the suit too, so he'd no argument really.

In the end they got too cold at the bus stop and Esme was beginning to get very tired, so they took a taxi. As soon as they walked into the shop, Michael wanted to leave. It was full of ponces. All talking like they'd a poker up their holes and pawing the lines of suits as if they were thoroughbred racehorses.

"Can I help you?" A young man with a gay-looking haircut approached them.

Esme smiled at him and explained that she needed a suit for Michael.

"It's not every day one turns seventy. I need him fitted out from top to tail, please, sir." She was, of course, using her telephone voice.

"If you would like to come this way, I will measure you properly and we can decide if you would rather choose a ready-made suit or a custom design." He smiled at them and motioned for them to go to the back of the shop.

They followed him obediently.

"Now, sir, I will measure your inside leg first."

"Esme, he just wants to fondle me jewels," Michael whispered. "I'm out of here. That fella's a queer and he's not sticking his measuring tape up my inside leg. He can get lost if he thinks I'm going to stand there and play his game."

"Don't be silly, love, it's his job. He's a designer – he's only doing the same thing he does every day. It's not a brothel, it's a bloody suit shop. Now stop your nonsense and don't make a show of me." She wagged her finger at him and gave him a dagger's stare.

Feeling a bit faint and hating every second of it, Michael did what he was told. The pain got worse. They made him try on piles of suits, everything from pale grey, which was like a school uniform, to a dark purple colour.

"*No way.* I'm not going dressed as a bruise. I've had enough. I'll take a black one, off the peg, with a plain shirt and no tie. I hate ties."

Half an hour later, they sat into the taxi the shop man had called for them. Michael was kitted out with a new suit, shoes, shirt and of course a tie.

"I'll look like a fucking eejit in that lot. The shoes and matching belt are like they're made out of a conker. Everyone will be able to see my knickers down the leg of the trousers, them shoes are so shiny. They're like wearing two mirrors on me feet. The tie makes me look like Daniel O'Donnell, and the matching hankie thing is a joke. I feel like a plank in it all, Esme. In fact, I feel violated after that assault on my person."

Esme wasn't even listening to him. He could grumble all he liked, she was thrilled. He looked dead handsome in his new gear, and she'd be as proud as punch on the night. The two girls always looked beautiful. They'd have the best London fashion on, she'd be in her knock-dead rig-out with her fascinator. The Golden Girls, Father Moriarty and the neighbours wouldn't see this coming, she chuckled to herself.

She was very short of energy due to the chemotherapy, so she decided to go to bed with her magazine when she got home. Michael was busy studying the form for the afternoon racing at Leopardstown. He had his cup of tea and a ham sandwich, made from leftover meat from the night before. Once he was happy, he wouldn't be shouting up the stairs to her, annoying her.

The first page she opened she saw it. The pink Hummer. One of the Wags was stepping out of it in a photo. It took Esme's breath away it was so beautiful.

The phone rang, it was Nora.

"You won't believe what I just saw!" Esme was so excited she could barely speak.

"What?" Nora smiled.

"A pink Hummer," Esme said it like it was a regal thing of beauty.

Nora laughed. She wasn't surprised at her mother lusting after the car. She thought it was a bit tacky, but if that was what she wanted, then so be it.

"Would it be able to collect us and then swing by and pick up Miriam and Mrs Murphy?"

"I thought you hated Mrs Murphy? You've always called her a sour old bag," Nora laughed.

"I do hate her, but it would be worth it to piss her off," Esme reasoned. "It would be the best bit of the night, pulling up outside that old bitch's house and making a fuss for all to see. Miriam would love it, and there'd be room for her Frank."

Declan, Miriam's son, had already said he wouldn't come to the party. They'd be better off without him. He'd only upset Miriam anyway. She said he'd a tendency to get pissed and start fights. They'd been at her niece's wedding and he'd gone up to the chap singing on the stage and snatched the microphone and started singing rude songs in front of everyone. Miriam had nearly died of shame. The hotel manager had asked him to get down and he'd lost the plot and boxed him. Miriam said his nose had burst and destroyed his dickey-bow and white shirt. Frank had ended up taking her home. She'd cried half the night after the shock of it all.

Esme had put Declan's name on the invite and all but, unbeknownst to her, Miriam had put it in the drawer in the hall table. She told Esme that Declan had a previous engagement that night, but the truth was that she didn't want him to come along and deck someone and embarrass the life out of her.

* * *

After she'd had a little sleep, Esme made her way to the front room to log on to the computer. She typed in *"pink hummer"*. At first her heart sank – it was all stuff in America. They'd never be able to get there on time if they had to come from Chicago, she mused. But there in one of those little ads on the right-hand column was exactly what she'd been searching for – *California meets Tallaght. Tallaghfornia Dreams, Limousine and Hummer Hire.*

Scrolling with the mouse, Esme looked down their web page. They had a black Hummer, a white one and finally there it was, shining like a beacon, a Barbie-pink one. They had pictures of the inside as well. It had a bar and a disco ball, with a ceiling that lit up. *A fluorescent kaleidoscope of colour as you make your way in style,* the ad read. Esme felt a flutter of butterflies as she read on. Without delay she picked up the phone and called them.

"That's no worries at all, Mrs Mulligan. If you can give me a credit-card number to secure your booking, I'll put all that through for you this second." Bucko was the man's name. He was the owner, so he said.

"Do yous want any doves?" he asked.

"What do you mean? Would they not peck us in the back of the car?" Esme had visions of them flying at her fascinator and trying to attack it.

"No, love, I'd keep them in a cage in the boot and we'd let them fly off as you make your grand entrance to the hotel. Did you ever see *My Sweet Sixteen* on MTV? Where all the American millionaires have big birthday bashes for their kids?"

"Yes, I've seen them alright. Some of them need a good hiding if you ask me!" Esme forgot her telephone voice for a second.

"Agreed, love, but they know how to do things proper in America. Loads of them, famous ones mind you, daughters of rappers and all, they wouldn't even consider having a do without the doves. If you want I can dip them in food colouring and make the tips of their wings pink to match the Hummer," he offered kindly. "For no extra charge, with regards to the colouring."

"Well, that's very nice of you, Bucko. I can't argue with that. I'll have the doves, and I'll take you up on the pink. That sounds lovely. I am doing a gold and cream theme throughout the ball room, but pink would indeed match the car."

"I'd put some gold glitter on them for you, but I'd say they'd only fly into the wall if I put glue on their wings. I'm only thinking out loud here. I haven't had a request for gold before, you know."

"Ah no, pink will be great, Bucko. Just a quick question before I let you go – we'll be collecting Mrs Murphy and she's a miserable old cow – will you be wearing a cap and uniform by any chance?"

"Oh yes, I wear the full Navy uniform with the hat with the gold braiding, with matching jacket. I take this all very seriously. There'll be no lack of professionalism on my part, Mrs Mulligan. Of that I can assure you."

"Mrs Murphy has looked down her nose at me and all the other Golden Girls for too long now. I'm not a nasty person by nature, Bucko, but I'll enjoy rubbing her nose in it, if you know what I mean?"

"I do indeed, Mrs Mulligan. Consider her nose rubbed raw."

Deciding that Bucko was a serious businessman, Esme hung up, delighted with the notion of the Hummer and the pink doves. Maybe I should have ordered the black one, she thought with a smile, so we can use it for the funeral, because Mrs Murphy is going to die of jealousy when she sees all this.

* * *

The following morning, the postman had to ring the doorbell on account of the large package.

"Sorry, Mrs Mulligan, I wasn't going to try and stuff it into the letterbox. I don't know what's inside, but things can get damaged if they're forced through, you know?"

"Will you come in for a quick cuppa, Mr Quinn?" Esme asked politely.

"Ah, just a very quick one so, if you insist. How are things with you? How's the chemo going for you? You look very well on it, if I might say." He followed her down the hall into the kitchen.

"Hiya, Jim!" Michael shuffled into the kitchen. "In for a quick cuppa, are ya?"

"Yeah, just a quick one, Michael."

"There's one left in the pot, you're in luck. What've you got there, love?" Michael nodded towards the package.

Esme had slit the top of the jiffy bag and pulled out the bale of invitations with matching envelopes.

*You are cordially invited to join in the celebration of Esme Mulligan's birthday.*
*70 years young!*
*Venue: The Regal Hotel*
*Time: 7.30pm sharp for a drinks reception*

*RSVP: Regrets only*
*Dress code: Smart*

As they all drank a cup of tea, they studied the invitation. It was on a cream card with black writing. In the top left-hand corner there was a small bunch of gold stars, with the number seventy in the centre.

"That is a thing of beauty, Mrs Mulligan." Jim the postman was very impressed.

"Isn't it just? Of course yourself and Mrs Quinn will come along, won't yous?" Esme elbowed him. Jim had been their postman for nearly thirty years. Since the day he started, he'd called Esme "Mrs Mulligan" and Michael, well, "Michael". In turn, Esme always called him "Mr Quinn". She'd be delighted to meet his wife. She always sent them a Christmas card each year and Mr Quinn always said his wife was very grateful for the tin of Fox's biscuits she sent on Christmas Eve. But they'd never actually met. Jim was always turned out perfectly. His uniform never had dandruff down the back of it like that other fella who came the odd time, Mr Duff, who snorted all the time too. No manners at all. She wouldn't be inviting him. He'd probably turn up in a bin bag and stand in the corner picking his nose. No, it was only people of distinction (and Mrs Murphy) who would be gracing her with their presence.

"That's terrible kind of you, Mrs Mulligan. I'll certainly say it to Nan, but I'm not sure if she'd come. She's very shy, you see. She gets a bit worried about her wheelchair too. Do they have a ramp at that hotel, do you think?"

"Oh, I'd say they have two or three, Jim. It's a fabulous place, the Regal. Were you never in it?" Michael sat back proudly.

"I never knew your missus was in a chair, Mr Quinn. I'm sorry to hear that. Is it recent?" Esme's ears pricked. All the more reason to get a look at her, she thought.

"Ah, she's always suffered with her legs, on account of her weight. Since she turned sixty, she's been a bit of a divil with the biscuits and chips. She got the chair from the community centre last May, and she goes everywhere in it now." Jim nodded, resigned to the fact that he had to push his wife around most of the time now.

"Very fat, is she?" Esme's mouth was agape.

"Ah yeah, she's a big woman, in fairness to her." Jim didn't seem offended by Esme's query.

"Sorry, love, that's not very politically erect of me. 'A larger lady', isn't that what you're supposed to say nowadays?" Esme corrected herself. "'Embracing her curves', what?"

"You're alright. I think you should call a spade a spade, meself. Half the time I don't know what people mean." Jim took a slug of his tea. "Don't waste the money on a stamp now with regards to my invite. You can just hand it to me."

"That's very good of you, isn't it, Michael? That's very thoughtful of Mr Quinn, isn't it? To save us the price of a stamp? One less, what?"

The whole invitation episode was so exciting, Mr Quinn ended up being half an hour late with the rest of the post. Nobody else minded except that old biddy, Mrs Murphy. She must've been waiting behind the net curtains for him to arrive. He was halfway up the driveway with her post when she flung the front door open. She didn't even have the grace to talk to him. All she did was point at her watch and glower. He wouldn't mind if she was waiting for the Crown Jewels to be delivered, but all she was getting that morning was a begging letter from Oxfam. The miserable old wench wouldn't give the steam off her own piss, never mind donating money. She snatched the letter and he turned on his heel and marched off as quickly as he could. He'd left his bike two houses up. He never even leaned his bike on her wall. It'd probably melt.

# 27

*Tanya, every day things happen and I look for you to be there. Will I ever manage to live without you? Do I even want that to happen?*

Alfie looked at the cream envelope and turned it over. It looked a bit like a wedding invitation. He certainly didn't feel like going to a wedding on his own.

A short time later, Zoe picked up a similar envelope from the kitchen table.

"That came for you yesterday, to the apartment, so Charlie dropped it in," Diana called over her shoulder.

Zoe ripped it open and smiled. Good old Esme. She was having a birthday bash. She'd written *Zoe + 1* on the card. A little yellow sticky note was attached. In perfect writing that almost looked like it had been typed, Esme had written.

*I got your address from Sian. I sincerely hope you can come. Hope to see you soon.*

*Yours sincerely*
*Esme Mulligan*

It was very nice of her, but Zoe didn't think she'd go. She wouldn't know anyone for a start and, secondly, she'd probably be the youngest person by forty years.

* * *

Sian opened her envelope too. She knew it was coming, as Esme had asked her for the addresses the previous week at their meeting. The older lady had been so excited. Although she was feeling tired and rather sick from her chemotherapy, she was doing exceedingly well. She'd only two more sessions to go and was dealing with the whole ordeal incredibly.

"I'm doing fine, to be honest with you, Sian. Having Miriam there with me has been a blessing. She's a great companion and we've kind of been a source of support for each other. Michael is great and her fella's alright, but nobody can understand unless they've been through it, can they?"

"No, I don't suppose they can. Well, I think you're marvellous. You've coped like a trooper," Sian smiled. She was very fond of Esme. She was a real character and one of the most positive people she could remember meeting. Zoe had more or less bowed out of the whole counselling thing, due mainly to the fact that she'd been in hospital so often, but Sian guessed it might not be her scene. Both herself and Esme were a lot older than her, and maybe it just didn't make her comfortable.

Esme had been fortunate during her chemotherapy so far that her bloods had remained in good order and she'd managed to avoid infections.

"I wonder is it because we eat liver once a week on a Saturday?" she asked Sian, as they sipped a cup of freshly brewed coffee. "My mother, Lord rest her, always swore by liver. Now, at the same time, she'd always have a bottle of Guinness on the go too. She kept it under the sink in the kitchen. She'd have a swig out of it while she was washing the delph."

"Well, they say both liver and Guinness are full of iron alright, so I'm sure it isn't doing you any harm," Sian smiled.

"Now, I know we're supposed to talk all about being sick and bowel movements and cancer and all, but I've a bit of news. I'm having a party! You know the way I'll be seventy in November? Well . . ."

Esme took off. She'd even brought her folder to show Sian. They had a lovely morning chatting about the preparations. Sian promised she'd come and even told Esme about her new purple dress and coat. She thought she'd bring Joan, if that was okay with Esme.

"Are yous lesbians?" Esme leaned forward. "Because Mrs Murphy's youngest is one of those. She lives with her girlfriend and they both wear men's army boots. So you needn't worry about people pointing and whispering. Mrs Murphy, old bitch that she is, she'd talk to you. You could tell her and introduce your 'friend'." Esme nodded and smiled and patted Sian's hand.

"No, Esme, we're not gay. We're both widows and simply friends. There's no funny business involved," Sian giggled. "But, if I ever decide to be gay, you'll be the first to know!"

Esme belly-laughed, before launching into the details of the Hummer.

By the time Esme left and Sian was washing the cups and wiping the coffee table, she felt lighter and happier than she had in ages. The thought of the party was keeping Esme going and, after hearing about the finishing touches, Sian couldn't wait to see it all.

This would be her last "occasion" as the current Sian. After a lot of deliberating and visiting Liam's grave, Sian had made her decision. She was going ahead with her facelift. She was booked in for the 10th of December. It would tie in with her Christmas holidays from the centre and she'd be able to hide while she looked like a car-crash victim.

Joan knew and had offered to come and spend Christmas with her.

"I'll be a regular Florence Nightingale. But I won't have to douse you with antiseptic or anything, will I?" She'd looked a bit fearful.

"Not unless the stitches all burst and you might have to reattach my face using a staple gun," Sian teased.

She'd gone through a catalogue of emotions in making her

decision. At first she'd been terrified. What if she ended up looking like a liver-lipped ageing Barbie doll? Further conversations with the surgeon had convinced her that she wasn't going to look that way.

The more she thought about it, the more she wanted it done. Eventually, she'd taken a deep breath and phoned through to Janet the secretary.

"Good for you! Now I know you won't broadcast this, but I'm going to slot you in before Christmas. I'd be shot if it gets out. Dr Burke has a huge waiting list, so Mum's the word," she'd whispered.

Now that it was November, the countdown was on. She was really excited about her new look. She imagined herself a bit like a butterfly. For the last ten years, she'd been cocooned, soon she would break free and emerge. She might not be beautiful, but she'd at least feel fresh and new.

She'd weaned herself off the sleeping tablets, and her body had got into the habit of sleeping. At least she wasn't devouring half the contents of the freezer at night anymore. Her nightdress was still stained with pink blobs after one particularly messy episode involving a packet of digestive biscuits, a jar of beetroot and a tub of cookie-dough ice-cream. She'd woken up in the morning and screamed, thinking she'd been attacked and stabbed in her sleep. Wildly flailing around in the bed, hair all over her eyes, she'd tried to piece it all together in her mind. Nothing. It was all a blank. She pushed the duvet back and heard clanking. A bowl, spoon, sharp knife and jar all bashed off each other. She'd been such a mess, what with the ice-cream melted into her hair and the beetroot juice staining her face and clothes, she'd had to get straight into the shower. Towelling her hair, she'd pulled on a track suit and made her way down stairs. The sight that greeted her was nothing short of a catastrophe. The beetroot juice was dribbled all across the kitchen. The rug would have to go in the bin. Before making her way up to the bedroom, she'd obviously savaged two packets of popcorn – the place looked like it had been showered in polystyrene – and she'd obviously been making lemon-curd sandwiches. She'd been wheat-free for months by that stage, and so must have dug the sliced pan out of the bowels of the freezer. No wonder she felt like she'd swallowed a sofa. Her tummy was round and bloated after the midnight feasting. Cleaning up the mess was a good start at working it all off. The fuchsia-pink beet juice mixed with the yellow sticky residue from the lemon curd was a challenge for any household cleaner.

All the bingeing aside, she was feeling so much better in herself due to the lengthy hours of sleep she was having. Slowly she'd weaned herself off the tablets, until she was managing to sleep by herself. She still woke a number of times in the night, but her body had got into the habit of needing the rest, so she usually managed to drift off again quite quickly.

As she propped Esme's party invitation on the mantelpiece, she dialled Joan's number. She knew she'd be on for going to the party – both of them always enjoyed a night out. It would be a good excuse to get their hair done and maybe even make an appointment for a manicure and fake tan. Seeing as she was going to be laid up in the house over Christmas, it would be nice to get out and about first.

\* \* \*

Alfie was sitting at the kitchen table with a feeling of unbearable sadness as he read the invitation. It was odd but the whole fact that Esme was celebrating being seventy hit him like a smack in the face. Tanya would never be old. Her memory would never be old. In one way, it was so right for Tanya to always remain in control and steady and fresh. In another, it was so awful that she would never experience any more of life. There were so many places she had never been to, so many things she'd never done. Alfie felt certain that he would never come to understand why she'd had to die. He might accept the fact she was gone, he might learn to move on and to live without her, but he'd never understand it fully.

His mobile phone made him jump as it sprang to life.

"Phone, Dada, quick!" Jenny hurtled in from the playroom.

Her latest thing was answering it and running off to another room, refusing to let him talk. Most people were very patient and enjoyed listening to her tinkling tones, as she asked question after question. He'd let her speak for a little while and then coax the phone away, usually with bribery.

She grabbed the phone. "Hi!" She hopped from one stripey-tighted leg to another.

"Hi, Jenny, this is Zoe. How are you today?"

"Fine. Do you like Barney or Barbie?" Jenny's speech had suddenly burst forth from mixed babbling baby talk to more understandable sentences.

"Well, I like both, but Barbie has much cooler stuff, hasn't she?"

"Uh-huh. She has a pink car. Pink is nice. I have a pink tutu. Do you have anything pink, Zoe?" Her little voice was almost screechy from excitement. Her breathing was heavy down the line as she waited to hear Zoe's answer.

"Guess what I have that's pink?" Zoe whispered loudly.

"What? A cat?"

"No, I have pink hair that I wear sometimes. Next time I see you I'll put it on if you like?"

"Like Stephanie from *Lazy Town*," Jenny shouted, accepting pink hair as the norm.

"Sort of, but mine is a bit paler. Can I speak to your daddy?"

"No, he's gone to the shops. I'm here by my own and he'll be back soon. He's gone to buy milk," she lied.

"Jenny, can Dada have a go of the phone now?" Alfie stood with his hand out.

"No," she pouted. She tucked it under her arm, ran to the other side of the playroom and crawled into her little pop-up tent. "Mine!" She stuck her head out momentarily and shot back inside.

"Jenny, please, I'll give you a bickie if you come out?" That was the last thing Zoe heard before Jenny pressed a pile of buttons and cut her off. Laughing, she waited for Alfie to call her back.

It took about five minutes.

"Sorry, Zoe. She had a complete melt-down when I tried to get the phone. No amount of bribery was going to work. She's got a vicious temper when you don't do what she wants. She's as stubborn as a mule and if you try to grab anything from her, she flips. I had to calm her down and put on the TV before I could call you back." Alfie sounded flat.

Zoe admired him so much. She'd no idea how he did all the parenting on his own. With nobody to talk to most of the time, nobody to back him up and nobody to share the good and bad times, he was an amazing guy.

"Did you get an invitation to Esme's party?" she ventured.

"As a matter of fact I did. I can't see myself going though. I think I'd find it too hard-hitting. I haven't been to anything like this on my own yet, apart from the funeral of course, but at least everyone understood why I was at that on my own!" He tried to sound frivolous, but his voice cracked and he ended up sounding miserable.

"I'm not too keen either, but I was kind of wondering if we might hook up and go together? Would your mother-in-law mind Jenny?" Zoe bit her lip, thinking he'd just scoff and fob her off.

"Well now, there's a thought. Do you know what? I'll ask Danielle if she'd take Jenny for the night. I've been sitting here feeling sorry for myself since I opened the invitation and had automatically assumed I would just decline and send Esme a bunch of flowers. But maybe I should change the record, so to speak?" He was tired of feeling like a hollowed-out version of himself. He was so used to being heartbroken and haunted, it was becoming a way of life for him. He knew he'd need a lot of time and energy to crawl out of the terrible hole of empty loneliness he now called life, but at some stage he had to make a move.

"I won't stay late, I've no energy, stamina, hair or resolve at the moment, so I'll be a fairly lousy date, but it'll mean you won't have to endure the night right to the bitter end if you're feeling too vulnerable," Zoe offered gently.

He knew she hadn't meant the word "date" to be serious but the word hit him nevertheless. She was still talking as he sat reeling. It felt like Tanya was only just gone and he couldn't possibly imagine "dating" another woman. In fact, right at that moment, he felt he could never love anyone else ever again. He'd been through it all in his mind, he knew it was all still too raw, too painful. But even stretching his imagination to its height, he couldn't see how he'd ever marry again or move on with a new relationship. He knew he wasn't the first person to lose a partner, and unfortunately he wouldn't be the last. But, the ones he'd heard of who moved on and went on to remarry, have another four children and live happily ever after – they simply mustn't have loved their partners the way he'd loved Tanya. It was the only thing he could think of. They mustn't have felt the same way. He couldn't see any amount of time healing the empty thudding pain where his heart used to be.

Zoe had stopped talking.

"Alfie? Are you still there?"

"Yes, sorry, Zoe. I don't think I can go to the party. I don't think I'm ready. I know Tanya would scoff and get irritated with me. I can almost hear her now, telling me not to be so soft, telling me to go the party, get pissed and forget the past, even for a couple of hours. God knows I'd love to do just that. But I don't think I can. I'm sorry, I appreciate your asking me, but I don't think I can physically bring myself to even carry out the motions."

"Why don't you think about it? I'd really appreciate you coming along. Other than Sian, I won't know a soul there and I feel obliged to go, even for a little while. If you change your mind, you can let me know. No pressure." Zoe tried to sound bright. She felt so inadequate. What could she say to the poor man? He sounded so lost and unreachable. Even though he had the constant company of little Jenny, at the same time his child must be a constant reminder that he was on his own.

Retail therapy was the first thing that sprang to Zoe's mind after putting the phone down. She'd pop over to Blackrock and look in on Charlie in the shop. The Christmas stock was all coming in. She'd see if there was a nice dress or outfit she could take for Esme's seventieth. She knew, if it came to it, that Charlie would come with her to the party. Reversing into the little parking space they owned at the side lane to the shop, she felt a familiar rush of excitement at seeing the new line of clothes. She missed the shop and the customers. She also missed her twin. They'd never been apart this much and, due to the flourishing relationship Charlie was having with Simon, her boyfriend of almost six months, she felt removed from her for the first time ever.

"Zo-Zo! How are you, lovie?" Charlie rushed and hugged her as soon as she entered the shop. "Love the hair. You look fabby. What's the story-Rory?" Charlie linked arms with her and led her to the wide counter. She hopped up to sit on it while Zoe leant against it.

"Not a lot. I'm invited to a seventieth party and I wanted to have a quick goo and see if there's anything suitable," she smiled.

"Jesus, that sounds happening alright," Charlie teased. "You'll have to swap that pink wig for a blue rinse to fit in there. Who's the old dear?"

"Ah, it's Esme, the lady I met at the Pink Ladies cancer support group. She's a great old bird and I'll definitely give it a look for a while. She's so excited – her daughters are organising it for her and she'd appreciate me going. Don't slag too much, m'lady – you might be coming with me." Zoe poked her sister in the ribs.

Just as Charlie was about to tell Zoe to sod off, that she would rather head-butt a brick wall than go to some antique tea party, a little girl with auburn curly hair and pink glittery runner-boots ran into the shop.

"Zoe, you do have pink hair!"

Charlie looked from the toddler to Zoe. What the hell was going on with her sister? One minute she's talking about an old fogey's version of *Come Dancing* and now she was chatting to a miniature person who appeared to be by herself.

Seconds later, a very harassed-looking man lolloped into the shop. *Tasty*, thought Charlie. He looked a bit like Michael Hutchence from that band *INXS*. All floppy curls and long eyelashes, with killer eyes – deep blue and iridescent. He was dressed in scruffy jeans, an army surplus anorak and battered leather boots, but he was undeniably sexy and gorgeous.

"Jenny, there you are. Zoe! Hi!" His expression changed and the smile made his eyes dance. Self-consciously, he pulled his hand through his rough dark curls and stuffed the other hand into his pocket. "We were in the neighbourhood and I was curious to see the shop."

314

Charlie was dying to know who this dude was.

"Hi Alfie, this is Charlie, my twin sister. Charlie, this is Alfie, and this little scamp is Jenny." Zoe scooped the little girl up and Jenny immediately stroked the pink wig.

"Look, Dada, pink!" she grinned, delighted with Zoe's hair. "Pretty Zoe," she nodded. Peeping at Charlie she looked briefly confused. "Two Zoes!" She opened her eyes really wide.

"Thanks, Jenny," Zoe beamed. It was quite a while since anyone had called her pretty. Even a two-and-a-half-year-old's compliment was welcome.

Alfie regarded Zoe. Her face wasn't as swollen as it had been before. The red raw rash had disappeared, and she had make-up and a trendy black dress on. Her elfin features and big brown eyes reminded him of Tinkerbelle. Realising he was staring at her, he shook himself up.

"I know! The pink hair – it's a girly thing, isn't it, Jenny?" She instinctively nuzzled the toddler. "I don't think your daddy likes my hair," she giggled.

"No, it's not that at all, sorry . . . I didn't mean . . ." He looked at the floor, and shuffled one foot awkwardly.

"Was that invitation I dropped into Mum and Dad's for this old dear's bash?" Charlie broke the uncomfortable silence.

"Yes," Zoe also looked at the floor.

"Rock on, Zo! Sounds banging alright!" Charlie laughed.

"She's actually a lovely lady, Charlie," Zoe protested, "and it was kind of her to invite us, wasn't it, Alfie?"

"Oh, you're going too, are you?" Charlie perked up. Maybe there was method in Zoe's madness after all.

"Well, no, we'd kind of said we wouldn't bother, isn't that right, Zoe?" Alfie looked at her for support.

"Maybe we should go," Zoe said uncertainly. "She'd appreciate us turning up – it's a huge deal for her. It mightn't hurt to show our faces. What do you think? I'll go if you go." Zoe looked a bit shy, deeply regretting her words. Christ, it sounded like she was asking him out!

"Okay."

Neither of them knew who was more surprised by the sudden arrangement. An odd silence descended once again.

"Well, that's settled then," said Charlie. "Zoe, you need to get your little tartan shopping trolley and Alfie you need your overcoat and tweed cap. You could even wear matching tartan slippers if you felt a bit cold. It is winter after all and at your ages you need to look after yourselves. You might end up with a devastating bout of chilblains. God forbid, bless us and save us!" Charlie poked Zoe in the ribs.

Grateful for the diversion, Zoe and Alfie laughed a little too hard at the joke. It wasn't *that* funny.

Jenny got fed up of being in the shop after a few minutes. There were only so many necklaces Charlie could point at while Zoe and her daddy chatted. Besides, Charlie was really not a baby person. She was quite happy organising her own schedule for the moment. The shop was enough seriousness for her. Outside of that, she was on the fun bus.

Alfie was hardly out the door before Charlie went off on one.

"Kept him very quiet, you sassy little minx! Spill. Jesus, there was I feeling all sorry for you, trotting in and out of hospital being all cancer this and chemo that, while all along you've been courting Mr Delicious. *Tell me everything!*"

"There's nothing to tell," Zoe snapped. "His wife just died, for Christ's sake. Have a bit of respect, Charlie. He's just a friend. Not even, he's an acquaintance. I've bumped into him a couple of times. I just feel sorry for him. He's kind of lost at the moment."

"*Ooooh*! Don't get shirty with me, Zoe Clarke! I was only saying what I saw. I think there's a bit of chemistry between you two." Charlie was delighted with the new gossip.

"Shut up, Cha, you haven't a clue. He's been through the wars. He was invited to this party too and we'd decided not to go. That's all."

"*We* had, had *we*?"

"Get a life, Charlie," Zoe huffed.

Stomping into the back room to inspect the incoming stock, Zoe felt a bit odd. There had been a funny feeling between herself and

Alfie just now. Of course she'd felt it too. But it was just the fact that the poor man was lonely.

He was stuck on his own with a baby. He was grieving for Tanya. She was a familiar face. Jenny recognised her. That was it. There was no issue either way. Charlie was just bored. She was settled with her boyfriend Simon and just felt like poking her nose in, adding two plus two and coming up with five. She'd always loved to annoy Zoe. That's what sisters did.

Zoe turned her attention to the rail of evening dresses, usually her favourite part of the whole year's collection. She found herself scrutinising each piece. Becoming a bit frantic, she dismissed dress after dress. None of them were suitable for Esme's party. They were too revealing or too over the top.

"Have we anything more suitable for this party? Where's the cocktail wear?" Zoe shouted through from the back room.

"I thought you didn't give a toss? You were only turning up to make the old lady happy?" Charlie teased.

"Look at me, Charlie. I need all the help I can get at the moment. I've been posing as a boiled chipmunk, with the complexion of an ageing alcoholic. With this rash all over my body, causing involuntary scratching. Add in the nice green pallor only a chemo patient can sport. Bald and missing eyebrows. Need I say more?"

"Okay! Jesus, I was going to say, keep your hair on!"

They both dissolved into cackling giggles. They had the ability to fight like cats and seconds later be the best of friends again.

Normally Charlie would be thrilled to have a reason to prod at Zoe. Something to tease and slag her about, but this time a weird sense told her to hold her tongue with regards to this Alfie guy. Fair enough, he'd just been through a terrible ordeal. But whether he or Zoe could see it or not, there was chemistry between them. Charlie hoped they would stay in touch. He seemed like a genuine guy, and although it would be a big problem for her personally, Zoe seemed to like the little girl too. Charlie shuddered at the thought of meeting a guy with baggage in the form of a toddler. Personally it would send her running for the hills, but Zoe didn't seem in the least bit phased by the little person.

Knowing the stock like the back of her hand, Charlie grabbed a few hangers and folded the dresses over her arm. "You pop into the changing room and I'll pass you in some stuff. There's an amazing range of jersey pieces, with some sequined detailing. They can be dressed up or down and wouldn't be too over the top. This one comes in a gorgeous midnight blue which I think would be kinder on you than black at the moment." Charlie flew off around the shop, picking accessories and shoes to finish off the look.

# 28

*It's party time!*

The day before Esme's party, Nora and Tracey arrived home. They'd booked an afternoon spa session for themselves and their mum, to make sure she looked her best. They were looking forward to the evening, and were hoping it would work well.

Just as they arrived at the beauty salon, Esme's phone rang.

"Esme Mulligan, how may I help you?" She blinked and put on her best Queen Mother voice. "Oh right. Yes, okay. That's nice. Yes, I understand. Thank you so much for letting me know. Alright then. Good day."

The girls were checking in with the receptionist as Esme wandered over, tucking her phone back into her bag.

At the top of her voice, from utter silence, she yelled: "Me cancer is gone! That was the hospital. The doctor has promised me the chemotherapy has worked!" Her face flushed and her eyes shining, she threw her arms up to her daughters.

"Mum, I can't believe it, that's the best birthday present you could ask for!" Tracey had tears running down her cheeks as she hugged her mother.

"That's the most fantastic news!" Nora joined in, hopping up and down with delight.

They all stood looking at each other in delighted shock. There was nothing like being told she was clear again.

"You've a lot to celebrate, ladies," the receptionist smiled. "I wish we had a little glass of bubbly or something, but I'm afraid coffee or herb tea is all we have."

"That'd be great but I'll have a coffee anyway." Esme's face was alight with glee.

She phoned Michael to fill him in. He said he'd head down to the pub for a quick drink, by way of celebration. He'd be back in time for his tea at half five.

"Do you know what, it was nearly worth getting the cancer to be told it's gone away now," Esme told the girls.

"Well, Mum, I don't think I'd go along with that, but I like your optimism all the same," Nora laughed. Their mother was renowned for coming out with beauts, and this was one of her better ones.

"At least now at the party tomorrow night, I won't have it in the back of my mind that I might be dead by next year," Esme laughed.

"Jesus, Mum, don't say things like that," Tracey scolded.

"I know, but you understand where I'm coming from, don't you? I get that we could all go at any minute, sure I could be struck down dead by the 10B bus tomorrow morning, but cancer can do that to you. Make you have to think about dying and all that. It makes you face it head on. Makes you plan things in your own head. I even said to your daddy that we should go and pick a grave and that type of thing. But Michael never liked talking about that, so I had to let it go. Had I got any sicker, I would have pushed him. But, hopefully now we can have that conversation when we're good and ready."

The girls had tears in their eyes as they hugged Esme. They knew the whole cancer thing must have frightened their poor mother half to death, but she never showed her dark side. She was always upbeat and never wanted to admit to feeling blue. Any time they called and asked her how she was, she'd brush it off. They'd always been afraid to push her to talk, especially when they were in England and unable to sit and hug her if she got worked up.

"It has to have affected you, Mum," said Nora. "That's natural. Nobody likes to think about dying and when it's put to you that you just *might* not survive, I can't imagine how that makes you feel. That sense of the unknown and teetering on the edge must be mind-bending." She shuddered at the thought.

"It has its good points too, you know? Look at this lovely party I'm having."

Tracey was quick to put her straight. "Mum, you'd be having your party even if you hadn't been sick. Being seventy is a wonderful achievement, but you've made it doubly fantastic."

"Ah, you're great, girls. I know you'd always look after me, but it's been a great source of amusement for the Golden Girls too. This party has them all excited. They do love to hear all about the chemotherapy and what it does for you. It's been an education if nothing else. But the party is different. It's something they can all join in with. I don't know what we'll all talk about when it's over. Now that my cancer is gone too, sure I'll have to start making things up. They've all become reliant on me for a bit of news. I feel a bit pressurised in a way now." Esme straightened her top and smoothed it down. "You just never know what life is going to throw your way next. At least it won't say on my gravestone that I died of boredom. I'll have to think of a new topic for conversation now. I think I know how those celebrities like Jordan and all of them decided to take their clothes off. They probably ran out of news and had to entertain people in some way."

"I'm not sure that would go down too well in the church hall – you flashing, I mean!" said Nora.

"Ah, not at all, sure nobody wants to see my auld wobbly bits – sure I can barely look at them meself. I might just have to retire to the background and let one of the other ladies take the limelight for a while," Esme sighed.

The three women had a fantastic time being pampered and preened. By the time they got home, with perfect paws and looking like they'd spent a month in the tropics, tanned to within an inch of their lives, they were barely recognisable.

Esme kept tapping and clicking her nails off the table when they got home. She'd phoned Michael who was still at the pub and told him to bring home fish and chips.

"I won't be able to cook, on account of me nails. Thank you." She went to hang up.

"I'm here on the feckin' phone, Esme! Why are you speaking to me like I'm the message-minder?" Michael was a bit put out.

"It's a bit hard to concentrate what with the nails and my fake tan. You won't recognise me when you get home!" she giggled, delighted with herself.

"You're a mad auld bat, do you know that?" he cackled.

Esme could hardly sleep that night, she was so excited. She took the fascinator in its box down from the wardrobe and peered in. She was going to be the belle of the ball.

She'd made Michael buy a cravat in a deep emerald green, to match her outfit.

"I feel like a plank, Esme," he said when she got him to dress up at home for her. "Men from the Northside of Dublin are not meant to wear silk knickers tied around their necks. If I'd appeared dressed like this as a young fella, they'd have beaten me up, and rightly so."

"Stop standing with your legs apart and your shoulders hunched like that. You're not going to stand in the doorway of a nightclub. You are a distinguished gentleman, so behave like one. Stand up straight like a good man. We know we're all descended from the apes, but we don't need to remind everyone right now."

Jaysus, this was like making his Holy Communion all over again. At least this time he didn't have his mammy smacking the back of his head and spitting on a hanky and mashing it all over his face.

"These shoes should come with a health warning. I'm going to skull meself in them. I'm not Frank Sinatra, Esme. People will feel sorry for me when they see me," he moaned.

"Indeed they will not. You'll have the Golden Girls all in a frenzy when they catch a goo of you. I'll be dead proud of you. I can just see you, with the fluorescent lights of the Hummer bouncing off the top of your head. You'll be gorgeous." She shrugged her shoulders and clasped her hands. Her nose wrinkled up and her eyes twinkled as she regarded him. She still loved him as much as she did the day they got married. Having this moment of clarity made her a bit overcome.

"What's wrong with you, love?" Michael asked. "I'm only messing. You know me! I wouldn't upset you. Why are you crying? I'll stand up straight and I won't pick me nose, arse or any other orifice and make a show of you." He went over to her, well, slid over, in his shiny new shoes.

"Ah no, love, I'm only counting me blessings here. Don't mind me. I'm just having a little cry here. Just being a silly old bat. Do you know, I'll be the only one of the Golden Girls with a husband? All the others are long since dead, Lord rest them. I'm very lucky really, Michael."

He would have given her a big bear hug and rocked her a bit better, but the suit was a bit like wearing a straitjacket and the shoes were like ice-skates, so he'd resorted to a little squeeze and few pats on the back, before side-stepping and starting to take off the offending articles.

\* \* \*

The day of the party finally dawned. The girls brought up a breakfast tray for their parents. There was even a little posy of pink carnations for Esme. As they sat drinking their tea and savouring their toast, Tracey handed Esme a little square package, tied with gold curling ribbon.

"What's this?" Esme was astounded.

"Your pressie. Happy birthday, Mum. It's from the three of us," Nora said proudly.

"But you're already doing the party and you bought me the clothes and the fascinator. I wasn't expecting anything else."

"Just open the box, woman. I'll be dead by the time you've finished your speech," Michael teased.

Esme fumbled with the parcel, her hands shaking with emotion. As she lifted the lid of the dark-red velvet box, she heard a tinkling sound inside. There, nestling in the plush soft fabric, was the most stunning gold charm bracelet she'd ever seen.

"Each charm has a meaning," Tracey began. "The number seventy is obvious."

"The two angels are us," Nora pointed out.

"The pint is to remind you of me." Michael pointed to the little gold glass proudly.

"The pink crystal twisted ribbon is to represent your fighting the cancer," Tracey said.

"The gold heart is because we love you," Nora continued.

"Finally the unicorn is eternal youth, because no matter what age the calendar says you are, you'll always be young at heart," Tracey finished.

The chain part of the bracelet was cut in such a way that it twinkled and shone when it moved. It was without doubt one of the most precious things Esme had ever laid eyes on. Michael reached over and after a good bit of fumbling – "I need me fecking glasses, I'm as blind as a bat" – he managed to put it around her wrist. It jangled and danced against her skin. She hadn't even got out of bed and already it was one of the best days of her life.

# 29

*Please – someone tell me that this is as bad as it gets.*
*The upward spiral has to begin soon.*

Zoe woke early the day of Esme's party. She'd been tossing and turning for most of the night anyway. She'd had chemotherapy only two days before. Her legs ached, as if she'd been running on a treadmill for hours the night before. Her head was stuffed and throbbing, like a vodka hangover. Her nose was running as if a cold was starting. Her skin was crawling, as if she was coming off heroin.

Of course, she'd done none of the above things. It was simply the drugs coursing through her system. She'd only managed a slice of dry toast and a cup of tea the day before. Her mouth was parched and she felt around with her tongue and noticed she'd two new mouth ulcers. The chemotherapy commonly caused the inside of the mouth to break down. She'd been meticulous about using mouthwashes, but sometimes the sores just came anyway.

Looking in the mirror, as she made her way to the shower, she barely recognised herself. Bald as a baby, with no eyelashes, eyebrows or colour in her cheeks, she felt like a leper. The feeling of the bumps in her mouth, which weren't visible from the outside, but felt the size of tennis balls from within, added to her general misery.

She was nearing the end of her chemotherapy, after which Dr Leah would send her for another set of scans. She'd asked Charlie to spray her with fake tan the night before, hoping it would miraculously camouflage the greeny-blue hue which had become her skin these days. Although the tan had added a slightly different shade to her complexion, she still looked like the walking dead.

As she stood under the warmth of the flowing shower and leaned her head forward, allowing the water pressure to gently pummel the back of her neck, she placed her arm on the tiled wall to steady herself.

Most of the time, she tried not to think too deeply about the cancer, or the fact that it might still be coursing its way through her body. She was trying to think positively. Surely if she was feeling so awful and struggling so much with nausea and lack of energy, it must be working? If the chemotherapy was making her feel this dreadful, surely it must be having a detrimental effect on the cancer too?

She hadn't meant to cry. She hadn't even tried to be sad. Perhaps being surrounded by water had encouraged her to join in. But once the tears started, she couldn't stop them. She heaved and sobbed until her throat and chest ached and the muscles in her tummy gave out. She had to crouch down and eventually kneel down to facilitate the wailing. Engulfed in grief, she cried like her life depended on it. It was almost as if a demon was trying to escape her body through her tear-ducts. As the warm water began to turn chilly, she used the handles on the bath to stand herself up again. Reaching back, she turned off the shower.

Stepping out of the bath, she wrapped a huge towel around herself and stood hiccuping for a few minutes. Perching on the closed lid of the toilet seat, she chewed on the end of the towel and stared into space. The steam in the room and the smell of the shower gel in the air was comforting. A bit like a milder version of a steam room in the gym. Rocking back and forth, she slowly calmed down and came to. Splashing her raw swollen eyes with cool water, she inhaled through her nose.

By the time she'd put on a bit of make-up and dressed herself, she actually felt better than she had done in a long time. That whole theory of crying being good for releasing happy endorphins made sense to her now. Leaning heavily on the banisters, she made her way down to the kitchen. There was a note on the kitchen table from Diana to say she'd gone to meet a friend and would be back in the early afternoon.

*I can be home at a moment's notice, just call if you need me. Love you x x*

Sighing deeply, Zoe was actually glad she had the house to herself. She poured herself a bowl of sugary kid's breakfast cereal, something she found she was usually able to stomach. Eating two full bowls of the stuff left her exhausted, so she ambled back up the stairs, fell into bed and woke to the sound of Diana calling her.

Sitting bolt upright, she looked at the digital alarm clock on the bedside locker. It was nearly three o'clock. She'd been asleep most of the day. Feeling like she should have a panic, she quickly decided against it. What did it matter that she'd missed most of the day? She'd only have felt rotten anyway, so getting a decent block of sleep was preferable. Stretching and yawning she smiled as Diana popped her head in the door.

"Hi, sweetie, were you having forty winks?" Diana came around to the side of the bed and plopped a little package in front of Zoe.

"More like two thousand winks. I've been asleep all day. What's this?" Zoe lifted the little cardboard bag, with pretty tulle ribbon handles.

"A little gift to cheer you up. I thought they might be cute with your outfit for this lady's party you're going to tonight."

Zoe opened the little gauze drawstring bag and found a pair of Swarovski crystal earrings. Like petite delicate chandeliers, in a deep inky blue, they made Zoe squeal with delight.

"Oh Mum, I love them. Thank you, they'll be gorgeous with my navy dress. I'm going to wear the short dark wig too, so they'll be shown off to perfection!"

Zoe's smile was the best thanks Diana could receive. Her previously happy-go-lucky daughter was so fraught with pain and sickness lately she had almost forgotten how beautiful she looked when she smiled. Gulping back tears, Diana swallowed the hard lump in her throat as she watched Zoe putting the earrings in place.

Zoe's mobile phone jumped into life.

"Hi, Alfie!" she smiled as she answered. "I'm fine – yes, I'm still on target for going tonight. What about yourself?"

Diana went to leave the room so Zoe could talk to Alfie, but Zoe motioned for her to stay while she confirmed the arrangements for that evening, saying she'd be ready when Alfie called in the taxi at seven forty-five.

She smiled at her mother as she put down the phone.

"That's good if you feel up to going out, lovie." Diana stroked her daughter's face. "So you're going with Alfie?" She cocked her head to the side. She wasn't sure how she felt about Zoe hanging around with him. He seemed like a lovely fellow and all that, but she hoped the whole situation wasn't just a bit depressing for Zoe to be involved in. That poor man was obviously going through a dreadful time and her heart went out to him and his little baby, but at the same time she didn't want Zoe to be his shoulder to cry on.

"Well, we made a pact that we'd go together and be moral support for each other. We won't know many people at it and it's Alfie's first time going out on his own. I promised I'd be there for him," Zoe said seriously.

"Darling, I know you mean well, and you've a heart of gold. But, do watch out, won't you? You're not exactly in a position to be another person's strength right now."

"Mum, how can you be so callous? The poor man has lost his wife. His baby has lost her mother. Christ, I'm only going to an old lady's function in a hotel, for a couple of hours. I'm not moving in and assuming the role of new wife and mother!"

"I know, I know, sorry, pet. I'm not trying to preach, I'm just concerned about you, that's all." Diana realised it was better not to voice her opinion about this Alfie guy.

Zoe's expression softened as quickly as it had shadowed and she announced she had a yearning for chocolate. Padding down to the kitchen, she rustled in the cupboards and found some milk-chocolate mini-bars. Unwrapping one, she took a bite, expecting the usual melting, creamy loveliness she adored. Instead, it tasted watery and bubbly, followed by slightly gritty and generally quite nasty. Running to the bin, she spat the mouthful out loudly and chucked the rest of the bar.

"Zoe! That's disgusting!"

"Not as disgusting as that bar tasted! God, my taste-buds are really skewy at the moment. Stuff that I normally love tastes vile. One of the only things that I like now is jelly. I've always hated jellies. They're too sweet and artificial, but lately they're all I can stomach. Do we have any more of those jelly babies?" She searched the cupboard for something to chew.

\* \* \*

Jenny was having a little sleep in her buggy. Alfie had been up since five in the morning with her. She was getting her back teeth, her cheeks were flaring and she was prone to crying at the drop of a hat. Another child had pushed ahead of her on the slide at the park and she'd been overcome with grief. She'd been so sad he'd had to put her into the buggy and walk around with her until she fell asleep. None of the usual medicine was working its magic, and she was utterly miserable.

For the first time in weeks she'd called for Tanya. Alfie had been glad of the deserted pathway as the toddler had pointed a little fat finger towards the sky, squinting in the November sun and crooning, "Mama, I want my mama! Mama in the sky!" Rubbing her eyes and throwing her head back against the buggy, she'd sobbed hoarsely until she'd eventually fallen into a fitful slumber. Breathing shakily, Alfie had marched the pavement until he knew she was sound enough asleep to go home. He'd gently pulled the buggy inside the front door, then tip-toed into the kitchen and shut the door. Hoping Jenny would sleep in the buggy for a little while at least, he'd leaned his forehead against the wall and cried.

He'd done quite well over the last two weeks. He'd even gone a couple of days in a row without crying. He'd been sleeping a little better too. The night demons and lilting mocking shadows had lessened slightly. He was able to turn the light off just as he drifted off to sleep now. The silence and the darkness didn't make him as petrified as before. Very slowly and subtly, things were improving. He was managing to pull himself through each day. Of course Jenny was his saving grace. Her constant babbling and need for love and attention was without doubt the only reason he hadn't curled into a ball and expired.

He sobbed until he felt he would burst, then slowly managed to regain his composure. He'd noticed the bursts of awful soul-destroying grief were shorter now. He was able to recover from them more quickly. In the early days, when something upset him, he would need the rest of the day before he could feel human. Now, he was better able to click back into normality. He didn't know if it was practice or whether he was actually beginning to heal.

Before Jenny woke, he dialled Zoe's number. He needed to check if she was well enough to go to this party tonight. If she couldn't go, he'd gladly give it a miss. If she was still on for it, he'd keep his side of the bargain and accompany her. Deep down, he was hoping she'd say she wasn't well.

Moments later, he hung up and took a deep breath. Okay, so Zoe wanted to go tonight. He'd better check if his suit was clean. Removing his shoes, he crept past Jenny in his socks, so as not to wake her. As he stood in front of the wardrobe, he hesitated. He needed a second to steady himself. As he opened the wardrobe door, it was almost as if a whoosh of ghostly voices hit him and made him stagger backwards slightly.

He hadn't looked at his suit since Tanya's funeral. It dangled there on the hanger, like a Halloween costume, reeking of grief. All cheerless and sullen, it was silently mocking him like a depressing uniform of sadness. Slamming the wardrobe shut, he pulled his fingers through his dark tangled curls.

Sweat formed on his brow, as he tried to steady his racing heart. Okay, he could do this, he was quite simply being irrational. It was only clothing. He would pull the suit out and lay it flat on the spare bed and check it for stains. He could carry out the motions.

As he scanned the fabric for stains he felt a bit better. It would be good to wear the thing again, to rid it of the ghosts. To take the fug of funeral desolation and dissolve it into the cold November night air.

Jenny woke up soon after that and screamed incessantly until Lauren, Tanya's sister, arrived to baby-sit at seven.

"Jesus, Alfie, you look rough. You're not going to the party like that, are you? The seventy-year-old bird will die of fright at the sight of you!" She hugged him and stepped back. She'd never really known what Tanya had seen in him. Fair enough, he had that rough-around-the-edges smouldering rock-star look that some people found attractive. She preferred the more coiffed suit-and-tie look herself. A nice corporate-banking-type person.

Lauren was waiting for a guy with plenty of money who treated her like a princess. She wasn't settling for someone who couldn't give her a good life. She wasn't going to be one of those mothers who went around looking like the walking dead, with a string of matted-haired, snotty-nosed kids trailing after her. She wanted beautiful children and a full-time nanny who'd do all the disgusting stuff, like nappy-changing and nose-wiping. Nor did she want to end up like Tanya had – working herself to the bone while her she-man stayed at home being a house husband, content with a career in pot-washing and trips to the supermarket.

Since Tanya's death, Lauren had tried to make an effort to help Alfie and to be there for him. If she was honest, it was just that – an effort. Earth Mother, she certainly wasn't. She loved little Jenny, of course she did. Especially now, as she was the one remaining part of Tanya, but she certainly couldn't imagine her body-clock ever starting to tick. Doing her duty and dipping in and out of Jenny's life was quite enough for her, thank you very much.

She had to admit, however, when Alfie appeared a few minutes later, dressed in a suit and shirt, with the top buttons opened, she got a brief momentary inkling of what Tanya had liked about him. He looked a damn sight better than he normally did, although she still felt he required too much imagination for her.

"You clean up well, brother-in-law." She fixed his collar. One side was up and the other turned down.

"Thanks, I know by the look on your face that you still think I'm a state, but thanks for lying all the same," he grinned.

Lauren giggled.

# 30

*If there is a God up there, please help me to get through this
evening. Sprinkle a tiny bit of fun-dust on me. Even just for
an hour. Zoe.*

*Hey, Tanya. Hope you can see me in my suit. I hope you
don't hate me for going out to a party. That's okay, isn't it?
Please, come with me, stand beside me and help me to say
and do the right things. I'm scared and so sad. I love you, my
angel girl. Alfie x*

As the taxi pulled up outside her house, Zoe spotted it from her
bedroom window. Shoving her pink notebook into the bedside
locker, she grabbed her bag and rushed to the front door. Every
time she stood up, she got a head-rush. The hospital had explained
that it was due to her poor bloods.

"When your platelets are low like yours are, it can cause this
light-headedness," the nurse had told her. "It's nothing to worry
about at the moment, unless it gets excessive or you actually black
out. Obviously, in that case, you'll need to come in immediately."

Zoe was so used to feeling dreadful that she'd actually forgotten
what it felt like to be "normal". She'd pushed her still-swollen feet

into high heels, thinking it was the first time in months she'd managed to dress up. Looking in the mirror, she'd been somewhat disappointed with the image that had greeted her. The wig might have been convincing to a bystander, but to her it looked like a squirrel had stopped for a quick snooze. Her complexion was a mixture between the Incredible Hulk and a blow-up doll. Her rash had died down a lot, but some scarring still remained. The lack of energy and nausea made every movement an effort. She knew she looked like she was climbing Everest when she was doing the simplest thing.

Her heart raced as she made her way to the taxi. She hoped she'd be able to stay for a decent length of time at Esme's party. She didn't want to abandon Alfie or disappoint Esme. The awful thing was that her body had taken over her mind. It wasn't like being out two nights on the trot for a healthy person, where you'd be sitting on night two in a pub wishing you could go to bed. This was a total knockout. She'd feel utterly whammied. Her head would spin, her hearing would dim, her limbs would almost refuse to hold her up. It was a no-choice-in-the-matter happening.

All she could do tonight was sit down as much as possible and try to conserve her energy and pray that she'd be able to stay for a little while at least.

Alfie got out of the car to greet her. Kissing her on the cheek, he rested his hand on her arm. She was surprised to feel his hand shaking uncontrollably.

"Sorry, Zoe. I'm a nervous wreck. I don't know if I can do this. I haven't been out since . . . I hadn't seen this suit since . . . I just don't know if I can do this . . ." He looked miserable.

"Oh Alfie, I'm so sorry. I should never have bamboozled you into coming to this thing. If it helps at all, I feel like I'm either going to keel over or puke. Do you want to give it a miss? We can always call Esme and tell her that I'm not well and you're not up to it?" Zoe half-hoped he'd agree.

Seeing Zoe's woeful state made Alfie feel ashamed of himself. He had to pull himself together and support the poor girl. "No, I'd love nothing more than to back out, if I'm totally honest. But this was never going to be easy. I was never going to just sail out to my first occasion without Tanya. At least I know you're as reluctant and uncomfortable as I am, albeit for different reasons. We can support each other."

"Okay, sir, plaster on your best smile and let's get going. Misery would look like a jester in our company, but hey, let's go out and feel shitty together!" She sounded a lot more enthusiastic than she felt. God love him, though, Alfie must be finding this a thousand times more difficult than she was.

When they arrived at the hotel, the taxi pulled up at the edge of a plush wide red carpet. The wind was whipping and it was drizzling slightly. That kind of squally spitty rain that blows your hair and wafts into your face.

"Jesus, I'll have to hold onto my hair!" Zoe yelled through the breeze.

It was just the comment they needed. As they stepped into the foyer, both were genuinely smiling. They were immediately greeted by the sight of a large crowd of people, all standing with drinks in their hands. A string quartet played upbeat pleasant music and the buzz was good.

"God, I feel like a toddler at this. It's quite good for the psyche being about thirty years younger than most of the others," Alfie whispered.

They nodded greetings to the other guests, and spotted Sian and another lady just to the side.

"Hi, Zoe and Alfie, this is my friend Joan. Joan, this is Alfie and Zoe, who I told you about," Sian smiled.

They all shook hands and made small talk. As they were taking a drink from a passing tray, there was a bit of a kerfuffle from outside.

A man dressed as a formal doorman in a navy and gold uniform hit a copper gong and formally announced: "Ladies and Gentlemen, may I have your attention please? Your hostess is about to make her entrance."

# 31

*I am the luckiest woman alive. I feel like a child on
Christmas morning. I'm seventy years old, and I have
never felt younger.*

The crowd shuffled and squashed themselves up against the
large floor-to-ceiling windows of the hotel.

As the huge pink Hummer slid into place at the end of the red
carpet, Esme and her entourage were giddy with excitement. The
whole mood was being nicely helped along by the champagne.
Tracey and Nora had been lashing it into them for the duration of
the journey while the others had been tippling away too.

Even if she had to go home now, Esme had had enough fun to
last her a lifetime.

The Hummer had collected herself, Michael and the girls, and
gone straight up the road to Mrs Murphy's house. Oh, she'd come
out sniffing as if she'd a bad smell under her nose, but Esme could
tell she was wildly impressed.

"Good evening, Mrs Murphy, how are you, love? Delighted you
could join us. In you get! Can I offer you a glass of fine champagne?"
Esme was using her best telephone voice.

Mrs Murphy looked like she wanted to swing Esme around by

the hair, but she had to be civil. "Thank you, Mrs Mulligan, how kind," she'd smiled tightly.

They'd gone on over the road and around to Miriam and Frank's house. The polar opposite to Mrs Mulligan, miserable old cow that she was, Miriam's curtains were twitching as they came up the road. The second the Hummer came into view, she flung the front door open and raced up her tiny concrete driveway, her long evening coat flapping in the wind as she moved with the lithe nimbleness of a seventeen-year-old. She was so enthusiastic she nearly knocked over the garden gnome pushing a wheelbarrow that she lovingly treasured.

"Esme, this is fab-lus! I never seen one of these in real life. God, it's like Hollywood in my estate!" she exclaimed, waving her arms around in delight.

Frank banged the door shut and turned the key in the Chubb lock. Looking all uneasy and awkward in his new suit and stiff shirt, he shuffled towards the huge car.

"You forgot your bag, Miriam." He shoved the glittery evening purse at his wife, and looked the car up and down. "Jaysus, the buses have come a long way, Michael, what?" he grinned.

"Hop in, Frank. Be my guest. No pints in here, mind you, only champagne if you'll excuse me." Michael was all delighted with himself, his chest puffed out like a peacock.

By the time they pulled up outside the hotel twenty minutes later, the noise level had risen and they were all ecstatic with excitement. In spite of herself, Mrs Murphy was almost smiling. The swishy music mixed with the bubbles (which were pink and emanating from a little machine stuck to the roof) and soft colour-changing roof-lights had worked their magic, even on her.

"Them lights must have some sort of a defrost mode built in, a bit like a posh microwave – the old goat nearly looks happy," Michael whispered to Esme.

"Daddy, shut up, she'll hear you," Tracey hissed.

As the car drew to a halt, Esme gasped.

"Oh Holy St Anthony, look at the crowd! It's like the Oscars, isn't it?"

Bucko slid back the glass and shouted in to them. "Yous stay here for a minute till I get the doves out of the boot and put them up above the door. The hotel have a lad waiting to prop the cage on a hook for me. I'll give yous the nod when it's time to get out. It builds the entrance to keep them waiting for a minute or two. They can all get a good look at the car too," he cackled and slammed the glass shut.

Hopping out of the car, he swung his cap into place. Smoothing his thin moustache, he yanked his trousers up and walked around the side of the Hummer to the boot. He could hear the doves cooing away in the cage.

"Alright, girls, are ya ready to do your party piece for Daddy?" he twittered at them.

Two porters from the hotel appeared and he handed them the long cage containing the twelve doves. As promised he'd coloured the tips of their wings pink. Not that anyone would really notice in the dark, but Esme would know. That was the main thing. It only took the two young guys a couple of minutes to prop the cage above the hotel's main door. When they gave Bucko the thumbs-up sign, he walked slowly and purposefully, for full effect, to the back door of the Hummer which was facing the red carpet.

With his eyes shut, and one hand behind his back, to add to the drama, he pulled the door open. The crowd inside were in full view of the proceedings and the automatic doors had been propped open, so Esme could see and hear them properly.

"All of yous get out first and make two little lines at each side of the red carpet. Esme, you emerge last and don't forget to smile and wave. This is it. Your big moment! It's show time!"

All the others piled out and stood as they were told. The wind whipped and the ladies all had to keep a hold of their skirts, to stop them flying over their heads and flashing their control-panel knickers to the watching crowd.

"Hurry up, Esme, before we end up on the top of a lamp-post!" Michael shouted in to her.

As she stood out of the car, an almighty cheer went up from inside the hotel. Tears pricked Esme's eyes as she stood for a second, waving her right hand forwards and backwards, just like the Queen did. Hitching up her coat, she walked the red carpet, linked to Michael, head held high with pride. The two girls followed, arms linked, closely trailed by Miriam and Frank. Bringing up the rear, muttering to herself about "bullshit" and "pretentious garble" was Mrs Murphy. As soon as Esme reached the top of the three wide steps into the hotel, and was about to enter the foyer, the doves were released.

Flying gracefully to the gasps of the impressed onlookers, they wheeled about. in a lovely little pattern. A round of applause broke out.

Esme felt like she might burst with the sheer joy of it all.

All the others had just stepped into the foyer, bar Mrs Murphy, who fuelled by the champagne had purposely decided to *use* the fact that she was last inside. Walking very slowly, she figured it might be nice to make a little entrance of her own.

Just as she neared the door, two of the doves dive-bombed her in poo. One purplish grey lumpy load landed on the front of her set fringe and the other on her shoulder. Shouting and yelling like a fishwife, she darted into the foyer where she jumped and danced in disgust.

"The fucken seagulls are after shitting all over me hairdo and me good frock!" she screamed.

Snorts and strangled yelps came from the crowd who were all desperately trying to conceal their laughter.

"I've a hanky in me bag, Mrs Murphy. That's a sign of good luck, when a bird does its business on you like that." Esme was weak with laughing.

"Good luck for who? I can't imagine you'd be quite so happy if them beasts had crapped all over you, Mrs Mulligan," Mrs Murphy snapped, eyes like flints.

Nora discreetly led her by the arm towards the nearest bathroom to help her pick the bird poo out of her hair.

Meanwhile the doves finished off their performance by flying back to the car where Bucko was waiting to place them into another cage where they could have some tasty seeds as a reward.

Accepting a glass of bubbly and a little canapé of a warm prune wrapped in bacon, Esme milled around and greeted her guests. All the Golden Girls were there in force.

"Hello, Father Moriarty, welcome and delighted you could join me!" Esme went to shake his hand but he hadn't a free hand, so he leaned forward and kissed her on the cheek.

"Tangs fer invding me, ish greash so far!" He'd one eye shut and was swaying from side to side, with a glass of whiskey in one hand and a cocktail in the other.

Michael banged him on the back enthusiastically and grinned at him. "Good man yerself, Father! Having a few bevvies there, fair play to ya. Why not, huh?" he boomed, delighted with the priest. Things were on the up – a little foreign girl arrived just then with a lovely looking creamy pint on a round wooden tray. "Good girl! Thanking you. Lovely. Sláinte!" He raised his glass and toasted the room.

About an hour later, the party was led into the function room. Mrs Murphy had been doused with champagne cocktails and needed to be helped to her seat by one of the staff.

"Them fucken pigeons have me hair ruined. Thirty euro I gave to have it set this morning. I've a good mind to sue that driver," she slurred to the Polish girl who helped her to her seat. Turning to her left, she instantly put on a smile and batted her eyes. "Fr Moriarty, if it isn't yourself. How are you this evening? Lovely celebration, isn't it? Lovely woman, Mrs Mulligan, God bless her."

"Howerya, Mrs Murphy. Sure ish a joy to shea ya." He swayed horribly to the side and Mrs Muphy thought he was going to fall off his chair.

Feeling quite shocked by his drunken behaviour, Mrs Murphy would have been very annoyed if she'd been clear enough of mind herself. But by the time her prawn cocktail was put in front of her, she'd forgotten all about being grumpy. Sometimes, it was simply exhausting being so uptight.

Zoe and Alfie took their seats at their table just across the way. Two people around Zoe's age introduced themselves as friends of Nora's. Miriam and her husband Frank sat down and the final two seats were filled by Sian and her friend Joan.

The atmosphere in the room was warm and bubbly. Esme and Michael were led to the table by Nora and Tracey, to a standing ovation. Esme did a little squeal when she saw the archway of balloons around her seat. The tables all sparkled courtesy of the little gold sequin decorations.

Fr Moriarty was helped up to the microphone to say grace. It consisted of a big prolonged mumble with some vaguely familiar words like God and Jesus every now and again.

At the end, he held up the microphone and yelled, "Habby birshday, Mrs Mulligan, you're shooper!"

The applause died down and Michael took the microphone.

"I won't keep yous from your prawn cocktails for long, God knows I'm bloody starving meself. Past eight o'clock and nothing but a few bits of fried rat on sticks in the hallway!" The crowd hooted. "The reason we are here is obviously to oversee this lady here becoming the ripe old age of seventy." The cheers and claps brought a tear to Esme's eye. "She's been a fantastic wife, a fabulous mother and of course as yous will all agree, a brilliant friend. Apart from her occasional bouts of verbal diarrhoea she's a real trooper. I couldn't have asked for a better partner. She finds fun when there's none, like recently with this cancer. She's a fighter and one of the most spirited people I know. I don't say this enough, because I find it all very embarrassing and cringy to be honest – but I love you, Esme, and I would like the whole room to join me in raising a glass. To Esme!"

The chairs were scraped back and everyone bar Fr Moriarty, who was too pissed, stood up. "To Esme!"

Just as the room was beginning to go from a mumble to a louder din, Tracey took the microphone.

"Sorry, everybody. I won't be long, I promise. Just on behalf of myself and Nora, I would like to say a few words if I may. We are so proud of our mother. From when we were children, she's always put Daddy and us first. She does all her day-to-day business with a nod, a wink and a smile. She's a character and yes, as Daddy pointed out, she certainly knows how to talk. But the most wonderful trait our mum has is positivity. Even faced with surgery and chemotherapy recently, she was totally unphased. She takes life and grabs it with both hands. She faces things head on, whether it be a dash around the shops or a trip to the operating theatre. Anytime Nora or I feel down, we know that all we have to do is lift the phone to our mum and our smiles will be restored. From the bottom of our hearts, Mum, we would like to thank you for all that you've done. We love you so much and we want you to know how much we appreciate and admire you. To our Mum!" Tracey stood and raised her glass, with tears in her eyes.

Once again the room rose to the occasion. Taking the microphone, Esme stumbled upwards.

"Well, well, well. After all them lovely kind words, I think I'd better join in. I'd like to thank you all for coming here tonight. There was a moment earlier on when I was at the saloon having me hair set, that I had a sudden fit of the nerves. I imagined what it would be like if nobody came tonight. But I soon put that thought to bed, as I knew you'd all do right by me, and you have. I want to thank Michael for being by my side for all these years. He can be a right grumpy old git, as we all know. But underneath it all, he's an auld teddy bear. Just so long as he gets his dinner on time. I want to thank my girls, Nora and Tracey, without whose help this event wouldn't be taking place. Especially on account of them paying and all that." Esme blinked as Tracey and Nora looked embarrassed. Forgetting she was even holding the microphone, Esme went off on a tangent. "Did yous see the Hummer outside? Wasn't it class? In case the light wasn't good enough, as well, just for your further information, the doves were pink to match it." Esme shrugged her shoulders in delight. "The food will be fantastic if the lunch we had here recently is anything to go by. The girls took me here for a meal not so long ago. I hope you all enjoy yourselves and that the anticipation and preparation was all worthwhile. Thanks again to one and all. *Over and out!*" Esme shouted the last bit, sending quite a few hearing-aids off into a whistle around the room.

"You're not on the bleeding *Starship Enterprise*, Esme!" Michael bellowed laughing.

"Wasn't I making an announcement? There's nothing worse than not knowing if someone's finished or not. You know the way you do be sitting there wondering if you can eat your dinner or not?" Esme confided. Not that she needed to tell Michael to get started – he was already munching on a bread roll and delving into his prawns.

By the time the moon-walking granny balloon, along with the others in the overhead net, fell on the dance floor, the crowd were raring to go. The band kicked off with a foxtrot and all the ladies filed onto the dance floor. What men were still alive and able-bodied were snapped up quickly by the waiting elderly women. Esme and Michael were well in time with each other and glided around happily.

Thinking quickly, Nora did ask one of the attendants to discreetly sweep the balloons off the wooden floor. "All we need is for one of them to slip and fall and break a hip," she whispered from behind her hand.

The music was the cue that Zoe needed to make her exit. Without wanting to draw attention to herself, she whispered to Alfie that she'd had enough.

"Please feel free to stay if you're not ready to make tracks yet," she offered.

"That's so kind of you, but you're my ticket out of here. I'm right there with you. I don't want to sound dreadfully mean but I don't want the first dance without my wife to be with a seventy-five-year-old scuttered priest!" He indicated Father Moriarty, who was suddenly awake, alert and on the lookout for a dancing partner.

Although he was trying to remain light-hearted, Zoe could see he was starting to feel upset.

"Would you like to dance for a moment before we leave? Would it tick a box for you, as another thing you've overcome?" Zoe looked up at him, her face filled with concern.

"Actually, yes. I would love that."

She held out her hand and, as they took to the floor, Zoe felt his tremble as they made contact. Her heart went out to him. She was feeling pretty terrible, but all her pain was physical. It would end, it would all get better. At least she had to believe that.

What Alfie was going through was different. A stranger on the street would be able to see that Zoe was unwell with her pallor, the look of weakness she couldn't hide even under a ton of make-up. If she wasn't wearing a wig, the world would be able to see that she was a cancer patient. But nobody would know the dreadful hurt and desolation Alfie was feeling, unless he told them. If she'd had to choose which to take, her own illness or Alfie's personal torture, she'd have been hard pushed to decide which was worse.

As she felt Alfie's arm around her, Zoe gasped. Guilt and pleasure washed over her in equal measure. She knew Alfie was grieving and she knew it was probably wrong on so many levels, but as they swayed she felt one thing was for certain: something felt right. She had to stop herself from resting her cheek against his chest as they moved in time to the music.

"Are you okay?" she asked, gazing up at him.

"I'm better than I've been for a long time," he answered.

When the song ended, Zoe longed to stay on the dance floor but two things stopped her. Firstly, her limbs were aching and, secondly, she didn't want to ruin the wonderful moment they'd just shared. If anything were to happen between herself and Alfie, it would have to be in baby steps. Zoe had no idea if Alfie felt the way she did, but whether it was right or wrong, she realised she was falling for him.

"Thank you, that was really special," Alfie said gently.

Zoe held his gaze as they shared a smile.

"Ah, there you are!" Esme bounded over. "Are you heading away already, Zoe love?" she asked as Zoe scooped up her handbag from the table.

"I'm sorry to be such a party-pooper, Esme. I've enjoyed every moment of your party, but I hope you'll understand. I've the energy of a gnat right now?" Zoe apologised.

"Don't you worry, pet. I'm thrilled you came along. Are you headed away together then?" she asked, tilting her head to the side as she regarded a blushing Alfie.

"I didn't want Zoe to have to go home in the taxi alone," he stuttered.

"You're doing the right thing, love. I love a fella with good manners. You mind this girl – she's a little dote. Safe home, folks, and thanks again for joining in with the festivities!" Esme flapped from one to the other, hugging and kissing them enthusiastically.

As Zoe and Alfie stepped out the main door of the hotel and waved to a waiting taxi, the wind whipped and the rain lashed. But neither of them felt cold.

They sat in comfortable silence for part of the way to Zoe's house, both lost in their own thoughts. Zoe was glad Esme was having such a great time. She hoped she would be as happy and content, with as many people who loved her, when she was seventy. With a mild stinging of fear, she fleetingly wondered if she'd even be around still. Until she had her scan results and knew her prognosis, she was constantly trying to quell that nasty thought in her head.

There was also a new feeling in the mix. One of tingling hope of something new and wonderful that she was certain she'd felt on the dance floor.

Alfie felt like he'd achieved the greatest feat. He was immeasurably glad he'd gone to the night out. He'd survived without Tanya – though he was certain she'd been there with him in spirit. More than that, he'd felt a real connection with Zoe. He certainly had no intention of rushing into anything, not for a long time to come, but a part of him was relieved to realise that he would at least have a new presence in his life. For the first time since Tanya's death, he felt some hope shining through.

# 32

*Beauty may be only skin deep, but I know I'll feel
prettier on the inside when my outer shell looks less like
a prune!*

Sian was awake well before the alarm clock went off on the
morning of her surgery. Her tummy grumbled and she wished
she could at least have a cup of tea. But she'd been warned to fast
from midnight, which meant not even water was allowed.

As the shower water washed over her, she wondered what she
would look like after the operation. The next time she stood in this
very shower, she'd be a newer, fresher-looking woman.

A ripple of excitement shot through her. Dressing in a soft comfy
tracksuit, she gathered up her toothbrush and last-minute bits for
her wash-bag. She had that same feeling she got when she was
going on holidays.

She heard Joan emerge onto the upstairs landing. She'd offered
to stay the night and accompany Sian to the clinic that morning.

"Good morning, did you get any sleep?" her friend called in.

"Come in, Joan, I'm just closing my bag," Sian called.

Joan padded in, dressed but in bare feet.

"I'll make you some coffee and toast – we've plenty of time,"
Sian said, stretching.

"No change of heart, I take it?" Joan scanned her friend for signs of indecision. Secretly she was hoping Sian would crumble and say she was happier the way she was, that now the whole thing was upon her she wasn't going through with it. Not because she disapproved – far be it from her to influence another person – she just didn't like the idea of the pain and discomfort. She hated the thought of Sian being chopped up and frazzled with acid.

"Do you know, I was half-expecting to decide to bottle it and not want to go through with it, but I can't wait. I feel ready, willing and able." Sian bounced down the stairs and into her kitchen.

* * *

As Sian sat in her surgical gown, ready to go to theatre a couple of hours later, Joan hugged and kissed her and wished her luck. The porter wheeled her towards the operating suite. Whistling as he went, the man seemed quite at ease with the whole thing.

"I suppose you don't give it a second's thought, bringing people to have an operation, seeing as you do it every day." Sian glanced behind to look at the man.

"It's run of the mill for me, love. Not the same for the person sitting in the chair though. You're playing a blinder so far. Can't be easy going under the knife. Fair play to you. Please God everything will go well for you. I always say a little prayer to myself after I bring a patient down to the basement for surgery, and you won't be any different, love." He patted her on the shoulder.

For a split second she *did* change her mind. She wanted to jump out of the moving chair and run.

"Sian, good morning. We're all ready for you. Won't be long now. It'll be over in no time at all. See you in a moment." Dr Burke retreated in his green scrubs before she had a chance to tell him she wasn't going through with it.

Her porter, appearing to be oblivious to her inner pain, wished her well and waved while muttering to himself. She hoped he was saying that prayer.

* * *

By the time she heard Joan calling her softly, Sian felt like she'd been asleep for five seconds. She tried to open her eyes, but they didn't seem to be able to comply. Raising her hand tentatively, she felt gently around her face. She was covered in bandages like an Egyptian mummy.

"How do I look?" she managed to utter through gritted teeth and slitted eyes.

"Honestly?" Joan leaned forward to whisper. "Like road kill."

Trying to giggle, Sian couldn't move or make the noise. Instead she made a rather nasty snorting kind of sound.

"Don't try and move or talk, lovie." A nurse breezed in the door and hooked up a drip. "This is just a bit of saline to keep you nice and hydrated. How is your pain?" she asked kindly.

"Fine actually. My face just feels kind of hot. I can't see much but I can't say my eyes are sore," Sian grizzled, trying to speak through the mesh of bandages.

Joan kindly stayed until the afternoon before leaving Sian to have a sleep. That night she was pretty uncomfortable and found it hard to get to sleep, what with all the nurses coming in and out and the noise of the hospital clinic.

\* \* \*

The check-up a week after the procedure came around so quickly. It was almost Christmas and the weather was brutal. Walking like a clockwork dolly, she made her way into Dr Burke's waiting room. Thankfully there were no small children sitting there, as she looked like a walking bloody rainbow. Every colour from yellow to dark red was bursting forth around her eyes. She was swollen and looked like she'd had a fight with a baseball bat. Her skin was sore and baggy-looking and beginning to come off in sheets.

She'd been applying her special cream four times a day diligently, both to help avoid infection and to encourage the new skin to shed the old.

Having the stitches picked out of her upper lids was an experience she wouldn't look forward to repeating – ever. Although it wasn't that painful, the tugging and knowledge that a very sharp metal instrument was at her eye was not good.

"You're healing very well, Sian. I'm very pleased with the results. You will look this messy for another week, and after that you'll be amazed by how quickly you begin to look more normal again," Dr Burke smiled.

True to his word, by the time she was putting her turkey crown in the oven and preparing Christmas lunch, she was starting to look well. Already she could see the shape of her eyes and the clarity of the skin that was beginning to shine through.

When she opened the door to Joan, the look of delighted surprise on her pal's face said it all.

"Ohmigod, you look fantastic. Really, I can't get over the difference in you. I honestly didn't know what to expect today. Happy Christmas! God, will you be able to sit with me now? I'll look like your mother instead of your friend." She hugged her.

"I'm so glad I did this. I know it's not for everybody, but I needed a boost, Joan. I think this will give me the confidence to make the most of myself," Sian smiled.

As they clinked glasses and toasted their husbands and each other, Sian felt an inner peace that she hadn't had before. She knew her life was never going to be the same without Liam, but for the first time ever she felt a new sensation. It was called hope.

# 33

*Happy Christmas, Tanya darling. I hope they don't make boned and rolled turkey where you are, I know you hate it so much. There are no words to describe how much I miss you.*

As Alfie stood beside Tanya's grave on Christmas morning, the air was oddly calm. It was bitingly cold and the sky was grey. It looked like it might even snow. Jenny was busy pushing the buggy and doll Santa had brought.

"Don't go too far away with your baby, Jenny," he called over his shoulder.

It was only ten thirty in the morning and he was already exhausted. Following Jenny down the stairs that morning, he'd had to grind his teeth to stop himself from crying. His heart felt like it was going to disintegrate as he watched his little girl squeal with delight.

"Dada, look! A baby and a buggy for Jenny!" She launched on her stocking and began to empty it upside down.

He'd never experienced pain like this. Even the funeral hadn't seemed so bad. Perhaps because he'd been so overcome with grief at the time, and so hugely surrounded by people. This was undeniably the most desolate and strangled moment of his existence so far.

He hated himself for feeling so blue. Jenny was enthralled with her presents and the thought of all the magic and excitement that Christmas brought. He wanted to feel it too. He wanted to be able to join in, but it was too difficult. Sure, he made the right sounds and watched his daughter like a hawk, making himself smile when she looked his way, but inside he felt like a knife was gouging his heart right out of his chest.

After a couple of hours, he'd put Jenny in the car and driven here to the graveyard. The little girl had never associated the stones and rows of flowers with Tanya. Any time she wanted to tell her mummy something or show her a new thing, she put her hands on her hips and shouted to the sky.

Alfie knew she would understand more when she was older, but for now he was on his own with his pain.

"I wish you were here with us, Tanya. Nobody scowls at the Christmas tree and decorations quite like you did. Do you remember when I bought the flashing lights that play music two years ago? You could barely eat your turkey you were so appalled by the tackiness. I wish you could tell me how to move on. I know you'd be so cross with me, being such a wuss about all this. But that's my problem, you see? I needed you to keep me strong. I never wanted to be without you. I hope you are organising heaven. I'll bet they don't know what's hit them."

As he looked up, Alfie saw the little old lady in the headscarf. The same one he'd met several times before at the church when he'd gone there to light a candle and say a prayer.

"Oh hello, Merry Christmas to you!" Alfie said in surprise.

She smiled at him and said gently, "Time will heal your wounds, love is waiting, love is already here. You just need the time to realise it. Soon you will be able to accept it."

As she turned to walk away, with a twinkle in her eye, an image of Zoe came to Alfie. Smiling spontaneously, he turned as he heard his baby approaching.

"Who are you talking to, Dada? Are you happy now?" Jenny looked mildly confused.

"I'm talking to the lady who was here," Alfie answered, pointing in the direction the old woman had walked. The scent of lavender filled the air.

"What lady?" Jenny looked up and down the graveyard. "There's nobody here but you and me, silly Dada!" She giggled and wrapped her arms around his neck.

He had been hunched down on his hunkers, but the force of Jenny flinging herself at him and the shiver that ran through him made him fall backwards. Jenny laughed out loud, loving the horseplay. Alfie felt like he'd seen a ghost.

# 34

*A Merry Christmas? You bet. I have never been so*
*excited. Fingers crossed Santa brings me the best gift of*
*all this year – life.*

Zoe stretched lazily as she heard her parents moving about
downstairs. Jotting her little note into her pink notebook, she
managed to stash it away just before Charlie burst into her room in
her pyjamas. They had both decided to stay at home with their
parents for Christmas.

"Up and at 'em, lazy bones! Let's see what Santa brought us!"
Charlie yanked the duvet off her sister and bolted down the stairs
like a puppy.

Zoe followed, feeling five years old again.

As the family sat around the tree, with the fire lit and clinked
their classes of Bucks Fizz, with freshly squeezed orange juice, Zoe
had tears in her eyes. Although she was feeling so much better and
Dr Leah had assured her they were very hopeful the cancer was
under control, Zoe wouldn't believe it until she had her scans in
early January.

What a year it had been. This time last year, they had done a
similar thing, in the same room, but never in her wildest dreams

could she have predicted the year ahead. She sincerely hoped she would never have to endure anything like it again.

"Aren't you going to open your pressies, Zo-Zo?" Charlie was like a small child, firing wrapping paper over her shoulder and squealing and clapping before moving on to the next thing.

Without touching a thing or moving a muscle, Zoe spoke.

"Thank you all." She looked from one face to the next. "Thank you all for minding me and getting me through the last year. I know it hasn't been easy for any of you. Cancer doesn't just affect the patient, it affects everyone. I love you all. Thank you." She raised her glass and her sister and parents toasted her.

"Group hug!" Charlie yelled. "Here's to a better year to come!" She winked at Zoe.

"Well, let's face it, it can't be much worse," Zoe agreed.

As they all embraced one another, she wasn't sure why, but Zoe fleetingly thought of Alfie. She wondered how he was doing. He must be gutted on this, his first Christmas without Tanya. She would give him a call later on, when she was on her own. She knew it wasn't the right time and maybe it never would be, but deep in the recesses of her mind, should she allow herself to go there, she knew she had feelings for Alfie.

She wasn't sure if it was admiration or if she felt sorry for him, but there was a small nagging voice in her head that reminded her of how her pulse quickened when he was around. The feeling of comfort and electricity she'd experienced when they'd danced at Esme's party had stayed with her ever since. Time also slipped by in his company, without her realising it. Little Jenny, when she called her name and put her chubby arms up to her, made her feel wanted and special.

But then an image of Tanya would play on her mind. Guilt would stab at her for even contemplating putting herself in the picture with Tanya's husband and child and she would instantly feel ashamed and rotten to the core. Besides, Alfie probably didn't give her a second's thought. He was in mourning and would probably never want to consider meeting anyone else.

Realising her entire family was waiting with bated breath for her to join the Christmas toast, Zoe raised her glass.

# 35

*God bless us all on this holy and special day. Please God next year will bring better health and continued happiness.*

Esme loved Christmas. She had her two girls home with her and Tracey had brought her young man with her.

They'd arrived in the door the previous evening, just as Esme and Michael had finished their tea, and the minute Esme had clapped eyes on her daughter she'd known there was something different about her.

"Surprise!" Tracey had held out her left hand and there, for all to see, was the most stunning diamond ring.

"Congratulations, love! Michael, look, our Tracey is getting married!" Esme had been overcome with emotion. Tears had coursed down her cheeks as Michael had shuffled forward in his slippers to have a look.

"No expense spared there either – nice one, son!" He clapped Harry on the back.

"I know I should have asked your permission first, but my excitement took over and I proposed in the airport earlier," Harry said anxiously.

"You did right, my son. Go with the moment," Michael grinned. "Now, I would of course appreciate a little man-to-man chat, on account of you taking on our eldest child."

Harry looked slightly flustered for a moment, fearing what the man was going to say. "Of course, Mr Mulligan," he answered in his lovely English accent.

"Firstly, it's Esme and Michael," Esme wagged her finger at him, "and secondly, this old goat is only looking for an excuse to go for a pint!" She chuckled, hugging Harry. "I hate the pub, especially on Christmas Eve, so he's been like a child waiting for you to come and accompany him."

"Got it in one, but we might indeed discuss the wedding, for five seconds at least." Michael rubbed his hands together and went to find his shoes and coat.

Looking mildly bemused, Harry found himself being trotted out the door with his future father-in-law, as Michael explained the importance of picking a venue that serves good pints. "It's an art, you know, Harry. Not any fool can pull a decent pint." The door banged.

"Poor Harry," Tracey giggled to Nora and her mum. "If he manages to survive the evening down the local on Christmas Eve with Daddy and his cronies, he'll be able to manage being married to me!" Her eyes shone with glee.

"He's lucky to be getting you." Esme looked affronted for a minute. "Now first things first, love. Daddy and I have a little fund put aside for each of you. God knows it's quite big by this stage. We've put a few quid aside each week since yous were small, in preparation for your weddings. So we'll be able to provide a large truncheon of the money for the reception." Esme looked very proud.

"*Tranche,* you mean, Mum," Nora smiled.

"That's what I said, love." Esme looked at her younger daughter as if she was a bit slow. "You'll be having your wedding in Buckingham Palace by the time you get around to it." She patted Nora's arm.

The girls laughed, and moved into the kitchen, where bowls of stuffing, prepared vegetables and half a pig were boiling on the stove, in preparation for the following day's dinner.

"I hope you don't mind," said Esme, "but Miriam, Frank and Declan too, after all, are joining us for their dinner tomorrow. Miriam is very weak after her operation. She had another surgery and the doctors think she has a better chance now." Esme looked sad for a moment. Miriam hadn't been as lucky as she was with her cancer. It seemed to like Miriam, that damn cancer, and wasn't wanting to leave her alone. So Esme felt it would be too hard for her to cook at the moment.

"That's fine, Mum, of course," the girls chorused.

"I know he's a bit of a spanner, but maybe you could hook up with Declan, Nora?" Esme didn't look too sure.

"You're alright, thanks, Mum. I actually have a new boyfriend. He's Irish and living in London like me. His name is Joseph, and he said he might call in tomorrow evening if you're up to it." Nora looked all thrilled.

"Up to it? I'll wear my fascinator for the whole day now!" Esme was beside herself. "I'll have to be careful I don't get any gravy splashes on the feathers though. I'd hate it to catch fire while I'm taking the turkey from the oven." Esme rubbed her chin for a moment.

"Maybe you could just save it for Tracey's wedding instead?" Nora suggested gently. She'd already explained to Joseph that her mum was slightly eccentric, but all the same it might be easier not to scare him away on the first meeting.

By the time Harry and Michael appeared from the pub, it was after midnight. The girls could hear the two men singing "Molly Malone," as they bundled in the front door together. Esme was in bed asleep. Nora and Tracey were sitting beside the fire having a glass of wine.

"I'm off for me beauty sleep. Tracey, I told Harry here that yous can stay in the same room. No funny business, mind." Michael pointed at them one by one and raised his eyebrows. He couldn't really concentrate on the pointing, so he had to close an eye for comfort. "I'm off to bed now, but I'll see yous all bright and early for Mass." He burped loudly as he went up the stairs.

\* \* \*

Esme was up and about before eight. The stuffing was inside the turkey, which was the size of an ostrich, and she'd peeled all the spuds and put them in a bowl of water before Nora even heard her.

"Happy Christmas, Mum," she yawned, with a sense of excitement rippling through her. It didn't matter how old she was, Christmas morning still held such magic. This one was particularly special after the terrible shock they'd all had with Esme's cancer. The girls both knew their parents weren't getting any younger, but the thought of losing either one was not easy.

They decided they'd all open their presents after dinner, when Nora's fella arrived, so they could all be together.

"Are you sure he won't have a bit of dinner?" Esme asked.

As Nora surveyed the amount of food on offer later that afternoon, she mused that she should have invited his entire family. As usual, Esme had an entire farm of animals on offer, from turkey, ham, spiced beef and a little bit of pork (should anybody want it) plus five types of vegetables.

"He'll have a dessert when he arrives," Nora smiled. Her boyfriend was great craic and she hoped her parents were going to like him. Especially as they were planning to come home to Ireland in the spring. She'd tell her parents later on. Yesterday had been Tracey's engagement and her news could be for today. She knew her parents would be delighted to have at least one of them back on home turf.

As they all sat, complete with paper hats and full bellies, the doorbell rang. The sound of bells came through the front door.

"What's going on out there?" Michael grumbled, as he roused himself and shuffled to the door in his new slippers. Esme always insisted on new pyjamas and slippers for everyone for Christmas.

As he pulled the front door open, Michael was met by Santa, round and red and white, with a flashing nose and bulging sack over his back.

"Ho, ho, ho, Merry Christmas! You must be Michael – I have a nice six-pack in my sack for you!" shouted Santa.

"Well, hallelujah, and you are most welcome, Santie, do come in!" Michael was thoroughly enjoying this strange bit of unexpected banter.

Back in the dining room, Declan was busy telling the almost suicidal diners another story about "eejits on the number 10 bus". Thrilled with a bit of a change of conversation, they all turned to see Michael leading Santa into the dining room.

"Look who I found! Let's hope he's a magician too. First things first, Santie – can you stop that gobshite from talking through his arse, or is that more the job of a surgeon?" Michael pointed at Declan, who was too pissed to even look affronted.

After he'd finished handing out gifts to all the people at the table, Santa went over to Nora. "Here's your pressie, because you've been a very good girl," he winked.

Nora heard the jingle of metal as he dropped a set of keys into her hand. Squealing with delight, Nora jumped up to hug him.

"Everyone, this is Joseph, and when he's finished his job as the man in the red suit, we're planning on moving back to Ireland together!" Nora looked up at him adoringly.

"Well, you will be most welcome, Joseph." Michael clapped him on the back and pumped his hand up and down. "At least she won't have her mother setting her up with the bleedin' bus stop on the end of the table," he whispered, gesturing to Declan with his thumb. He'd deaden the head of even the most skilfully pulled pint with his dreary talk. Worse than a teetotaller he is. As much fun as a dose of the piles he is."

Nora smiled at him gratefully. She'd been fretting about whether or not Joseph would get on with her family. She adored her parents, but knew they could be what most would class as slightly unconventional. This was the best way she could imagine for him to both get them on side and make her feel comfortable. She had a good feeling about Joseph and this was the icing on the cake.

"Fair play to you, Joseph. Now you'll have a bit of sweet, won't you?" Esme got out of her chair and motioned to him to sit down.

Within minutes, he had a glass of wine and a large plate of assorted desserts put in front of him. The mood was jovial and Esme had never felt happier. Not only would she have the wedding to tell the Golden Girls about but her baby, Nora, was coming home. Imagine what the ladies would say when she told them her daughter was going to be living in sin with Santa!

# 36

*December 31st*

*Please let next year pass by quietly. I've had enough exciting events to do me a lifetime. 'Normal' would be extraordinarily wonderful right now.*

Zoe had texted Alfie on Christmas Day. To her the message hadn't warranted a response.

Thinking of u and Jenny. Hope the day passes as best as can b expected. Am here if u need a friend. Zoe x

Thanks Zoe. Many happy returns. Hope to c u soon. Alfie x

Zoe smiled as she read his answer. She had no doubt it was an extremely difficult day for Alfie, but she hoped that little Jenny was helping him get through.

On the morning of New Year's Eve, when her phone had beeped, she had scrolled down to read the message, with mild surprise.

Hey Zoe. R u able to talk? Alfie.

Without hesitation, Zoe dialled his number. It hadn't even rung properly once, when he answered.

"Thanks for calling so quickly. How are you?"

"I'm good, Alfie. How are you, more to the point?" She was genuinely worried about him.

"I've been sincerely okay, but I'm at the park with Jenny and I had a sudden downwards dive, and I didn't know who to call, so I chose you. Do you mind?" He sounded so desolate and unsure.

"I'm thrilled you called. Meet me in fifteen in Starbucks? Whoever gets there first buys the latte and chocolate cake, and that doesn't mean you deliberately walk slowly so I get stuck with the bill."

Zoe rushed to the bathroom and applied her make-up. Checking herself in the mirror, she made a snap decision. It would take her five minutes to change and she'd look much more respectable. Selecting a gorgeous fitted leather jacket and skinny jeans, she pulled on her short and funky styled wig, which looked the most like the hair she'd once owned. It was actually beginning to slide around on the new growth of hair which had just begun to show itself.

A quick spritz of perfume and a slick of lip gloss and she was ready for action.

"Mum, Dad, I'm going down to the shopping centre for a couple of hours. Catch you later!" She was about to bang the front door shut when Diana appeared.

"We're going to the Cardiffs for their New Year's party at seven thirty – are you not coming along? Charlie and Simon are," Diana encouraged.

"I don't think so, Mum. I'm not really in a party mood. I'll text you later when I decide what I'm doing."

Diana was so glad to see Zoe looking like a normal early-twenties girl, she didn't argue.

Giggling and hugging instinctively, Zoe met Alfie at the door to Starbucks.

"We didn't say what happens if we arrive at the same time," she chuckled as she bent to snuggle Jenny hello.

"I'll tell you what, you get to mind Jenny and snatch the next available table and I'll get the drinks and cake. Deal?" Alfie had already abandoned the two girls.

Zoe skilfully manoeuvred the buggy to the far corner of the café where a group was starting to gather up their pile of 'Sale'-emblazoned carrier bags.

"Out, Zoe, out!" Jenny wriggled and held her hands up to Zoe.

"Sure thing, little lady. Let's sit and wait for Daddy to bring our things." As the toddler was freed of the reins and Zoe pulled her out, their eyes locked. Not sure why the little girl was staring at her, Zoe smiled.

"What's wrong, Jenny?"

"Ah-oh! Zoe's hair is broken." Jenny pointed and stared intently at Zoe.

Putting her hands up to feel her head, Zoe's heart almost stopped as she realised her wig had slid halfway around her head. Before she had a chance to fix it, Alfie banged a laden tray onto the table.

"Poor Zoe, Dada. Look, broken hair!" Jenny extended her little finger once more.

Zoe felt embarrassment rise and the sweating begin. "Sorry, this is awful. My hair has started to grow like weeds. I have a little covering all over now. I'm a bit like a tennis ball under this thing. But as a result the wig keeps sliding around. I'd better go and try to make it look a bit more normal." She really felt like she was going to cry.

"Wait." Alfie put his hand on Zoe's, stopping her. "Let me fix it." Gently, he swivelled the wig around and tugged it into place. "There, all done."

"That better!" Jenny clapped and smiled. "Good boy, Dada. Now Zoe is all fixed."

As the toddler munched on her cake and played peep-o with another small person, the two adults sat in silence. The bags under Alfie's eyes were the only window to his grief.

"See," Zoe began through a mouthful of cake, "this is why we need to be friends. You phone me because you're having a bad moment, and I appear and instantly make you feel better. At least your hair stays in one spot."

"No, you don't win. You're not a widower. Imagine being one of those. Shouldn't there be a law saying that nobody under the age of forty is allowed to gain that title?" he quipped.

"Well, if that's the case, why shouldn't the same law extend to being bald prior to your fortieth birthday? No, sorry. I'm a girl, and

I'm only in my twenties and I'm both infertile and bald. I'm gonzoed. I win." She pointed vigorously at herself for effect.

Alfie paused for a moment and squinted. "Nice try, but no cigar. Your hair will grow back and you have youth on your side. I am a single father, whose hair is likely to fall out shortly and never grow back. I am destined to never love again, and one day, Jenny will grow up, realise I'm a sad bastard and run off with the circus. I'll be left alone and sad."

Zoe drew breath at the dreadful picture Alfie was painting. Spontaneously, the two of them burst out laughing. They rocked back and forth, holding the side of the small round coffee table for support. The hysteria dislodged Zoe's wig again. The shaking of her head made the mesh slide around, until the sideburns part covered her left eye.

"Oh bloody hell, this is ridiculous. I wish I could just take this blasted thing off for good," Zoe continued to giggle.

Alfie grew serious momentarily. "Why don't you then? If you have hair underneath, throw caution to the wind, take it off. Fling it across the coffee shop. I dare you. Frighten the living daylights out of some unsuspecting innocent bystander."

The look of challenging mischief in Alfie's eyes gave Zoe such a rush. "You dare me, do you?" Rising to the moment, she reached her hand up to her head slowly, holding his gaze all the while. With a flick of her wrist, she dislodged the wig and in one swoop it flew across Starbucks and landed on the counter, making a tall man scream like a little girl.

The cackling and rocking that erupted between Zoe and Alfie made the whole place stop and stare.

"Sorry, everyone," Zoe tried to force the words out, but the tears and giggles took over.

Quickly the other customers went on with their business, ignoring the giddy couple in the corner.

When they eventually managed to control themselves, Zoe sighed and looked over at Alfie. "So how do I look? Tennis ball or just a dodgy skinhead?"

"Can I touch it?"

"If you want," she smiled again.

"It's like velvet. For the record, you look beautiful. I think I prefer you without much hair. You have the most amazing face. You're so brave." Alfie took her hands in his and smiled warmly.

The light had faded outside and Jenny was beginning to get antsy. They gathered their things, including the wig, which had been perched on the side of the counter. As they made their way outside, Alfie looked at the ground as he spoke.

"I'm sure you have plans already, but if you're at a loose end, you're so welcome to come over and ring in the New Year with us." He gestured towards Jenny.

"I'd love to. I'm invited to a party with my family, but I don't think I'm quite in the mood for insane drinking and dancing just yet."

They fell into step together and decided to go to Marks and Spencer and pick up some party food and sparkling wine.

Alfie insisted on paying, ushering Zoe to the side with Jenny's buggy. The air-conditioning in the shop blasted down on her fuzzy head. But instead of it feeling terrible, it made Zoe feel free and bizarrely hopeful.

She glanced over at Alfie who was chatting easily to the lady behind the cash register. He was a wonderful man, and she was lucky to have him as a friend. She bit her lip as she thought of his words earlier in the café. In her opinion, he wouldn't be alone forever.

\* \* \*

When the bells tolled on the television at midnight, signalling the dawning of the New Year, Alfie held his arms out to Zoe. As he drew her into his embrace she felt safe and secure. She had no idea what the future held, but she allowed herself to dare to hope that Alfie and Jenny might play a part in it.

If you enjoyed *The Pink Ladies Club*
by Emma Hannigan why not try
*Miss Conceived* also published by Poolbeg?
Here's a sneak preview of Chapter One.

# Miss Conceived

EMMA
HANNIGAN

POOLBEG

# 1

tweeting@angiebaby.com

*I do not need a man to make my life complete ... I am a modern woman ... I will learn to be happy with what I've got ... I am in charge of my own destiny ...*

Even bloody Seamus was married. Come on! He wore brown nylon trousers and had two pockets of white spit on either side of his mouth. Granted, his wife looked scarily like Shrek, but all the same they'd found love. *Well*, Seamus did what he was told and his wife was only short of poking him with a cattle prod by way of communication. But, at the end of the day, they had each other. They had *someone*.

As she looked around the dimly lit room, Angie sighed. Eyeballing the Bacardi and Coke she'd just paid far too much for, she was tempted to pour it into the plastic pot plant beside her and leave.

"All right there, Angie baby?" Ken from Accounts staggered towards her, with one eye shut, spilling his pint up his own sleeve.

"Not really, Ken – in fact, I'm about as far from all right as I've ever been." She downed the drink, figuring she might as well get the value out of it at this stage.

"Ah, what's wrong with you? Tell me all about it!" Ken tried to sit on a bar stool, but the combination of his jockey-sized physique and ten pints meant he shunted sideways and drenched his own

371

shirt and the front of her skirt. "Oh no, I'm such a gobshite! Angie, I'm really sorry. I'll wash your frock for you – bring it in tomorrow and I'll get it back to you as good as new." He bit his lip.

Angie took a deep breath. "It's okay, Ken, could happen to a bishop. It's just another disaster to add to the multitude of others that I call my sad life." She slumped forwards to lean on the bar, resting her chin in her hands.

"Hello!" Seamus was standing like he'd a pole up his arse and waving like a clockwork dolly from the end of the bar. His wife, who was actually more manly-looking than he was, elbowed him and he swiftly turned his attention back to her.

"At least you're not with someone like that yoke Seamus has to endure." Ken shuddered.

"Shrek, you mean?" said Angie. "That's true."

But, deep down, Angie would settle for a mongrel on a piece of string and living in a shoe box if it meant she could find a decent man. She was starting to wonder whether she had an invisible, negative, magnetic force surrounding her. For years she had attracted all the wrong men. Cheapskates, don't-give-a-tossers, I'll-call-tomorrowers. Liars, every one of them. Maybe she should go to the doctor and ask if there was a scan available to tell her whether or not she's been chipped by aliens with a "nice guy" repellent.

Ken began to tell her about his new flat-screen TV. "Ah, you'd love it, Angie," he slurred.

"Um-hum." Angie sighed inwardly, thinking about the line-up of men in her life. From time to time, she'd manage to convince herself that she could get a man. How hard could it be? She wasn't too picky. As long as he possessed dangly toilet parts and could mutter "I love you" occasionally, he'd do. But over the years, she'd never found The One.

Her first boyfriend was in school in Senior Infants, when she was six. His name was James and he'd stolen his mother's engagement ring and brought it into school to give to her. They'd been in the toilets "getting engaged" when the teacher had found them. In fright, James had swallowed the ring so he wouldn't get caught having nicked it.

His mammy had given him two tablespoons of castor oil and he'd had to shit into a sieve for two days. Hardly the makings of a wonderful relationship. But at least he'd given her a ring.

Lately, as her thirties were slipping into her forties, the pickings were getting slimmer. She'd go out on the pull, full of intentions of scoring, just to prove a point. But, *wham* (or dead silence to be exact) – nothing. Not an available mutant in sight. Instead, to avoid feeling like a reject, she'd decided it was better to take the assertive, defensive approach. She maintained to all and sundry her firm assurance that all men should be evenly covered in dog poo and then rolled in leaves.

"You've the right idea, Angie," one of the girls in work used to say to her. "Steer clear of men. You've got your super-cool apartment, a gang of friends and you're your own woman. A lot to be said for being your own woman, I can tell you."

That was all very well for her to say – she had a husband and three kids at home. But who was Angie trying to kid? Here she was, at the after-conference drinks with the people she worked with day in day out, and even now she couldn't manage to relax and enjoy herself.

"What the hell is wrong with me?" she asked Ken. "Okay, quick CV, correct me if I'm wrong at any stage, right?" Choosing to ignore his pained look, she decided, fuelled by the Bacardi Bus, that right here and now was the right time to get some answers.

"Well, in fairness, Ange, I bat for the other team so I'm probably not the best choice to be asking."

Ken was one of the few people in the world who Angie didn't feel the need to be Superwoman with. He was her emotional crutch when times were fractious – usually after several units too many of mixing the grape and the grain, which was of course a total no-no.

"No, Ken, you're spot on. You're a man but you're gay, so you won't be foggy in your judgement. Just hear me out and let's work from there, yes?"

That day the team-building conference had been about trust and communication, which Ken had been all fired up about, but he hadn't thought in his wildest dreams it would mean having to listen to Angie's man troubles. Feeling more than a little boxed-in, he tried to resist the urge to lie on the floor and fall into a loud snoring drunken slumber. Keeping his focus away from the floor tiles, which looked alarmingly enticing, he turned his attention back to Angie, who was going hell for leather on the ranting front, God bless her.

"I'm an honest, decent and fairly intelligent woman. I have a sense of humour, I can laugh at myself." She lurched a little and snorted to demonstrate this fact.

Ken nodded with a fixed smile.

"Okay," she held her hands up, "I know I mightn't be Elle MacPherson, but am I offensive-looking? Especially in the right light, with enough make-up on and assuming the fella has a few drinks on board?" She tried to stand up straight, keeping her tummy in and her boobs out.

She could see herself in the mirror over the bar. She had shoulder-length brunette hair. (Well, that's how the magazines might describe it. In reality it was the same colour as a muddy puddle and, no matter what hairstylist she went to, it stubbornly remained unkempt and not-bothered-with-looking.) She had piercing blue eyes, which Ken felt were her best feature.

"You're a real firecracker, Angie, you have stop-'em-dead eyes and all you need is to give it a bit of time." Ken rubbed her arm, hoping to God she'd melt and thank him, and shut the hell up. No such luck.

"So," she slurred, "why is it that the only men who are attracted to me are either comparable to pond life, mentally deranged or, recently, non-existent? I'm nearly forty, Ken. My body clock is ticking so loudly sometimes I feel myself looking around to see if anyone else can hear it."

She was gripping his arm so tightly by this point that Ken was becoming increasingly alarmed.

"Another drink?" He smiled and tried to release his arm, which was in danger of bruising.

Ken ordered some of those tiny mouse's-pints-of-Guinness cocktails, which Angie hated at this stage of attempting to get ossified.

"They take half an hour to mix, two seconds to drink, they cost an arm and a leg and they have the potency of a Mr Whippy. I'm ordering us some real drinks. Tequila time! Barman, if you please, two shots of your finest tequila!"

"You, my dear, are going to end up in a pool of your own vomit. I am merely trying to slow you down a bit and provide a sophisticated little tipple that we can actually enjoy the flavour of."

The mouse's pints arrived and Ken made her giggle as he raised his pinkie and downed his in one.

"I'll see your posh fairy drink and we'll hammer this night home," said Angie, swaying a little as she grabbed a tequila shot from the barman. "Are you a man or a mouse?"

"I'd settle for the fairy description," Ken winked.

Angie had started working with Ken and Seamus at Stacks and Co IT eight years previously. It was a small company which had grown steadily over the years. Situated in a Georgian house just behind Shandon church in Cork city, the main office was open plan, with big blue screens dividing her and Ken's desks. Her area was usually messy and laced with chocolate wrappers, while Ken's was pristine and orderly.

Angie had grown up in a small remote village, with a higher ratio of cattle to people. So when she'd first got her job at Stacks, she'd shared with a college friend, Ed. His parents owned the flat and he subsidised his dope and lack of work by renting the spare room to Angie. Within two years she had moved from her shared accommodation into her own one-bed place. The sale of the last ten acres of land meant her parents were able to give her enough for a decent deposit on her apartment.

She thought back to those first few months in her lovely apartment. She was like a child in a sweetshop. The sheer joy of not having to label her milk and cheese in the fridge was beyond exciting. There was nothing worse than coming home from work to find her hairy, smelly, stoned flatmate sitting in *her* sweatshirt, eating the only food she had left. Ed was a lovely guy, but he had long dark hair which congregated in the plugholes and he was usually too stoned to go outside, and so he'd help himself to her stuff. Her flat was decorated in a minimalist way, which translated as having only the absolute necessities in place. A battered old sofa her father had found in a barn, an old iron bed and very little else. As she balanced her beans on toast on her lap, while watching the tiny portable TV with the coat-hanger stuck in the top (not a satellite dish in sight) she couldn't have been happier. There were no carpets on the floors and, as yet, no curtains on the windows, nor was there a resident stoned hippy. Best of all, the sinks weren't full of Ed's tangled dark hair. No more brushing her teeth and then retching when she discovered the plughole looking like a spider colony. She'd got on the right side of the builder and managed to get him to throw in her white goods in exchange for a cheaper bathroom suite. When she put food in the pristine new built-in fridge, it was still there when she came home from work. She could walk around in her underwear. In fact she could walk naked from the bathroom to her bedroom and decide what to wear without being confronted by a confused druggie with the munchies. She could leave her toiletries in the bathroom. (Ed used to use her toothbrush if she left it in his.)

"I was so happy when I moved to my flat, Ken. I don't know why but I thought that if I had my own place the man and babies would follow." She slumped and drained her drink. "My round. Thanks for listening and I'm sure you're dying to go the toilet and you're sick to the back teeth of listening to me moaning. No doubt you're ready to head home and wrap your arms around Barry and thank your lucky stars you're gay," she sniffed.

Ken made some limp attempt at telling her he was glad she'd talked to him, before excusing himself, tapping his watch. "Sorry, hon, you know I'd love to stay and chat for longer, but Barry will be worried and it's a work night and all that jazz." He kissed her cheek and tried not to trip on the carpet as he ran out.

She sat in the bar watching the work crowd. Not just Seamus but one of the new girls who was sweet and all that but certainly no supermodel – and she was engaged.

For the first years after she'd taken possession of the apartment, every spare cent was put back into making her place more homely.

But now that she had full furniture, matching towels, pretty bed linen and even optional extras like a coffee table and a tiny patio table with chairs for her miniscule balcony, she knew she wanted the most important accessory – a man.

She'd arranged to meet a group of friends in the city's newest and trendiest tapas bar. She wasn't a fan of all those tiny bits of stuff that could be a marinated rat's arse covered in spicy tomato sauce and presented on a big cocktail stick, but it seemed to be all the rage, so there might be some choice men floating around. Her friend Rachel was also single, and she and Angie were a great twosome. There were fewer and fewer "going out" buddies still unattached.

Slinking out of the work drinks, which had emptied out considerably at that stage, leaving only Seamus, Shrek and some other randomers, she tried to fix her lipstick as she walked. There was no sign of a taxi, so she strode steadily towards the city-centre bar. It was late July but, as it was Ireland and nobody had told the weather it was supposed to be summer, without warning the skies opened and the rain bucketed down.

"Bugger it," she muttered, trying without any success to shield her hair, face and body with the light jacket she'd brought. She was, of course, not organised enough to own a little handbag-sized umbrella, so instead she got soaked. Unlike in the movies, when the women get wet and look all sexy with stunning corkscrew curls framing their delicate features, making them look vulnerable and in need of love from a heroic, toned man, Angie just looked a state. By the time she reached the bar she was more haystack than Audrey Hepburn. Her hair was matted and wiry, her eye make-up was careering down her face, and the front of her trousers was soaked.

Angie hugged her friend hello. "Have you managed to have a scope around? Any nice-looking men?"

"Jesus, girl, what have you been drinking? Your two eyes are facing different directions already," said Rachel. "And you look like something from Fossetts' Circus – what's all over your face?"

"I touched up my lipstick on the way." Angie fished in her bag for a mirror. Sure enough she looked like she'd been attacked by a visually impaired toddler with a crayon. "Here, grab us some drinks, I'm going to fix myself." Angie shoved a note into Rachel's hand.

Spreading her make-up all over the sink in the toilets, she tried to make herself look half-decent. She was always aware that tonight might just be the night she met Mr Right. (Or even Mr Sort of Okay.)

She began to panic then. She wasn't one of those people who could mix and match clothes and come up with a stunning outfit. She never knew what clothes suited the occasion. She was happier in her work suits, with a clean shirt and her black shoes. Her "going out" gear was safe to say the least. In fact, all she was missing was the wooden cross and the rosary beads and she would have passed for a nun. Even when she'd just had a shower and dried her hair and put on make-up, she never looked polished or svelte. She unintentionally sported the just-got-dressed-in-the-dark look. When she saw an outfit in the window of a shop, she had to buy the whole thing. Picking up "key pieces" and making them her own just never happened for her. If she tried to move away from black and went for a gorgeous pink skirt or top, she just ended up looking like a nun going to a special occasion, or a policewoman who didn't have the right shirt clean to put with her uniform. Much as she hated to admit it, she knew she lacked natural style.

She'd always had friends, both male and female, but the boys always seemed to treat her as either a confidante or one of the lads. They never seemed to fancy her. None of them wanted to date her, vie for her attention or make a move on her. They were all more likely to challenge her to a pint race, followed by a congratulatory dig in the arm, than try and put their hand up her skirt.

Feeling a bit hungover already, she tried to dry herself with the hand dryer and gave up, spritzed herself with perfume and said a silent prayer. *Please God, let me meet my soul mate tonight.*

Everyone said it happened when you least expected it, that love came along when you weren't looking. Well, she would make sure she looked as carefree and unsuspecting as possible.

"I don't have a drink problem as such . . ." It was midnight and she was hugging a pillar in the bar with one arm and slurring to Rachel, who was equally trollied, "I just find it can work as a kind of anaesthetic for my broken heart, ya know?"

"Don't you need to have actually had some sort of catastrophic relationship-tragedy to be broken-hearted?"

"That's just it, Rachel, I'm such a disaster that I can break my own heart."

"Ah, come off it, you're not a total disaster. If you asked me to rate you, I'd say above Mother Teresa and below Joan Collins." Rachel giggled so much her sangria came out her nose.

"I'm actually two steps above Mother Teresa, I'll have you know. One relationship lasted two months, and the other almost three!" She did exaggerated counting on her fingers for effect.

"Ah yeah, but you were always the one to make all the effort, and still ended up being dumped in the end," teased Rachel. "It's been two years since a man stayed in that neat, minimalistic, tasteful, built-in-a-good-area apartment, with outdoor space overlooking Shandon."

"Now that was harsh, Rachel. It's hardly for a lack of effort. You and I," Angie poked herself and Rachel repeatedly, "would go to the opening of an envelope, at four in the morning on a Tuesday night, up the back of a field, if we thought we might meet a nice guy. Isn't that true?"

"It's true for you, girl," Rachel agreed.

"I think I'm good fun too. It's not like I walk around with a sandwich board on my back, with 'desperate for a husband,' in big black letters written on it. But, if the truth be known, all this being an independent woman looking out for myself is bloody boring and fecking exhausting. I'd love to come home even one night a week and have someone else make the dinner. To come home and be met with something other than silence would actually do it." She felt too drunk, quite sick and utterly miserable.

* * *

At two o'clock that morning, she swayed and shut one eye as she wrestled with her key, trying to make it fit in the lock of her apartment,

"I don't understand why this fucking key won't work," she slurred loudly to herself.

At that moment the door opened and a rather bleary-eyed man stood there in a pair of striped boxer shorts, staring at her with his arms folded.

"What the hell are you doing in my apartment?" she shouted.

"I live here," he answered rather snottily.

"I think you'll find you've made a mistake. This is my apartment and I've been living here since it was built. Now if you'll kindly move aside!" She shoved him out of the way and pushed her way in rudely. "What have you done with all my furniture?" she asked, feeling really confused.

Then it dawned on her.

"Oh Jesus, Mary and Joseph, I'm on the wrong floor, aren't I?" She turned around and met his gaze. "I am so embarrassed. I think I'm a bit drunk and I decided to take the stairs instead of the lift and I don't think I went up enough flights . . ." She trailed off feeling like a complete idiot. "I'm sorry I'm such a spanner – if it helps you at all, I do intend on going to the vet tomorrow morning and having myself put down."

"Don't worry about it, could happen to a bishop," he replied yawning. "Will you be able to find where you live?" He scratched the back of his head.

"Yep, that'll be no problem. So, sorry again, you go back to sleep – I'm off to slip into something a little more comfortable, like a coma." She staggered away. She was glad she was so pissed, otherwise she'd have died with embarrassment. He was bloody cute too, more was the shame. But, odds were, he was probably either gay or married, so there was no point in even thinking about him.

\* \* \*

When the alarm clock went off at six forty-five the next morning, Angie did hear it but it was very far away and quite muffled. By the time her brain managed to register it was intended for her, it was seven fifteen.

"Oh God," she groaned. Hauling herself out of bed, she berated herself for getting so drunk last night. She hardly ever drank mid-week any more, it just wasn't worth the hassle. She knew she would spend the day shovelling in junk food, washed down by dissolvable painkillers, counting the hours before she could go to bed again.

She'd staggered halfway to work by the time she recalled all the events of the night before. Her heart stopped as she halted.

"Oh God no!" she said out loud, to no one in particular. She felt her cheeks flush with embarrassment. She would have to move house. She would definitely have to sell her apartment now. There was no way she could risk seeing that man ever again. The shame of it, how was she going to cope? She couldn't even go home alone in a dignified manner.

By the time she reached work, her boss was standing at her desk looking agitated.

"Oh Angie, there you are. Nice of you to join us. You look rough. Come into my office when you've had a cup of coffee and made yourself look halfway decent. The team-building days are meant to be a positive thing, not an excuse to get yourself inebriated and insult colleagues. Seamus mentioned to me this morning that you were comparing his wife to an ogre last night. I'm not impressed, just chalk it down." He looked her up and down and walked off muttering.

Brian O'Leary was an utter prick. There was no two ways about it. He had balls of steel and that was why he'd made so much money. His company was going strong and he paid well, but he had the personality of a pre-menstrual she-devil and Angie had always felt he had it in for her. How typical that Seamus and Shrek had overheard her talking to Ken. She'd a good mind to stomp over to Seamus and tell him to keep his whingey little trap shut. What was he like? Telling on her like that?

Angie had worked hard to get to the position she had now, but being head of marketing was no easy feat. Especially when she was dealing with Brian O'Leary. She'd never forgiven him for his snide comment when she'd sent in her CV for the job application. He'd phoned her to organise a meeting, way back when he was only getting going and didn't have a shower of minions to do his dirty work.

"Your credentials look promising on paper but, looking at your passport photo, if you actually look like that in reality all I can say is that what you need is a holiday!" He'd proceeded to snort and laugh at his own wit.

Only her foresight that the company might be a good place to climb the success ladder made her hold her tongue. She could easily have hung up saying, "Give my regards to your arsehole if and when you remove your head from it." Instead, she'd made an extra-special effort just to prove him wrong and had done a great interview and secured the job.

The jury was still out on Brian O'Leary all the same. Angie wasn't convinced that he was definitely human. She often wondered what might happen if the fire-extinguishing sprinklers were ever activated. Would sparks fly out the back of his head?

Snapping back to the present time, putting her contempt for her boss aside and doing her best to look neutral as opposed to seething, Angie staggered into the bathroom and frightened herself. In fairness to O'Leary, she did in fact look like she'd just survived a holocaust. Riffling in her handbag, she found the makings of a face. Concealer, blusher, mascara, eyeshadow and lip gloss. Her skin had that ruddy, post-boozy complexion which no amount of product bar building materials could rectify. Knowing she was simply wasting her make-up, she knew she had to be seen to make the effort nonetheless. In the hope of feeling fresh, she spritzed herself with perfume, which she knew would just clash horribly with the smell of stale alcohol emanating from every pore. Lastly, she finished off by pulling a brush through her hair. Surveying her work, she grudgingly admitted that she felt and looked a damn sight better.

Taking a deep breath she strode purposefully towards Creepy O'Leary's office. He'd been in his pacing-panther mode, which always meant either a big deal on the cards or trouble in the camp.

She knocked on his door and he answered in his usual abrupt tone.

"Come in!" he barked. "You look slightly more human. Sit down, Angie."

The bloody nerve of him! With his old-fashioned trousers, greasy grey comb-over, and his patchy reddish beard. He was hardly Brad Pitt himself. More like an ageing fox with a dose of the mange. Cheeky bastard.

"I'm going to cut right to the chase here. There's a big deal coming through the pipelines. I need a strong team on board. How would you feel about relocating to Dublin for a year?" He was eyeing her like a vulture.

"Well, I don't know. I'm not sure. Why?" Angie looked astonished. Why the hell did he have to dump this on her today? Why in the name of God did she choose last night to go out and get rat-arsed? She hardly ever went on the batter on a work night and this was exactly why. She couldn't cope with the aftermath. She was a mess. On cue, her stomach did one of those dreadful angry-sounding gurgles as she felt cold sweat engulf her.

O'Leary was on the move again. Striding up and down his murky oatmeal carpet, in his squeaky cheap shoes, hands clasped behind his scrawny back.

"Okay, the deal is this. I need you to head the marketing strategy. You are the best person for the job. You've headed all the big campaigns over the last eight years – with ease and talent, I might add. You are well able to do the job. There's a good package in it for you to boot. I'm collaborating with an American company on this one. I've swung your rent in Dublin, as well as your mortgage to be paid here in Cork while you're away. A good expense account – in fact, you could eat in a Michelin-starred restaurant every night if you like. Your current wage and a ten-thousand-euro bonus at the end for your trouble. Will you think about it?" He was smiling, which was actually rather unnerving.

He was so unaccustomed to being cheerful, it really didn't suit him. In fact he looked a bit like a deranged squirrel, with his strawberry-blonde beard, as he revealed little sharp teeth. He stroked his bristly beard and then leaned on his desk to focus on her.

"I'll need to think it over. When is all this supposed to go ahead?" Angie asked, her hungover head reeling with this information overload. Not to mention her discomfort at having O'Leary in such close proximity, being all thrilled with himself.

"The deal is done. I need you to sign and agree to move to Dublin in two weeks' time. I know it sounds rushed, but believe me it will be worth it. These guys are big time. If we do well with this deal, it could become a regular trade-off. Why don't you go home, get some rest and mull it over? See me back here at three o'clock, and for Christ's sake, Angie, take the boiled sweet out of your hair, girl. If you're going to be a real high flyer, you'll have to get the finger out."

Angie reached up and felt around her head in confusion. There, nestled in her stringy locks, was a half-wrapped, sticky cough sweet, which must have been suctioned to her hairbrush at the bottom of her bag.

O'Leary never told anyone to go home, so she didn't wait to be told twice. She grabbed her coat and told her secretary she would be out for the morning.

The muggy city air hit her nostrils but it still felt fresh in comparison to the stuffy building. She headed straight for a coffee shop, knowing she needed some soakage before she could even begin to think about this opportunity. Intending to buy a low-fat bagel and black coffee, she waited in line at the nearest café. Of course by the time she reached the counter all ideas of being sensible and health-conscious went out the window. She figured her liver was already in distress after the night before and her growling stomach needed some proper sustenance.

"A breakfast roll, a piece of double-chocolate fudge cake and a large cappuccino with an extra shot to go, please." She dumped her bag on the sliver of counter space available in front of the cash register.

As she fumbled for her wallet, her oversized faux-leather supposed-to-be-a-handbag-but-really-should-have-wheels bag decided to empty itself all over the hard tiles of the crowded shop. Close to tears, she bent onto her hunkers, her head throbbing at being tilted at such an angle, and tried to steady herself while shoving her personal items back into the privacy of her bag.

"That's twelve euro and eight cent," the bored Eastern European girl, with jet-black hair and enough make-up to secure tiles to a bathroom wall, stood with her hand rudely shoved out.

"Can you just give me a sec? I'm trying to put what's left of my belongings into my bag."

"Next!" the girl yelled, as Angie put her smashed eyeshadow compact away.

"*Shiiiiit*!" she cursed under her breath as her leg got showered in greyish glittery powder which she stupidly tried to wipe, causing a greasy stain on her good work skirt.

She paid and tottered home, trying to sip her boiling coffee, which she reckoned would melt metal it was so hot, and flopped on the sofa feeling violated. The salt of the bacon and sausages, followed by the dense sugary cake, at least helped with her shaking hands and eased the hollow churning in her stomach.

This time in Dublin could be just what she needed. She knew it sounded sad, but it would also mean a fresh start. New men to meet, a new scene to crack into. Maybe this was Cupid's way of lining up his bow for her. Rachel could come up to Dublin on the train and the capital city would be their new playground. Sighing, firstly with relief that her hangover was shifting slightly and secondly at the thought of what could lie ahead, Angie felt hope springing forth.

If you enjoyed this chapter from
*Miss Conceived* by Emma Hannigan
why not order the full book online
@ www.poolbeg.com

Poolbeg wishes to

# THANK YOU

for buying a Poolbeg book.

If you enjoyed this why not
visit our website:

**www.poolbeg.com**

and get another book delivered straight to
your home or to a friend's home!

All books despatched within 24 hours.

POOLBEG

WHY NOT JOIN OUR MAILING LIST
@ www.poolbeg.com and get some
fantastic offers on Poolbeg books

ALSO BY POOLBEG.COM

# Designer Genes

## EMMA HANNIGAN

Emily Cusack's got it all sorted. A loving husband, two adorable kids and a gorgeous home. All she needs now is an au pair, for life to be truly perfect.

Her friend Susie is content too. A brilliant psychotherapist, she's got an elegant flat, a wardrobe full of ball-busting suits, a sleek sports car and doesn't need a man, thank you very much.

The only jeans the friends normally encounter are the designer version. Then Emily learns about genes of a different kind and why she could be a carrier of a
cancer-causing one. Emily doesn't take much lying down and deals with this in her decisive way. But can her marriage survive the aftershock?

Emily's news rocks Susie and makes her take a long hard look at her own self-sufficient life. Brought up by her loving but ditzy single mum, Susie has never known her father. Now she decides to do something about it.
But she's in for more than she bargains for! One thing's for sure –
life will never be the same again after a trip on this roller-coaster of discovery.

978-1-84223-382-5